In the Shadow of the Crown

As the cherished and only surviving child of Henry VIII's marriage to Katharine of Aragon, Mary Tudor faced an assured future – until her father decided to rid himself of her mother, and so brought devastating changes not only to Mary, but to the entire country. Young and inexperienced, Mary was left alone to face the dangers of those who live in the shadow of the crown.

Anne Boleyn's reign; the birth of Anne's daughter, Elizabeth; the death of Mary's mother, persecuted and neglected – the perilous years that followed were filled with drama. Mary saw the break with Rome, the suppression of the monasteries, two Queens lose their heads and another come near to it, one die in childbirth and another discarded. Yet she longed for a happy married life and children. And by this time she had reached a conviction that she was preserved for a divine purpose: to restore the Church of England to Rome.

As Queen, Mary believed she must give the country an heir. Long ago she had thought herself in love with the Emperor Charles; she had tender feelings for the noble Reginald Pole; Philip of Bavaria had been charming; but there had been hindrances to these matches. And now there was Philip of Spain . . .

D0198178

JEAN PLAIDY

In the Shadow
of the Crown

FONTANA/Collins

First published by Robert Hale Ltd 1988
First issued in Fontana Paperbacks 1990

Copyright © Jean Plaidy 1988

Printed and bound in Great Britain by
William Collins Sons & Co. Ltd, Glasgow

CONTENTS

The Betrothal

I have taken for my motto 'Time unveils Truth', and I believe that is often to be the case. Now that I am sick, weary and soon to die, I have looked back over my life which, on the whole, has been a sad and bitter one, though, like most people, I have had some moments of happiness. Perhaps it was my ill fortune to come into the world under the shadow of the crown, and through all my days that shadow remained with me – my right to it; my ability to capture it; my power to hold it.

No child's arrival could have been more eagerly awaited than mine. It was imperative for my mother to give the country an heir. She had already given birth to a stillborn daughter, a son who had survived his christening only to depart a few weeks later, another son who died at birth, and there had been a premature delivery. The King, my father, was beginning to grow impatient, asking himself why God had decided to punish *him* thus; my mother was silently frantic, fearing that the fault was hers. None could believe that my handsome father, godlike in his physical perfection, could fail where the humblest beggar in the streets could succeed.

I was unaware at the time, of course, but I heard later of all the excitement and apprehension the hope of my coming brought with it.

Then, at four o'clock on the morning of the 18th of February in that year 1516, I was born in the Palace of Greenwich.

After the first disappointment due to my sex being of the wrong gender, there was general rejoicing – less joyous, of course, than if I had been a boy, but still I was alive and appeared to be healthy and, as I believe my father remarked to my poor mother, who had just emerged from the exhaustion of a difficult labour, the child was well formed, and they could have more . . . a boy next time, then a quiverful.

Bells rang out. The King and Queen could at least have a child who had a chance of living. Perhaps some remembered that other child, the precious boy who had given rise to even greater rejoicing and a few weeks later had died in the midst of the celebrations for his birth. But I was here, a royal child, the daughter of the King and Queen, and until the longed-for boy arrived to displace me, I was heir to the throne.

I enjoyed hearing of my splendid baptism from both Lady Bryan, who was the lady mistress of the Household, and the Countess of Salisbury, who became my state governess. It had taken place on the third day after my birth, for according to custom christenings must take place as soon as possible in case the child did not survive. It took place in Greyfriar's Church close to Greenwich Palace, and the silver font had been brought from Christ Church in Canterbury, for all the children of my grandparents, Henry VII and Elizabeth of York, had had this silver font at their baptisms, and it was fitting that it should be the same for me. Carpets had been laid from the Palace to the font, and the Countess of Salisbury had the great honour of carrying me in her arms.

My father had decreed that I should be named after his sister Mary. She had always been a favourite of his, even after her exploits in France the previous year which had infuriated him. It showed the depth of his affection for her that he could have given me her name when she had so recently displeased him by marrying the Duke of Suffolk almost immediately after the death of her husband, Louis XII of France. She was more or less in exile at the time of my christening, in disgrace and rather poor, for she and

8

Suffolk had to pay back to my father the dowry which he had paid to the French. In the years to come I liked to remind myself of that unexpected softness in his nature, and I drew a little comfort from it.

My godfather was Cardinal Wolsey who, under the King, was the most important man in the country at that time. He gave me a gold cup; from my Aunt Mary, the wayward Tudor after whom I was named, I received a pomander. I loved it. It was a golden ball into which was inserted a paste of exquisite perfumes. I used to take it to bed with me and later I wore it at my girdle.

The best time of my life was my early childhood before I had an inkling of the storms which were to beset me. Innocence is a beautiful state when one believes that people are all good and one is prepared to love them all and expect that love to be returned. One is unaware that evil exists, so one does not look for it. But, alas, there comes the awakening.

A royal child has no secret life. He or she is watched constantly, and it is particularly so if that child is important to the state. I say this as no conceit. I was important because I was the only child of the King, and if my parents produced the desired boy, my importance would dwindle away. I should not have been watched over, inspected by ambassadors and received their homage due to the heir to the throne. It is difficult to understand when one is young that the adulation and respect are not for oneself but for the Crown.

There are vague memories in my mind, prompted no doubt by accounts I heard from members of my household; but I see myself at the age of two being taken up by my father, held high while he threw me up and caught me in his strong arms and held me firmly against his jewel-encrusted surcoat. I had felt no qualms that he would drop me. I never knew anyone exude power as my father did. As a child I believed him to be different from all others, a being apart. Of course, I had always seen him as the most powerful person in the kingdom – which undoubtedly he was – and my childish mind endowed him with divine qualities. He was not only a king; he was a god. My mother and Sir Henry Rowte, my priest, chaplain and Clerk of the Closet, might instruct me in my duties to One who was above us all, but in my early days that one was my father.

I was so happy to be held in his arms and to see my beloved mother standing beside me, laughing, happy, beautiful and contented with me.

I remember my father's carrying me to a man in red robes who reverently took my hand and kissed it. My father regarded this man with great affection, and it seemed wonderful to me that he should kiss my hand. It meant something. It pleased my father. I knew by that time that he was my godfather, the great Cardinal Wolsey.

That had been when I was exactly two years old. I think the ceremony must have been in recognition of that fact. It was not only the great Cardinal who kissed my hand. I was taken to the Venetian ambassador and he was presented to me. I had been told I had to extend my hand for him to kiss, which I did in the manner which had been taught me, and I knew this caused my father's mouth to turn up at the corners with approval. Several people were presented to me afterwards and I believe I remember something of this. While I was in my father's arms, I saw a man in dark robes among the assembly. I knew him for a priest. Priests, I had been told, were holy men, good men. I was drawn to them all throughout my life. I wanted to see this one more closely, so I called out, 'Priest, Priest. Come here, Priest.'

There was astonishment among the company, and my father beckoned to the man to come forward. He did and stood before me. He took my hand and kissed it. I touched his dark robes and said: 'Stay here, Priest.' The man smiled at me and, basking in my approval, he overcame his awe of

10

the King and stammered out that the Princess Mary was a child of many gifts and the most bright and intelligent of her age he had ever seen.

People remember that occasion more for the manner in which I summoned the priest than that it was my second birthday and that the King was showing his love for me and that he was becoming reconciled to the fact that he might never have a legitimate son to follow him, which would make me, his daughter, his heir.

I was at that time at Ditton in Buckinghamshire. On the other side of the river was Windsor Castle and there was frequent traffic between the two places. I looked forward to those occasions when the ferryman rowed us across the river. I had my household governed by the Countess of Salisbury, who was a mother to me when my own beloved mother was not able to be with me. She deplored these absences, I knew, and had made me understand that she loved me dearly, and in spite of my reverence for my father, she was the person I loved best in the whole world.

Whenever she visited the household, she and the Countess would talk of me. My mother wanted to know everything I did and said and wore. She made me feel cherished; and the greatest sorrow of my early life was due to those occasions when we had to part.

She would say: 'Soon we shall be together again and when I am not here the lady Countess will be your mother in my place.'

'There can only be one mother,' I told her gravely.

'That is so, my child,' she answered. 'But you love the Countess as she loves you, and you must do everything she tells you and above all remember that she is there . . . for me.'

I did understand. I was wise for my years. I had, as Alice Wood, the laundress used to say, 'an old head on little shoulders'.

11

Soon after that, when I was two years and eight months old, my first betrothal took place.

A son had been born to François Premier, the King of France, and my father and the Cardinal believed that it would strengthen the friendship between our two countries if a marriage was arranged for us. Although I was almost exactly two years older – the Dauphin was born on the 28th of February 1518 – we were of an age. I had no notion of what this was all about. I do vaguely remember the splendid ceremony at Greenwich Palace, largely because of the clothes I had to wear. They were heavy and prickly; my gown was of cloth of gold, and my black velvet cap so encrusted with jewels that I could scarcely support its weight. My prospective bridegroom, being only eight months old, was naturally spared the ceremony and a somewhat solemn-looking Admiral Bonnivet represented him. I remember the heavy diamond ring he put on my finger.

The great Cardinal celebrated Mass. I was too uncomfortable in my unwieldy garments to be anything but pleased when it was all over.

The Countess told me that it was a very important occasion and it meant that one day I should be Queen of France. I need not be alarmed. The ceremony would not be repeated until the Dauphin was fourteen years old – by which time I should be sixteen . . . eons away in time. Then I should go to France to be prepared for the great honour of queenship.

My mother did not share in the general rejoicing. I learned at an early age that she did not like the French.

I was three years old when an event took place which was of the greatest importance to my mother and therefore to me, although, of course, at this stage of my life I was blissfully ignorant of it and of the storms which had begun to cast a cloud over my parents' marriage.

Later I heard all about it.

I had sensed that there had been a certain disappointment at my birth because I was not a boy, and I was aware some time before my third birthday that there was an expectancy in the Court which had seeped into my household. People whispered. I caught a word here and there. I think I must have been rather precocious. I suppose any child in my position would have been. I did not know what the undercurrents meant but I did somehow sense that they were there.

My mother was ill and I heard it murmured that this was yet another disappointment, though 'it' would only have been a girl. The King was angry; the Queen was desolate. It was yet another case of hope unfulfilled.

'Well, there is time yet,' I heard it said. 'And after all there is the little Princess.'

And then a boy was born – not to my mother, though. He was a very important boy, but he could not displace me. He was flawed in some way. He was – I heard the word spoken with pity and a touch of contempt – a bastard.

But there was something special about this bastard.

I learned the story later. Bessie Blount was not the King's first mistress. How my poor mother must have suffered! She, the daughter of proud Isabella and Ferdinand, to be forced to accept such a state of affairs. Men were not faithful . . . kings in particular . . . but they should veil their infidelities with discretion. I heard many tales of Bessie Blount; how she was the star of the Court, how she sang more prettily and danced more gracefully than any other; and how the King, tiring of his Spanish Queen who, in any case was more than five years his senior, was like every other man at Court fascinated by her.

There had been another woman before Bessie Blount's arrival on the scene. She was the sister of the Duke of Buckingham and was at Court with her husband. The Duke of Buckingham considered himself more royal than the Tudors. His father was descended from Thomas of

Woodstock, who was a son of Edward III, and his mother had been Catherine Woodville, sister to Elizabeth, Queen of Edward IV. So he had good reasons – particularly as the Plantagenets were inclined to regard the Tudors as upstarts. My own dear Countess of Salisbury was very proud of her Plantagenet ancestry but she was wise enough not to talk of it.

However, the erring lady's sister-in-law discovered what was happening and reported it to her husband the Duke, who was incensed that a member of his family should so demean herself as to become any man's mistress, even if that man was the King. Being so conscious of his heritage, he was not the man to stand aside and had gone so far as to upbraid the King. It was really quite a storm and I could imagine the interest it aroused throughout the Court and the anguish it brought to my mother.

The woman was taken to a convent by her brother and kept there. The King and the Duke quarrelled, with the result that Buckingham left the Court for a while. I suppose it was not considered to be a very serious incident but I believe it was the first time my mother had been aware that the King looked elsewhere for his comfort.

The Bessie Blount affair was quite another matter – no hole in the corner affair this. My father was now petulantly showing his discontent. All those years of marriage and only one child – and that a girl – to show for it! Something was wrong and, as my father could never see any fault in himself, he blamed my mother. He convinced himself that he had nobly married his brother's widow; when she was helpless, he had played the gallant knight as he loved to do in his masques and charades, and out of chivalry he had married her. And how had she repaid him? By producing children who did not survive . . . apart from one daughter. It was unacceptable in his position. He must have heirs because the country needed them. He had been cheated.

There was no longer pleasure to be found in the marriage

14

bed. God had not made him a monk, so it was only natural that he, so bitterly disappointed in his marriage, should turn aside for a little relaxation to enable him to deal effectively with matters of state.

So there was the delectable Bessie, the star of the Court, so enchanting, desired by many. It was natural that she should comfort my father.

Perhaps it would not have been so important if Bessie had not become pregnant; and even that in itself could not have made such a stir. But Bessie produced a boy – a healthy boy! The King's son – but, alas, born on the wrong side of the blanket, as they say.

A ripple of excitement ran through the Court, so obvious that even I, a child of three years, was conscious of it.

When my mother visited me, I noticed a sadness in her. It grieved me momentarily but when she saw this she was determined to hide it and became more merry than she usually was.

I forgot it. But later, of course, looking back, I saw that it was, in a way, the beginning.

The boy was named Henry after his father. He was a bright and good-looking child, and the King was proud of him. He was known as Henry Fitzroy so that none should forget whose son he was. Bessie was married to Sir Gilbert Talboys, a man of great wealth, for it was considered fitting that as she was a mother she should be a wife. The boy must have the best and his father saw much of him. My mother used to talk to me about it during those dark days when the King's Secret Matter was, in spite of this appellation, the most discussed subject at Court.

When I was four years old, my parents went to France. There was a great deal of excitement about this visit because it was meant to mark a new bond of friendship between France and England. The King of France and my father were going to show the world that they were allies;

but mainly they were telling this to the Emperor Charles, who was the rival of them both.

I wondered whether they would take me with them. But they did not. Instead I was sent to Richmond. This was a change from Ditton, although I had my household with me and the Countess and Lady Bryan were in charge. But the Countess did try to impress on me that it was different because my parents were out of the country and that put me into a more important position than I should have been in if they were here. I tried to grasp what this meant but the Countess seemed to decide that she could not explain. I heard her say to Lady Bryan: 'How can this be expected of a child?'

There was a great deal of talk about what was happening in France and there were descriptions of splendid tournaments and entertainments. The occasion was referred to as 'The Field of the Cloth of Gold', which conjured up visions of great grandeur in my mind. My mother told me later that it was not all they had thought it was while it was in progress.

I have always deplored the fact that I missed great events and that they came to me by hearsay. I often told myself that, if I had been present, if I could have experienced these important occasions when they happened, I could have learned much and been able to deal more skilfully with my own problems when they arose.

It was while my parents were in France that three high-ranking Frenchmen came to the Court.

This threw the Countess into an agony of doubt. I heard her discussing the matter with Sir Henry Rowte.

'Of course, we have to consider her position. But such a child . . . Oh, no, it would be impossible, and yet . . .'

Sir Henry said: 'Her extreme youth must be considered by everyone. Surely . . .'

'But who is to receive them? She is . . . who she is . . .'

I understood that they were talking about me.

16

A decision was arrived at. The Countess came to my schoolroom where I was having a lesson on the virginals.

'Princess,' she said, 'important gentlemen have come from France. If the King or Queen were here, they would receive them, but as you know, they are in France. So . . . as their daughter . . . you must greet these arrivals.'

It did not occur to me that this would be difficult, and I suppose, as I felt no fear, I carried off the meeting in a manner which, on account of my youth, surprised all who beheld it. I knew how to hold out my hand to be kissed. I knew that I must smile and listen to what was said and, if I did not understand, merely go on smiling. It was easy.

I was aware of their admiration, and the Countess looked on, pursing her lips and nodding her head a little as she did when she was pleased.

One of the gentlemen asked me what I liked doing most. I considered a while and then said that I liked playing on the virginals.

Would I play for him? he asked.

I said I would.

I heard afterwards that everyone marvelled at my skill in being able to play a tune without a fault. They said they had never known one so young such a good musician.

The Countess was gratified. She said my parents would be delighted to hear how I had entertained their guests during their absence.

Often during the years that followed, I would look back on those early days and fervently wish that I had never had to grow up.

In due course my parents returned from France. There was still a great deal of talk about the brilliant meeting of the two kings. I kept my ears open and heard scraps of conversation among the courtiers when I was with the Court. I learned how the two kings had vied with each other, how they were determined to show the world – and the Emperor Charles – that they were the best of friends.

When they were in church together, each king had stood aside for the other to kiss the Bible first, and at length the King of France had prevailed on the King of England to do so, as he was a guest on French soil. My mother and the Queen of France had been equally careful of each other's feelings. I knew my mother had great sympathy with Queen Claude. I heard the whispers: François was a libertine with whom no woman was safe, and poor crippled Claude had a great deal to endure.

That occasion when the King of France had forced his way into my father's bedroom when he was in bed was much discussed. My father had said: 'I am your prisoner,' but the King of France had charmingly replied: 'Nay, I am your valet.' And he had handed him his shirt. It was all elaborate play-acting to show the amity there was between them and to warn the Emperor Charles – who was a most ambitious young man – that he would have to face the might of the two countries, so he had better not think about attacking one of them.

On that occasion my father gave François a valuable jewelled collar, and François responded by giving him a bracelet of even greater value. That was how it was at the Field of the Cloth of Gold. Each king had to outdo the other; and because of the shift in interests, because of the wily and unpredictable games they played, very soon it became clear to both participants that the entire venture had been an enormous waste of time and riches.

When my mother returned from France, young as I was, I detected that she was not happy. I understood later that she did not like the French; she did not trust François – and how right she was proved to be in that. Moreover, she had been most uneasy because the entire farce of the Field of the Cloth of Gold had been an act of defiance against the Emperor Charles. My mother was Spanish and, although she was devoted to my father, she could not forget her native land. She had loved her mother as passionately as I

18

was to love her and she me. It could not give her any pleasure, considering her strong family feeling, to witness her husband joining up with an ally in order to stand against her own nephew.

At this time there were three men of power astride Europe; they were François Premier of France, Charles, Emperor, the ruler of Spain, Austria and the Netherlands, and my father, the King of England. They were all more or less the same age – young, ambitious, determined to outdo each other. There was a similarity between François and my father; Charles was different. Not for him the extravagances, the lavish banquets, the splendid tournaments, the glittering garments. He was quiet and serious.

My mother was torn between husband and nephew. It grieved her greatly to think of them as enemies. She could not, of course, explain this to me at that time.

When my parents returned from France, after a short stay with them I went back to Ditton Park; but the following Christmas I was with them. Although I dearly loved the Countess of Salisbury, Lady Bryan and all my household, I looked forward with great pleasure to being with my parents. My father was such a glittering figure, and it delighted me, even at that early age, to see how he inspired a certain awe in everyone near him; even the greatest men, like the Cardinal, whom all respected and feared, bowed to my father. He had a loud laugh and when he was merry his face would light up with joy and everyone around him would be happy. I had seen him, though rarely, in a less than merry mood. Then his eyes would be like two little points of blue ice and his mouth would be such a small thin line that I thought it would disappear altogether. A terrible fear would descend on the company, and it appeared to me that everyone would try to shrink out of sight. It was awesome and terrible. Someone usually hurried me out of the way at such times.

So, while I worshipped him, I did experience a little fear

even in those days. But that only made him the more godlike.

With my mother I felt safe and happy always. She was dignified and aloof, as became a queen, but always warm and loving towards me and while I was proud to have such a glittering, all-powerful father, I was more deeply contented in the love of my mother.

That Christmas I spent with them was one I remember well. There were so many presents – not only from my parents but from the ladies and gentlemen of the Court. I remember the gold cup because it came from the Cardinal, and the silver flagons I think were from Princess Katharine Plantagenet, who was quite old, being the daughter of my great-grandfather, King Edward IV. In contrast to these valuable presents was one from a poor woman of Greenwich. She had made a little rosemary bush for me all hung with gilt spangles. It gave me as much pleasure as any.

My mother made it a Christmas to delight me and sent for a company of children to act plays for me. I remember some of those plays well. They were written by a man called John Heywood who was later to make quite a success with his dramatic works.

Those early years were spent mainly in the calm serenity of Ditton, with occasional visits to my parents. These memories are of laughter, music and dancing, of cooks and scullions rushing hither and thither with great dishes of beef, mutton, capons, boars' heads and sucking pigs, and in fact any meat it was possible to think of; of eating, drinking and general merrymaking, with my father always at the centre. He could sing and hold the company spellbound – perhaps as much by his royalty as his talent; but there was no doubt that in the dance he could leap higher than any; he was indefatigable. No stranger, seeing him for the first time, could have doubted that he was the King and master of us all.

I was proud to be his daughter, and if I could have had

one wish it would have been that my sex might be changed, so that I could be the boy who would have delighted him as Henry Fitzroy did and so rid my mother of that look of anxiety which I saw more and more frequently in her face.

But perhaps Henry Fitzroy felt something of the same, for he could not give my father complete pleasure because he was illegitimate. So he was flawed even as I was.

Shortly after my parents returned from France, something happened which caused anxiety to my godmother, the Countess of Salisbury. At my tender age I was aware only of a ripple of disturbance, and it was not until later that I understood what it meant.

It concerned Edward Stafford, Duke of Buckingham, whose rank brought him close to the King, and on the surface they were good friends. Just before the party went to France, Buckingham had entertained the King lavishly at Penshurst. I heard people talking about the masques and banquets which had been of such splendour as to surpass even those given by the King himself.

Buckingham was not a wise man. He could never forget his royal descent and would remind people of it in any way which offered itself. He should have remembered that, although he was so proud of it, in the mind of a Tudor it could arouse certain suspicions. A clever man would have been more subtle, but from what I heard of Buckingham he had never been that. The King might enjoy the entertainments while they lasted, but afterwards might he not ask himself: Why should this man seek to outdo royalty? The answer was, because he regarded himself as equally royal . . . no, not equally, more so.

It was true that the Tudors' grip on the crown was not as secure as they would wish. My grandfather, Henry VII, had seized it when he defeated Richard III at Bosworth Field in 1485; and many would have said that his claim to it was not a very strong one. Buckingham was one of those.

21

Later I was to see my father's eyes narrow as he contemplated such men. At that time he was more tolerant than he became later. Then he delighted in the approval of his subjects, but later he only wished them to accept his rule. It was up to them to like it or risk his displeasure. My father was a man who changed a great deal over the years. At this time he was only just passing out of that phase in which he appeared to be full of bonhomie and good will towards men, which made him the most popular monarch men remembered. It was the growing discord in his marriage which was changing him; he was turning from a satisfied man to a disgruntled one, and that affected his nature and consequently his attitude towards his subjects.

Buckingham had powerful connections in the present as well as the past. He was married to a daughter of the Percys, the great lords of the North. His son – his only one – had married the Countess of Salisbury's daughter, so that made a family connection between him and my godmother. Small wonder that she was worried. He had three daughters, one of whom had married into the Norfolk family, one to the Earl of Westmorland and the third to Lord Abergavenny. So it was clear that Buckingham was well connected.

Someone said of him: 'My lord Buckingham is a nobleman who would be a royal ruler.'

Knowing my father, now I can guess that such a remark would set up warning signals in his mind. His father had been plagued by pretenders to the throne – Perkin Warbeck, Lambert Simnel, to name the two most important. A king who sits warily on the throne has to be careful.

Buckingham was a stupid man. It was a great mistake to antagonize Wolsey. Obsessed by his nobility, I suppose it was natural that he should resent a man of lowly birth who had climbed so high that the King relied on his judgement and had more affection for him than he had for the greatest nobleman in the land.

He should have had more sense than to pit his wits

against Wolsey. Precarious as his position was with the King, he could not afford to challenge the cleverest man in the kingdom.

For some time my father must have been toying with the idea of ridding himself of the arrogant Buckingham who, in time, would doubtless be laying claim to the throne.

Matters came to a head over a simple incident, as such matters do.

It was the custom for one of the highest-ranking nobles to hold the basin while the King washed his hands. This was Buckingham's duty. Wolsey was standing beside the King, chatting amiably to him as they did together, for if my father liked someone he never hesitated to show it and would allow that person all sorts of privileges; and when the King had finished washing his hands, Wolsey attempted to use the basin too.

Buckingham was incensed that he should be holding the basin for a low-born son of a butcher, as he called him. Wolsey's father had owned land in Ipswich and may have bred sheep and cattle; if so, he doubtless sold the carcases. In any case the epithet 'Butcher's Cur' was often bestowed on him by his many enemies and frequently used by those jealous of his power. The Duke tilted the basin and poured the water onto Wolsey's shoes.

The King was amused and nothing was made of the incident at the time, but naturally it was not brushed aside. Wolsey would not forget; Buckingham had to be taught a lesson; and as the King was already uneasy about Buckingham's pretensions to royalty, it was not difficult to bring a charge against him.

Men in high positions can be sure of one thing: they have many enemies. It was not long before a case was brought against Buckingham and he was committed to the Tower on a charge of treason.

I believe it was easy to prove a case against him. He was supposed to have listened to prophecies of the King's death and his own succession to the crown and of even expressing an intention to kill my father, but that was mainly hearsay. The King wanted to be rid of him. He would always be a menace. He must have remembered the uneasiness of his own father, and Buckingham was condemned as a traitor. He was beheaded on Tower Hill, and his body was buried in the church of Austin Friars.

I should not have known anything of this at the time, as I was only five years old, but I was aware of the effect it had on the Countess, for the Duke's son was her son-in-law and it was a family tragedy. The Countess was a clever woman. She knew that the Duke had not lost his head because of treasonable acts. He had died because of his closeness to the throne. And she herself? She was even closer. Her father had been the brother of Edward IV. My father was the grandson of that Edward through his mother, so they were closely related; but the Countess through the male line.

My dear Countess, being astute and a very wise woman, would have realized that the Duke was a very foolish man who had himself to blame for a great many of his misfortunes. But also it would have been brought home to her that, in view of her own royal connections, she was in a very precarious position.

Children are perceptive and perhaps, being brought up as I had been, I was particularly so. But I do remember that time and I was very conscious of a change in the Countess. She must have been a very worried woman.

One day my mother arrived at Ditton. I was then six years old but being close to events such as the birth of Henry Fitzroy and the death of the Duke of Buckingham, I was beginning to acquire a greater understanding than would have been expected from one of my tender years.

My mother looked happy and, having been mildly conscious of the Countess's distress and that my mother had previously been anxious about something, I rejoiced to see her so.

She embraced the Countess and they talked together for a while. Then I was brought to them. My mother kissed me with great affection.

The Countess said: 'I doubt not that Your Grace will wish to talk to the Princess alone.'

'Oh yes,' replied my mother. 'I can scarcely wait to impart the good news.'

When we were alone, she sat down and drew me to her. I stood beside her, her arms encircling me. I watched the happiness in her eyes and eagerly waited to hear this good news.

'My dearest child,' she said, 'you are to be betrothed.'

I was puzzled. I thought I *was* betrothed. When I was sixteen I was to go to France to learn how to be Queen of that country when I married the boy who was now Dauphin.

'Yes, my lady,' I said. 'I know I am.'

She shook her head. 'You do not understand, dear child. This is wonderful news. You are going to marry the Emperor Charles.'

The Emperor Charles! But he was our enemy! The Field of the Cloth of Gold had taken place to let him know how friendly we were with my future father-in-law, the King of France.

'But, my lady,' I stammered, 'what of the Dauphin?'

My mother smiled tenderly at me. 'That, my dearest, is over, and it greatly pleases me that this should be. It would have been a great tragedy. But let us rejoice. The Emperor Charles is the greatest ruler in Europe . . . next to your father,' she added quickly. 'He is half Spanish . . . the son of my own dear sister Juana. It is what I have always wanted for you.'

I glowed with pleasure. If my mother wanted it, it must be good. And it was wonderful to see her so happy.

25

'Does my father wish this?' I asked.

She laughed. 'He wishes it . . . or it would not be. You see, it is better for our country to be friendly with the Emperor than with France. Everything is good about this match. You are half Spanish through me . . . and the Emperor is through his mother. Friendship with the Emperor is better for England. The alliance with France brought us no good. It would have ruined the wool trade which is so important for England for our wool goes to Flanders, and Flanders is in the dominions of the great Emperor Charles – as is so much of Europe. But you are too young to understand . . .'

'Oh no, my lady. I want to know. I want to know . . . all.'

She took my face in her hands and kissed it. 'This is a happy day for me,' she said.

So if it was a happy day for her, it must be for me, too.

After that my mother, Lady Salisbury and Lady Bryan talked to me often about the Emperor. They made me feel that I was the most fortunate girl in the world because I was to be his bride.

He was powerful; he was clever; he was handsome; he was everything that a young girl could hope for in a husband. By great good fortune I had been saved from a match with the wicked and corrupt Court of France, and now I was to be awarded the greatest prize in Christendom.

My bridegroom-to-be was twenty-three years old. I was six, so there did seem to be a certain disparity in our ages. This was nothing, my mother told me. I would soon grow up. I wanted to say that Charles would grow too and as I grew older so must he. In eight years, they told me, when I was fourteen, Charles would be in his prime.

It was wonderful to see everyone happy; so I was happy, too, for I believed that everything that pleased my mother must be good and right and please me.

One day she told me that Charles was so delighted with

26

everything he had heard of me that he was coming to England to see me for himself and that if I pleased him there would be a formal betrothal.

I was a little anxious that I might not please him, but the Countess soothed my anxieties with a tender smile. 'You are your father's daughter, Princess,' she said. 'That is enough to please anyone.'

All the women of the household used to talk of my romance with the Emperor Charles.

'The Princess is in love,' they would say. 'I declare she is always dreaming about her bridegroom. And who can wonder? Such a bridegroom! The great Emperor himself.'

It was a game to me. I laughed with them. It seemed wonderful to be in love because it made everyone so happy.

My mother came to Ditton. She was very excited.

'I have wonderful news for you, little daughter. The Emperor will soon be here.'

I clasped my hands. I should see him . . . this wonderful creature, this god who, in my mind, would be rather like my father but not frightening, tender like my mother, in spite of the fact that he was as powerful – or almost – as my father.

'Yes,' said my mother. 'Although at this time he is engaged in a war, he is coming to see you.'

It seemed marvellous. No one told me that it was *because* he was engaged in a war, because he wanted my father's support against the French, that he had agreed to take me as his bride, even though he would have to wait years before I could take up that position, and that in his mind this was something which might never happen.

I believed then that he loved me. I had been told so, and it did not occur to me, at that time, that my elders did not always mean what they said. They had told me that I was going to live happily with him for the rest of my life, and this would begin as soon as I was old enough to go to him. What could be more enticing than a rosy future in the far distance, so that I could contemplate it with a comforting pleasure knowing that nothing could be changed for many years?

It seemed so simple as my inexperienced imagination grappled with the scraps of information I received. I saw the wicked King François, with his long nose and satanic eyes, who had betrayed my father at the Field of the Cloth of Gold, who, all the time he had been professing friendship, was trying to humiliate him, who had greeted him as brother merely because he wanted help against that knight of shining virtue, the Emperor Charles.

In due course Charles arrived in England. It was June, four months after my sixth birthday. I was at Greenwich, in a state of immense excitement because this most wonderful being would in due course arrive here and I should come face to face with him.

The Countess talked continually of him – of what I must do, of how I must not speak unless spoken to. I must practise the virginals, for he would surely wish to hear me play. I danced well, but I must dance better. I must outshine all other dancers. He would be interested in my learning perhaps more than my social graces. He was that sort of man. So I must be at my best in every way. There were discussions with the seamstress. What should I wear for the great occasion?

I was in a fever of excitement.

'The Princess is in love,' giggled the women.

Each day I awaited his arrival and was disappointed.

'Why does he not come?' I demanded of Lady Salisbury.

'Your father will not let him go,' she replied. 'You see, the Emperor is a very great ruler. He is as important in his own country as your father is here. They will have much to speak of. Your father will wish to give him great entertainments and, although the Emperor would rather come to see his bride, etiquette demands that he must partake in all the banquets, witness the masques and enjoy the pleasures

28

which have been prepared for him. That is why he cannot come immediately.'

There were accounts of what was happening. London, I heard, was eager to welcome the Emperor. I thought this was because everyone was aware of his excellence. I did not know that our recent friendship with the French had threatened the trade in wool which was our country's greatest export, and that the merchants realized that alliance with the Emperor was more beneficial to us than that with France. I did not know that the Emperor was most anxious for England's support against his enemy King François and that there was nothing more calculated to make firm alliances between countries than marriages. I also did not know that betrothals were undertaken with an ease only to be compared with that with which they were set aside when it was expedient to do so.

How could I at the age of six be expected to know such things? It is only by bitter experience that one learns.

So I listened to the reports of the meeting between my father and the Emperor, and I could visualize the banners in the streets, the Lord Mayor and the Aldermen, so splendidly attired, all the citizens of London, and the King and the Queen riding out to welcome my betrothed, surrounded by their retinue of noblemen, each trying to outdo the others in his glory.

I imagined the pageants, the speeches of welcome, the plays performed for the Emperor's enjoyment. I wished that I could see them: the wonderful tableaux which sprang to life as the Emperor approached, representing the two rulers embracing. There was one, I heard, representing England. It was quite magical. It was of the countryside and depicted birds and animals, and above it was an image of God with a banner proclaiming: 'Blessed are the peacemakers, for they are the children of God.'

Every day I heard of the tournaments and masques which were performed for the Emperor's pleasure. They

29

were very extravagant and many of them reviled the wicked French and depicted the determination of the new allies to suppress the sly François.

'The Emperor,' said the Countess, 'is a very serious young man. It is said that he would prefer to talk of diplomacy, but the King is determined to show him how he welcomes his friends.'

What the Emperor wanted was something more than a mockery of the French; he wanted more than sympathetic talk; he wanted action from my father; in other words, he wanted the English to declare war on France; and in exchange for this he was ready to be betrothed to the King's daughter.

My mother came to Greenwich. There was great excitement. At last it was about to happen. I was to see my bridegroom.

My mother was all smiles and happiness. She said to me: 'He is coming to see you. Your father and he have come to an agreement. All is going well.' Then she took me into her arms. 'This is the dearest wish of my life. My dear sister's boy and my own daughter. If I could only tell you what this means to me!'

She was brisk suddenly. 'Now we must prepare,' she told me. 'We must be ready when he comes. We must not disappoint him. We must make sure that you are all that he has been led to believe you are.'

There was little time left. I practised the virginals. I danced, twirling as I had never twirled before; and in due course I donned the most splendid garments I had ever worn and was standing beside my mother when the barge containing my betrothed came sailing along the river to Greenwich.

I could hear the music and the cheering of the people on the banks of the river. I felt my mother's reassuring touch on my shoulder.

'Soon now, daughter,' she murmured. 'Soon he will be here.'

He stood there beside my father in the barge. The contrast was great. Every man looked insignificant beside my father so I was accustomed to that. In cloth of gold with diamonds in his bonnet my father scintillated; and with him was the Cardinal in his magnificent red. Charles . . . he was so different. His clothes were black and sombre, lightened only by the heavy gold chain about his neck. But when he took off his cap I saw how fair his hair was, and I thought: He is as kingly as my father and he does not need fine clothes to remind people of this. They had told me that I was in love with him and I believed I was. It suddenly seemed to me that there was something more dignified in garments that were sombre than those of a gaudy richness. Such thoughts might have been disloyal to my father, but I had to remember that I was in love. I must be, because they had told me so; and I was happy to see my mother so contented.

My mother and he looked at each other in silence for a few moments, then they embraced.

He spoke to her in Spanish and she answered him. There was a trill of happiness in her voice. She told me afterwards that meeting him brought back memories of her childhood and her sister and dear mother. His first words were of the happiness it gave him to see his dear aunt and his charming cousin, whom he already loved.

Then he knelt and, as I had been told to do, I stretched out my hand; he took it and kissed it.

I was able to study him. He was tallish, though no man looked tall beside my father. Being so fair, he did not look Spanish. His father had been Austrian and one of the handsomest men in Europe. He had been known as 'Philip the Fair'. Charles was very pale, and his eyes were of light blue. His teeth were a little discoloured and he had a heavy jaw which I learned he had inherited from the Hapsburgs.

He was not handsome after the manner of my father, but his eyes were gentle and his smile told me that he liked me.

My father was watching with good humour, so I knew that all was well.

It was a happy time. I played the virginals for him; I danced; and he looked on with approval.

People said: 'The Princess is enchanting.'

I suppose those were some of the happiest days of my life.

It seemed that he was with us for a long time. When I look back, I feel sure that he looked without amusement upon those merry masques. When my father entered the great hall in an assumed disguise – as if his royal dignity could ever have been concealed; he was himself and there was none other like him – Charles would rather have been discussing ways of defeating the French than partaking in frivolous dances.

He was always kind and attentive to me. We rode together. He told my mother that I must learn the Spanish tongue, and she agreed with him. She had spoken it with me now and then, so that I was not entirely ignorant of it – a fact which pleased Charles very much.

* * *

After a week or so at Greenwich, we travelled to Windsor, where the matrimonial treaty was signed. It was a very solemn ceremony presided over by the Cardinal, and when it ended I was the affianced bride of the Emperor, destined one day to rule over many lands.

It was awe-inspiring, and I thought I should be happy for the rest of my days.

I learned that I was to be married when I was twelve years old.

England had declared war on France, and my father and the Emperor had agreed as to how they would divide that country between them when they had conquered it.

I was dismayed when I heard that Charles wished me to go to Spain that I might be brought up in the Spanish manner. Fortunately my parents would not allow this. I was delighted and flattered that they did not want to part with me.

My father said that, if I was to be brought up as a Spanish lady, who better to supervise the upbringing than my own mother?

I could see that the idea delighted her, for she could spend more time with me than previously her duties as Queen had allowed her to.

There always had been a special love between my mother and me and as we grew closer she talked to me more openly than she had before. I was growing up; and she was delighted that I was destined for Spain.

'My dearest child,' she said. 'I always knew that a daughter has to leave her mother at some time. I left mine to come to England. But I shall know that you will be in Spain, my country . . . the land where I spent my childhood, and you will go there as a bride. You will love Spain, Mary. You will love it because it was your mother's home and you will love it for itself and because it will become yours. We are more serious than the English. We are more restrained . . . more formal. Your father is one whom the English love — although in truth he is half Welsh . . . but he has become an ideal Englishman. He is greatly loved by his subjects. You, my child, are more as I am. Spain will be your natural home. I am so happy for you.'

She talked then of her mother and her father, Isabella and Ferdinand. 'My mother was the most wonderful lady I ever knew. She was a great ruler and a loving mother. It is not always easy to be both. You are an only child.' I saw the look of terror pass over her face, and it frightened me. 'I was the youngest of the family,' she went on. 'I had a brother and three sisters. I was happy in my family, and in spite of the fact that my mother was much engaged in matters of state, she had always time to spend with us, to listen to what we had to say and to make us understand that, whatever else she was, she was first our mother.'

Her sad eyes looked back to those days and I saw them light up with the pleasure which comes from happy memories, even though they must be tinged with sorrow because they are past.

'I was only five . . . more or less your age . . . when my sister Isabel was betrothed in Seville to Alfonso of Portugal. It was a grand ceremony. My sisters Juana and Maria were with me. Two years later I was present at the triumphant entry into Granada. That was when my parents had driven out the Moors. They were stirring times . . . and yet I remember more clearly our family life than these great events.'

'You must have been sad, my lady, to leave it.'

'Ah, my dear child, how sad I was . . . and how frightened! I was sixteen years old when I set sail for England. I came to marry your Uncle Arthur, you know. Poor Arthur, he died soon after our marriage.'

'And then you married my father.'

'Yes, but it was not until some time after.' She shut her eyes as though this was something too painful to contemplate.

'So you have had two husbands, my lady.'

'Arthur was not really a husband. Well, we had gone through the ceremony but he was too young for marriage, and all the time we were together he was ill . . . so ill.'

'You loved him, did you?'

She hesitated. 'He was a kind, good boy, but he was so sick . . . so different from your father. It was hard to believe that they were brothers. We were sent down to Ludlow because, as he was Prince of Wales, he must have his own Court. We had only been there a few months when he died. Poor Arthur, his was a sad life. And then your father, who had been destined for the Church, became the Prince of Wales and future King.'

'It is hard to imagine my father's being anything but King, and certainly not a priest.'

She nodded. 'Yes. He was made for kingship. Ah, I grow sad, thinking of the old days, and now we have so much for which we can rejoice. You are going to be happy, my daughter. And we have to prepare you for your future. I am glad Dr Linacre is with us. He was tutor to Prince Arthur and I know his value.'

I liked Dr Linacre. He was a very old man – a scholar as well as a doctor of medicine. He had written several books – chiefly on grammar. There was one he had produced for Prince Arthur and he had done another for me. He was rather feeble now and very different from Johannes Ludovicus Vives, whom my mother had brought from Spain to supervise my studies.

With the coming of this man, my life changed. It was my first encounter with a fanatic. He was pale, aesthetic and lean. He was one of those people who enjoy tormenting themselves as well as other people. It was his firm belief that we were not sent on Earth to enjoy our lives, and that there was a great virtue in suffering. The more thorny our earthly path, the greater glory we should come to in Heaven. He was completely different from my father, who, while he always kept a wary and placating eye on the life to come, had a great determination to enjoy his time on Earth; and I was sure he believed that it was God's will, since he had been endowed with special means to do so. They had one thing in common though; they were both tyrants, but I did not discover this in my father until later. It is amazing, looking back, how clearly one sees things. My firm belief in the Catholic Faith and my conviction that all those who diverged from it were sinners who deserved to die were instilled into me at an early age – and I could never rid myself of them. My frail health might have been due to long hours spent over my books and anxiety to please my exacting tutor.

My half-sister Elizabeth, who at this time was not born, but who later became so important in my life that she seemed at times to dominate it, was given a similar education, but she was different. She never felt the same fidelity to religion; she had her eyes set on one goal throughout her life; she wanted to rule the country, and rarely did she stray from the path of self-interest. She would have been a Catholic if that was what people wanted. She was not there to plague me at this time, but later I did fall into the habit of comparing myself with her.

Vives had made it clear that if he was to have charge of my education, he must have complete control. My mother was absolutely under his influence. He was Spanish and I was to be Spanish. From my marriage with her nephew, she could find consolation for all that she had suffered in England. As for my father, he was immersed in his own schemes at this time and they did not include me . . . only when I became a minor nuisance, but this was not so at this early stage.

He had said: 'If the Emperor could search all Christendom for a mistress to bring up the Princess Mary and frame her after the manner of Spain, who could be found more meet than the Queen's Grace, her mother, who comes of the royal House of Spain and who, for the affection she beareth the Emperor, will nurture her and bring her up to his satisfaction.'

It sounded very flattering to my mother, and I was delighted that he was anxious that I should not go to Spain as the Emperor wished. In my innocence I thought it was a measure of my father's love for me.

How bitter I became later and it was small wonder. In fact, he did not wish me to go because in his heart he was already wondering whether the match would ever take place and whether he should soon reverse his loyalties and it would be the French for whom he would show friendship, which could mean offering up his daughter on a different sacrificial altar.

But at that time I lived in my dreams, and I must obey the rules which Vives had drawn up and submitted to my parents. I must be governed by these rules, and there must be no divergence from them. Then he said I should remember my mother's domestic example of probity and wisdom and, except all human expectations fail, I should be holy and good by necessity.

My mother had been brought up most virtuously, but she had had sisters and a brother, and I used to long for some of my own. If only I had a sister – someone to play with, to share things with. I knew enough to realize that I was echoing the wishes of my parents.

I had been rather fond of stories of romance and chivalry. It had been pleasant after lessons and outdoor exercise to settle down and read with the Countess or perhaps Margaret Bryan.

When Vives heard this he was shocked. 'Idle books!' he declared. 'There shall be an end to this. If there are stories for recreation, they must be from the Bible, though the classical and historical might be permitted occasionally.'

Everything I did must be with the object of improving my mind. Fiction was out of the question. No more romances, such as Lancelot du Lac and Pyramus and Thisbe. I might read the story of the patient Griselda, for this would strengthen my character.

Card-playing was definitely forbidden. I must not preoccupy myself with finery of any sort. Instead of gloating over silks and fine brocades, I should commit to memory certain Greek and Latin passages which would be set for me; and I was recommended to repeat them at night until I was word perfect. Only then could I go to bed with the knowledge that I had earned my rest.

I was spending a great deal of time at my desk. I had

always been a studious child and fond of learning, but I did want a chance to be out of doors, to train my goshawk, perhaps to play games with other children. I grew rather pale. I was already a little thin.

The Countess was worried. She had long conversations with my mother.

'The Princess is but a child,' she said. 'There is too much work and too little play.'

'She has to be trained for a great role,' explained my mother. 'Johannes Ludovicus Vives is one of the greatest living scholars. We must keep to his rules or he will turn his back on us and go back to Spain.'

'Better that than the Princess's health should suffer.'

My mother began to worry about my health but she felt that Vives must not be offended.

The Countess was adamant. There were occasions when she remembered that she was a Plantagenet, and this was one of them. She declared that she would not be responsible for my health if the rules were not relaxed a little.

'It is true that the Princess must study,' she said, 'but she is already beyond the standard expected of a princess of her age. There should be leisure in everyone's life, particularly for the young.'

She so thoroughly alarmed my mother that I did study less. Sometimes I think they were right to drive me, for although my health has at times been frail, I was always able to enjoy the company of some of the wisest men in the kingdom, which must have been due to my excellent education.

When the question of my being overstrained was brought to the notice of Vives, he pointed out that the daughters of Sir Thomas More were examples of educated women, and they could be regarded as a lesson to all. Sir Thomas's daughter Margaret was the most highly educated woman of the time and she was in good health. When I learned something of the More household, I realized that in such a

38

happy family, which was full of fun and laughter, learning had been something to be enjoyed; and Sir Thomas would never force his children to do what they did not wish to. It was not that I did not *want* to learn. I did. It was just that I was often so tired and in danger of falling asleep at my desk.

All the time I thought of the Emperor Charles. I built up a picture of a hero in my mind. My mother, the Countess and all the women of the household constantly told me how much I loved my future husband. He was always in my thoughts. When I read my books, when I translated my Latin passages, I thought of him and how proud he would be of me.

* * *

This state of affairs continued for two years, until I was nine years old. It was the year 1526 – an eventful one for me because, I suppose, during it I grew up. I ceased to be an innocent child, for many things were revealed to me.

I had been vaguely aware that a great deal had been happening in Europe during that time. I had known that my father and my beloved Emperor were friends and allies and that we were at war with that wicked man of Europe whose evil schemes the heroes were determined to suppress. That was François Premier.

One day I saw my mother in a state of great excitement. It was good news, she told me. The war would soon be over. François, attempting to take Pavia, had been captured and was now the Emperor's prisoner in Madrid.

It was wonderful. It was good triumphing over evil, which I believed to be always the case in the end.

'Your father and the Emperor will now jointly invade France, and between them they will share that land.'

I listened, starry-eyed.

The Cardinal came to see me. I was not sure that I liked

him. He was always rather unctuous but at the same time giving an impression that it would be unwise to cross him.

He kissed my hand with reverence and asked after my health. Then he told me he had brought something to show me. He opened a case and in it was a magnificent emerald ring.

'It is very beautiful,' I said.

'His Grace, your father, and I believe it is time you showed the Emperor your true feelings for him. I know you regard him with great tenderness.'

'Yes, my lord Cardinal.'

He smiled at me. 'That is well. Did you know that the emerald is often a gift bestowed by lovers? It is said that the brilliant green will fade if the lover who receives it is unfaithful. Would you not like to send this to the Emperor as a token of your love for him?'

'Oh yes,' I said. 'Yes, I should like to do that.'

He smiled benignly. 'I have written a letter telling him that your love for His great Eminence has raised such a passion in you that it is confirmed by jealousy, which is the first sign and token of love.'

'Perhaps one should not say that, there being no cause for jealousy.'

'Ah, but you would be jealous if there was a cause.'

'Oh . . . mayhap,' I agreed.

'Then it shall be sent. I am sure the emerald will retain its brilliant green for many a year.'

So the emerald was sent and the Cardinal visited me again to tell me that when the Emperor received the ring he had said he would wear it for the sake of the Princess. Those were his very words.

The Cardinal seemed very satisfied, smiling inwardly, it seemed to me, by which I mean not at me but at his secret thoughts.

I wondered why, after so many years, I should have been given this emerald to send to my betrothed. Why so

40

suddenly? But then he had said he would wear it for my sake, and that warmed my heart.

I was to learn later. It was all part of the rude awakening.

Everything began to go wrong in that year. Perhaps it was because I was getting to an age of understanding. I had not seen the evil which existed all around me. Perhaps I should have noticed my mother's tragic looks, the furtive glances which members of my household gave each other; perhaps I should have noticed the whispering in the corners. I was so immersed in my studies that I had no time to observe what was going on.

My father was preparing to join the Emperor in the campaign against France. François was the Emperor's prisoner and my father wanted to help Charles complete the conquest.

An army was being raised and taxes were being levied throughout the country. Those with high incomes had to pay as much as three shillings and fourpence for every pound they earned. I heard some of the lower servants talking of it.

It was causing a great deal of trouble. I must have been aware at that stage of the growing tension, for I was constantly listening to conversations not meant for me – not of those who were close to me, for they were very careful to keep me in the dark, but sometimes the scullions and serving maids would pass below my window and I would stand there trying to catch what was said.

One day I heard three or four of them talking together. There was excitement in their voices. 'It could spread . . .' one maid was saying. 'I know it started in the eastern counties on account of the cloth workers . . .'

'Who can blame them? What do they care for wars in France if they have no bread to give their children?'

'Left without work, they were . . . on account of their masters not having the money to pay them.'

'On account of paying the tax for the King's war.'

41

'All very well . . . but I tell you what. It's spread to London. That's going to mean something.'

'What do you think? Revolt?'

"'Twouldn't be the first time.'

I was trembling with indignation. They were speaking treason. They were criticizing my father. They were talking of uprisings against him.

There were times when the Countess was on the point of telling me something. She would start to speak and then stop and frown, perhaps shrug her shoulders and then begin to talk of something else.

My mother, too, was preoccupied. I felt they were both holding something back from me and, when I heard talk such as that of the servants, I began to grow alarmed.

Pliny and Socrates lost their interest. It was the present day . . . my father, the Emperor and the King of France . . . the Cardinal and the cloth workers who began to take possession of my mind. I was nine years old – a precocious nine. I wanted to know what was going on.

It was not often that I saw my mother, and those occasions when I did were very precious. I did not want to spoil them by making her more unhappy than she already was. I could not ask her the questions I longed to, for my reason told me that they would be upsetting to her; so I sought subjects which I thought would please her.

It was different with the Countess. As I was sure she had often been on the verge of telling me something, perhaps a little prompting would urge her to tell me what I felt I ought to know.

'Countess,' I said, when we were alone together, 'what is happening? Is it true that there are riots in the country?'

'Where did you learn such things?'

'I hear scraps of conversation.'

She frowned. Then she shrugged her shoulders and said: 'There has been a certain amount of trouble in some parts of the country.'

42

'The cloth workers of the eastern counties,' I said, 'and now in London.'

She was astonished.

She said: 'I forget how you grow up. You are too old for your years. I suppose you should know these things.' She hesitated and then seemed to come to a decision. 'Yes,' she went on. 'There has been trouble. It is the new tax. It was crippling to the manufacturers who could not pay their workers. It was for the war against France. The King and the Cardinal saw that it would be unwise to have trouble at home. So the tax was withheld and the people paid just what they liked.'

'Was that enough?'

'Well . . . yes . . . as it turned out, because there was not to be a war in France after all.'

'But was not my father fighting with the Emperor against France?'

'My dear Princess, at one time that was so, but relations between countries . . . politics . . . they change so quickly. An enemy of one day is a friend the next.'

'How can that be?'

She was silent for a while, then she said: 'A ruler has to consider what is best for his country.'

'But the Emperor is a good ruler and so is the King, my father, but the King of France . . . he is wicked.'

'Dearest Princess, it may be that one day you will be a ruler.'

I caught my breath.

'Well,' she went on, 'you are the King's only child.'

'But not a son.'

'You are the next in line. I have always thought you should learn more of affairs of state. Latin and Greek are all very well . . . but they are not going to help you rule a country.' She seemed to come to a decision. 'I think you should know that at the moment relations between your father and the Emperor are . . . a little strained.'

'You mean they are not good friends?'

'Heads of state are not really good friends in the sense we think of in our ordinary relationships. If what is good for one's country is good for another, then those rulers are friends. If not . . . they are enemies.'

'But the King of France has no right to his crown. France belongs to us.'

'The King of France could say we have never had a right to it. It is just a matter of the way one looks at these things.'

'But right must be right and wrong wrong.'

'My dear Princess, you are very clever, but you are young and no matter how clever the young are, they lack experience. You will remember that not long ago we were friends with the French. You remember the meeting at Guisnes and Ardres?'

'The Field of the Cloth of Gold!'

'Ah, I see you do.'

'But they deceived us. All the time they were pretending.'

'Perhaps everyone was pretending. However, that could be treasonable talk, so let us avoid it and not concern ourselves with who was dissimulating. It is past and it is the future we have to think of. The King of France is the prisoner of the Emperor Charles, and the Emperor is in a strong position. He no longer needs the help of England as he once did. I have to tell you something which may be a shock to you. Of course, you have met the Emperor only once.'

'It was enough to tell me that I loved him.'

'Dear Princess, you know nothing of love . . . not the sort of love between a man and his wife. Your mother loves you dearly; so does your father; so do I and Margaret Bryan. Many people love you. We want everything that is good for you. It is different with the Emperor.'

'What do you mean? He is going to be my husband.'

The Countess shook her head. 'You see, my dearest Princess, these marriages are arranged in accordance with

44

what is best for the country. The Emperor and your father wanted to make an alliance against France; he was unmarried, and the King has a daughter – you. But you must realize that the disparity in your ages did make your marriage rather a remote possibility.'

'Do you mean that the Emperor doesn't want to marry me any more?'

She was silent and I felt blank with dismay.

Then she went on: 'It has not gone as far as that. Oh, I shall tell you, for I think you should know. I, who am here in your household, know you better than anyone perhaps. You are older than your years and I do not believe you should be deluded any longer.'

'Please tell me, Countess.'

'It may be something of a shock. You see, you did not really know the Emperor. People have told you that he is a hero . . . the greatest match in Christendom. They have represented him as benevolent and powerful. Powerful he undoubtedly is, but he is first of all a ruler. Through his father and his mother he inherited great territories. A ruler has first of all to think what is best for his country.'

'What are you trying to tell me, Countess? That I am not good for his country?'

'He no longer needs your father. He has the King of France in his hands. No ruler wants to impoverish his country in useless wars. The Emperor, it seems, is not one who wants glory for showy conquests; he wants to bring prosperity and power to his dominions. He no longer needs your father's help.'

'So you mean that it was solely because he wanted that, that he became betrothed to me?'

'That is how royal marriages are made. In fact, the marriages of most of us come about because of the advantages they can bring to our families, and with the sons and daughters of kings it is for the good of the country.'

'You mean that he really did not love me. But I . . .'

45

'No, Princess, you did not love him. You did not know him. You were told you loved him. You thought it was love, as in those romances which Vives forbade you to read. Perhaps he was right, for they gave you idealistic ideas which are not always true to life.'

'What has happened? Please tell me, Countess.'

'The Emperor is considering marrying Isabel of Portugal.'

'But how can he do that?'

'With the greatest of ease. He has asked your father to send you to Spain immediately, with your dowry of 400,000 ducats, and he wants an undertaking from your father to contribute half of the expenses of the war with France. Those are his terms. He knows they are ones which your father cannot fulfil for he could not raise the money without plunging this country into disorder.'

'So that means . . .'

'It means that the Emperor is hinting that the agreement with your father is coming to an end.'

'So it was not I whom he loved . . .'

'Little Princess, it never was. We do not live in a dream world where gallant knights in shining armour die for their ladies. It is a harsh world, and the realities are quite different. There is love. You have mine. I would do anything I could for your happiness; and you know how dear you are to your mother. But we live close to you. We know you. You are a living human being to us. You are not a counter in a game to be moved this way or that. You are our own dear Princess whom we love. That is the love to seek and cherish; and perhaps, in time, when a husband is found for you, you will grow together and love each other in due course. It happens again and again.

'I was eighteen years old when I married. It is a good age to marry, for although one is young, one has had time to glean some experience. My husband was chosen for me.' Her eyes were reminiscent, as she went on: 'He was Sir

46

Richard Pole and owned lands in Buckinghamshire. The King, your grandfather, approved of the match and he made him a Squire of the Body and a Knight of the Garter. He served the King faithfully. He distinguished himself in the Perkin Warbeck revolt and he fought well for the King in Scotland. Then he went to Wales as a Gentleman of the Bedchamber to Prince Arthur, who, as you know, was married to your mother before she married the King.'

'Yes, I know,' I said, 'but it was no real marriage. He was too young and sick.'

She nodded. 'My husband and I were married for nearly fourteen years and then he died.'

'You must have been very sad.'

'Yes . . . but I had my children. You see, there are compensations. They made it all worth while. We had five children: Henry, Arthur, Reginald, Geoffry and Ursula.'

'My mother must envy you. She is sad because she has only one.'

'But that one is more precious to her because she is the only one.'

'But all yours are precious to you. I know by the way you speak of them . . . particularly Reginald.'

'Parents should not have a favourite.'

'But they do . . . and yours is Reginald.'

She smiled at me. 'So you see, my dear, you must not grieve. You must look for happiness. You must accept your lot, and if the marriage with the Emperor does not take place, after all, you will say to yourself, perhaps it was for the best.'

'I cannot forget him as easily as that.'

'Dear child, you did not know him. You have built up a picture of him. You are so young. You know nothing of these matters.'

'Because no one tells me.'

She was silent for a while. Then she said: 'Perhaps I

have talked too much. Your mother is very unhappy at this time.'

'She wanted so much for me to marry the Emperor because he is half Spanish and her nephew.'

'Yes. You should wait until she talks to you of these matters. She has much on her mind. When she is with you, you must try to distract her from her melancholy. Do not let her see that you are affected because this marriage with the Emperor is not to take place.'

I nodded gravely. She took my hand and kissed it.

'You are a good child,' she said and there were tears in her eyes. 'I hope and pray that all goes well with you. It has been my great privilege to serve in your household, and you will always be as my own to me.'

I kissed her tenderly. I loved her very much and I could see how anxious she was, fearing that she had said too much. What she had said could have been construed as treason. Since her brother, Edward, Earl of Warwick, had been murdered on the orders of my grandfather, Henry VII, for no other reason than that he was a Plantagenet with a claim to the throne, the Countess had lived under the shadow of the axe, for it could descend upon her if she were to utter one careless word which could be construed as treason.

She had taken certain risks in talking to me so frankly, and I knew that it was because of her love for me that she had done so. She had realized that certain events could not be kept from me much longer and she wanted to prepare me for them.

I was desolate. I told myself that I should be heartbroken if it really came to pass that the Emperor jilted me.

* * *

Now that the Countess had spoken to me more frankly than ever before, the ice was broken and she was less restrained than she had been hitherto. She must have felt that, having

48

gone so far, there was no point in holding anything back which it would soon be impossible to keep from me for long.

But I was still in the dark regarding the really great trouble which was to make such a difference to both my mother and me and which was to cast a dark shadow over our lives. I thought at the time that my mother's tragic looks were due solely to the fact that she was upset because of the strained relationship between my father and the Emperor, but I soon learned this was not so.

An event took place in June of that year which I found irritating, though little did I understand its significance at that time.

I had always been aware of the existence of Henry Fitzroy and what a trial he was to my mother because he was a continual reproach to her. *She* could not give the King a son but another woman could, which pointed to the conclusion that the fault lay with the Queen.

Henry Fitzroy had been born in June six years before, and to celebrate his birthday there was a very grand ceremony, and on that day he was made a Knight of the Garter.

To bestow such an honour on one so young seemed in itself ridiculous but the King was anxious to show his feelings for his son, and at this time – though I learned this later – he was calling attention to the sorry plight in which he and the nation had been placed by his marriage to a woman who could not bear a son.

I did not see my mother at this time. Even my father would not expect her to be present at such a ceremony, for he must have realized how painful it would be to her. It was an indication of his resentment that he had allowed it to take place. Later I saw how every act of his at this time was working towards one end.

This ceremony concerned me too. I was the heir to the throne. What did the King mean by bestowing such an honour on his bastard? It must have occurred to many that he intended to set the boy above me. It would never be tolerated. The people of England would not have a bastard on the throne.

Being but nine years old, and only just made aware of the perfidy of rulers, I could not grasp the significance of these events; but at the same time I was aware of disaster looming. It was like the shivering of aspen leaves when a storm is approaching; it was in the silences of people around me and the sudden termination of conversations when I approached.

Soon after the ceremony the French envoy, De Vaux, came to London. He had been sent, the Countess told me, by the mother of François who was acting as the Regent of France during the King's absence in Madrid.

'Why is he here?' I asked.

'It is to make terms with your father.'

'That means there is peace with France?'

'There will be.'

'What of the Emperor? Our alliance with him is over?'

'Well, the war is over now.'

'So we are no longer friends with him?'

'Oh, it will be amicably settled . . . but no one has any wish to continue with the war.'

'But why does the French envoy come here?'

'He will make peace terms with your father.'

'It seems so strange. We hated them so much and now there are lavish entertainments for the French.'

'That is diplomacy.'

'I do not understand it.'

'Few people understand diplomacy. It is a veil of discretion and politeness covering the real meaning.'

'Why do people not say what they mean?'

'Because that could be very disturbing.'

I did know that I was one of the subjects which was

being discussed by my father, the Cardinal and the French envoy. First it was announced that I was to go to Ludlow.

My mother came to tell me this. I noticed that she looked older. There was grey in her hair, more lines on her face, and her skin had lost its healthy colour.

'You are to go to Ludlow, my dear child,' she told me. 'You will like it there.'

'I wonder why I am so suddenly to go,' I said. I was beginning to realize that there were usually reasons.

'Your father thinks it would be good for you to go. You see, Ludlow is an important place. Your Uncle Arthur was there just before he died. I remember it well. It is a very beautiful spot. Prince Arthur was Prince of Wales when he was there, and you will be the Princess of Wales. Your father is going to give you that title.'

I was pleased, particularly as I had felt that fluttering of alarm because of the honour done to Henry Fitzroy.

'Your household will go with you,' my mother explained. 'It will be just as it is here.'

'And you, my lady?'

Her lips tightened as though she were trying to control some emotion.

'I shall, of course, be with the Court. But we shall meet often and there will be no change. Your father will wish you to go very soon.'

The Countess told me that it was good that we were going. 'It means,' she explained, 'that your father is telling the world that you are Princess of Wales.'

'That means the heir to the throne, does it not?'

'It does indeed.'

'Perhaps he thought that people wondered after the honour done to Henry Fitzroy.'

'Oh, that was not important. You must not think that it detracts from you. You are his daughter. Everyone knows that. They know the respect that is due to you. Now we shall have to prepare for your departure, which I believe is to be soon.'

* * *

My parents and the Court accompanied me to Langley in Hertfordshire, and there I said goodbye to them. There was some constraint between my parents, and I thought there was something forced in my father's laughter. He was almost boisterously merry. He embraced me warmly and referred to me as his Princess, the Princess of Wales.

The Countess had told me that it was the first time the title had been bestowed on a member of the female sex, so I should be very proud. My mother smiled on me warmly but she could not hide her sorrow from me. I wanted to protect her, to share her unhappiness – if she would but tell me the cause of it. I still thought it had something to do with the Emperor and believed we might have comforted each other.

There was a certain sadness when we parted, although my mother said we should meet often and my father took every opportunity of showing his affection for me.

At length they had gone and I, with my entourage, made my way to Ludlow.

The countryside is exceptionally beautiful, and the castle stood on the north-west side of the charming town. Some of the people came out of their houses to cheer me as I passed, and that pleased me.

The Countess told me that in the castle I should have a larger household than I had had before. Princess Mary had become the Princess of Wales, and there was a distinction.

I was gratified. I had been foolish, I told myself, to have had qualms about the little bastard Fitzroy. How could I have thought that the King would contemplate putting him above me just because he was a boy? The people loved me. They had shown that. 'God bless the little Princess,' they had shouted. They could not call Henry Fitzroy a prince.

He was, after all, only Bessie Blount's son and I was the daughter of a princess of Spain.

The castle was a fine example of Norman architecture, having been built very soon after the Norman Conquest by a certain Roger de Montgomery. In a way there were sad memories within its walls for there, after the death of his father, little Edward V had lived for a while. It was in this very castle that he had been proclaimed King, and three months later he had been in the Tower with his young brother the Duke of York where, it was said, he had been murdered by his uncle, Richard III. I could not help thinking of that little boy who had lived here with a terrible fate hanging over him. It was a reminder of what harm could come to princes from those who coveted the throne.

My mother's first husband had lived here with her for five months before he died in this very castle. I imagined her living here . . . a young girl . . . in a new land. How sad for her when, so young, she found herself a widow.

She had spoken of those days with sadness. It was as though she looked shudderingly over her shoulder at the past. She had been alone and poor for so long before my father, like a gallant knight, had rescued her and made her his bride.

And now here was I, wondering now and then why I had been elevated and given a larger household. I did not know then that it was less grand than that which had been bestowed on Henry Fitzroy.

Life was different here. It was my first taste of queenship, for I was a little queen here. I was made to feel important. I had certain duties, and they were those of a ruler. I realized I was *learning* how to rule. People brought petitions to me and I presided over a Council. The Countess was invariably at my side. She taught me how to speak to the Council, how to deal with the people who came asking favours. There was less time spent at my desk. These were different lessons.

My household consisted of an impressive number of officials. I had my Lord Steward, the Chamberlain, Treasurer and Controller and many more, including fourteen ladies, all of high birth and in the charge of the Countess who ruled over us all and to whom I could always turn in moments of uncertainty.

I was forgetting my disappointment over the Emperor, although I could not entirely believe that he would not marry me. All the same, I was enjoying my new status. This was a miniature Court and I was learning to become a queen. I realized that I should enjoy that very much.

How different life had become from those long days of study under the guidance of Johannes Ludovicus Vives. The only thing lacking was the company of my mother. I thought of her often and used to say to myself: I wonder whether she sat here? Did she and Arthur walk along this path? It was long, long before I was born. It is hard when one is young to imagine a world without oneself.

Christmas came. It was a very merry one. I was at the centre of the revelry. We had our Lord of Misrule and many masques and I led the dances.

The Countess said she was delighted that I was enjoying the fun. I had a faint impression, though, that she was keeping something from me, which brought a little uneasiness into the jollity; but in those first months at Ludlow I was a little intoxicated with my new power. I had learned that I cared passionately about my position. I had not known before how much I wanted to be a queen.

It was March when I heard the news.

The Countess told me.

'You never talk of the Emperor now as you used to,' she said.

'I think of him still,' I told her.

'But you now understand, don't you, that the betrothal was in truth a matter of state . . . and such are laid on flimsy foundations?'

54

'What do you want to tell me, Countess?'

She sighed. 'Well, you have to know, but I believe it will not be such a shock as it might have been if you had not been warned. The Emperor has married Isabel of Portugal.'

I stared at her unbelievingly. Although it had been hinted that this marriage might take place, I had never expected that it would. He had been promised to me and I to him. How could he have married someone else?

The Countess was looking at me helplessly. 'You were only six,' she reminded me, 'and you only saw him for such a short time. It was all built up in your mind. You will see that when you look at it more clearly.'

'Yes,' I said, 'it was all built up in my mind.'

I pretended not to care. But I did; and often, when I was alone in my bed, I shed tears for the perfidy of rulers, for the loss of my beliefs, for the fact that my childish innocence had gone for ever.

Reginald Pole

The Emperor's marriage cast a blight over my life for some weeks. I would wake in the morning and ask myself how he could have behaved so. It could not be that he had been forced to. No one could force emperors. He could do as he wished, just as my father could. And he had abandoned me.

I tried to console myself that it was simply because of my youth. Had I been as old as Isabel of Portugal, he would have married me.

I wished that I could see my mother. I thought of how sad she would be, for she had so wanted me to marry her nephew and live in Spain.

But it was not to be, and life at Ludlow was very pleasant because I had tasted power and found that I liked it very much.

It was soon brought home to me that happiness was a fleeting emotion.

The Countess came to me one day and with some hesitation made a revelation to me that I found quite horrific.

What a wonderful person she was. She thought of me at every turn, and I knew she would without hesitation put herself in danger for my sake. At the time, of course, I did not fully realize how precariously placed were those who had Plantagenet blood in their veins.

The Countess knew that she must step warily but she was not lacking in courage and would always do what she considered right, no matter what the risk. On this occasion I was sure she felt she must prepare me for what was to come.

She began: 'You know, Princess, that the question of your marriage will be of considerable importance to your father. It is necessarily so because of your position.'

'Yes, I know that,' I said. 'But what is the use of making engagements when no one really considers them seriously?'

'They are of importance when they are made.'

'To be honoured only when people don't change their minds,' I remarked with some bitterness.

She put her arms round me as she sometimes did when we were alone.

'My dearest, the difference in your and the Emperor's age was so great. You see, if you could have been married immediately . . .'

'I am glad we did not. If he could not be faithful . . . if he could not keep his promises . . . it was better as it is.'

She held me against her soothingly. Then she said: 'There will be other arrangements.'

'I shall not regard them with any seriousness.'

'Well, you are young and it would be a year or two before any plans came to fruition.'

'Are you trying to tell me something, Countess?' I asked.

'Yes. But you must not take it seriously. It would never come to pass. It is just a gesture.'

'Who?' I asked.

'The King of France.'

I stared at her incredulously. The King of France! My father's enemy! The man who had been described to me as the most wicked in Europe. The man who had tried to humiliate my father at the Field of the Cloth of Gold. It was impossible to believe.

'But we were at war with him.'

'That is over. There is now peace, and our two countries are friends again. We are against the Emperor now.'

'Oh no . . . *no!*' I cried.

'You must not be upset. It will never come to anything.

I did not want it to shock you. That is why I warn you. You should not be unduly alarmed. It will never happen.'

'I thought he was the Emperor's prisoner.'

'There has been a treaty between them . . . the Treaty of Madrid. François is free, but there are harsh terms. He is having to give up much land to the Emperor . . . Milan, Naples and Burgundy, I believe, among much else. In the meantime he has been allowed his freedom, but he has sent his two sons to Madrid as hostages.'

'And he has agreed to that?'

'His sons are there now.'

'How could he? They are only little boys.'

'It is necessary that he return to his country. It is all very complicated.'

'And my father would marry me to this man!'

'I doubt there is any serious intention of doing that. It is just a gesture to the Emperor. You see, no ruler likes to see another too powerful, and several states are forming a league against the Emperor now.'

'It's horrible,' I said. 'I hate it.'

'It is the way states are governed.'

'I shall never govern that way.'

She smiled at me. 'You will be a wise and benign ruler, I know. But, just now you must not be disturbed about this proposed alliance. I will be ready to swear that nothing will come of it. There is another matter. One of the terms of the Treaty of Madrid is that François shall marry Charles' sister, Eleanora. He cannot evade his obligations because he has to think of his two hostage sons.'

'How old is the King of France, Countess?' I asked.

'About thirty-two.'

She did not add that most of those years had been spent in debauchery and that, coupled with the fact that he had been languishing in a Madrid prison where he had come near to death and probably would have died if his sister,

58

Marguerite, had not gone out to nurse him, he would probably seem older than his years warranted.

The King of France! He haunted my dreams. I had never seen him but I had often pictured his dark, satanic face. I had heard it said that no woman was safe once he had cast his lecherous eyes on her. Could it really be that my father would contemplate marrying me to such a man?

Not only had I lost my hero, the Emperor, but there was a possibility that I should be thrown to this monster.

Just as I had thought I was growing up and having power was going to be a wonderful experience, the truth was borne home to me. I was a woman. I could be snatched from my home at any moment. I could be given to any husband who happened to be important in the game of politics. It was the fate of princesses.

I lived in trepidation of the arrival of messengers from Court, demanding my presence that I might be betrothed to the fearsome and terrifying King of France.

* * *

The days began to pass and no one came to Court. The Countess said that it was such an absurd proposition that no one could take it seriously. I could rest assured that it was just an attempt to show the kindly feelings of England to a recent enemy.

My status at Ludlow had made me more interested in politics. But perhaps that was just because I was growing up. I should have liked to hear more of what was happening among the states of Europe than what occurred in the ancient Roman Empire. I had had a taste of authority and had seen how possible it was that one day I should rule England. My mother was now past childbearing and there was no one but myself; and the fact that I had been made Princess of Wales and given my own little Court at Ludlow was surely significant.

The defection of the Emperor had made me more aware.

I must thrust aside sentimentality. I must cease to dream of chivalry and romance. That was not for such as I was, and oddly enough I did not wish it to be different. My little taste of power had changed me. I felt a glow of satisfaction when I thought of the crown.

And then we had a visitor to Ludlow. The Countess brought him to me and said with great pride: 'Your Highness, may I present you to my son?'

And there was Reginald Pole. I held out my hand; he took it and kissed it.

He was very handsome and I liked him as soon as I saw him. He had a good face, and in spite of my growing cynicism, I very much wished to retain my belief in the triumph of goodness over evil. I warmed to him.

He was respectful but by no means subservient. I might be a Tudor but he was of the Plantagenet line, as royal as I – some would say more so.

He was of middle height and very slender, with a fair complexion, light brown hair and blueish grey eyes – a handsome man, but he had more than good looks. There was a nobility about him which came from within and coloured his entire personality.

'Reginald has just returned from Padua, where he has been studying,' went on the Countess.

'Do you intend to stay here in England?' I asked.

'I am as yet unsure, Princess,' he replied. 'So much depends on what happens.'

'The King received him with great pleasure,' the Countess told me.

'Yes,' agreed Reginald. 'He was very gracious to me. I told him that I should doubtless go to the Carthusian Monastery at Sheen to continue my studies.'

During the next days I was in the company of Reginald Pole a good deal. Although he was several years older than I – about sixteen, I believe – we were drawn to each other. I was glad then that Johannes Ludovicus Vives had made me study as I did because I could see now that I astonished Reginald with my learning.

The Countess was delighted by our friendship, and I believe she contrived it so that we should often be alone together. He used to talk to me as though I were of his own age which flattered me considerably. In Reginald's company I forgot my disappointment at the Emperor's perfidy and the impending dread of a possible marriage with François Premier.

Reginald had a great admiration and love for my father, which delighted me; he was also deeply attached to my mother.

His conversation was erudite but never condescending, and I always felt elevated after my sessions with him. He was frank about the past and my family's accession to the throne. Reginald was the sort of man who would maintain the truth at all costs and have died rather than deny it. He gave me back my belief in mankind. I shall always be grateful to Reginald Pole because he came into my life when I was bewildered and needed to have my faith restored. While there were such men as he was, I could believe in the human race again and should always do so.

He talked about his grandfather, George, Duke of Clarence who had died in the Tower at the instigation, some thought, of his brother King Edward IV.

'Oh,' he said, 'it is indeed dangerous to live close to the crown. You will always have to be on your guard, Princess.'

'I know that now.'

'One day you could be Queen of this country. You must be prepared.'

'I will be,' I told him. 'I am determined to.'

'You are so young,' he said, smiling tenderly.

'I feel I have advanced far in the last year.'

He understood at once. He knew that I had been bandied from the Emperor to the King of France. I think that when a closeness grows up between two people they can often

61

understand what is in each other's minds without the use of words.

'The match with François will never take place,' he assured me.

'I fervently hope and pray that it will not.'

'You can put your fears away. François will have to marry the Emperor's sister. He dare not refuse. His sons are in jeopardy. The match with you was never meant to be taken seriously.'

He told me how delighted he was to see the friendship between me and his mother.

'You are as dear to her as her own flesh and blood,' he told me.

'We have been together so long.'

'My mother is a wonderful woman. The King has been good to her. He restored her estates when he came to the throne and that was to compensate for the murder by the previous King of my uncle, the Earl of Warwick, who had a claim to the throne.'

'I know. I am sorry it was my grandfather who behaved so.'

'It is the lust for power. The glitter of the crown. Your grandfather felt it necessary. He was a man who never murdered for the sake of revenge or such motives – only when he feared the security of the crown.'

'Does that excuse him?' I asked.

'In the eyes of some who believe his motives were for the good of the country, yes. Those who think it is for the love of personal aggrandisement and power, no. And some believe that to murder in any circumstances is a mortal sin. You see, when there is more than one claimant to the throne the result can be civil war. Your grandfather, I am convinced, thought that should be stopped at all costs, and if the death of one man can save the lives of many which would be lost if there were war . . . his actions could be justified.'

'And what do you believe?'

'That each case should be judged by its merits.'

'Then you would excuse the murder of the Princes in the Tower?'

'Ah, you are getting into deep water, Princess. That remains a mystery, and it is always unwise to judge without being in possession of all the facts.'

'Is one ever in possession of all of them?'

'Hardly ever, I imagine.'

'Then it is always unwise to judge.'

He smiled that very sweet and gentle smile which I was growing to love. He said: 'I see you are a very logical princess. One must be sure of one's premise when in discussion with you.'

I liked to lure him into talking about himself. He had stories to tell of his first five years at Stourton Castle with his brothers and sister. Henry and Arthur were older than he was, and after his birth Geoffry and Ursula had joined the nursery. I had often heard the Countess talk of them, and I could well imagine that happy household presided over by my dear friend and governess, for most certainly she would give to her own children the same loving care which she had bestowed on me.

He told me how he had loved the Charterhouse at Sheen, where he had spent five years. Like myself, he had taken to learning and had always had the desire to add to his store of knowledge. In many ways we were very much alike. I suppose that was why, in such a short time, we had become such good friends.

'Your father always interested himself in me,' he told me. 'He could not forget what happened to my uncle. He carried his father's conscience.'

I glowed with pleasure because of this. I wanted so much for my father to be a good man as well as handsome and distinguished and able to shine above all others. I had uneasy twinges when I heard about the birth of Henry

Fitzroy after his elevation, both of which had caused great sorrow to my mother.

'The King insisted on paying for part of my education,' Reginald told me. 'He always calls me cousin. Then I went to Oxford, and there my tutor was Doctor Thomas Linacre who, I believe, was concerned with your education.'

'Oh yes – and my Uncle Arthur's too. He is a great scholar.'

'I owe him much. My mother always intended that I should go in the Church. I think my father expressed the wish that I should do so before he died.'

'And do you intend to?'

'Yes . . . but later. It is a decision I do not want to take just yet. I want to do more study. I want to travel more. I might wish to marry.'

'Yes,' I said. 'Perhaps you will.'

He smiled at me and I felt a sudden lifting of the heart. I thought: Suppose they were to choose Reginald for my husband, how should I feel? But of course they would not. In my position I should be reserved for a ruler. I should be betrothed when it was convenient to make some treaty. That did not matter much – the treaty would surely be broken before the marriage took place.

'In the meantime,' he was saying, 'I have seen something of the world and I shall see more if I am as fortunate as I have been so far. People have been good to me in my travels abroad. Oh, it was not myself who was honoured. It was the King, for I was his representative. There were times, I confess, when I might have been guilty of pride; but I always reminded myself of the truth.'

The days passed with astonishing speed. I was constantly afraid that one day he would tell me he was leaving. But he lingered and his mother smiled benignly on us.

'I believe, Princess,' she said to me, 'that my son finds it difficult to tear himself away from Ludlow.'

Then one day messengers arrived. I was terrified that

they might bring news of my proposed marriage to François. I had been lulled into a sense of security, for everyone had assured me that there was no danger of the match's ever taking place. But when I saw the messengers I awaited their revelations in trepidation.

In due course the Countess came to me.

'We are to leave Ludlow tomorrow and go to Greenwich,' she told me.

I looked at her apprehensively but her smile told me that my fears were without foundation.

'There will be no marriage with the King of France,' she said. 'He has said that he knows of your erudition, your beauty, your virtue, and of course you are of royal birth. He says he has as great a mind to marry you as any woman, but he is sworn to Eleanora, the sister of the Emperor Charles, and she is the one he must take to wife; and while the Emperor has his sons, he has no alternative.'

I clasped my hands together in relief.

'Was that not what I always said?' demanded the Countess.

. 'It was,' I replied.

She hesitated for a moment, then she said: 'There is another proposition.'

I stared at her in growing concern.

'This marriage could not take place for a very long time. As you cannot marry the father, you are to be affianced to his son.'

'He . . . who is in captivity?'

'With his elder brother, yes. It is to be the little Duke of Orleans for you – the second son of the King of France.'

'He is only a child.'

'That is all to the good. There will be a long delay before the nuptials.'

My pleasure in the knowledge that I was no longer to marry the King of France was dampened a little because I was to take his son. So from a bridegroom who was thirty-two I was to be given one who was three years younger than myself.

I felt frustrated and humiliated. It was distressing to be passed from one to another in this way. At the same time I must rejoice in having escaped a man whose reputation for lechery was notorious; and the little prince did not seem so bad in comparison, particularly as he had such a long way to go before he grew up.

'The French envoys will be coming over soon,' said the Countess, 'and you know what this will mean.'

'Yes. We are to leave Ludlow tomorrow.'

'For Greenwich.'

So that pleasant interlude was over. It had lasted for about eighteen months; but it was the last weeks which had been the most enjoyable, and that was due to the presence of Reginald Pole.

* * *

Greenwich had always been of especial importance to me. I suppose the place where one was born always must be. My father was born there too. He loved it, and it was natural that he should choose it as the place where he would receive the French envoys who had come to draw up the terms of my betrothal to the Prince of France.

My grandfather, King Henry VII, had enlarged the Palace and added a brick front to it where it faced the river. The tower in the park had been started some years before, and he finished it. My grandfather was a man who could never bear disorder. He was, I gathered, constantly anxious lest someone should take the throne from him, and I imagine he felt guilty for having snatched it from the Plantagenets. He was frequently trying to placate God, and at Greenwich he did this by building a convent adjoining the Palace and putting it at the disposal of the Grey Friars.

Everything my father did must be bigger and better than

others had achieved before, and when he came to the throne, loving Greenwich dearly as his birthplace, he enlarged it, and it was now more magnificent than it had ever been before.

So it was not surprising that he, who always wished to impress foreigners with his grandeur – and none more than the French – should entertain their envoys at Greenwich.

I was received with affection by him and my mother. My father, ebullient and boisterous, lifted me up as though I were a child and looked at me. He laughed, as though delighted with what he saw, and gave me a hearty kiss on the cheek.

'Ah, you are fortunate, sweetheart,' he said. 'You see how I plan for you? You are to have a grand marriage . . . as you deserve, I know full well. Such reports we have had from my Lady Salisbury. And now for the merrymaking.'

My mother was quiet. The change in her gave me a sick feeling of fear. All was not well. I noticed the grey in her hair; she had put on weight – not healthily – and her skin was sallow.

She smiled at me with great tenderness and I longed to comfort her.

I sensed that something terrible was wrong, though there was no sign of this from my father.

I learned that I was to take a major part in the revels for the French envoys, led by the Bishop of Tarbes, and I must be prepared.

In my apartments, which I shared with the Countess, I was to continue with my studies. I must perfect my French because naturally I should have to converse in that language with the envoys. I must practise my dancing because I should be required to show them how proficient I was in that art. I had to remember that the French set great store on social grace and I must not be found lacking.

I was in a strange mood. I might have been nervous; I certainly was a little resentful that I should be paraded to

67

make sure I was worthy to be the wife of a boy younger than myself; but all these emotions were overshadowed by the fear for my mother's health.

I mentioned to the Countess that she looked ill.

'She has much on her mind, I doubt not,' said the Countess evasively.

There was a strange atmosphere at Court. I noticed whispering, silences, watchful eyes.

I wished I knew what was going on, but no one would tell me.

At length the envoys arrived.

For weeks the banqueting hall at Greenwich had been in the process of refurbishing. Many workmen had been toiling at great speed that the work might be finished in time; there were to be such balls and banquets as never seen before. My father was noted for his extravagant displays, and this was to outshine all that had gone before. In spite of my fears for my mother and my apprehension on my own account, I could not help feeling a certain gratification that this was all done for me.

The banqueting hall astonished all who beheld it. Much had been made of the theatre which adjoined the great hall. The French regarded themselves as the great arbiters in the field of the Arts, so my father wished to astonish them with his taste for and appreciation of beauty. He had had silk carpets decorated with fleur-de-lys in gold laid on the floors; and on the ceiling were depicted the moon and stars. Perhaps less tact was shown in the banqueting hall, where there was a picture painted by Hans Holbein at the time of the battle of Thérouanne to celebrate my father's victory over the French, which I thought might dampen their joy in the fleur-de-lys.

In this room I was to perform. Special masques were written for the occasion, and I had to rehearse them with the other ladies who would dance with me.

I enjoyed dancing but there were certain matters which .

must be thrust to the back of my mind before I gave myself to pleasure. Besides my mother's melancholy, there was the real meaning behind all these lavish celebrations. After all, did I want to marry this little boy? I certainly did not, and it was consoling that he was so young. My marriage was in the future and, as I kept telling myself, such marriages rarely take place.

In due course the envoys arrived. I went to meet them. I was very much aware of my father, beaming happily, but I had already noticed how quickly his moods of affectionate bonhomie could change, and I dreaded to see the frown come over his face and his eyes narrow to points of icy blue, and – most expressive of all – the mouth become a tight line. It was then one must beware.

But all went well. I spoke my French fluently and the envoys were impressed. They paid me gracious compliments, and my father stood by, beaming benignly. All was well. I was passing the test.

We sat down to dine. My father and mother were together at the great table which commanded a full view of the hall. I was at the centre of another table with the French envoys and some ladies, all from the most noble families in the land. The feasting seemed to go on interminably, and all the time I must speak graciously in French, which somehow I contrived to everyone's satisfaction. The food was served on gold and silver plate. There was meat, fish and pies of all description and while we ate the musicians played soft music.

When the banquet was over, the entertainment began. Children were brought in to sing and recite. There was a mock battle between righteousness and evil – righteousness naturally victorious.

I had slipped away, as arranged, to play my part. The curtain which divided the theatre from the banqueting hall was drawn back to disclose a cave from which I emerged with seven ladies. We were all dressed in cloth of gold and crimson tinsel, with crimson hats covered in pearls and precious stones. As we came out of our cave, seven young gentlemen came out from another and we danced the ballet as we had practised it. I am glad to say that everything went even better than it had at rehearsals.

There was tremendous applause, and the company made it clear that they had been particularly enchanted by my performance.

The meeting had been very satisfactory, and my father was pleased. That night I went to bed happy, flushed with my triumph.

There were other entertainments, and always I was there, seated close to the French envoys. They were all very gallant to me and I was told that they were astonished by my beauty and my erudition.

There was, however, one word of criticism. Turenne, the French ambassador, remarked that I was undoubtedly handsome and well endowed mentally, but I was spare, sparse and thin and would not be ready for marriage for at least three years.

The Countess, when she heard of this, said with an air of 'I told you so' that they had kept me at my desk too long and I had not had enough fresh air and exercise, because Johannes Ludovicus Vives had insisted and she had always been against it. I should be allowed a more normal life – a little more time for recreation in place of so many lessons.

Perhaps she was right, but at least I had been able to converse and impress people with my erudition.

At one entertainment my father led me in the dance and we performed the stately pavanne together. He treated me with great affection and showed everyone, as we danced, how fond he was of me. There was that about my father – and this was so later when much was not well between us – that made any show of affection from him warm the heart; he could banish resentments with a smile; it was this quality which made him what he was and later led him to believe that he could act in any way he pleased.

So happily I danced with him, and that was one of the happiest occasions of the French visit.

Something happened on that night. It was when the music was playing one of the dances that each gentleman asked the lady of his choice to dance with him. The rule was for the King to select his lady and the rest would follow. I had expected him to dance with my mother, but he did not. He had walked across the room and was standing before a girl. I had seen her at some of the revelries before. She was the sort of person whom one would notice. I cannot say what it was about her. She was not beautiful . . . at least not in the conventional way. But there was something distinctive about her. When I came to compare her with the other ladies, it seemed that there was a uniformity about them and often one could mistake one for another. That could never happen to this girl. No one else looked in the least like her. Her dark hair fell to her waist. Her enormous eyes were sparkling and luminous; her dress was not exactly in the fashion of the day and yet it was more stylish. It had long hanging sleeves and there was a jewel on a band about her neck. I was even more struck by the grace with which she moved.

I noticed that people watched her all the time. I believed they were whispering about her. I meant to ask someone who she was, but I had not done so at that stage.

She seemed a little reluctant to dance but, of course, she could not refuse the King.

The music was playing. The King took her hand, and the dance began. The French ambassador asked me to dance and we fell in behind the King and his partner.

* * *

I was alone with my mother. Such occasions were rare and therefore very precious to me. She told me how proud she

71

was of me. My father was pleased; the French were satisfied; they would carry back a good report of me to the King.

She said suddenly: 'The Emperor has become a father.'

I stared at her. I felt my face harden.

She went on: 'He has a son . . . a little boy. He is to be called Philip after the Emperor's father. I wonder if he will be as handsome.'

I was silent. I could not speak.

My mother took my hand and gripped it. I saw the tears on her cheeks.

'Dear Mother,' I began, dropping formality. I stood up and put my arms about her. It seemed as if that were the wrong thing to do, for the tears came faster.

She said: 'He has been married such a short time and already he has a son. Why cannot . . . ? Why? Why? What have I done to deserve this? Why is God punishing me?'

I said: 'You have me . . .'

Then she began to weep openly. 'You mean more to me, my daughter, than any son could mean, except . . . except . . . You see, your father wants sons. Oh, you will have to know sooner or later. How much longer can it be kept from you?'

'Tell me, Mother, tell me,' I begged.

'But you are a child still . . .'

'The envoys thought I was far from stupid.'

She stroked my hair. 'You are my clever daughter. I want you to know that I love you. It has been my great sorrow that we have had to be apart so often.'

'I always understood,' I told her, kissing her hand. 'Please tell me. Perhaps I can comfort you.'

'Your father would be rid of me.'

'But . . . no . . . how . . . ?'

'He seeks means. He says he is afraid our marriage is no true marriage and that is why I have been unable to give him sons.'

'But you are the Queen . . .'

'You know I was married before.'

'Yes, to Prince Arthur. Everyone knows.'

'In the Bible it says that if a man marries his brother's widow the union shall be childless.'

'But why . . . ?'

'It is said to be unclean. Again and again I have told him that I was never Arthur's wife in the true sense.'

'And you are not childless. You have me . . . and there were others.'

'You, my dearest, are the only one who survived and you are a girl.'

'I see, he thinks God is punishing him for disobeying His Laws.'

'I would never disobey God's Laws. I was never Arthur's wife. Your father is the only man I have known as a husband.'

'You have told him that.'

'A thousand times.'

'Dearest Mother, do not grieve. Everyone will understand.'

'Your father is determined. He says he must have a son . . . a legitimate son. And the only way he can do that is by ridding himself of me.'

I was puzzled. It seemed impossible to me. My mother was the Queen. My father was married to her, so how could he marry someone else in order to get a son?

I said: 'I know he wants a son. All rulers do. They despise our sex. It is very sad. But my father is married to you and if it is God's will that he shall not have a son, there is nothing he can do about it.'

'Kings are very powerful, daughter.'

'But . . . he is married . . .'

'Marriages are, in some circumstances, set aside.'

'Set aside!'

'A dispensation from the Pope . . .'

'But even the Pope cannot go against the Holy Laws of the Church.'

She said: 'We shall fight for our place. I will fight . . . and it will be mainly for you.'

'For me?'

'Oh, I forget your youth. You make me forget it, daughter, because you are so serious and I am so distraught.'

'Dearest Mother, I do understand. I know how you have suffered for a long time.'

'You knew that?'

'I have seen it in your face . . . because I love you so much.'

'My poor child. I will fight for your position as well as for my own, for you see, if this terrible thing came to pass, you would no longer be the Princess of Wales.'

'But I *am* the Princess of Wales. I am the King's daughter . . .'

'It is hard to explain. If the King were to prove that his marriage to me was no true marriage, although we have lived for all those years as husband and wife, in the eyes of the Church our marriage would be no true marriage and therefore our child would not be the legitimate heir to the throne.'

As the enormity of this swept over me, I felt deeply shocked.

'That could never be,' I said.

My mother answered: 'We must see that it never comes to pass.'

We sat for a long time, I at her feet clinging to her hands. We were silent, she no doubt brooding on the past years, perhaps remembering the happiness she had enjoyed with my father during the first years of their marriage and I shocked and bewildered by the sudden realization of what had been going on for so long.

It was the reason for my mother's sadness, the silences

of the Countess. They had believed me too young at eleven to understand that which could have had a devastating effect on my future.

I was afraid of the future; I was afraid of my powerful father. Young as I was I knew that my fate, and that of my mother, was in the hands of a ruthless man.

Yet, I was glad that at last I knew what it was all about.

* * *

Reginald had come to Court with us from Ludlow and I had an opportunity of talking to him.

I said bluntly: 'I know now what has been troubling my mother for so long. My father fears theirs is no true marriage. You know of it, I suppose.'

'Yes,' he answered.

'I dareswear everyone at Court knows of it.'

'Many do,' he admitted, 'although it is known as the King's Secret Matter.'

'What will happen?' I asked.

'What can happen? Your father is married to the Queen. There is an end of it.'

'But if the marriage was no true marriage . . . ?'

'It was a true marriage.'

'My father thinks that, because my mother was married before to his brother Arthur, it was against the laws of Holy Church that he and she should marry.'

'It has taken him a long time to come to this decision.'

'It has been brought to him because God has denied him sons.'

'There could be a number of reasons for that.'

'But he thinks it is because he married his brother's widow.'

Reginald shook his head.

'My mother prays for a son,' I went on. 'If only she could have one, all would be well.'

75

Reginald looked at me sadly. 'My dear Princess,' he said, 'you are too young to bother your head with such matters.'

'But they concern me,' I pointed out.

'You are thinking of your right to the throne. If your father does not have a son, you will be Queen one day. Would that mean so much to you?'

I hesitated. I was remembering the months at Ludlow where I had had my own little Court. Power. Yes, there was an intoxication about it. It would be my right to follow my father, to rule the country . . . unless there was a brother to replace me. 'I see,' he said, 'that ambition has already cast its spell over you.'

'Are you not ambitious, Reginald?'

He was silent for a while. 'I think we all have the seeds of ambition in us,' he said at length. 'Some might have ambition to possess a crown; others for a peaceful life. It is all ambition in a way.'

'You could advance high in the Church.'

'I am not sure that I want that. I want to see the world . . . to learn. There is so much to be discovered. When you are older, you will understand. And now . . . do not grieve. This will pass, I am sure. Your father is restive. Men sometimes are at certain periods of their lives. He is disappointed because he has no son. He looks around for reasons. This will pass. It must pass. The Pope will never grant him what he wants. There is the Emperor Charles to be considered.'

'Why the Emperor?'

He said gently: 'The Emperor is the Queen's nephew. He would never agree that your mother should be set aside. It would be an insult to Spain. The Emperor is the most powerful man in Europe . . . and his recent successes have made him more important than ever. The sons of the King of France are his hostages.'

'My bridegroom is one of them.'

'Oh, these treaties, these marriages! They hardly ever come to anything when they are between children.'

'You comfort me, Reginald.'

'That is what I shall always do if it is in my power.'

He stooped and kissed my forehead.

I was thankful for Reginald.

* * *

The only brightness during that anxious time was due to his presence and the fact that I was under the same roof as my mother.

She and the Countess were often together; they had always been the best of friends. They were often in deep conversation, and I was sure my mother was completely frank with the Countess, for she trusted her absolutely.

I had grown up considerably since leaving Ludlow; and when I was in that pleasant spot I had emerged from my childhood to get a notion of what it really meant to rule.

But to be plunged into this tragedy which surrounded my mother had brought a new seriousness into my life.

I wished that I knew more. It is frustrating to be on the edge of great events and to be afforded only the sort of view one would get by looking through a keyhole.

Reginald was often with us, and the four of us would be alone together – my mother, the Countess, Reginald and myself. I am sure that both the Countess and her son did a great deal to sustain my mother, but there was little anyone could do to lift the menacing threat which hung over her.

She had suffered neglect and poverty after Prince Arthur's death, when her father did not want her to return to Spain and my grandfather did not want her in England. For seven years she had lived thus until my father had gallantly and romantically married her. I think she feared that she would be forced into a similar position to that which she had suffered before, if the King, my father, deserted her.

She had great determination. She was going to fight . . . if not for herself, for me, because my fate was so wrapped up in hers.

She was pleased to see my friendship with Reginald, and it suddenly occurred to me that she and the Countess would be happy to see a marriage between us. Instinctively I knew it was a subject often discussed between them. I was excited by this prospect. How wonderful it would be to marry someone one knew, rather than to be shipped off to some hitherto unseen prince because of a clause in a treaty.

I began to think how happy I could be with Reginald. I was eleven years old. He was twenty-seven or -eight. That was a big difference but we were good friends and could be more, for I, brought up on the rules of Vives, was more learned than most people of my age and there had been a rapport between myself and Reginald from the start. It was not so incongruous as it might seem. He was a royal Plantagenet, and if I were to be Queen one day he would be King. The people would like to see the two Houses joined. That was always a stabilizing factor. It would be like the alliance of the Houses of Tudor and York, when my grandfather Henry VII had married Elizabeth of York, daughter of Edward IV, thus putting an end to the Wars of the Roses.

It was a wonderful, comforting thought during those months.

I was often present when the Countess and my mother talked together. I think they had come to the conclusion that now I was aware of the King's Secret Matter, it might not be harmful for me to know more of it, for, after all, I was deeply involved in it.

Thus it was that I learned of those farcical proceedings when my father had been summoned to York Place where the Cardinal lived in sumptuous splendour.

There the King had allowed himself to be charged with

immorality because he was living with a woman who was not, in the eyes of the Church, his wife.

The idea of my father's being summoned anywhere by his subjects was ludicrous. But meekly he had gone; humbly he had listened to their accusations – which, of course, he had ordered them to make. Archbishop Warham had presided.

'John Fisher, Bishop of Rochester, was present,' said the Countess; 'I have always held him to be one of the most saintly men I know.'

'It was Doctor Wolman, I believe, who was making the case against the King,' added my mother.

'And Doctor Bell was the King's Counsel,' said the Countess. She added scornfully: 'I can imagine it. "Henry, King of England, you are called into this archiepiscopal court to answer a charge of living in sin with your brother's wife."'

'It is so false. It is so untrue!' burst out my mother. 'I was never Arthur's wife in truth.'

They seemed to have forgotten my presence, and I sat there quietly, trying to efface myself lest they should remember me and cease to talk so frankly.

I could imagine it all . . . that scene with my father looking shocked and anxious. It was a grave charge which they were bringing against him. If he had not wished it to be made, those who made it would have doubtless lost their heads by now. The case for the validity of the marriage was that, on account of Arthur's health, the marriage had not been consummated. Pope Julius II had given a dispensation, and the King had innocently believed that all was in order.

'And now the Bishop of Tarbes has said this monstrous thing . . .' said my mother.

She looked at me and stopped, and the Countess abruptly changed the subject.

But they had aroused my suspicions. I must discover what the Bishop of Tarbes had suggested.

They were subdued after that, and their conversation was constrained. I knew I was ignorant of a great deal regarding this matter. But after a while they could not resist the temptation to talk of it, and then they seemed to forget my presence.

The Countess said: 'Archbishop Warham is an old man. Old men seek comfort. He wants to live peacefully in his old age. He will agree with all the King wishes him to.'

'And we know what that is,' said my mother tragically.

'Warham declares that, if the marriage with Arthur was consummated, you were truly his wife and therefore the King has married his brother's widow.'

'It was not. It was not. I tell all it was not. I was a virgin when I married the King.'

'John Fisher is an honest man. He declared that the Pope had given the dispensation so that the King could suppress his fears. He had no doubt that his marriage was a good one. There was a Bull from the Pope to legalize it. There was no need for the King to question the validity.' The Countess looked at my mother with the utmost sympathy and, seeking to comfort her, went on: 'The King spoke so well of you. He said that through the years of your marriage he had found in you all he could hope for in a wife.'

'Save this one thing,' said my mother, 'and that of the greatest importance.'

'It is only the suggestion of the Bishop of Tarbes . . .' She paused. Then she went on: 'We know differently. It is not an unusual occurrence. It is just that this is the King . . .'

'And his need for sons.'

'He said that, if he had to marry again and if it were not a sin to choose you, you are the one he would marry. He would select you among all others.'

'Words,' said my mother bitterly. 'Words hiding the truth.'

They were silent again. Then the Countess said briskly: 'Well, they have settled nothing.'

'I believe the King is very disappointed with them. He greatly desired the matter to be settled.'

The Countess took my mother's hand and held it firmly.

'It cannot be,' she said. 'The good men of the Church would never allow it . . . nor would the people.'

'I think you under-estimate the determination of the King,' said my mother sadly.

I sat there quietly watching them. I knew this was by no means an end of the matter.

* * *

Iñigo de Mendoza, the Spanish ambassador, called to see my mother and was with her for a long time.

The Countess was silent and withdrawn. It was no use trying to get her to talk. I wished that they would not leave me so much in the dark. They were thinking that I was too young to understand. I chafed against my youth. My future was involved. I should know. This matter concerned me. And I was determined to find out all I could.

In time I learned what was said to have aroused the trouble. It had come about during the betrothal celebrations. The Bishop of Tarbes had said that, since the King was questioning the validity of his marriage to the Queen, did that not throw some doubts on my legitimacy? The King of France was very ready to agree to a proposed marriage between his son and me if I were Princess of Wales. But how would he feel if I were an illegitimate daughter of the King?

Henry Fitzroy would be heir to the throne if he were legitimate – as a bastard he could never be that. And now some people – including my own father – were attempting to prove that I was in like case.

My father lived in fear of offending God by living with a woman who was not in His eyes his wife. My father was emphatic. He could have accepted the judgement of the Bishop of Rochester but he did not.

He had his reasons.

It was the first time I had heard the name of Anne Boleyn.

* * *

While this was going on, a terrible event took place which was to shock the world for years to come.

It was the sacking of the City of Rome. Everyone was talking about it. Tales of horror were on every lip. It was incredible that such terrible deeds could be perpetrated by man.

Reginald talked to me about it. As a deeply religious man, he was much affected.

'There has never been such a tragedy in the history of the world,' he said. 'It was the Constable of Bourbon's men.'

'The French . . .'

'No. No. Bourbon was on the side of the Emperor. Bourbon and François had been warring together for years, and Bourbon was fighting with the Emperor.'

'So the Emperor's allies did this terrible thing.'

'The Emperor would never have agreed to it. Nor would Bourbon himself if he had been alive. He was killed at the beginning of the affray. Had he not been, he would have controlled the rough soldiery, I doubt not. No man of education would ever have allowed that to happen. It is a blot on Christendom. I do believe Bourbon had no wish to attack Rome, but his men were unpaid, they had marched for miles and they were hungry. There was only one way to retrieve something from the campaign: loot. And where could they find it in more abundance than in the City of Rome? They stormed the city. There was no defence. They decimated the churches, they stole rich ornaments. They

82

were all determined to make up for their months of hardship, lack of spoils, lack of food.'

It was hard for a girl of eleven to understand all the horrors which took place during those fearful five days when the soldiers pillaged Rome. I heard later of the terrible happenings. The nuns, hoping their robes would protect them, were seized at the altars where they knelt in prayer and were lewdly stripped of their robes and raped in the most horrible manner. Drunken soldiers roamed the streets. There were mock processions in the churches. The fact that foul deeds were performed in holy places had lent a fillip to the disgusting behaviour of these wicked men. They brought prostitutes into the churches. They mocked God, the Pope and all Rome stood for.

Pope Clement VII had escaped to Castel Sant' Angelo with thirteen of the cardinals. There he was safe from the mob.

But he was at the mercy of the Emperor, and my father was seeking papal help in annulling his marriage. The Emperor would never allow the Pope to help my father divorce his wife.

So the Sack of Rome had a special significance for the King.

* * *

When I heard the name of Anne Boleyn, I determined to find out all I could about her.

There was no doubt that she was the most attractive woman at Court. Before I had known what part she was going to play in our lives, I had noticed her. She dazzled. She had all the arts of seduction at her fingertips. Brought up in France, there was a foreignness about her which I suppose some men found attractive. Her magnificent dark hair and her big, luminous eyes were her great beauty, but everything about her was arresting. It was clear that she paid great attention to her dress. I heard she designed her own clothes. The outstanding feature of her elegant gowns was the hanging sleeves which hid the deformity on one of her fingers. Her enemies used to say that she had a mark on her neck which few had seen because it was always covered by a jewelled band. It marked her as a witch, they said. I was not sure about that, but there were times, when my hatred for her was at its height, when I made myself believe it.

She had come from the Court of France whither she had gone when a child in the train of my Aunt Mary Tudor who went there to marry the ageing Louis XII. She had not returned until soon after the occasion of the Field of the Cloth of Gold, on account of the rapidly deteriorating relations between France and England. She was then to marry Piers Butler because there was some dispute in the Boleyn family about a title, and the marriage of Anne to the son of the Butlers had been arranged to settle the matter.

My father must have been aware of her at that time, for the proposed marriage was mysteriously prevented. I could not believe that at that time he thought of marrying her. The suggestion would have been too preposterous. I was shocked to hear that Mary Boleyn, Anne's sister, had been my father's mistress for some time.

These rumours of his philanderings upset me very much when I first heard of them. Now I know that that is the way of men. Well, Mary Boleyn was his mistress and I suppose that at the time of Anne's return to England the King became aware of her and decided to replace one sister with another.

I heard, too, about the passionate love between Anne and young Henry Percy, the eldest son of the Earl of Northumberland, and how they planned to marry. That would have been a very good match for Mistress Anne Boleyn, for although her father had received many honours, largely because of the favour the King showed to Mary

Boleyn, and Anne's mother was a Howard of the great Norfolk family, her father had his roots in trade. There was some story of an ancestor's being a merchant. True, he had acquired a title and become Lord Mayor, but still trade.

Anne no doubt thought all was set fair. She had been so much in love with Percy, people said. As for Percy, he was besotted. People used to marvel at her devotion to him, because he was not a heroic sort of young man but rather weak. That he adored her was not surprising but her genuine love for him was amazing, for they said it was not due to the great title he would one day inherit.

I grew to hate her so much that I could not see any good in her; but later on, when her terrible fate overtook her, my bitterness diminished a little and I often thought that, if she had been allowed to marry Percy, she could have been a happy wife and mother and much anguish spared to many.

My father, by this time, was beginning to be deeply enamoured of her and ordered Wolsey to prevent the marriage with Percy going ahead. Young Henry Percy was humiliated by the Cardinal, and the Earl of Northumberland was sent for. He came to London and berated his son for his folly. Henry Percy was banished to Northumberland, and Anne Boleyn to Hever.

I could imagine her grief and anger. She would be passionate in her emotion, although at the time she would not have known that the breaking up of their match had been due to the effect she was having on the King and that he was forming plans for her. She thought it was because she was not considered of noble enough breeding to mate with the mighty House of Northumberland, which had deeply wounded her dignity.

The rest of the story is well known: her return to Court at the instigation of the King, a place in my mother's household as one of her ladies-in-waiting, where she could grace the Court with her special talents of dancing, singing and writing masques with the young poets of the Court, most of whom were her slaves.

She was one of those women who I believe is called a *femme fatale*. My father was not the only one who desired her.

I did not know – I am not sure even now after so many years have passed – whether she deliberately set out to wear the crown. She could not in the beginning have believed this possible – she, from a family associated with trade – and in any case the King already had a wife. It seemed quite preposterous. No, I think at that stage she might have been sincere.

When he made it clear that he wished to be her lover she told him that she would not be the mistress of any man and as, by reason of her unworthiness and the fact that he was married, she could not be his wife, that must be an end of his aspirations.

It was bold. But then, she lived by boldness. It had served her well in the beginning, but it was to be her downfall in the end.

My father could not bear to be crossed; in any case, he was obsessed by the woman. He wanted her so desperately that he contemplated drastic steps to get her.

We could not believe it at first – not even Wolsey, who knew the King as well as any of us. Wolsey was our enemy – my mother's and mine. He was a clever man who believed there was a need to produce a male heir, but for him there was a greater need than that, which was to placate the King. But he was an astute politician who would immediately see the folly in divorcing my mother in order to put Anne Boleyn on the throne. He had his eyes on an alliance with France. Divorce my mother, yes, but only in order to marry a princess, possibly of France.

I did not know how much the proposed divorce was due to the lack of a son and how much to the King's desire for

Anne Boleyn. My father was adept at dissembling. He had the gift of being able to deceive himself in the face of logic, and he did it so effectively that one was inclined to believe him . . . as he believed himself.

He came to my mother one day and I was present. Looking back now, I think that made a turning point in our relationship.

My mother and I were embroidering together, which was something we often did. The Countess said it had a soothing effect and calmed the nerves. It did seem to do so, for my mother would become quite interested in the stitches and we would sometimes talk of happier subjects than that one which was uppermost in our minds.

When my father arrived, I rose and curtsied. He came towards us, smiling benignly.

'Well, Kate,' he said to my mother, 'I would speak with you.'

He turned to me and laid a hand on my shoulders.

'So . . . you are keeping your mother company? Good. Very good. And getting on with your studies so that you do not disgrace us, eh?'

There was a faraway look in his eyes, and his mouth showed signs of tightening. They were aspects which always alarmed me as well as others because I was beginning to recognize what they meant.

His hand went to my head and he patted it.

'Growing up now. Well, well, I would speak with your mother. Go now. Go to your governess. Leave us . . .'

I curtsied and went, but on the other side of the door I paused. There was a small ante-room which led into the chamber in which they now were. I slipped into that room. I was going to commit the sin of eavesdropping. I could not restrain myself. So often I had felt I was groping in the dark, and how could I comfort my mother, how could I protect myself, if I did not know fully what against?

Shamelessly I hid myself and listened. The door was slightly ajar, and I could hear every word.

'It is time we discussed this matter which is causing me so much grief,' he said.

'I wish to do so with all my heart,' she replied.

'Ah,' he went on. 'How well I remember the time we went through the ceremony of marriage. Do you recall it? You were so desolate.'

'Yes, neglected by all . . .'

'I suffered with you . . . my brother's widow . . . unwanted in Spain and no place for you here. I shall never forget.'

'I also have good reason to remember.'

'Unhappy days . . . until I changed all that.'

'Yes, you changed it.'

'All seemed set fair. We were young. We were in love. I was a romantic boy. I wanted to do what was right. I wanted to help you.'

'You were pleased with my person, I believe.'

'Kate . . . I have always been pleased with your person. It is this question which they are raising. It gives me sleepless nights. I cannot rest. It is on my mind . . . on my conscience. I feel a great anger against these probing churchmen who have raised this question. They believe ours is no true marriage. Think what that means, Kate.'

'I do not have to. It is untrue.'

'They quote the scriptures. That cannot be ignored. I vow my desire is to tell them to hold their peace . . . to leave us . . . but I cannot do that, Kate. My conscience . . . it plagues me . . . night and day it asks me to stop and consider. I am committing a sin in the eyes of God.'

'Your conscience must have been troubling you for some time,' said my mother coldly, 'regarding Bessie Blount and Mary Boleyn.'

'Oh come, come, such talk does no good. It was that

88

fellow Tarbes . . . that monstrous suggestion about our daughter.'

'It is unforgivable.'

'Unforgivable . . . but is it true, Kate? Think of what has happened to us. We have been denied that which we most desire . . . a son, Kate. God has made it clear that He is displeased. Every time . . . every time . . .'

'We have our dear daughter.'

'Yes . . . yes . . . and none dearer . . . a cherished child, but a girl, Kate. A girl . . . when the country needs a man to follow me.'

'There have been worthy queens.'

'A queen cannot lead an army.'

'I was your regent while you were in France.'

'My mother did, and a good one, too. Ah, Kate, if only this man had not raised that question! It is too late now for us to get sons. My concern for your health . . .'

'And your desire for a new wife.'

'You joke. You know that is not my desire . . . though I could be forced to it . . . for the people, Kate, for the sake of the country . . . for the hope of a son.'

'And to satisfy your own desire.'

'For a son, Kate, only for a son. By God's Holy Blood, I would He had granted us a son . . . just one healthy son . . . and I would shake my fist at this Tarbes and anyone who dares raise such a question. I would not have it.'

'Yet you will,' said my mother softly.

'If I could quieten my conscience . . . if I could turn my face from the truth . . . I would be the happiest man on Earth.'

'You need not concern yourself, for it is lies. I was never Arthur's wife.'

'If I could but ease my conscience . . .'

I was almost on the point of dashing into the room and shouting at him: 'Stop it. Stop talking of your conscience.

We know too much. It is not your conscience you must appease but your desire for a new wife.'

I stood uncertain for a moment but I knew I must not betray my presence. I wondered what would happen if he knew that I had listened to their conversation, that I knew he was living a lie, that he wanted this divorce. He wanted to be rid of my mother even though I should be proclaimed illegitimate.

He was untrue to us and to himself.

I could not bear to hear him mention his conscience once more. I crept silently out of the ante-room and made my way to my bedchamber.

* * *

Now that I saw my father afresh, I placed myself firmly on my mother's side. My father had said they should no longer live together, for he feared it was sin in the eyes of Heaven. His talk about his conscience had seemed to me so blatantly insincere; and I had heard the whispers about Anne Boleyn. As she was at Court, one of my mother's women, I saw her now and then. She fascinated me. She scintillated and dazzled all those about her. She was surrounded by the wittiest of the young men, all the poets and the musicians; she planned the masques; laughter rang out round her; and the King wanted all the time to be close to her.

I was deeply aware of her blinding brilliance, her quick wits, her sharp, clever face. It frightened me. My tenderness for my mother was almost painful. I would sit and watch her sad, sad face and feel sick at heart. I longed beyond everything to comfort her.

Once she caught me looking at her and, taking my hand, she smiled at me.

'You must not grieve, dearest child,' she said. 'It may not come to pass, you know. He cannot put me away from him. I am his true wife. Moreover I am the daughter of a great King and Queen. They are both dead now, it is true, but I am still a Princess of Spain as well as a Queen of England.'

'The Emperor would not allow it to happen,' I said confidently.

'I think you are right.'

'Does he know of it? It is called the King's Secret Matter, so it must be secret to some.'

'It is not easy to keep such secrets. The Court knows what is happening. In the streets they are talking of it. The Emperor would never allow the King to harm me, and the Emperor is more powerful than ever since he defeated the French. Your father has tried to get the Pope's sanction to a divorce but, as you know, the Pope is now virtually a prisoner in Castel Sant' Angelo. One could say he is the Emperor's prisoner. Your father is very angry about that.'

'His conscience worries him, he says.'

My mother smiled wanly, then she said: 'This is too much to burden you with, dear child. You are too young fully to grasp the significance of this.'

'I do grasp it,' I said.

'Perhaps you should, for it could be vital to your future.'

'I know that, my lady.'

'Then listen. I will tell you a secret. I have sent one of my servants to Spain. He has taken a letter from me to the Emperor in which I have told him exactly what is happening.'

I clasped my hands together in relief.

'Everything will be well now,' I said with conviction.

I still remembered the hero of my youth.

* * *

My mother was jubilant, for she had received an answer from the Emperor, brought to her through the ambassador Mendoza.

She called me to her, for she knew what my feeling for the Emperor had been.

'Here is his reply,' she said. 'He is deeply shocked. He says that, because I have been married to him for so long, the King has forgotten that I am a Princess of Spain, and the Emperor will not allow a member of his family to be treated thus. He is sending Cardinal Quiñones, General of the Franciscans, to Rome without delay. He will be in charge of the affair there. He writes: "My dear Aunt . . ." Yes, he calls me his dear Aunt. "You can be assured that Clement, still in Castel Sant' Angelo, will not be in a position to flout my wishes."'

'What a wonderful message!' I cried.

I threw myself into her arms, forgetting all formality owed to the Queen, and we laughed together although we were near to tears.

* * *

There was so much about this affair that I learned later, and I was able to fit the information together like pieces in a puzzle. Consequently I now understand more than I did at the time it happened.

I think few of us believed then that the King really meant to marry Anne Boleyn. It seemed then preposterous; but my father was a most powerful man; he was the despotic ruler of our country, and it was only the heads of other countries who could prevent him having his own way. The divorce would have been settled in a few months but for the fact that the Queen was the aunt of the most powerful man in Europe; and, this being a matter for the Church, the Pope was involved – and that Pope was now virtually the Emperor's prisoner.

I can well imagine how my father raged against fate which had arranged the Sack of Rome at this time. An amenable pope could have given the divorce as popes had done in the past to powerful men who sought such – and the matter would have been at an end.

But what was accursed bad fortune for my father was

good for my mother and me. I knew she believed right until she was proved wrong that the delay would bring the King to his senses and that he would tire of the waiting game. So prevarication and any obstacles which would stand in the way of my father's attaining his goal were welcome.

Now that so much is clear, and looking back on the facts that are known to many, it is easy to understand. He really did intend to marry Anne Boleyn. He was so enamoured of her, and she was adamant. His mistress she would not be, so that if he would possess her he must marry her. Someone had to give way. I often wondered about his conscience. He talked of it often, and it was always there to help him get what he wanted. It was serving him well over this matter of the divorce. It must have been so comforting to blame his conscience and not his lust. Oddly enough, sometimes I am sure that he really did believe in that conscience. It forced him to work against Wolsey and was probably the beginning of the rift between them.

Wolsey was not averse to the divorce. No doubt he agreed that a male heir would be an advantage, and it was clear that my father would never get one from my mother. She was so much older than he was, and even when she was younger she had shown how difficult it was for her to bear healthy children. The constant theme all those years had been: All those attempts and only one daughter!

So Wolsey was for the divorce but certainly not for marriage with Anne Boleyn. He must have feared the increasing power of her family. Anne Boleyn was his proclaimed enemy. She blamed him for breaking up the betrothal between her and Henry Percy though she must, by this time, have known that he was acting on the King's orders. There could be no joy for Wolsey in a marriage between Anne Boleyn and the King, so he was scheming to bring about a stronger alliance with a French princess to replace my mother.

The King, who normally would have stated his pleasure

and expected everyone to fall in with his wishes, was wary of Wolsey, for he knew that he was proposing something which must seem outrageous to most of his courtiers. First he wanted his divorce, and Wolsey to be presented with a *fait accompli*. I often wondered why he was not as frank as he might have been with Wolsey. It might have been because he respected the man and really had a great fondness for him. In any case, he allowed Wolsey to go to France and get François' approval for the divorce and to suggest the King's marriage to one of the princesses of France.

My father had called on his conscience so many times that it began to have a life of its own and would not always be guided by him. It now began to disturb him on account of his previous relationship with Mary Boleyn and, since he had lived on intimate terms with the sister of the woman he intended to marry, was he not in a similar position to that of which he was trying to accuse my mother? I knew this because it came to light later that he had sent one of his secretaries, a certain Dr Knight, to the Pope to get a dispensation in advance so that he could feel perfectly free to marry Anne.

This mission had to be kept secret from Wolsey, who was at this time presenting himself to François suggesting a French marriage for the King. So my father was playing a double game in his own immediate circle. Poor Wolsey. Although he was no friend to my mother and me and would have cast us off without qualm if need be, I could spare a little pity for him. He had risen so high, and it is always harder for such people when the fall comes.

I did catch a glimpse of Wolsey setting out on his mission. Pride and love of splendour would be his downfall, I thought then. He rode with as much pomp as the King himself. He was at the centre of his entourage on his mule caparisoned in crimson velvet, with stirrups of copper and gilt. Two crosses of silver, two silver pillars, the Great Seal of England and his Cardinal's Hat were all carried before him. It was a magnificent show, and people came out of their houses to catch a glimpse of it as it passed. They watched it sullenly, murmuring under their breath 'Butcher's Cur'.

I have come to learn that the lowly, instead of admiring those who have risen, are so consumed with envy towards them that they cannot contain their animosity. I often wondered why they did not regard them as an example to be emulated; but no, they prefer to hate. Wolsey's exaggerated splendour increased their anger against him, I always believed. They did not like his habit of carrying an orange which was stuffed with unguents as an antidote to the foul smells which came from the press of people. This seemed to stress the difference between them and himself. It was small wonder that it added to the resentment.

It must have been during that visit to France that Wolsey realized his influence with the King was in decline, for one of his spies managed to steal papers from Dr Knight's baggage, and so the Cardinal knew that my father had sent Dr Knight to act in complete opposition to him. It was the writing on the wall. What could Wolsey do? How could he assume any authority if the King was working against him? He must have returned from that visit to France a disillusioned man.

I heard about his return. The King was surrounded by his courtiers, Anne Boleyn at his side, when Wolsey sent a messenger to tell him of his arrival, expecting my father to tell him he would receive him at once and naturally in private. He was travel-stained and wished to wash and change his linen before meeting the King, but Anne imperiously ordered him to come to them as he was there in the banqueting hall. Wolsey was dismayed. This was not the treatment he was accustomed to, but when the King did not countermand Anne Boleyn's order, he must have known this was the end.

The King intended to marry the woman; and farseeing, clever as he was, Wolsey could see that there would be no place for him at Court while she was there.

When my mother heard what had happened, she was very melancholy.

It seemed that the King was determined.

She said: 'But time is on our side. He will tire of her in due course. I am sure of it.'

She was right in a way, but she did not see it. Perhaps she knew him too well to trust in his fidelity. Heaven knew, she had had experience of his nature in this respect.

There was little comfort for us except in the love and support of the people. When my mother and I took barge from Greenwich to Richmond, they lined the banks of the river to cheer us. The sound was heartening. 'Long live the Queen! Long live the Princess!'

Did we imagine it or was there an extra fervour in their cheers? How much did they know of the King's plan to replace my mother and disinherit me?

* * *

There was trouble everywhere. My father was on unfriendly terms with the Emperor. There was no doubt that he was shocked by my father's attempts to divorce my mother and regarded it as an insult to Spain. I rejoiced that she had such a strong champion. This meant a halt to trade, which caused unrest in the country. England did a certain amount of business with Spain but that with the Netherlands was vital to our people and especially the clothiers of Suffolk. As before, the manufacturers found it necessary to discharge workers and there was a return of the riots.

My father had always dreaded to lose his subjects' affection. I had never seen anyone so delighted by approval as he was. Despot that he was, he wanted to be loved. It was a measure of his infatuation with Anne Boleyn that he risked their displeasure.

However, there was an immediate truce with the Netherlands.

Then disaster struck. The sweating sickness came to England.

This was the most dreaded disease which seemed to strike our country more than any other, to such an extent that it was often known as the 'English Sweat'. There was a superstition about it because it had first appeared in the year 1485, at the time of the battle of Bosworth Field when my grandfather, Henry VII, had become King after defeating Richard III. People said it was revenge on the Tudors for having usurped the throne; and now here it was again when my father was contemplating divorcing my mother.

It was dreaded by all and was so called because the victim was struck until his death – which was usually the outcome – by profuse sweating. It was a violent fever; it rendered those who suffered from it with pains in the head and stomach and a terrible lethargy. The heat the patient had to endure was intense, and any attempt to cool it meant instant death.

When victims were discovered in London, there was great consternation.

The Court broke up. The King believed that the best way to escape the disease was to leave for the country without dclay and move from place to place, and this he proceeded to do.

I could not help feeling great satisfaction when I heard that Anne Boleyn had caught the disease. She was immediately sent to Hever, away from the Court.

My father was deeply distressed and sent his second-best physician – but only because his first was away – to look after her. This was Dr Butts, a man of great reputation. I heard my father was in a panic lest she die.

I frankly hoped she would.

I said to my mother and the Countess: 'This is God's answer. When she is dead, all our troubles will be over.'

My mother answered: 'It may be that her death would not be the end of our troubles.'

I retorted angrily: 'My father says that he is afraid his marriage is no true marriage but the truth is that he wants to marry Anne Boleyn.'

The Countess looked at me steadily. Since they had known I was aware of what was happening, they had treated me more like an adult, talking to me frankly – and at least I was grateful for that.

She said: 'He wants to marry Anne Boleyn, but it is true that he wants sons, too.'

'And he thinks she will provide them.'

'He has two desires – one for her, and one for sons.'

'Suppose she could not have them?'

The Countess said slowly: 'Well, then it would depend . . .'

'On what?'

'How deep is his feeling for her? Is it love? We shall never know perhaps. I will say this: I have a feeling that these negotiations will drag on for a long, long time.'

'But I wish she would die,' I said. 'It will save us all much unhappiness if she does.'

The Countess was silent. I was sure she agreed with me that that would be the best solution.

* * *

During that period everyone at Court realized how obsessed the King was by Anne Boleyn. I was in dark despair. My hatred for the woman overshadowed everything for me; she was never out of my thoughts. I gloated over the fact that she was suffering from the dreaded disease. I reminded myself again and again that there were not many who survived. People said it was a punishment from God. Surely, if God's wrath should be turned against anyone, that should be Anne Boleyn. So I whipped up my hatred. I prayed for her death. What a wonderful release that would be!

My father wrote often to her. He was plunged into melancholy. Hourly he waited for news from Hever. So did I . . . for the news that she was dead.

But she did not die. She was nursed back to health by her devoted stepmother. My father was joyful. His sweetheart was saved. Meanwhile my mother and I had been travelling from place to place with the Court.

'God is not on our side,' I said bitterly, and my mother admonished me.

'Whatever happens,' she said, 'we must endure it because it is God's will.'

So when the epidemic was over, we were in the same position as we had been in before it started.

That year was the most unhappy I had lived through – up to that time. I did not know then, mercifully, that it was only a beginning. I thanked God that I was surrounded by those I loved. I was with my mother each day, I had my dear Countess, and there was also Lady Willoughby, my mother's greatest friend. Maria de Salinas had been with her when she came from Spain and had stayed beside her ever since. She had married in England and become Lady Willoughby but their friendship had remained steadfast.

Then, of course, there was Reginald. How grateful I was for his company. He had said that he would not stay in England but I think perhaps my need of him made him change his mind. He was very fond of my mother and, like us all, greatly saddened by her suffering.

I would be thirteen years old in the February of the following year. Perhaps I flatter myself but I am sure I was like a girl at least four years older. My education and upbringing had done that for me. Moreover at an early age I had been aware of my responsibilities and of a great future either as the wife of a monarch or as ruler in my own right.

I was often in Reginald's company – indeed, I believe he sought this, for he was clearly eager that it should be. The only brightness in those days was provided by him. What was so gratifying was that he treated me like an adult, and from him I began to get a clearer view of the situation. My father was very fond of Reginald, for he had a great respect for learning. He would summon him and they would walk up and down the gallery talking of religion and, of course, the subject which was uppermost in his mind: his desire to do what was right; his fears that he had offended God by living with a lady who was not in truth his wife. All that he told Reginald, seeking to win his sympathy in his cause, I believe, for he cared very much for the opinions of scholars.

It must have been difficult for Reginald, whose sympathies were with my mother and me, to choose his words carefully, for I was sure if my father thought he did not agree with him he would be very angry. Sometimes I trembled for Reginald during those encounters, but he was clever; he had a way with words and he did learn a great deal of what was in the King's mind during these interviews. But I knew my father's temper and I was uneasy.

My father was, in some ways, a simple man. He made much of Reginald, calling him cousin and when they walked along the gallery putting his arm round Reginald's shoulders. At the back of his mind would be the memory of what his father had done to the Earl of Warwick because he feared people might think that Plantagenet Warwick had had a greater claim to the throne than Henry Tudor. Later, when I began to understand my father's character more I could believe that he wanted to make much of Reginald because he was placating Heaven in a way for the murder of Reginald's uncle.

What uneasy days they were when we never knew what momentous event was going to erupt.

So my consolation was Reginald.

He it was who told me that the Pope had now been released and was at this time in Orvieto trying to build up a Court there.

'He is in a dilemma,' said Reginald. 'The King is demanding judgement in his favour, and he is too powerful to be flouted. But how can he defy the Emperor?'

'He should do what he considers right.'

'You ask too much of him,' said Reginald with a wry smile.

'But surely as a Christian . . .'

Reginald shook his head. 'He is still in the hands of the Emperor. But, who knows, next week everything could be different. He is in too weak a position to defy anyone.'

'Then what will he do?'

'My guess is that he will prevaricate. It is always the wise action.'

'Can he?'

'We shall see.'

And we did. It was Reginald who told me: 'The Pope is sending Cardinal Campeggio to England.'

'Is that a good thing?' I asked.

Reginald lifted his shoulders. 'We shall have to wait and see. He will try the case with Cardinal Wolsey.'

'Wolsey! But he will be for the King.'

'It should not be a case of either being for one or the other. It should be a matter of justice.'

'I fear this will make more anxiety for my mother. I worry so much about her, and I think she worries too much about me. I think she is fighting for me rather than herself.'

'She is a saint, and it is true that she fights for you. But you are her greatest hope. The people love you. You strengthen her case. The people cheer you. They call you their Princess, which means they regard you as heir to the throne. They will not accept another.'

'I never thought anything like this could happen.'

'None of us can see ahead. None of us knows what the future holds for us.'

'Reginald,' I said, 'you won't go away yet?'

He looked at me tenderly. 'As long as I am allowed to remain here, I will.'

He took my hand and kissed it.

'I hope you will never go away,' I told him. He pressed my hand firmly then released it and turned away.

I knew there was some special feeling between us, and I was glad that there had been no marriage with the Emperor Charles. My betrothal to the little Prince of France I did not consider. I was certain that it would come to nothing.

It must . . . because of Reginald.

* * *

It is an old story now. Everyone knows that Cardinal Campeggio did not arrive in England until October, although he had left Rome three months before. He was so old, so full of gout, that he had to take the journey in very slow stages, resting for weeks when the attacks brought on by discomfort were prolonged.

Reginald, who was very far-sighted in all matters, confided in me that he believed Campeggio had no intention of making a decision. How could he when the Emperor would be watching the outcome with such interest? He dared not give the verdict the King wanted, because it would displease the Emperor, and to go against the King would arouse his wrath.

'What a position for a poor sick old man to be in!' he said. 'It is my belief that the Pope sent Campeggio because of his infirmity. Why should he have not sent a healthy man? Oh, I am certain Campeggio has his instructions to delay.'

Reginald understood these matters; he had travelled widely on the Continent and he had an insight into politics and the working of men's minds.

102

How right he proved to be!

I heard from Reginald that the King was in a fury. He had told him that this man Campeggio was determined to make things more difficult. '"He has come here not so much to try the case as to talk to me. As if I needed talking to!" he cried. He cited his sister of Scotland, who divorced her second husband, the Earl of Angus. Louis XII of France had been divorced from Jeanne de Valois with little fuss. Why all this preamble because the King of England was so concerned for his country, to which he must give a son, and was merely asking for a chance to do so? So he went on. He gripped my arm so fiercely. I was glad he did not expect me to speak.'

'Oh, you must be careful.'

'My dear Princess, you can rest assured I shall be. What alarmed me – forgive me for disturbing you, but I think you should see the case clearly – is that the King flew into a rage when the Cardinal suggested that the Pope would be only too ready to amend the dispensation and make it clear that the King's marriage to the Queen was valid.'

'I know he does not want that. He is blinded by his passion for this woman.'

'That . . . and his desire for a son.'

'How can he be sure that she can give him one?'

'He has to risk that, and he is determined to have the opportunity to try.'

I was glad we were prepared, for shortly after that Campeggio and Wolsey called on my mother.

I was with her when they arrived and made to leave but she said: 'No, stay, daughter. This concerns you as it does me.'

I was glad to stay.

They were formidable, those two, in their scarlet robes, bringing with them an aura of sanctity and power. They wanted to impress upon us the fact that they came from the highest authority, His Holiness the Pope.

They hesitated about allowing me to stay, but my mother was adamant and they apparently thought my presence would do no harm.

Wolsey began by citing cases when royal marriages had for state reasons been annulled. The one my father had referred to with Reginald was mentioned – that of Louis XII and Jeanne de Valois.

'The lady retired to a convent,' said Wolsey, 'and there enjoyed a life of sanctity to the end of her days.'

'I shall not do that,' replied my mother. 'I am the Queen. My daughter is the heir to the throne. If I agree to this, it will be said that I am expiating the sin of having lived with the King when not his wife. This is a blatant lie, and I will not give credence to it. Moreover the Princess Mary is the King's legitimate daughter, and unless we have a son she will remain heir to the throne.'

Wolsey begged her to take his advice.

She turned on him at once. 'You are the King's advocate, Cardinal,' she said. 'I could not take advice from you.'

Campeggio leaned forward in his chair and stroked his thigh, his face momentarily contorted with pain. 'Your Grace,' he said, 'the King is determined to bring the truth to light.'

'There is nothing I want more,' retorted my mother.

'If this matter were brought before a court, it could be most distressing for you.'

'I know the truth,' she answered. 'It would be well for all to know it.'

'Your Grace was married to Prince Arthur. You lived with him for some time. If the marriage were consummated . . .'

'The marriage was not consummated.'

'This must be put to the test.'

'How?'

'Those who served you when you and your first husband were together might have evidence.'

My mother gave him a look of contempt. She had for some time regarded him as one of her greatest enemies.

'Would your Grace confess to me?' asked Campeggio.

She looked at him steadily. She must have seen, as I did, a poor sick old man who had no liking for his task. He might not be her friend but he was not her enemy. Moreover, he was the Pope's messenger and she trusted him.

'Yes,' she said, 'I would.'

I was dismissed then, and she and Campeggio went into her private closet. She told me afterwards that he had questioned her about her first marriage. 'I told the truth,' she said. 'I swore in the name of the Holy Trinity. They cannot condemn me. The truth must stand. I am the King's true wife and I will not be put aside.'

* * *

I was now passing into one of the most distressing periods of my life up to that time. It is well known how the legatine court opened in Blackfriars in 1529 and when my parents were called to state their cases, my mother threw herself at my father's feet and begged him to remember the happiness they had once shared and to consider his daughter's honour.

I could imagine his embarrassment and how he declared that, if only he could believe he was not living in sin with her, she would be the one he would choose above all others for his wife.

I wondered how he could utter such blatant hypocrisy when everyone knew that his passion for Anne Boleyn was the major reason for his desire for a divorce, for she would not become his mistress but insisted on marriage.

It is common knowledge that my mother declared that she would answer to no court but that of Rome, that she withdrew and when called would not come back. I still marvel at my father. I wondered how he could possibly maintain that his reason for wanting the divorce was solely

105

due to his fear of offending God when all knew of his obsession. Because he felt I was an impediment to the fulfilment of his wishes on account of the people's attitude towards me, and the fact that I was undoubtedly his daughter, he was eager to get me married and out of the picture. The possibility of my marrying the little French Prince was becoming more and more remote, and in any case it would not come about for years. And at one stage the King had the effrontery to suggest a marriage between myself and Henry Fitzroy, Duke of Richmond. How could he, while pretending to be so disturbed because of his connection with his brother's widow, suggest marrying me to my half-brother!

It was well that this suggestion did not become widely known, but I did marvel that the possibility had entered his mind and that the Pope should consider the idea and be prepared to provide the necessary dispensation. It brought home to me the fact that most men were completely concerned with their own grip on power and would do anything, however dishonourable, to keep it. I was developing a certain cynicism.

I was not surprised that my mother was in despair. How could she, in such a world, ever expect justice!

'What think you?' she said to the Countess. 'Will any Englishman who is the King's subject be a friend to me and go against the King's pleasure?'

Reginald grew more and more convinced that Campeggio had received orders to bring the matter to no conclusion and that his task was to delay wherever possible. This he seemed to do with a certain skill, while my father grew more and more angry as the case dragged on and nothing was achieved.

That which Reginald had prophesied came to pass. The Pope recalled Campeggio. It was announced that the case was to be tried in Rome. My mother was jubilant, my father incensed. They both knew that Rome would never

106

dare offend the Emperor as far as to give the verdict the King desired. He naturally refused to leave the country.

During those weary weeks my mother and I were sustained only by each other and our friends. The scene around us was changing. Anne Boleyn was now installed at Court; she was the Queen in all but name; but still she kept my father at arms' length. Thus she kept her power over him. Wolsey was in disgrace; he had failed; according to the King, he had served his master, the Pope, against the King, and that was something my father would not endure. Poor Wolsey! I could feel it in my heart to be sorry for him. To have climbed so high and now fall so low – it was a tragedy, and one could not fail to commiserate just a little even though he had been no friend to us. He had worked for the divorce; where he had failed was not to work for the marriage of the King and Anne Boleyn.

Campeggio had left the country, and the King was so furious with the old man that he commanded his luggage be searched before he embarked for the Continent. Campeggio complained bitterly at this indignity – a small matter when one considered what was happening to Wolsey.

Thomas Cranmer had leaped into prominence by suggesting the King appeal to the universities of England and Europe instead of relying on a papal court. This found great favour with the King who guessed – rightly – that bribes scattered there could bring the desired result.

I was heartily sick and weary – and completely disillusioned – by the whole matter.

When I look back on those three years 1529 to 1531, I am not surprised that my mother's health, and mine also, deteriorated. She was really ill and I was growing pale and suffering from headaches. But at least we were together most of the time, although I had a separate household at Newhall near Chelmsford in Essex. My mother was still living as the Queen and moving from place to place with the Court, but she was being more and more ignored, and often the King would leave her and go to some other place with Anne Boleyn. I at least was comforted by the constant company of the Countess and her son.

I knew I gave some concern to the King. Not that he cared for my welfare but he believed I was an impediment to the granting of the divorce and that, if it were not that she was determined to fight for my rights, my mother would have gone into a convent by now and the whole matter could have been settled.

It was sad to see my mother growing more and more feeble in health, although at the same time her resolve was as strong as ever and grew stronger, I think, with every passing day and new difficulty.

We would sew together and read the Bible. She liked me to read to her. She told me once that the path to Heaven was never easy and the more tribulations we suffered on Earth the greater the joy when we were received into Heaven. 'Think of the sufferings of our Lord Jesus,' she said. 'What are our pains compared with His?'

We used to pray together. She it was who instilled in me so firmly my religious beliefs. Religion was our staff and comfort. I shall never forget how it maintained us during those days.

My mother and I were so close that I think we sometimes knew what was in each other's minds. I know she longed for death – though she clung to life because she believed she must fight for me. She would never give the King what he asked, for that would mean that she accepted the fact that I was their illegitimate daughter. She wanted me to be a queen. She wanted me to rule the country with a firm and loving hand. She believed that there were not enough religious observances in England. The people, on the whole, were not a pious race. They were too preoccupied with amusement and finery and bestowed too little attention on sacred matters.

'You need a strong man beside you,' she said to me once.

'My lady, I am betrothed to the son of the King of France.'

'That will come to nothing. The friendship of kings is like a leaf in the wind. It sways this way and that, and when the wind blows strongly enough, it falls to the ground, is trampled on and forgotten. I do not wish to see you married into France.'

'I dareswear I shall marry where it pleases my father.'

'My dear daughter, if I could see you married to a good man, a man of deep religious convictions, someone whom I could trust, I could die happy. I want to see you protected from the evil of the world. I want someone who will stand with you, for your position could be difficult in the days ahead. It is my most cherished dream to see you on the throne of England, and I want you to have the right man beside you when you are there.'

'Where is such a man?' I asked, although I knew of whom she was thinking.

Again she read my thoughts: 'My child, I think you know. His mother and I have watched the growing friendship between you. It is more than friendship. His mother has seen it . . . and we are of one mind on this matter.'

I flushed and said quietly: 'But it would be his choice?'

'Has he not made that clear? He was to leave England. He was to go back to Italy to complete his studies, but he is still here.'

I was suffused with happiness. If it could only be! If I could be spared that fate which befell most princesses, to go to a foreign land, to a husband whom I had never seen . . . if it could be Reginald!

My mother was smiling and looking happier than she had for a long time.

She said: 'It would be a suitable match. He is of royal blood. He is a Plantagenet and you know how the people feel about them. Now they are no longer ruled by them, they see them as saints or heroes. Some of them were far from that . . . but that is human nature and in this case serves us well. Ah, my child, if only it could be. If I could see this come about, I should die happy.'

'Please, my lady, do not talk of dying. You must not leave me now. What should I do without you?'

She put down her needlework and held out her arms to me. We clung together.

'There,' she said, 'my dearest daughter, do you think I should ever leave you if it were in my power to stay? Rest assured that wherever I am I shall be with you in spirit. You are my reason for fighting, for living . . . always remember that.'

I wondered later whether she had a premonition of what was to come.

Soon after that, Reginald came to me in a very serious mood.

He said: 'Princess, I have to go away.'

My dismay was apparent.

He was in a great quandary. He wanted to be a supporter of my mother's cause, but the King was fond of him and he was expected to be in his company. It was very difficult for him to be frank as to his feelings.

'I cannot stay here,' he told me, 'without letting the King know that I do not agree with his plans for divorce.'

'Have you let him see that you do not approve?'

'Not yet, but I fear I soon shall. I find it hard to deceive him. There was a time when he talked of other matters but this is never far from his mind and soon he will discover my true feelings.'

'Reginald . . . be careful.'

'I will try but I cannot dissemble for ever. This could cost me my head.'

'No!'

'Remember I am in a vulnerable position already because of my birth. If I showed opposition to the King, my life would be worth very little.'

'Oh, it is cruel . . . cruel,' I cried.

'My dearest Princess, we have to face facts. I have asked his permission to go to Paris to study. I have deserted my books for so long.'

'You are going away,' I said blankly.

He took my hand and looked at me earnestly. 'I will come back,' he said. 'As soon as this miserable business is over, I shall be with you. We have much to talk of.'

He kissed me tenderly on the forehead.

'It is you, Princess,' he said, 'whom I hate leaving.'

So he went and that added a gloom to the days.

'I persuaded him to go,' the Countess told me. 'Life can be dangerous for those who do not agree with the King.'

I suppose we were all thinking of Cardinal Wolsey, who had so suddenly lost the King's favour and had died, some said, of a broken heart.

I heard that the King had sent orders to Reginald to get favourable opinions on the divorce from the universities of Paris. Poor Reginald! How he would be torn. I did not believe for one moment that he would obey the King. It was well that he was out of the country. Perhaps I should feel happier for that but it was so sad to lose him.

So we lived through those days. Often my mother was not with us but the Countess and I talked frequently of her and Reginald, and then it did not seem that they were so very far away.

The Countess told me that Reginald had such a distaste for the task the King had set him that he had written back asking to be released from it on the grounds that he lacked experience. But my father was certain of Reginald's powers and he sent Edward Fox out to help him. I was hurt when I heard that the answer the King wanted had come from Paris until I discovered that this had come through the intervention of François Premier who, as his sons were now released and he was married to Eleanora, was a free man.

Then the King sent for Reginald to return home.

He visited his mother immediately, which meant that he came to me.

We embraced. He looked less serene than he had when he went away. He was very perturbed by the situation.

'The King remains determined,' he said. 'The more obstacles that are put in his way, the stronger is his desire to overcome them. It is now a battle between the power of the Church and that of the King. And the King has decided he will not be beaten by the Church. He will have his way no matter what the consequences. Instead of a battle for a woman, it is becoming one between Church and State.'

'And if this is so, it means that everyone will have to take sides. I know which side yours must be.'

He nodded. 'I must defend the Church.'

'And now the King has sent for you.'

He nodded. 'Do not fret,' he said. 'I know how to take care of myself.'

I was delighted to have him home but I was worried about what would happen. I tried to console myself with the fact that the King had always been fond of him. Reginald was summoned to his presence.

The Countess was in a state of great anxiety; so were we all. We kept thinking of Wolsey's fate.

It seemed that, apart from the fact that the matter of the divorce remained in the same deadlock, everything else was changing . . . my father most of all. He was irascible and feared by all. He could suddenly turn on those who had been his best friends. The conflict obsessed him day and night. It was said that his hatred against the Pope was greater than his love for Anne Boleyn.

He guessed where Reginald's sympathies lay and, apart from his affection for him, he had a great respect for his learning. If he could get men like Reginald on his side, he would be happier. Moreover, Reginald was a Plantagenet. People remembered that.

He was still a layman, though he did intend to take Holy

Orders later in life. People said afterwards that he delayed doing this because he had it in his mind that a marriage might be possible between him and me. This might have been so but, layman as he was, the King offered him an alternative choice of the Archbishopric of York and that of Winchester.

This was a great honour, but Reginald knew it was an attempt to get his support. It was difficult for him to refuse it for fear of offending the King but, of course, he must.

He talked of this to his mother, and I was present.

He said: 'This cannot go on. Sooner or later I shall have to tell the King that I cannot support him in this matter of the divorce.'

'Perhaps you should return to Paris,' suggested his mother. 'Much as I hate to lose you, I have no peace while you are here.'

'I feel I should talk to him,' said Reginald.

'Talk to the King!'

'I believe I might make him see that he can find no happiness through this divorce.'

'You would never do that. He is determined to marry Anne Boleyn and how can he do that if there is no divorce?'

'I will go to him. I will appeal to his conscience.'

'His conscience!' said the Countess contemptuously.

'He refers to it constantly. Yes, I have made up my mind. I will go to him. I will ask for an audience. I know he will see me.'

What agonies we lived through when he left Newhall for the Court. The Countess and I sat together in silence imagining what would happen. We were terrified for him. I was glad my mother was not with us. I was sure she would have been deeply distressed.

When Reginald returned to us from York Place we hurried to meet him. He looked pale and strained. It had been a very uneasy meeting, he told us.

'I begged the King not to ruin his fame or destroy his soul by proceeding with the matter.'

'And what said he?' whispered the Countess.

Reginald was silent for a moment. Then he said slowly: 'I thought he would kill me.'

I covered my face with my hand. Reginald smiled and laid a hand on my arm. 'But he did not,' he said. 'See. I am here to tell the tale.'

'He listened to you?' asked the Countess incredulously.

'No. Not after my first few sentences. He was very angry. He thought I had come to him with one of the suggestions such as he is getting from Cranmer and Cromwell. While I was talking, his hand went to his dagger. I thought he was going to plunge it into my heart without more ado. The King is a strange man. There are such contradictions in his nature. He can be so ruthless . . . and yet sentimental. He changes from one moment to another. That is why one sometimes believes what he says, however outrageous. One could accept that he wants this divorce solely because of his conscience. One believes that he really is worried about the fact that he married his brother's widow because when he says it he seems to believe it . . . sincerely. Then, the next minute one knows it is the desire for this woman. I do not understand him. I do not believe he understands himself. Just as he was about to lift his dagger and strike me, he seemed to remember that he was fond of me. He looked at me with rage . . . and sorrow.'

'And he let you go.'

Reginald nodded.

'He shouted at me: "You say you understand my scruples and you know how they should be dealt with." It was like a reprieve. I said: "Yes, Your Majesty." "Then set it down. Set it down," he cried. "And let me see it when it is done. And go now . . . go . . . before I am tempted to do you an injury." So I went, feeling deeply wounded and at the same

114

time rejoicing that he was no longer in doubt as to my true feeling.'

This was an addition to our worries, but at least Reginald seemed at peace, and he set about writing his treatise.

I think my father was genuinely fond of him, because he read it with interest and showed no displeasure, although Cromwell said it must not be made public because it was contrary to the King's purpose; and he added that the arguments were set down with wisdom and elegance but would have the opposite effect of what the King wanted.

We trembled afresh when we heard this.

'This man Cromwell is an evil influence on the King,' declared Reginald. 'I do believe he is trying to undermine the supremacy of the Church. Pray God he does not succeed. The King does not like the man but he is very taken with his arguments. I am greatly in fear of what will happen next.'

We had many serious talks after that. His mother was in constant fear for she was convinced he was in acute danger. She was persuading him to go abroad. She said to me: 'I know we do not want to lose him, nor does he wish to leave us, but I am terrified every day he remains.'

'What do you think will happen?' I asked.

'Cromwell's idea is that the King should break with Rome and set himself up as Supreme Head of the Church of England. That is what Reginald thinks will happen. The King will then demand to be accepted as such, and those who refuse to accept him – as all good churchmen must – will be accused of treason.'

'Surely my father would never go so far!'

'He is caught up in this matter. It is more than a desire to marry Anne Boleyn. It is a battle between Church and State, and it is one he must win to satisfy himself.'

'And you think that Reginald . . .'

'Is in danger if he stays. He must get out now . . . and stay away until it is safe for him to come back.'

115

At length his mother prevailed on Reginald to go; but first he must get the King's permission.

I remember that day when Reginald presented himself to the King. The Countess had been all for his going away and writing to the King from Paris, Padua or some safe distance; but Reginald would not agree to that. He thought it cowardly.

He presented himself to my father and told him he wished to continue his studies abroad. He told us afterwards what happened. The King was pleasant to him, and Reginald was able to tell him frankly that he could not go against his conscience. Perhaps the King was particularly sympathetic about consciences, for he listened with sympathy. Reginald told my father that he believed it was wrong to divorce the Queen and, no matter what happened to him, he could not go against his convictions.

The King was sorrowful rather than angry and at length he agreed to allow Reginald to go.

How relieved we were to see him arrive back to us but that relief was tempered with sadness that he should be leaving us.

I was very melancholy. I had lost one of my few friends; and one of the best I should ever have.

Enter Elizabeth

Time was passing. It was nearly six years since the King had first thought of divorce, and still he was without satisfaction. There had never been such a case in royal history.

We were at Greenwich with the Court, my mother and I, when we heard there was to be a move to Windsor.

Relations between my parents had become even more strained. Although my mother was still treated in some ways as the Queen, the King was hardly in her presence, and Anne Boleyn had her own apartments within the household.

We awoke one morning to find the Court ready to depart but to go to Woodstock instead of Windsor. We began to prepare to leave in the usual way when we were told that the King would not require our presence at Woodstock and we were to go to Windsor.

We were astonished. The Countess was very anxious. I had not seen her so disturbed since those days when she was urging Reginald to leave the country.

'I cannot think what it means,' she said to me. 'But mean something it does.'

We remained at Windsor for three weeks before a messenger came from the King.

He was coming to Windsor to hunt and when he arrived he desired that we should not be there. My mother was to go with her household to the Moor in Hertfordshire. Then came the blow. I was not to go with her. I was to go to Richmond.

We were dismayed and clung to each other.

'No, no,' I cried. 'I will not endure it. Anything but this.'

'Perhaps it is only for a while,' said the Countess soothingly.

But we none of us believed that. We understood. When we rode out together, the people cheered us. Anne Boleyn received very different treatment. She was 'the Concubine' and they shouted abuse at her, calling her the King's goggle-eyed whore. They felt differently towards me. I was their dear Princess, the heir to the throne. They would have none other but me.

This must have been infuriating to my father and his paramour; and I guessed she had had a hand in this.

So they would separate us and we should not be seen together. No doubt then we might come to our senses if we realized the power of the King.

'I will not leave you,' I cried passionately. 'Oh, my mother, we must be together. Let us run away and hide ourselves.'

'My dearest child,' she said. 'Let us pray that we shall be with each other again soon.'

'What is the use of prayers?' I demanded. 'Have we not prayed enough?'

'We can never pray enough, my child. Always remember my thoughts are with you. Let us be resigned to our cruel fate. It cannot endure, I am sure of that. Say your prayers while we are apart. It may well be that soon we shall be together again.'

But how sad she looked in spite of her brave words. I was in an agony of fear for her. He had taken so much away from us. Why could he not leave us each other?

My heart was filled with anger − not towards him so much as towards her, the goggle-eyed whore, the woman who was his evil genius. I blamed her for all the trials which had befallen us.

My mother took a sad farewell of the Countess. They embraced tenderly.

'Care for my daughter,' said my mother.

'Your Highness . . . you may trust me.'

'I know, my dear friend, I know. It is my greatest comfort that she is with you.'

I had loved Richmond until now; the view of the river, the irregular buildings, the projecting and octagonal towers crowned with turrets, the small chimneys which looked like inverted pears . . . I had loved them all. But now it was like a prison, and I hated it because my mother was not there with me.

* * *

I did try to follow my mother's instructions. It was difficult. I thought of her constantly. I was afraid for her health; the anxieties of the last years were clearly undermining it – as they were my own.

I said to the Countess: 'If we could only be together, I would suffer anything. But this separation is unendurable.'

'I know,' she replied. 'It cannot continue. There are murmurings among the people. They are with you and your mother. They will never accept Anne Boleyn.'

'They will have to if it is my father's will. He is all powerful.'

'Yet he has failed so far to get this divorce.'

'I hope he never does. I wish she could die. Why did she not when she had the sweat?'

'It was God's Will,' said the Countess.

And there was no disputing that.

We heard that Anne Boleyn was living like a queen, and of the jewels she wore – all gifts from the King. But every time she appeared in public, insults were hurled at her.

'Bring back the Queen!' cried the people. 'Long live the Princess!' It was gratifying but ineffectual.

119

We had no friends. There was only the Spanish ambassador, Eustace Chapuys, who could visit my mother, advise her and comfort her and keep her in touch with the Emperor, because of whom the Pope would not grant the divorce though beyond that he could do little. He could not go to war with England on my mother's account. Moreover my father and François were allies now.

There seemed no way out of this situation. My mother was alone and almost friendless in a country which had been her home for some thirty years and now was an alien land to her.

Then, to my delight, six months after my separation from my mother, I was allowed to join her again. What joy there was in our reunion and what anxiety when I saw how ill she looked!

'The hardest thing I have had to bear in this sad time is my parting with you, my daughter,' she told me. 'Oh dear, there is so much to say . . . so much to ask. How is your Latin?'

We laughed together rather hysterically because at such a time she could think of my Latin.

We were together every moment of the day. We cherished those moments, and we were right to do so for there were not to be many left to us.

We would sit talking, reading, sewing . . . each of us desperately trying to take hold of each moment, savour it and never let it go. We knew this was to be a brief visit. They were three weeks when I realized how much my mother meant to me and that nothing in my life could ever compensate for her loss.

How could they be so cruel . . . my father, revelling with his concubine, and she, the black-browed witch – had they no sympathy for a sick woman and her frightened daughter?

Compassion there was none, and at the end of those three weeks came the order. My mother and I were to separate. The brief respite was over.

I became listless. The Countess worried a good deal about me. She was constantly trying to think of something to cheer me. Something must happen soon, she said, and she was sure it would be good.

Dear Lady Salisbury, she provided my only comfort. We talked of Reginald. We heard from him now and then. He was in Padua studying philosophy and theology and meeting interesting people whose outlook on life was similar to his own. He mentioned Gaspar Contarini, a good churchman, and Ludovico Priuli, a young nobleman whom he found of the utmost interest. He wrote of these friends so vividly that we felt we knew them and could enjoy their conversation as he did. He was following events in England, and it was amazing how much he could learn from his friends, as there were constant comings and goings, for the King's affair was of the utmost interest to all.

He would come home soon to us, he wrote. We were never out of his thoughts, and it was a great consolation to him to know that we were together.

We would sit, the Countess and I, and talk of Reginald and try to look into the future. Life had its troubles and its joys, the Countess maintained, and when I said there seemed no hope for a better life for us, she chided me and assured me that God would show us a way and that tribulations were often sent for a good reason. They made us strong and capable of dealing with the trials of life.

Letters from Reginald sustained us during that time; but when one day followed another and we heard nothing but news of the concubine's triumphs and the King's besotted devotion to her, I began to lose heart. I knew that my mother was ill, and that threw me into despair.

It was not surprising that I myself began to grow pale and thin, and one morning I awoke in a fever.

The Countess was horrified, for soon it became obvious that I was very ill indeed.

I heard afterwards that news of my illness spread quickly

through the country and it was thought that I might not live. There would be rumours, of course. The concubine's spies had poisoned me. The King had been duped by her. She was a witch and a murderess.

When the King rode out with her, the hostile crowds shouted at them. That would disturb him for he had always cared so passionately for the people's approval; and he had had it until now. But he had disappointed them and they – particularly the women – had turned against him. His treatment of the Queen shocked them. She had done nothing except grow old and fail to produce a son, and the little Princess Mary, who was the true heir to the throne, was, because of the wickedness of the King's paramour, lying at death's door.

My father hastily sent one of his best physicians to treat me.

I can remember lying in bed longing for my mother. I called her name, and the Countess sent an urgent plea to my father begging him to let my mother come to me.

He was adamant. She was to stay away from me. He may have feared what would happen if we met. Perhaps he thought of the crowds following my mother on her journey to me, shouting their loyalty to her and to me. Riots could so easily arise.

No. He could not grant me what would have been the best remedy for my sickness. But he did send one of his doctors to me.

I was young; I was resilient. And I recovered, thanks to Dr Butts and the Countess's constant care.

Although I believed that both my father and his mistress would have been glad to see the end of me, they must have felt a certain relief that I had not died. Such an event at that time would most certainly have aroused the people to some action, and they would know that.

I hoped my mother was aware of the people's feelings. It

might have brought her a grain of comfort. It would have made her feel less of a stranger in an alien land.

There were some brave men who were ready to face the King's wrath for their beliefs. William Peto was one. He was the Provincial of the Grey Friars, and on Easter Day at Greenwich he preached a sermon in the presence of my father. Frankly, he said that the divorce was evil and could not find favour in the sight of Heaven.

I exulted to think of my father's sitting listening to him. He would be seething with anger. It was a very brave preacher who could stand up before him and utter such words. I could so well imagine his anger. I could see the small eyes growing icy, his expressive mouth indicating his mood. But this was a man who could not be entirely flouted; and there was the mood of the people to be considered.

For some time Peto had wanted to go to Toulouse, for he was writing a book about the divorce and he wished to get it published there; for of course he would not be able to do so in England. My father may have had some inkling of this, for he refused permission, but now, on the advice of one of his chaplains who feared that such a man could do much damage, my father summoned him and coldly told him to leave the country immediately. Then he sent for Dr Curwin, who would preach a sermon more to his liking.

He was right. Curwin did this to my father's satisfaction, even hinting that Friar Peto, after his disloyal outburst, because he was a coward, had fled the country.

There are some men who court martyrdom. Peto was one; Friar Elstowe was another. Elstowe immediately declared publicly that everything Peto had said could be confirmed by the Scriptures, and this he would eagerly do to support Peto and hopefully give the King pause for thought before he imperilled his immortal soul.

Such talk was inflammatory, and Elstowe, with Peto,

was arrested at Canterbury, where they were resting on their way to the Continent; they were brought before the Council, where they were told that such mischief-makers as they were should be put together into a sack and thrown into the Thames, to which Elstowe retorted that the men of the Court might threaten them if they would but they must know that the way to Heaven lies as open by water as by land.

However, the King wanted no action taken against them. I think he feared how the people would behave.

But the attitude of these men did much to add to his exasperation, which must at that time have been almost unbearable for a man of his temperament and power. I suppose it was the only time in his life that he had been baulked. All through his golden youth his wish had been law; his height, his good looks, his jovial nature – until crossed – had made him the most popular monarch people remembered. They had loved him, idolized him, and now they were criticizing him; and it was all because his unwanted wife was the aunt of the Emperor Charles. If she had been of less consequence, he would have been rid of her long ago.

There were others more powerful than Friars Peto and Elstowe. Bishop Fisher was one, and he had set himself against the divorce and had no compunction in letting it be known. The Countess said she trembled for him. She thought he would be arrested and sent to the Tower. This was not the case as yet. My father must have been very disturbed by the attitude of the people.

All that came out of this was that my mother was moved from the Moor and out to Bishop's Hatfield, which belonged to the Bishop of Ely. I worried a good deal about her. It hindered my convalescence. I had become pale and thin and I looked like a ghost. If only I could have been with my mother, I should have been more at peace; anything would have been preferable to this anxiety about her. I looked back with deep nostalgia to those days when we had all been together – my mother and I, Reginald and the Countess. And now there were just the Countess and myself. Reginald was in Padua, my mother at Bishop's Hatfield. Was it warm there I wondered? She suffered cruelly from rheumatism, and the dampness of some of the houses in which she had been forced to live aggravated this. I wondered if she had enough warm clothing. It was unbearable that she, a Princess of Spain, a Queen of England, could be treated so.

But I knew that we were moving towards a climax when I heard that the King was going to France and was taking Anne Boleyn with him.

'This cannot be true,' I cried to the Countess. 'How could he take her with him? She cannot go as the Queen.'

'The King of France is now his friend, remember. If he receives Anne Boleyn, it is tantamount to giving his approval.'

'He will do what is expedient to him.'

'Yes, and François needs your father's support and he will go a long way to get that.'

'But how could Anne Boleyn be received at the Court of France!'

'We shall hear, no doubt.'

'But my mother . . . what will she think when she hears of this?'

The Countess shook her head. 'These things cannot go on. But I can't really believe he will take her to France. It is just one of those rumours, and Heaven knows there have been many of them.'

But it was no rumour. My father showered more honours on Anne Boleyn. He created her Marchioness of Pembroke. That was significant. She was no longer merely the Lady Anne.

So he really did intend to take her to France. He was

telling the world that she was his Queen in truth and that the marriage was imminent.

I think my hopes died at that time. I was sunk in gloom; my mother was ill and we were parted by a cruel father and his wicked mistress. If we could have been together, what a difference that would have made! How could they be so cruel to us? Our love for each other was well known, and in addition to the trials we were forced to endure was the anxiety we felt for each other.

As we had feared, events moved quickly after that. They went to France; they were received by François, though not by the ladies of the Court, who, I was glad to hear, rather pointedly absented themselves.

But when they returned, the result was inevitable. There was a rumour that Anne was pregnant with the King's child, and they were secretly married.

* * *

I could not believe this. It was a false rumour, I insisted to the Countess. Nobody seemed to know where the marriage had taken place. Some said it was in the chapel of Sopewell Nunnery, others at Blickling Hall.

What did it matter where?

Of course it was kept a secret. It was a highly controversial step, for there would be many to ask how the King could marry Anne Boleyn when he was the husband of the Queen.

The ceremony had to take place though and without delay, for Anne was pregnant and it was imperative that the child should be born legitimate.

I often wondered later which was the greater – my father's longing for a son or his passion for Anne Boleyn. Knowing him so well, I believe he considered it a slur on his manhood that a son should be denied to him; and as he wished the world to see him as the perfect being, that irked him considerably.

They must have been in a state of some anxiety, for the marriage had to be legal and it was clear that they were getting no help from Rome. How could they pretend that she was his wife when the people knew he was still married to the Queen? I exulted in their difficulties.

It was May of that year 1533, after my seventeenth birthday, when Cranmer, now Archbishop of Canterbury, presided over a tribunal at Dunstable. There was no need for a divorce between the King and Katharine of Aragon, he stated, for their so-called marriage had been no marriage. The ceremony through which they had gone had been contracted against the Divine Law.

After this declaration they felt free to go along with Anne's coronation.

It was incredible that such a thing could be. But my father was determined on it.

My mother had been moved once more and was at Ampthill. I think my father feared to leave her too long in one place. I constantly asked myself why he would not let us be together, but if he would not allow us to see each other during my illness – when he really did fear what effect my death would have had on public opinion – he surely would not now. I was very, very worried for I knew that my mother suffered from constant ill health and I feared the worst was kept from me.

Events were moving fast. We heard, of course, about the splendid coronation, how Anne Boleyn left Greenwich dressed in cloth of gold, looking splendid, they said, with her elegance and her long black hair and great glittering eyes – witch's eyes, I called them. Many believed that she was a witch and that only her supernatural powers had been able to lure the King to act as he had.

I could imagine the guns booming out and my father's waiting to greet her when she reached the Tower. There she stayed for several days in accordance with the custom of monarchs coming to their coronations. How it sickened me to think of this woman, this upstart Boleyn, whose family by astute trading and noble marriages had climbed to a position where Anne might be noticed by the King. All this honour for her while my mother lay cold and ill, neglected, and while everything possible was done to degrade her.

How I hated that woman! How I wished her ill! I remembered my mother once said: 'Hatred it not good for the soul, my child. Pray for this woman rather. It may well be that one day she will be in need of our prayers.' But I could not. I was not the saint my mother was.

So I gave vent to my hatred. I prayed that the child she was about to bear would be misshapen, a monster, a *girl*! I prayed that she might die in childbirth – that they both should die and I might never have to consider them again.

I could picture her making her procession through the streets of London. She would look magnificent in her evil way. Even her greatest enemies could not deny that she had something more than beauty. It was the spell of witchery. I could see her in silver tissue and her ermine-decorated cloak. I could picture the litter of cloth of gold and the two white palfreys which drew it.

Would the people cheer her? They would be overwhelmed by the pageantry for they loved a spectacle. They would forget temporarily, perhaps, the wrongs against the true Queen. They would remember only that this was a holiday and the conduits ran with wine.

All through the day of the coronation, I brooded, nursing my hatred, thinking of my mother, wondering what would be in her mind on this tragic day. I thought of that woman, crowned Queen, in purple velvet and ermine; I could imagine the King's eyes glazed with desire for this witch who had seduced him from his duty and was leading him along the path to Hell.

What was the use of praying for a miracle?

There was no miracle, and Anne Boleyn was crowned

Queen of England which she could never be to me – and to many, I hoped – while my mother lived.

* * *

How well I remember those months before the birth of Anne Boleyn's child. She was constantly in my thoughts. I tortured myself with pictures of her – imaginary, of course. My father doted on her, sure that she was about to give him the longed-for son.

But there began to be rumours that all was not well, and that, after having waited so long for her, he was now asking himself why he had endured so much for her sake; and he was looking at other women – something he had not done for a long time, since he had first become obsessed by her. Were these merely rumours or was this actually taking place? As much as I wanted to believe them, I could not accept the fact that his mad desire had evaporated so rapidly.

And she was pregnant – that should make her doubly attractive. She was about to give him what he craved.

A messenger came to Newhall with a command from the King. I was to go to Court that I might be present at the birth of the child.

I was furious. I stamped and raged. 'I will not go,' I cried. 'I will not.'

The Countess looked sorrowful. 'Dear Princess,' she said. 'Consider. This is a command from the King.'

'I care not. How can he expect me to take part in the rejoicing at the birth of *her* child?'

'He does, and you must.'

'Never,' I cried. 'Never!'

The Countess shrugged her shoulders. 'What do you think the King would say to that? You must tread carefully. You could be on dangerous ground.'

'You mean he might kill me?'

The Countess was silent.

129

'You really believe that might be, do you not?' I demanded.

'I think life could be very unpleasant for you if you disobeyed,' she answered.

'It is unpleasant now.'

'More unpleasant. Dangerous in fact. Princess, I do beg of you. Be careful.'

'Do understand me,' I pleaded. 'I must refuse.'

She shook her head.

There was a letter from my mother.

'You must obey the King,' she wrote. 'It is your duty. He is your father. Do not add to my anxieties. They are many and would be more if I thought you defied your father and so roused his anger against you. At present he remembers you are his daughter. Do not, I beg of you, do anything to make him turn against you.'

Then I knew I had to accept what was asked of me. I should have to be there when the odious child was born.

So I set out for Greenwich. Until the baby was born I must live under the same roof as my father and the woman I continued to call his concubine.

From the moment I arrived I was made aware of the fact that my situation had changed a good deal from those days when my father had fondled me and delighted in his daughter.

I did see him briefly. He gave me a cool nod and somehow managed to convey that I had better behave in a seemly manner or it would be the worse for me.

I was presented to her, too. There she was, large with child, smug, complacent, carrying the heir to the throne, she thought. How I hated her! Elegant, she was, in her rich velvets apeing the Queen.

She gave me her hand to kiss. I could have spurned her but I seemed to hear my mother's voice pleading with me; and I could guess at my father's rage if I showed my contempt for her.

130

So I was cool to her, as she was to me, and if ever hatred flowed between people, it flowed between us two.

'Please God, do not let her live,' I prayed. 'Let her and the child die. Let the King realize his cruelty and let all be well between us.'

It was September. The baby was expected hourly. The King was in a state of high excitement, certain that at last he would have his son. I wondered what he would say if he knew I was silently praying for the death of the witch and her offspring.

Then Anne Boleyn was brought to bed.

A special chamber in the Palace of Greenwich had been prepared for the birth. It had been hung with tapestries depicting the history of holy virgins. My father had given her one of the most beautiful beds he had ever possessed to receive his son when he came into the world. The bed was French and had come to him through the Duc d'Alençon as a ransom when he had been my father's prisoner.

It was a long and arduous labour. Seated with others in the chamber adjoining that in which she lay and of which the door was open, we could hear her groans of agony, and at each one I have to admit I exulted.

'Oh God,' I prayed, 'let this be her last. Let her die . . . and the bastard with her.'

I seemed to see my mother's face admonishing me. 'The woman is in labour. My child, you have no notion of what this means. She suffers pain such as you cannot imagine. Did not Our Lord teach us to be merciful?'

Merciful to that woman who had deprived my mother of her health, strength and happiness? How could I? I was honest at least. Desperately I wanted her dead. Somewhere in my heart, I believed that if a benign God – benign to us, of course, not to her – would arrange her death, all would be well between my parents.

The King did not come to see her. He knew that as soon as the child appeared he would be told.

Through the night we sat. The next day dawned. I shall never forget that day – September. It must have been between three and four o'clock in the morning when I heard the cry of a child.

Breathlessly I waited, angry with God for not answering my prayers. They were alive – both of them. Anne Boleyn had given the King the child for which he craved.

And then the news. My heart began to sing. A girl! I wanted to laugh out loud. My mother had done as well as that. She had given him a girl – myself. And he had gone through all this for the sake of another! It was a joke. Hysterical laughter bubbled up within me.

How was *she* feeling now, the concubine? Witch that she was, this was something she could not achieve.

And the King? How was he feeling? He would be realizing now that his efforts had been in vain.

The Countess had not been allowed to accompany me, and I was desolate without her. There was no one whom I could trust as I did her, and I was old enough to know how easily I could commit some indiscretion which could do me great harm.

I did, however, see Chapuys, the Emperor's ambassador. I believe my father would rather have kept us apart but he could hardly do that without arousing hostile comment, and probably at this time he was feeling too frustrated to give much thought to it.

'The King is bitterly disappointed,' Chapuys told me. 'He cannot altogether hide it, although at her bedside he told her that he would never desert her. But that in itself betrays that the thought of doing so must have entered his mind. They will have more children, he said, sons . . . sons . . . sons. She is still the Queen but his eyes stray and it seems there are others.'

'But for so long he sought her! She was the only one for him all those years.'

'It may be that now he regrets what he had to pay for

132

her. He has taken great risks, and we do not yet know what will be the outcome of that. But what I have to say to you is this: You are the Princess of Wales but there is now another whom he might try to put ahead of you.'

I was aghast. 'He cannot!' I cried.

'He can and if it is possible he will. You must be prepared.'

'What can I do?'

'We will wait and see.'

'What of the Emperor?' I said. 'Why does he stand aside and see my mother and me treated thus?'

'The Emperor watches. He cares what becomes of you. The King's actions towards you are an insult to Spain, but the Emperor cannot go to war on that account. The time is not ripe, and the French and English are allies to stand against him.'

I covered my face with my hands.

'Be prepared,' he said.

I remembered those words when I was told I must attend the christening of the child, this Elizabeth, my half-sister who was destined to plague me in the years to come.

* * *

It was four days after her birth – four days of bitter foreboding for me. Why had I been submitted to this extra torture? Why did I have to see honours showered on her? Wasn't it enough that she was born?

After his initial disappointment the King was expressing a certain delight in the child. I sometimes thought in the years ahead that she had inherited her mother's witchery. She was beautiful and healthy. 'Oh God,' I asked in anguish, 'why did You not listen to my prayers?' From the beginning she charmed all those who came into contact with her.

It was the cruellest act to make me attend her christening.

There was a letter from my mother which had been smuggled in to me. I was sure that woman and my father would have stopped our correspondence if they knew her letters were reaching me.

She told me that Anne Boleyn had had the effrontery to write to ask her for the special robe which had been used at the christening of that son who had briefly brought her and the King such joy and then almost immediately died.

I remembered my mother's showing me the robe. She had brought it with her from Spain. It was to be worn by her sons at their christening. How ironic that she had been able to use it only once, and then for little purpose. Even I – as a girl – had not worn it. And that woman had dared to ask for it for her daughter!

My mother had refused, amazed that my father had known of his concubine's request and had not stopped it.

My mother wondered whether they would come to her and take it by force; but they did stop at that, and although the young Elizabeth was carried in a gown of purple velvet edged with ermine, it was not the Spanish christening robe.

To me it was like a nightmare. I kept marvelling how they could have been so insensitive as to insist that I take part. It might have been to show the people that my father was not casting me out. I knew a great many rumours were circulating about his treatment of my mother and me and that they disturbed him.

This was a very grand ceremony. The walls between the Palace and Grey Friars were hung with arras, and the path was strewn with fresh green rushes. Elizabeth was carried by the Dowager Duchess of Norfolk, who was her great-grandmother, and the canopy was held by Anne's brother George Boleyn, now Lord Rochford, Lords William and Thomas Howard and Lord Hussey, another of the Boleyn clan recently ennobled.

The Dukes of Norfolk and Suffolk walked beside the baby.

It was indeed a royal christening.

I was so wretched. Why had they insisted that I be present? At least my mother had escaped this.

Then came the final blow. I felt stunned when Garter-King-at-Arms proclaimed: 'God, of His infinite goodness, send a prosperous life and long to the High and Mighty Princess of England, Elizabeth.'

Princess of England! But *I* was the Princess of England. How could she be so?

I heard the shouts and trumpets through a haze of apprehension.

What did this mean? Need I ask myself? I knew. This was the final insult.

* * *

When I look back over that time, I think it must have been one of the most dangerous of my life. There have been many crises, and my life has been at risk many times, but then I was so young, so inexperienced in the ways of the world, so inadequate to cope with situations in which I found myself; I was so reckless, so lacking in good counsel. Lady Salisbury was not with me at this time and I did not realize then how much I had relied on her. My mother had written warning me, but my natural resentment made me one of my own worst enemies.

I was seventeen years old and had already faced as many dangers in a few short years as most people face in a lifetime.

I know now that there are people in the world who revel in the troubles of others and find excitement in fomenting them. They take a delight in seeing what will happen next. There was I, once Princess of Wales, heir to the throne . . . and now there was this child who had usurped my place and had been named Princess of England.

How they beguiled me – those people about me – with their gossip. They treated me as an adult. Was it not shocking the way in which Queen Anne behaved with all those men about her? She was never without a bevy of adoring young men. They had seen the looks which passed between them . . . and looks told a great deal. And the King? He was not so enamoured of her as he had once been.

I was too young, too foolish, to restrain myself. Of course I should not have listened. I should not have told them of my hatred for her and how I had prayed that she would die in childbirth . . . and her child with her.

Lady Salisbury would never have allowed it; my mother would have forbidden it. But I was parted from them; I was alone in a hotbed of treachery, and these gossipers seemed so sympathetic towards me that they lured me into expressing my true feelings.

I did not know that my remarks were recorded and taken back to Anne Boleyn.

I was bewildered and bitterly humiliated. *I* was the Princess of England, I declared, and foolishly not only to myself. A bastard did not count. The King was still married to my mother and I was born in wedlock.

In due course I was sent back to Beaulieu. At least the Countess was there.

I fell into her arms and sobbed out what had happened.

'They called her the Princess of England!' I sobbed. 'What does that mean?'

The Countess was silent. She knew full well what it meant.

But at least I was back with her and I found a certain comfort in going over my experiences while she stroked my hair and soothed me with gentle words, but she could not hide the fear in her eyes.

Sir John and Lady Hussey arrived at Beaulieu. He was to be my Chamberlain, he informed me, and his wife was to join my household.

The Countess was disturbed. She told me that Hussey

was one of the King's most trusted servants. I guessed now that he had been sent because of the remarks I had made and which had been reported to Anne Boleyn, who would have convinced my father that I was dangerous. Hence he had sent Hussey to watch over me. He might be suspicious of the Countess – after all she was a Plantagenet, and her son Reginald had openly expressed his feelings about the King's marriage in no uncertain terms.

Hussey had been a long and tried friend to the Tudors; he had fought for my grandfather when he came to the throne and had been made Comptroller of his household. When my father had become King, he had felt the need to win the people's approval by taking revenge on those who had helped his father collect the taxes, and he had executed Dudley and Empson, the hated enforcers of the royal extortion: Hussey had been involved with them, but shrewdly guessing that he would be a good friend, my father pardoned him and granted him land in Lincolnshire. So he had a loyal servant in Hussey. He was quite an old man now, therefore very experienced; and he had been useful to my father during the devious negotiations for the divorce.

My heart sank when he was presented to me as my Chamberlain; and I believe the Countess's did too. She guessed more accurately than I could what this meant. One of Hussey's duties was to tell me the doleful – though not unexpected – news of what the Council's ministers had decided.

Hussey looked uneasy, and I thought I caught a glint of sympathy in his eyes.

'My lady,' he said, 'I have received orders.' I felt a twinge of uneasiness as he had not addressed me as Princess. 'It is with regret I have to tell you of them.'

'Then tell me,' I said as coolly as I could.

He was holding a piece of paper in his hand. He looked

at it and bit his lips. I had not suspected him of such
sensitivity.

'The orders are that you are no longer to be addressed as
Princess.'

'Why not?'

'It . . . er . . . it seems that this is no longer your title.'

I stared at the man. 'How can that be? I am the King's
daughter.'

'Yes, my lady, but . . . in view of the fact that the King's
marriage to the Princess of Spain was no true marriage,
you are no longer entitled to be called Princess. Indeed,
my lady, we are forbidden to address you as such.'

'I do not believe it. May I see that paper?'

He nodded and handed it to me.

It was there, plain for me to see. I was to be called the
Lady Mary, the King's daughter. But I was no longer the
Princess of England. That title had been passed to the little
bastard whose christening I had been forced to witness at
Greenwich.

Hussey bowed his head. He said: 'I will send the
Countess to you.'

She came and I threw myself at her.

'There! There!' she said. 'At least you have a shoulder to
cry on. Do not grieve, Princess.'

'You must not call me that any more.'

'When we are alone together . . .'

I had grown up suddenly. I saw dangers all around us.
'Oh no, dearest Countess. You must not. Someone might
hear. They would tell tales of you. I believe those who call
me by my rightful title will be punished.'

'It is so,' she confirmed. 'We have been warned.'

'But I *am* the Princess. I shall call myself Princess, but I
will not bring trouble to you. They would take you from
me. Perhaps put you in the Tower.'

'Oh,' she whispered. 'You are growing up, Princess. You

138

are beginning to understand how dangerous are the times in which we are living.'

'But I will not accept this,' I said. 'I am the Princess. That trumped-up divorce is wrong. It is a sin in the eyes of God, and Anne Boleyn is no true Queen.'

'Hush. Did I say that you were growing up? Now you are behaving like a child.'

'My father does care something for me, surely.'

'Your father wants complete obedience. We must wait quietly . . . not calling attention to ourselves.'

I did not answer.

I was young and I was reckless. I was telling myself I could not endure this. I would not stand aside and let them treat my mother and myself in this way. She had cautioned discretion but she was weary and sick and had not the heart for the fight. I was different.

My household might be intimidated into dropping the title of Princess when addressing me, but I would continue to use the title. It was mine. And it was not for the Council to take it away from me.

When I went out into the streets there were always people to cheer me. They would cry: 'Long live Princess Mary.' I must have caused much anxiety to the King and his concubine for they knew what support there was throughout the country for my mother and me. The people knew that we had been separated and they thought that cruel. Yes, my father and Anne Boleyn must be having some very uneasy moments.

There would always be those fanatics who seemed to court martyrdom and make a great noise doing so. There was one known as the Nun of Kent. She was a certain Elizabeth Barton who had begun life as a servant in the household of a man who was steward to the estate owned by the Archbishop of Canterbury. She appeared to have special powers of prophecy and was taken up by a number of well-known people which gave her great prestige. Sir

139

Thomas More was said to have been interested in her. She sprang into prominence when my father had returned from France with the newly created Marchioness of Pembroke. Elizabeth Barton had met him at Canterbury and warned him that if he married Anne Boleyn he would die one month later.

She had begged my mother to see her. My mother was too wise to do this and refused to do so.

I wondered that my father had not had her removed long ago. But he was always somewhat superstitious and because the nun had been taken up by prominent people – and in particular Sir Thomas More – he was a little in awe of her. He was very anxious at this time to win back that public approval which he had lost since his Secret Matter was revealed.

After the marriage everyone waited for the prophecy to come true. A month passed and nothing happened. Now Anne Boleyn had come through the ordeal of childbirth and had a healthy child, albeit a girl. As for Anne, she was as well as ever. The nun's prophecy had not been fulfilled.

For two months after my return I waited in trepidation for what would happen next. The baby Elizabeth had remained at Greenwich with her mother for those two months; then the King decided that she should have a household of her own. I heard that Hatfield had been chosen.

Much to my horror, Hussey came to me, with further instructions from the Council. I, too, was to be moved. I imagine my recalcitrant attitude had been reported to him.

'Your household is to be broken up, my lady,' he said. 'You are to go to Hatfield.'

'My household broken up!' I repeated stupidly.

He nodded slowly and horror dawned on me. 'The Countess of Salisbury . . .' I began.

He did not meet my eyes. He said: 'The new mistress of your household will be Lady Shelton.'

140

'Lady Shelton!' I cried in dismay. 'Is she not related to . . . to . . . ?'

'To the Queen, my lady.'

'To Anne Boleyn!'

'She is the Queen's aunt.'

Anne Boleyn's aunt – a member of that hated family – to take the place of my beloved Countess! This was intolerable. I might bear other humiliations which had been heaped on me, I might endure insults, but to be deprived of the one to whom I had turned when I lost my mother . . . that was just not to be borne.

'This cannot be true,' I stammered.

'I fear so, my lady.'

'No one could be so cruel. If the Countess could be with me . . . if . . .'

'These are the King's orders, my lady.'

I turned and ran out of the room.

She came to me almost immediately. 'You have heard,' she said.

'How can he? How can he? Everything else I have borne, but this . . .'

'I know, my dearest. I shudder with you. We have been so close . . . you have been as one of my own . . .'

'Since they would not allow me to be with my mother, you took her place.'

She nodded and we just clung together.

'It will pass,' she said at length. 'It can only be temporary. We shall be together again . . .'

'Oh Countess, dearest Countess, what am I to do?'

'There is nothing to be done but to remain quiet and confident of the future. We must pray as Our Lord did in the wilderness.'

I was not as meek as she was. I could never be. She was like my mother, and they were both of the stuff of which martyrs are made. But I was not. I was filled with hatred

141

towards this woman whom I blamed for all our misfortunes. I hated the innocent baby who had taken my place and for whose sake I was being made to suffer thus.

I took up my pen and, against the Countess's advice, wrote to the Council. I gave vent to the rage I felt. The very act of picking up a pen, though, brought me back to my senses a little. I knew I should have to go to Hatfield, to part from the Countess, and that it was no use protesting about this. But I could call attention to the deprivation of my title which was mine by right of birth, and that I would do.

'My lords,' I wrote, 'as touching my removal to Hatfield, I will obey His Grace as my duty is . . . but I will protest before you all, and to all others present, that my conscience will in no wise suffer me to take any other than myself for Princess or for the King's daughter born in lawful matrimony, and that I will never wittingly or willingly say or do aught whereby any person might take occasion to think that I agree to the contrary. If I should do otherwise I should slander my mother, the Holy Church and the Pope, who is judge in this matter and none other, and I should dishonour the King, my father, the Queen, my mother, and falsely confess myself a bastard, which God defend I should do since the Pope hath not so declared by his sentence definitive, to whose judgement I submit myself . . .'

It was foolish. It was rash. But I was beside myself with misery because my dearest friend, who had been a mother to me, was about to be taken away from me.

There was a further blow. The Princess Elizabeth was to go to Hatfield with her household, and it seemed that, with no household of my own, I should be a member of hers. A lady-in-waiting perhaps! It was intolerable. This was proclaiming to the world that she was the Princess, the heir to the throne, and I was the bastard.

I could not understand how my father could do this to me. I remembered those days when he had shown great

142

affection for me. How could he have changed? It could only be because he was under the influence of witchcraft.

On impulse I wrote to him. I told him that I had been informed by my Chamberlain that I was to leave for Hatfield and that, when I had asked to see the letter and had been shown it, it stated that '. . . the Lady Mary, the King's daughter, should remove to the place aforesaid'. I was not referred to as the Princess. I was astonished and could not believe that His Grace was aware of what had been written, for I could not believe that he did not take me for his true daughter born in matrimony. I believed this and, if I said otherwise, then I should earn the displeasure of God, which I was sure His Grace would not wish me to do. In all other matters I should always be his humble and obedient daughter.

I signed myself 'Your most humble daughter, Mary, *Princess*.'

It was an act of defiance. I was stating clearly that in my opinion his marriage to Anne Boleyn was no true marriage, and as I was legitimate, Elizabeth was a bastard.

As soon as I had dispatched the letter, I realized the enormity of what I had done. Both my mother and the Countess would have been horrified.

The result was to bring the Duke of Norfolk down to Beaulieu with Lord Marney, the Earl of Oxford and the Duke's almoner, Dr Fox. Their purpose was, I think, to warn me of the folly of continuing in my stubborn mood, to administer the breaking up of my household and to see me on my way.

I knew from the attitude of the Duke towards me that I could expect no sympathy from him or any of his hench-men; and that was an indication of my father's feelings towards me.

The Husseys would remain in my household, and I might take two personal maids. I had to say goodbye to all the rest. Even now I cannot bear to brood on my parting with the Countess. It was one of the most harrowing experiences through which I had passed. When my mother had been separated from me, she had handed me over to the Countess and we had been able to mourn together.

I had never felt so alone, so bereft, as I did when I left Beaulieu behind and made my way to Hatfield.

News travelled fast and spread through the neighbourhood. The people of Beaulieu knew I was leaving and those of Hatfield that I was coming.

Courtiers are subservient to their masters; not so the people. They have means of expressing their feelings which are often denied those in high places.

They were on the road . . . groups of them . . . cheering me.

'Long live our Princess Mary! Long live Queen Katharine! We'll have no Nan Bullen!'

That was music to my ears – particularly when they called me Princess.

I smiled, acknowledging their greetings. I hoped my father would hear of the people's attitude towards me. I was sure it would give him a few qualms of uneasiness.

All too soon the journey was over. I had arrived at Hatfield Palace, and I felt as though I were being taken into prison.

* * *

Misery descended upon me. Lady Shelton was anxious to let me know that I was a person of no importance and that if I gave myself airs it would be the worse for me.

I treated her with a cold contempt which so aroused her anger that she told me that if I persisted in my stubborn ill behaviour she had been advised to beat me.

'Advised by whom?' I asked.

She did not answer but I knew. She was so proud of the fact that she was related to the woman they called the Queen.

During the first days of our encounter I knew that she would never lay hands on me. When she insulted me, I would draw myself up to my full height and merely look at her. I was royal and perhaps that was apparent. I could see little lights of apprehension in her eyes. What was she thinking? 'One day this prisoner could be Queen of England? It would be wise not to antagonize her too much. To strike her would be quite unforgivable.'

I found just a slight elation in the midst of my gloom to know that, although she might make me uncomfortable in a hundred ways and abuse me verbally, she would never lift her hand against me.

Hatfield is a beautiful place, but I was alone and desolate, deserted by my father and separated from my beloved mother and the Countess.

All the attention in the household was for the baby. The Princess, they called her. I would not call her that. To me she was sister, just as the Duke of Richmond was brother. There was no difference. They were both the King's illegitimate children.

Sometimes I dream of those days. They are remote now but I can still conjure up the infinite sadness, the deep loneliness, the longing for my mother and the Countess, the abject misery. I felt then that whatever happened I could never be truly happy again.

Sometimes I thought the object of the household was to humiliate me. The Duke of Richmond had a fine household; the King made much of him. But, of course, it was different with me. I was a continual reproach to him. I was there at the back of his mind, jerking that mighty conscience of his so that it refused now and then to do his bidding. Hatfield! The very name means blank misery, a certain feeling of hopelessness which is what comes to those in prison with no indication of how long their incarceration will last, wondering if only death can release them from the wretchedness of their days.

But I suppose nothing is complete gloom. Although in the beginning I had resented the Husseys, I was now rather glad that they were with me . . . particularly Lady Hussey, who, I was sure, had great sympathy with me. Once or twice she had addressed me as Princess. It may have been deliberate. On the other hand she had been accustomed to referring to me thus before it had been forbidden to do so. But so bereft was I of friends that I was grateful for that little show of sympathy.

Then I had the two maids who had come with me to Hatfield. They served me loyally and showed in a hundred ways that they regarded me as their Princess.

There was another blessing. It so happened that Elizabeth's governess was Lady Bryan, who had held the same post to me during my early years.

There seems to be a bond between a motherly woman and a child to whom she has been close in infancy. It may have been because Margaret Bryan was a kindly woman, or it may have been because there was that early bond between us, but it soon became clear that she deplored the way in which I was treated under Lady Shelton's rules. Looks were exchanged between us, and then we found opportunities of talking. She brought me some comfort, and I shall always be grateful to Margaret Bryan.

A great deal was happening. I suppose that year was one of the most momentous in history.

The Nun of Kent had been arrested soon after I arrived at Hatfield. She was sent to the Tower with some of her associates. When they were brought before the Star Chamber, they all confessed to fraud, and Elizabeth Barton was accused of trying to dethrone the King, which was, of course, treason.

Christmas came – the most dreary I had ever spent. It was cold. It was long since I had had new clothes, and I saw no means of getting any. I was not allowed to have my meals served in my room. If I wished to eat, I had to go

146

down to the hall and seat myself where I could; and if I did not go, nobody seemed to care. Except, of course, Margaret Bryan, who surveyed me with some anxiety. She assumed the role of nurse and talked to me as though I were a wayward child.

'What good is this doing?' she demanded. 'It is hard for you but you must make the best of it. Going without food is not going to help you.'

I said: 'You and my two maids are the only friends I have. Perhaps Lady Hussey is . . . in a way.'

I saw the tears in her eyes. I knew it was difficult for her to speak to me, for she might be noticed, and if she were she would be sent away. But as she saw I was growing more and more wan, she became reckless. I had once been her charge and she could not forget it. Moreover as any good woman would be, she was appalled at the manner in which my mother was treated.

She said to me: 'If I came to your room after the household has retired, we could talk.'

I was overcome with emotion. I felt as though a light had appeared in a dark room, and it brought with it a glimmer of comfort.

It was Margaret Bryan who kept me sane during that long time. Sometimes I felt an urge to throw myself out of a window. It was a sin to take life . . . even one's own. It was that thought which restrained me. My great comfort was in prayer. I was sustained by reading the holy books, by remembering the sufferings of Jesus and trying to emulate his example. At least I had managed to subdue Lady Shelton sufficiently to escape the humiliation of physical punishment.

And there was Margaret Bryan.

When the house was quiet, she would come to my room. I was terrified at the risk she was taking, for I knew that, if Lady Shelton discovered, she most certainly would be sent away; she might even be imprisoned. I was sure both the

147

King and Anne Boleyn were very much afraid of the people's feelings for my mother and me.

She was helped in this by one of the maids who was a sweet girl and wanted to do more for me. I was afraid her devotion would be noticed and she sent away; I told her that would sorely grieve me.

There was a secret understanding between us that she should pretend to be brusque with me, in common with the others around me. It was very important to me that she should stay near me, and although she thought of me as the Princess, it was necessary that she did not show this.

It was little incidents like this which sustained me. Later she became bolder, and it was through her, with Margaret Bryan's help, that letters from my mother and even Chapuys, the Emperor's ambassador, were smuggled in to me.

One day Margaret told me that the King was coming to Hatfield to see the Princess.

Now was my chance. If I could speak to him face to face, surely he would not fail to be moved by my plight. I would plead with him. I would make him understand. I must see him, I told myself.

The house was in tumult. The King was coming! I wondered whether *she* would be with him. Surely she would, for it was the baby they would come to see . . . her baby. If she came, there would be no hope of my seeing him. I was sure of that.

I thought of what I must do. I would throw myself at his feet. I would beg him to remember that I was his daughter.

The great day came.

My little maid was agog with excitement. 'They say Queen Anne is not coming to Hatfield because you are here,' she told me.

'Surely she will come to see her own child.'

'They say she will not.'

'If he comes alone . . .' I murmured. The girl nodded. She knew what I meant.

148

And at length he came. It was true that Anne Boleyn had stayed some miles away and he would rejoin her after the visit.

I could smell the roasting meats; I was aware of the bustle of serving men rushing hither and thither in the last throes of preparation for the royal visit. And at last there he was, riding into Hatfield.

I was in my room . . . waiting. Would he send for me? Surely he must. Was I not his daughter? He had come to see one; surely he must see the other, too.

The hours wore on. Margaret came to tell me that he had been with Elizabeth and seemed mightily pleased with her. Margaret glowed with pride every time she mentioned Elizabeth. 'He is now feasting in the hall,' she went on. 'They are in a panic in the kitchens lest anything go wrong.'

Surely he must ask: Where is my daughter Mary? Why is she not here?

But I could not go unless he sent for me.

The hours were passing. He was preparing to leave and he had not sent for me. Perhaps he had not asked about me. I must see him, I must.

But he was not going to send for me, and already they were riding out of the palace.

I dashed to the balcony. There he was. I stood there, looking down at him.

I did not call his name. I just stared and stared, my lips moving in prayer. Father . . . your daughter is here . . . please . . . please . . . do not leave without seeing me. Just a look . . . a smile . . . but look at me.

And then something made him turn, and for a few seconds we looked full at each other. He did not smile. He merely looked. What thoughts passed through his head, I did not know. What did he think to see this pale-faced girl who had once been his pretty child, shabbily clad, when once she had been in velvet and cloth of gold, an outcast in his bastard daughter's household . . . what did he think?

He had passed on. He did lift his hat, though, in acknowledgement of my presence as he turned away.

All the gentlemen around him did likewise.

I had been noticed. And that was all his visit meant to me.

* * *

I was hearing news of my mother through Margaret and my maid.

When they moved me to Hatfield, they had tried to move her from Buckden to Somersham, at the same time dismissing part of her household. I had been worried about her being at Buckden which is a most unhealthy place, but Somersham is worse. It is in the Isle of Ely and notoriously damp, and as she was suffering from excruciating pains in her limbs, I was sure that would have been disastrous for her. I often marvelled at my mother's indomitable spirit and the manner in which she clung to life. She must have known that she could not live long in Somersham, and the thought occurred to me that my father – lured on by his concubine – might have thought it would kill her to stay there long. Her death would make things easier for them, and I was sure it was what the concubine desired – if not my father.

My mother had defied the commissioners sent to carry out my father's orders; she had shut herself in her room and sent word down to them that if they wished to remove her they must break down her door and carry her off by force.

They could have done this, of course, but there was a rumour that the people in the neighbourhood were bringing out their scythes and other such implements implying that, if the Queen were taken, her captors would have to face the people, and this made them hesitate.

The result had been that my mother had remained at Buckden.

150

I heard what her life was like there. She found great comfort in prayer. I did too, but she was more intensely involved. Religion was all-important to her. It was becoming so with me, as it does with people who have nothing else to cling to. She, however, would never rail against her misfortunes, but meekly accept them. That was the difference in us. She passed her time in prayer, meditation and sewing for the poor. There was a window in her room from which she could look down on the chapel, and there she spent a great deal of her time. I was thankful that she had a loyal chamberwoman who cooked for her. Several new servants had been assigned to her, and naturally she must feel suspicious of them.

It is a terrible state when someone you once loved can be suspected of trying to poison you. I understood so well what she was suffering. After all, I was undergoing something similar myself.

She was constantly in my thoughts. I worried about her and the Countess. I often thought of Reginald and wondered what he was doing now. All I knew was that he was on the Continent and that he had further enraged the King by writing to advise him to return to my mother. Should we ever see each other again? Would that love between us which had begun to stir ever come to fruition?

I thought then what little control we have over our destinies. It was only the all-powerful like my father who could thrust aside those who stood in their way – but even they came up against obstacles.

In January of that momentous year 1534, anticipating the verdict of the court of Rome, my father ordered the Council to declare that henceforth the Pope would be known as the Bishop of Rome, and bishops were to be appointed without reference to the See of Rome. It was the first step in the great scheme which he had devised with the help of Cranmer and Cromwell. It was to have far-reaching effects which must have been obvious to everyone.

151

Very soon after, the Rome verdict was announced. My father's marriage to my mother was legal, and the Pope advised the King to put Anne Boleyn from him immediately.

My father retaliated by announcing that the children of Queen Anne were the true heirs to the throne and that all those in high places must swear on oath to accept them as such. All over the country preachers were instructed to applaud the King's action and revile the Pope.

It could not be expected that this would be received quietly by everyone, and there were naturally those who were ready to risk their lives and stand in opposition to the King's command. Bishop Fisher and Sir Thomas More were two of those who were sent to the Tower.

There were murmurings of revolt throughout the country. People continued to blame Anne Boleyn.

I was more frustrated than ever. It was maddening to receive only news which was brought to me through Margaret Bryan and my maid. I often wondered how true it was. Could it really be that the country was in revolt, that they were calling for the restoration of Queen Katharine and the religion they – and their ancestors before them – had known throughout their lives?

How could the King suddenly sever his country from Rome? And just because the Pope would not grant him the right to put his good wife from him and set up his concubine in her place?

I think he must have been very disturbed. He had always courted popularity so assiduously; he had revelled in it, sought it on every occasion; and now when he rode out he was met by sullen looks, and when that woman was with him there were some bold spirits who dared give voice to their disapproval. He must fear that we were trembling on the edge of disaster . . . perhaps even civil war.

There were rumours that the Emperor was going to invade England, to rescue the Queen, depose the King and set me up as Queen. It was frightening to be in the midst of such a storm.

Attention was turned on Elizabeth Barton, the Nun of Kent. Cromwell had made much of her confession – and those of her adherents. He wanted the whole country to know of the deception. I supposed that was why she had not been executed at the time of her arrest. I think they were trying to incriminate others . . . all of those who were making things difficult for the King. Sir Thomas More had once listened to this woman's prophecies with interest, and he was incriminated, but, clever lawyer that he was, he was able to extricate himself from the charge, although he was still in the Tower because he refused to agree that my father's marriage to my mother was invalid and he would not accept that Anne Boleyn's children were the true heirs to the throne. Panic was spreading all over the country; people were discovering that their bluff and hearty King could be cruel and ruthless. They did not yet know how cruel, how ruthless – but they were beginning to suspect.

All those who had professed interest in the Nun – and there were some in high places – now wished to dissociate themselves from her.

However, the King was determined to show the people what became of those who opposed him; but in spite of all the trouble she had caused him, the Nun's confession was gratifying to him. She said, before the crowds who had come to witness her last hours at Tyburn, that she was a poor wretch without learning who had been made to believe she had special powers by men who encouraged her to fabricate inventions which brought profit to themselves.

Poor creature, she was hanged with those who had been her close associates.   •

Each day we waited to hear what would happen next. Lady Bryan was very fearful on my account. She tried to hide it but she asked my chambermaid to take special care with my food.

If I was in this dangerous situation, I asked myself, what of my mother? How was she faring? If only I could have seen her, if only we could have been together, I could have borne this. I was growing thinner and very pale; I suffered from headaches and internal periodic pains and difficulties. I would find myself babbling prayers and asking Heaven to come to my aid.

My little maid came in one day and said: 'Madam . . . Princess . . . there are two cartloads of friars being taken to the Tower. People watch them. They stand in the cart, their hands together in prayer. People are asking, is that going to happen to us all?'

Later Margaret told me that the Franciscan Order had been suppressed.

Then I knew that the King's attention had turned on me, for his commissioners came to Hatfield. They searched the rooms of all those about me; and to my horror they took Lady Hussey away with them.

I was appalled. She had not been a great friend to me in the way that Margaret Bryan had but she had shown a certain sympathy for me. She had always treated me with respect and had on occasion called me Princess. I trembled lest they should take Margaret. She had been very careful, but I could not think of any misdemeanour Lady Hussey had committed.

Later I learned that she had been imprisoned because she had been heard to address me as Princess and on one occasion had said, 'The Princess has gone out walking,' and on another asked someone to take the Princess a drink.

What a pass we had come to when a woman could be in fear of losing her life because she had made such a remark!

I worried a great deal about her; I prayed for her; and I was delighted when I heard later that, after a humble confession and a plea to the King for mercy, she was released.

There was a change in my household. Everyone was

terrified. It says a great deal for Lady Bryan's courage that she continued to visit me and bring messages, taking mine in return. It would have been certain death for her if she had been discovered.

My mother might hear of Lady Hussey's arrest. What anguish that would cause her, for her fears would not be for herself but for me.

I was fortified by messages from Chapuys, the Spanish ambassador. My maid, being in a humble position, was not watched as some like Margaret would be; she had sources outside the palace, and through her I kept in touch with the ambassador.

I had his assurance that the Emperor was watching events with the utmost care. If it had been possible, he would have come to rescue my mother and me. He could not do this. François was now an ally of my father and the Emperor had to be watchful and could not leave his own dominions. I understood this, and it was comforting to know he was aware of what was going on.

Chapuys wrote that he had information of a plot to execute my mother and me because we refused to accept Anne as the true Queen. That was what others were suffering for, and the King could never be at peace while we lived.

There were times when I thought death would be a way out of my miseries; but when one comes close to it, one changes one's mind.

Now, I hesitated every night before lying down; I searched my little room for an assassin; I paused before taking a mouthful of food. I found I would tremble at a sudden footfall. I was eating scarcely anything. I prayed for guidance. And then suddenly, the idea came to me that I might escape.

Could I do that? I had friends to help me. Would they be prepared to risk their lives for me? Perhaps my father would be glad to see me go and rejoice . . . even reward those who helped me get away. Oh no, wherever I was, I should be a menace to him, and particularly so in the care of the Emperor, my cousin. It was dangerous but I needed some stimulation at that time.

So I planned my escape. I had a letter smuggled out to Chapuys. He must help me. I could no longer endure this way of life.

Chapuys was considering what could be done and, I supposed, how my escape would affect the imperial cause. That was always a first consideration. But I imagined the Emperor would not find me an encumbrance, and if I were in his care I should be a continual anxiety to my father, which would please my cousin. So . . . there seemed a possibility that the escape might be arranged.

It was at this time that all the months of anxiety, the lack of food and my deep depression took their toll of me. I awoke one morning and was too ill to lift my head.

Lady Shelton came to me. She was in a panic. They wanted me dead but everyone was afraid of being accused of killing me.

There was much activity in the house. Vaguely I was aware of it.

Then I found myself being carried out in a litter. By this time the fever had taken such a hold on me that I was not aware of what was happening to me.

They took me to Greenwich.

I learned about this later when people were more ready to talk to me. The King was in a dilemma. He must have been hoping for my death and at the same time afraid of the stir it would raise. For six days I lay at Greenwich, unseen by a doctor, while the fever took a greater hold on me. I was delirious, they tell me, calling for my mother.

My father sent for Chapuys, to tell him that I was dangerously ill and that he wanted the ambassador to select doctors to send to me. If he would do so, my father told him, they should be sent to me with the royal doctors.

Chapuys was uneasy. If he sent doctors and they failed to cure me, how would that affect the Emperor?

It amuses me now to imagine those men all watching me on my sickbed and wondering what my life or death would mean to their politics.

My father was surely hoping for my death and thought I could not live long when Dr Butts announced that I was suffering from an incurable disease. Chapuys, on the other hand, had said that Dr Butts' words were that I was very ill indeed but good care might save me, and that if I were released from my present conditions the cure would be quick.

I was now under the sole care of Lady Shelton. I had been robbed of Margaret, who of course remained with Elizabeth; and my little maid had been suspected of working for me. She had been threatened with the Tower and torture if she did not confess, so, poor child, she admitted to a little. It was enough to bring about her dismissal. So there I was, sick until death and friendless.

I kept calling for my mother, but there was no one to hear me or care if they did.

I owe a great deal to Chapuys. He may have used me as a political pawn for the advancement of his master's cause, but he saved my life. If the King was sending out rumours of my incurable illness, Chapuys had his own way of refuting that. There were hints of poison.

My mother sent frantic messages to the King. 'Please give my daughter to me. Let me nurse her in her sickness.'

The requests were ignored. But the people heard of them and they did not like what they heard.

My mother had at this time been sent to Kimbolton Castle — a grimly uncomfortable dwelling in the flat Fen country where the persistent east winds I feared would greatly add to her discomfort.

People gathered about the castle as they did at Greenwich where I lay. They mumbled their displeasure; they cried:

157

'God save the Princess!' in defiance of those who declared that I no longer had a right to that title.

There was an uneasy atmosphere throughout the land. The King was now Supreme Head of the Church in England, and the break with Rome was complete; so it was not only the treatment of my mother and myself which was threatening revolt all over the country.

I often wondered whether my father paused to think what he had done when his desire to marry Anne Boleyn had possessed him. He would have visualized an easy divorce, marriage to his siren and a succession of sons. And how differently it had turned out! The break with Rome, the cruelty to his wife and daughter and still the longed-for son had not arrived. What he had done could not possibly endear him to his people.

And there was I – expected to die. Then at least one of the causes for disquiet would be removed. It was a realization I was forced to face. My father must be praying for my death. Nevertheless he dared not withhold help from me entirely, and Dr Butts was attending me. He was a man whose loyalty to his profession came first. I was his patient now and he was determined to save my life. He knew the cause of my illness. It was not the first time that I had been ill, though I was not fundamentally weak. I had been made to suffer deprivations and such anxieties as I hope few people have to endure; and these had had their effect on me. My mother was ill, too, but her ailments were more of a physical nature – rheumatism, gout, chest complaints brought about by cold and uncomfortable dwelling places. She was saintly and her religion sustained her; she was made for martyrdom. Not so myself. I too had suffered from deprivations but it was not they alone which had brought me to my sickbed. I suffered from a smouldering resentment, a hatred against my persecutors. Mine was more an illness of the mind. If I could have been with my mother, if I could have taken the example she set, I would recover, I knew.

Now I must lie in my bed, sickly and alone, longing to be with her that we might comfort each other. If Lady Salisbury could have come to me, that would have helped. But my father did not want me to be helped . . . unless it was to the grave.

He did come to visit me because of the grumbling discontent in the country. I was vaguely aware of him at my bedside.

I heard him mutter to Lady Shelton: 'There lies my greatest enemy.'

Afterwards I discovered that he had not asked to see me but that the good Dr Butts had forced himself into his presence and told him how ill I was and that he knew the cause and begged him to send my mother to me; whereupon the King rounded on him, calling him disloyal and declaring that he was making too much of my illness for political reasons.

The doctor was abashed but nothing could shift him from his ground. He insisted that if I could be with my mother that would do more for me than a hundred remedies.

Why did I want to go to Kimbolton? demanded the King. So that I and my mother could plot against him, raise armies against him? 'The Dowager Princess Katharine is another such as her mother, Queen Isabella of Castile,' he said; and he went on to rave about my stubborn behaviour, which was part of a plot to raise people against him. Already people in high places were turning to us.

Yes, he was certainly afraid.

I wondered if he knew then that certain nobles in the North were intimating to Chapuys that they would be ready to support the Emperor if he invaded England in an attempt to bring the Church back to Rome and restore my mother

159

to her rightful place and make me the Queen after dethroning my father.

A story was being circulated about a girl of seventeen or so – my age – who impersonated me in the North of England, where it was unlikely anybody had seen me. She went from village to village telling a sad story of the persecution she had suffered, explaining that she had escaped and was trying to reach the Emperor. Her name turned out to be Anne Baynton and she collected a fair amount of money, so she did succeed in deceiving people. It showed their sympathy to me that none attempted to betray her and instead were willing to help her on her way.

Meanwhile I lay sick in my bed, hovering between life and death.

At length I did begin to recover, for Dr Butts was determined that I should. He had to prove that my sickness was not incurable. I had always known that he was the best doctor in the kingdom. He was aware of the cause of my illness, and although it was due to a certain extent to ill-nourishment, it was the sheer misery which I had suffered which was the chief cause.

And as I returned to health there was born in me a determination to live to fight for my rights. I had been through so much that there was little worse that could happen to me. I was denied the company of those I loved; those of my friends who would visit me were turned away. I was kept from my mother; I was deprived of the company of my dear Countess; and Lady Bryan was no longer with me. I told myself I had touched the very nadir of my suffering.

I was very weak and scarcely able to walk across the room; but at least I was alive.

To my surprise, one day I had a visitor.

I was astonished when Lady Shelton came to my room. She said: 'Her Grace the Queen commands you to her presence.'

160

I felt suddenly very cold, and my hands began to tremble.

Lady Shelton was smiling at the prospect, I presumed, of a royal princess having to obey the command of that woman.

I said: 'You know my condition. I am unable to walk across the room without help.'

She smiled secretively with a lift of her shoulders.

'Her Grace the Queen commands your presence,' she repeated.

'If she wants to see me, she will perforce have to come to me.'

With a smirk, Lady Shelton nodded and disappeared.

I sat down on my bed, putting my hand to my heart. It was beating wildly. What had I done? I had shown my contempt for her. What would be the punishment for such conduct? Should I be sent to the Tower?

The door of my room was opened. I stared in surprise, for it was the woman herself. I could not believe it. I half rose.

She shook her head and signed for me to remain seated.

She was impressive, I could not deny it. She had an air of distinction. In that moment I could almost understand my father's obsession with her. She was most elegantly attired – not flamboyantly and yet more outstanding for the sheer elegance, the cut of her clothes and her style of wearing them.

I noticed the band about her neck which many had copied but none wore as she did. I noticed the long hanging sleeves to cover the sixth nail. Marks of the devil, I thought, which she has exploited to add to her grace.

Her enormous dark eyes held mine. I was trembling, unable to believe this was really happening. It must be something in a dream. I had thought of her so much. I had conjured up this vision. But there she was. She had seated herself on the bed facing me. She smiled. It changed her face. She was dazzling.

She said in a gentle voice: 'You have been very ill.'

I did not answer and she went on: 'But you are better now. This rift . . . it has gone on too long. I do not want it to continue. I understand your feelings, of course, and I have come to talk to you, to make a proposition. If you will come to Court I will do all in my power to restore your father's love for you.'

I listened dazed, becoming more and more convinced that I was dreaming.

She smiled graciously. What did it mean? I reminded myself that I hated her. There was some ulterior motive in this . . . some evil purpose. She must be thinking that I was overwhelmed by this show of friendship. Did she expect me to fall on my knees and thank her?

I remained silent. I could find no words to answer her.

She went on: 'There must be an end to these differences between you and your father. It is not good for the King, for you or for the country. So let us put an end to them.'

I heard myself stammer: 'How?'

She smiled confidently. 'You will return to Court. I promise you, you will be well treated. There shall be no discord. Everything that you had before will be yours. Perhaps it will be even better. There is only one thing you must do to achieve this.'

'And what is that?' I asked.

'You must honour me as the Queen. You must be respectful . . . and accept that this is now a fact.'

I could listen to no more. I saw it all. She and my father wanted me there to tell the people that I was not being shut out and ill treated. They did not want *me*. They would not accept me as the Princess Mary. I was not to be a princess. That title was reserved for this woman's bastard.

I said to her: 'I could not acknowledge you as Queen

162

because you are not Queen. I know of only one Queen of England, and that is my mother.'

Her eyes narrowed. 'You are a fool,' she said. 'A stubborn little fool.'

'I can only speak the truth,' I retorted. 'If you would speak to my father on my behalf . . . if you would persuade him to allow me to join my mother . . . I should appreciate that.'

'You know that is not what I meant. I am suggesting that you come to Court. All you must do is acccpt the fact that there was no true marriage between the King and your mother, that I am the King's wife and Queen of this realm and that my daughter, Elizabeth, is the Princess of England.'

'But I accept none of this. How can I when it is not true?'

'Do you know you are in danger?' she said. 'You incur the wrath of the King. Do you realize what could happen to you? I am giving you a chance to save yourself . . . to leave all this . . .' – she looked round the room with contempt – '. . . all this squalor. You shall have a luxurious apartment. You shall have all that is due to you as the King's daughter.'

'As the King's bastard, you mean.'

'There is no need for you to stress the point.'

'I stress it only to show its absurdity. I am the King's legitimate daughter. It is your daughter who is the bastard.'

She had risen. I thought she was going to strike me.

'I see that you are determined to destroy yourself,' she said.

'It is others who will try to destroy me,' I replied. 'They have already tried persistently, God knows, but they have not succeeded yet.'

'I see I have made a mistake,' she went on. 'I thought you would have more sense. You are stupidly blind. You do not see the dangers of your situation. You carelessly provoke the King's wrath. That can be terrible, you know.'

I took a shot in the dark. I had heard life was not running smoothly for her and the King, that he looked at other women now and then and was perhaps beginning to regret the hasty step he had taken. I said: 'As we both know.'

It is true, I thought. I noticed the sudden colour in her cheeks, the glint in her magnificent eyes.

She turned to me. 'You will regret this,' she said. Then she shrugged her shoulders. 'Well, I have given you a chance.'

After that she left me. Lady Shelton was hovering.

I heard Anne Boleyn say: 'The girl is a stubborn little fool. I will see that her Spanish pride is brought low.'

It had been a shattering experience. I sat on my bed, my limbs trembling so violently that I could not move.

* * *

We were into another new year, 1535. Could there ever be another like that which had gone before, when my father had shocked the whole of Europe by the unprecedented action of breaking with Rome?

I could not believe that even he could look back with equanimity on what he had done. He was never one to admit himself wrong, but surely he must suffer some disquiet in the secret places of his mind. How could he not? He was a religious man, a sentimental man. Oh yes, if he paused to think, he must suffer many an uneasy qualm.

The rumours about the differences between him and the concubine were growing. Life had not gone smoothly for her since her marriage. She had failed again. The longed-for boy had not appeared. There had been great hopes for him until she – as my mother had so many times – miscarried. There seemed to be a blight on my father's children. Even that golden boy, the Duke of Richmond, was very ill at this time and not expected to live. If he died, as he surely would soon, there would only be two of the King's children left – and both girls.

People's attitude towards me changed at the beginning of that year. Even Lady Shelton was less insolent. It may have been that she feared she had gone too far. This was because the concubine was falling out of favour. She had a fierce temper; she was dictatorial. I daresay she found it hard to believe that she, who had kept a firm hold on the King's affection all those years, could so quickly lose it. He was becoming enamoured of a lady at the Court who it seemed had decided to champion me. Whether she did this to strike a blow against Anne Boleyn or whether she was genuinely shocked at the manner in which I was treated, I could not tell. The outcome was that people were beginning to wonder whether they ought to take care how they behaved towards me.

I was allowed to walk out now. I could even take my goshawk with me. I was feeling a little better, recuperating, and when I left Greenwich and went to Eltham, I was allowed, because I was so weak, to ride in a litter.

And how the people cheered me along the route!

'Good health and long life to the Princess!'

Those words were music in my ears.

* * *

In the early part of that year there was indeed danger of revolt. There was nothing weak about my father. He was every inch a king. Everyone would grant him that; and when he was confronted by danger, those qualities of leadership were very much in evidence. All that happened had changed him visibly. I could hardly recognize the jovial fun-loving man in the ruthless autocrat who was now emerging.

Those who were not with him were his enemies – as had been seen in the case of his own wife and daughter.

His peace would be destroyed by the rumblings of discontent throughout the country; he knew that if my cousin Charles, the Emperor, had not been so deeply involved in Europe, he might have attempted to invade England. So he took action and, being the man he was, it was drastic. There were no half measures with him.

In April of that year the first proceedings were taken against those who refused to accept the fact that he was Supreme Head of the Church. Five monks – one of them the Prior of the London Charterhouse – were condemned as traitors and submitted to the most brutal of executions: they were hanged, drawn and quartered. There were many to witness this grisly scene, which was what my father intended. It was to provide a lesson to all those who opposed him. I was reminded of the masques my father had so loved when he appeared among the company in disguise. Now he had thrown off his mask, and in place of the merry, jovial bluff Hal was a ruthless and despotic monarch who would strike terror into all those who thought they could disobey his command.

Bishop Fisher and Sir Thomas More were in everyone's thoughts. Those two noble men had done exactly what the monks had. What would their fate be? The King had been a close friend of Sir Thomas More. He had loved the man – as many did; he had often been seen walking in Sir Thomas's riverside garden, his arm about his shoulders, laughing at one of those merry quips for which Sir Thomas was renowned.

What will happen to Sir Thomas? people wondered. The King must find some excuse to save him. One thing was certain: Sir Thomas was a man of high principles. He was not one to deny what he believed merely to save his life.

All over the country bishops were ordered to insist that the King's supremacy should be preached.

The Pope intervened. He created Bishop Fisher a

166

cardinal. I could imagine my father's fury. He retorted that he would send the bishop's head to Rome for his cardinal's hat.

That seemed significant. Nothing could move the King.

On the 22nd of June Bishop Fisher went out to Tower Hill and was beheaded. On the 6th of July Sir Thomas followed him. A silent sullen crowd looked on.

This was the King's answer. No matter who disobeyed him, they should die.

The execution of Sir Thomas More sent a shiver through the country and waves of indignation abroad. The Emperor was reputed to have said that he would rather have lost his best city than such a man. The Pope – a new one now, Paul III – declared that Sir Thomas More had been excellent in sacred learning and courageous in his defence of the truth. He prepared a Bull excommunicating my father for what he called the crime. The King, of course, snapped his fingers at the Pope. He was nothing now. He could send out bulls for excommunication as much as he liked. They meant nothing in England, which was now free of his interference.

Even François Premier was shocked and remarked on my father's impiety and barbarism . . . as did the Emperor, but the former needed him as an ally, and political power came before pious indignation. There were nobles all over the country who would have welcomed the Emperor if he came in arms, but he could not do that. He was engaged in the conquest of Tunis, and he could not start a war on another front.

So these monarchs of Europe could do nothing to prevent my father's keeping a firm hold on his power and changing the course of religious history in England.

The country had submitted to the new Head of the Church and he had given examples of what would happen to those who acted against him. They had seen his treatment of his wife and daughter; and they had seen the execution of his friend, Sir Thomas More.

They knew their master.

* * *

Everyone was aware that the King's passion for Anne Boleyn was fast waning, and he made no attempt to hide it. She was a woman who could never be humble; it seemed that she had complete belief in herself. And who would not, after the lengths to which he had gone to get her?

I had passed into a new phase, for, as the concubine's star waned, mine . . . well, not exactly rose but it began to show a faint light below the horizon; for if the King should discard Anne Boleyn, what excuse would he make for doing so? If he should decide that his marriage with her was no marriage, might he not discover that that with my mother was?

It was all wild speculation, but when a man breaks with the Church of Rome he is surely capable of anything.

If it should so happen that I be taken back in favour, it would be unwise for people to treat me scurvily. I was sure this was the thought in many minds and I had suffered such hardship that I could only rejoice in the change.

Many of my women talked freely now, and I began to learn more of what was going on.

Then there was a change again. The concubine was pregnant. It was a setback to those who had been hoping to see the end of her. Everything depended on the child. If it should be a boy she would be safe for ever.

Disquieting news was brought to me of my mother. It was December and bitterly cold. I used to lie in bed wondering what it was like at Kimbolton with that icy wind blowing over the fens. I could visualize her on her knees praying. She would not stop doing that. I could picture the comfortless room, the inadequate clothing, and I would think of her as I knew she would be thinking of me.

The news was whispered to me by one of my women. 'Madam . . . my lady . . . the Emperor's ambassador is going to the Queen, your mother.'

'What?' I cried. 'But how? It is forbidden for her to have visitors.'

'Madam, the King is permitting it because . . .'

I felt sick with fear.

'Because . . . the Queen is very ill?'

She nodded.

A terrible despondency descended on me. This was what I had feared for so long.

I was avid for news. I asked everyone who might know something, and there were several who were eager to please me now. There was nothing to comfort me.

Christmas had come – a joyless season for me now.

My mother's health was a little improved, for she had seen Chapuys, and there was something else which had cheered her. My women told me all they knew of it.

The Emperor's ambassador went to Kimbolton on New Year's Day, and later that day there appeared at the castle gates a woman begging for shelter. She was cold and had fallen from her horse and was in dire need. Because she was clearly a lady of noble bearing, she was allowed to enter the castle.

'Who do you think she was, Madam?' asked my woman.

I shook my head.

'Lady Willoughby, the lady who came with your gracious mother from Spain. The Queen and Lady Willoughby embraced and swore that they would never be parted again. Lady Willoughby said she would die rather. That and the visit of the ambassador cheered her mightily.'

I was greatly relieved.

She has spirit, I told myself. She will recover.

* * *

It was the 11th of January . . . a date I shall never forget. Lady Shelton came to my room. She said: 'I have come to tell you that your mother is dead. She died four days ago.'

Her face was a mask. She had lost a little of her truculence now but she managed to convey her dislike of me. Perhaps it was more intense for being subdued, now that her mistress Anne Boleyn was no longer sure of her position.

I was stunned. I had been expecting this for so long but now that it had come I was deeply shocked. I wanted desperately to be alone with my infinite sorrow.

'Leave me,' I said and I must have spoken imperiously for she obeyed.

Dead! I should never see her again. For so long I had been parted from her but I had always hoped to. And now she was gone and there was no hope. Never again . . .

Oh, the cruelty of life . . . of people who satisfy their wanton desires by trampling on the lives of those about them.

How had she been at the end? There would be no more pain for her. I should rejoice that she was safe in Heaven and far from her miseries. I should have been with her. I thanked God that Lady Willoughby had found a way of getting to her. That would have been a great comfort to her.

My woman came in. She stood looking at me, her eyes brimming with sympathy. I shook my head at her. 'I wish to be alone,' I said.

She understood and left me, and I was alone with my grief which was what I wanted.

How had it been at the end? I asked myself. I wondered if I could see Lady Willoughby, who could tell me how she died. But I should not be allowed to, of course.

I sat in my room. I could face no one. I dressed myself in black and thought of all we had been to each other. I recalled endearing incidents from my childhood – some of

170

them when my father had been present. We had been a loving, happy family then.

I was horrified when I learned that, hearing of my mother's death, my father's first words were: 'God be praised! We are now free from all fear of war.' Did he remember nothing of those happy days? Had he not one morsel of tenderness left for her?

He was justifying himself, of course. He wanted to believe that my mother's death was a reason for rejoicing. There was no court mourning. Instead there were celebrations – a grand ball and a joust. The people must remember that her death had delivered them from war. In the tiltyard at the joust he performed with great skill. He was the triumphant champion. He was telling the people that he was the leader, the one they could trust to take them away from the devious Church of Rome. At the ball he dressed in yellow – yellow jacket, yellow hose and yellow hat with a white feather. The concubine was dressed in yellow too.

How could he care so little for one who had never harmed him and who had always been a dutiful wife?

I became obsessed with the idea that my mother had been poisoned. It would have been so easy and, as they made no secret of their delight in her death, my suspicions might be well founded. I could think of nothing but that. How had she died? I must discover. I asked that my mother's physician and apothecary should come to see me.

When he heard this, my father asked why I should need a doctor. He could understand that I felt a little low in the circumstances, but I should get over that. Chapuys, however, talked to my father and, to my surprise, at last he agreed to allow me to see them. No doubt he was softened by his pleasure in my mother's death; moreover he knew there would be silent criticism of his treatment of her, and he did not want to show more harshness towards me at this time.

One of my maids brought me a letter from Eustace

Chapuys in which he advised me to be brave and prepared for anything that might happen, for I could be assured that there would be changes. He also sent me a little gold cross which my mother was most anxious that I should have.

I was deeply moved and I was in a state of indifference as to what might happen to me. There were times when I wished with all my heart that I was with my mother.

In due course the physician arrived, with the apothecary, and from them I learned the details of my mother's last days, and of how delighted she had been at the arrival of Maria de Salinas, so much so that briefly her condition improved. The two friends had not been parted for an hour since Maria arrived, and my mother was in better spirits than she had been for a long time. Her talks with the ambassador had cheered her also. Eustace Chapuys had departed on the morning of the 5th of January. He had left her in a mood of optimism, believing that, if she could continue with the companionship of Lady Willoughby, she would recover.

'It was in the early hours of the morning of Friday the 7th that it became obvious that she had taken a turn for the worse,' said the physician. 'At daybreak she received the sacrament. Lady Willoughby was, of course, with her. Her servants came to the chamber, for they knew the end was near. Many of them were in tears. She asked them to pray for her and to ask God to forgive her husband. Then she asked me to write her will, which I did. She told me that she wished to be buried in a convent of the Observant Friars.'

I said: 'But the King has suppressed that order.'

'Yes, my lady, but I did not tell her. It would have distressed her. It was ten o'clock when she received Extreme Unction and by the afternoon she had passed away.'

'Was there anything . . . unusual about her death?'

'Unusual, my lady?'

'Did you have any reason to suspect it might have been something she had eaten or drunk?'

He hesitated and I shivered perceptibly.

'Yes?' I prompted. 'There was something?'

'She was never well after she had drunk some Welsh ale.'

'Do you think . . .?'

He took a deep breath and said quickly, 'She was not ill as people are when they are poisoned by something they have taken. It was just that she seemed . . . feeble after taking the beer.'

'Did the thought occur to you that her condition might have something to do with the beer?'

'Well . . . there have been rumours . . . Yes, the thought did occur to me that it might have had something to do with the beer. But it would have been an unusual substance . . . not one which would be recognized as a poison.'

'Ah,' I said. 'So the thought did occur to you.'

He was silent.

Then he went on: 'After she died . . .' He paused. Evidently he was trying to decide how much he should tell me. He seemed to come to a decision. 'Eight hours after she died she was embalmed and her body enclosed in lead. I was not allowed to be present . . . nor was her confessor.'

'It seems as though they were in something of a hurry.'

He lapsed into silence.

I wanted to ask him outright if he believed she had been poisoned, but I could see how uneasy he was. One simple remark could lose him his life.

I felt I could ask no more; but the suspicion remained in my mind.

How had she died? Had she been poisoned? Heaven knew her health was in a sorry state, and those who wanted to be rid of her would surely not have had to wait very long.

The thought hung over me, and I felt it always would. I should never know the truth now.

I was angry and desperately unhappy. I had lost the one I loved most in the world, and I should never recover from that loss. But she would be happy now. She had lived a saintly life; she would be at peace in Heaven. It was what she had been craving for over the last years.

* * *

One of my maids came to tell me the news. My father had had an accident. It was at Greenwich during a joust. He had been riding a great warhorse when suddenly the creature had fallen to the ground, taking my father with him.

There was terrible consternation. Everyone present thought my father had been killed, for he lay unconscious on the ground. They carried him to his bed and gathered round it. It would seem that this was the situation which had been most feared. The King dead . . . and no heir to take his place except the baby Elizabeth. And might there not be some to think that she was not the true heir to the crown?

He was not dead and very soon recovered but this incident did stress the need for the King to live a good many more years until a healthy son could appear to take over from him. At such a time as this, his death would cause great trouble in the country.

No one would have thought that my father could be near to death. He was strong and could still outride all his friends; he was always the champion of the games – though perhaps there was a little contriving to reach that result, and the most agile always managed to fall in just behind him. To win in a paltry game would be foolish if by doing so the winner risked the King's displeasure. But this did bring home the fact that even one as hale and hearty as my father could be struck down at a moment's notice.

There had been the usual murmurings. This was God's revenge for the manner in which he had treated his wife.

This was his punishment for raising up his harlot and living in sin with her while his poor wife was neglected and left to die.

But that was soon over. Within a day or so he was his exuberant self again.

My mother was given a dignified funeral. My father dared not further offend the Emperor by giving her anything less. It had to be remembered that after all she was the daughter of the late King Ferdinand and Queen Isabella.

I longed to go, though I knew it would be a harrowing experience; but that was not permitted.

She was to be buried at Peterborough, in the abbey church there, and three weeks after her death her body was conveyed there by two stages. I should have been there. I was the one who mourned her more than any. I wished that I could have shared my grief with the Countess of Salisbury, but I was denied that comfort. The daughter of Mary Tudor and the Duke of Suffolk were the chief mourners in my place. The King's sister had always been a friend to my mother and had deplored the manner in which my father had put her from him. It seemed fitting therefore, that if I could not be there, her daughter should take my place. The procession rested for a night at Sawtry Abbey before proceeding to Peterborough; and there my mother was solemnly laid to rest.

Perhaps it was better that I should not be there, for the bishop who delivered the funeral sermon stated that on her deathbed my mother had admitted that her marriage to the King was no true marriage.

All those who had been close to her were shocked by this, for they knew it was a lie. I was deeply hurt that my father could do this. Was it not enough that she was dead, brought to an early grave through his cruelty?

It was almost like a sign from Heaven. First my father had his accident, which some would say was a warning to

175

him; and on the very day of my mother's funeral Anne Boleyn miscarried. And to make matters worse, the three-month foetus was proved to be a boy.

How did she feel, I wondered, lying there? All her hopes had been on this boy. And it had happened again. It was a sign of Heaven's displeasure, I was sure. Anne Boleyn was doomed from that moment.

There were many to report the King's reception of the news that he had lost his longed-for son. He had not been able to hide his fury and disgust. He blamed her, of course. That was because now he wanted to be rid of her, as once before he had wanted to be rid of my mother.

It was emerging as a terrifying pattern. I exulted. The concubine would be put from him . . . just as my mother had been.

He had told Anne Boleyn, as she lay there exhausted from her ordeal, weighed down as she must have been with anxiety and fear of the future: 'You will get no more boys from me.'

Everyone knew we were on the edge of great events and were waiting to see what would happen next.

* * *

Lady Shelton was no longer insolent but mildly placating. I treated her coolly but I was not so foolish as to reject my new concessions. Her attitude told me a great deal about the rapidly declining importance of Anne Boleyn.

Eustace Chapuys came to see me. I was amazed that he had been allowed to do so, and my delight was profound.

He told me that there would almost certainly be a change in my position. He understood my deep sorrow at the death of my mother, but that event had made my position safer. There were rumours about Anne Boleyn. She would be removed in some way, there was no doubt of that. The King was working towards it.

'We do not know,' went on Chapuys, 'what method the

176

King will choose. Anne Boleyn has no royal relations to make things difficult for him. Her family owe their elevated position to the King's favours through Anne and her sister Mary before her. They will be put down as easily as they have been raised up. Her fall is imminent. The Seymours are promoting their sister. Edward and Thomas are a pair of very ambitious gentlemen, and Jane is a quiet, pale creature . . . a marked change from Anne Boleyn. But rest assured, events will move fast and we must be prepared.'

'Yes,' I answered.

'If the King puts Anne Boleyn from him, his next move will be to marry again. If his plan is to declare the marriage to Anne invalid, then his marriage to Queen Katharine was a true one and you are his legitimate daughter. We cannot guess how he will do it, but in any case it seems your status must change. There is a rumour that he had been seduced by witchcraft and now is free from it. We must hold ourselves in readiness for whichever way he turns.'

The intrigue was helpful to me in a way. It lifted me out of my overwhelming sorrow and imposed itself on the despondency which had enveloped me.

It was action . . . and whatever happened seemed preferable to sitting alone in my room brooding on the death of my mother.

I was now hearing more because I could have visitors.

Anne Boleyn blamed her miscarriage on her uncle, the Duke of Norfolk, because he had broken the news of the King's accident to her too suddenly. She had been so worried about the King that the shock had brought on the premature birth of her child.

It did not help her. Nothing could help her now. The King was as determined to be rid of her as he had once been to possess her.

I had thought the last two years, when I had been more or less a prisoner, were the two most eventful through which I had lived. But there was more to come.

It was a relief to me to be able to talk to Chapuys and to learn that the Emperor's concern for me had been great and that he had always been eager to seize an opportunity to help me.

Now it seemed there was a chance.

'If you were out of this country, in Spain or Flanders . . . under the Emperor's care, he would be happier,' said Chapuys. 'The King, your father, has shown himself to be capable of any rash act which momentarily serves his purpose. He broke with Rome so that he might marry Anne Boleyn. To take such an unprecedented step for such a reason must give us all some concern. Whether Queen Katharine was poisoned – and poisoned at his command, we cannot be sure, but it is a possibility which we must not lose sight of. The Emperor would feel happier if you were out of the country.'

'My father would never let me go.'

'Certainly he would not. It would be a great blow to him if he thought you were with the Emperor, for if he declared his marriage to Anne Boleyn null and void, you are the heir to the throne.'

'But he has declared his marriage to my mother was no true one, and it was said by the bishop at her funeral service that she admitted it, which was a lie, I know . . . but it was all done at my father's command.'

'That was before he knew that Anne Boleyn had lost the child. All is different now. Her reign is over.'

'They say that he plans to put another in her place.'

He nodded. 'We cannot be sure which way events will turn but you must be prepared.'

'What do you suggest?'

'This is highly secret. If it were mentioned outside these walls, it could cause trouble . . . great trouble. It would cost you your life and there would be little I could do to save it. I should immediately be sent back to Spain. You understand the importance of secrecy?'

'I do.'

He nodded. 'My plan is to get you out of this place. There will be horses waiting to take us to the coast, and there we shall cross to Flanders.'

'I shall be taken to my cousin?'

He nodded.

'Now, we must plan. Could you get away without your women's knowledge?'

'I have few servants now, you know.'

'That is good.'

'There are some whom I can trust.'

Chapuys shook his head. 'Trust no one. You must slip away unseen. No one must know that you have gone until you are on the sea.'

'They are here. They would see me leave. Unless I gave them a sleeping draught.'

'Would that be possible?'

'I think so . . . if I had the draught.'

'That would be an easy matter.'

'I should have to avoid Lady Shelton.'

'Would that be difficult?'

'Less so now. She is not so watchful as she once was. She no longer acts like my gaoler.'

'This sounds plausible. We should have horses waiting. We could get to Gravesend easily from here . . . and there embark. You will be hearing more of this from me.'

After he had gone, I lay in my bed thinking of it. I should be taken to my cousin. I remembered so well that occasion – years and years ago it seemed now – when my mother had held my hand and we had stood on the steps at Greenwich while the barge came along. I could see my dazzling father and beside him the young man in black velvet with the gold chain about his neck . . . the young man with whom I had been told I was in love.

He had broken our engagement, but I had forgiven him that now. I understood that monarchs such as he were

179

governed by expediency. I forgave him for that and for not coming to my rescue as a knight of chivalry and romance would have done, however difficult.

I was no longer romantic. Events had made me cynical, yet still there was a softness in me. I was capable of loving deeply, which was clear by the sorrow the loss of my mother was causing me.

* * *

So we planned and Chapuys visited me often. Lady Shelton made no objection. Chapuys was deeply anxious that all should go well, for if it did not, there would be dire consequences.

He told me that he was making arrangements with the utmost secrecy and would bring the sleeping draught to me when it was to be administered. I had practised what I must do. I had made a careful study of how I should go without passing Lady Shelton's window. We must wait for a moonless night when all would be ready.

Lady Shelton came to me the day after I had had a visit from Chapuys and he had told me that, as soon as the moon waned, we would put our plan into action.

She said: 'Madam, my lady, we have orders. We leave tomorrow for Hunsdon.'

'But . . .' I cried, 'why?'

She lifted her shoulders. 'Orders,' she said tersely.

After she had gone, I sat on my bed and stared at the window. This would change everything. We could not go tonight for the moon was too bright. Someone would almost certainly see me creeping across the garden. Besides, the horses would not be ready. Everything had to be perfect. Had someone heard? How could I be sure? There were spies everywhere. I could not believe that it would be someone in my household.

Chapuys came to see me in some consternation.

'Hunsdon,' he said. 'Hunsdon! It will be too difficult

180

from Hunsdon. We could not do it in a night. We should have to ride through the countryside. We should have to change horses. We should be detected. Everything depends on the closeness to Gravesend.'

'What do you suggest that we do? That we give up the plan?'

'Not give it up. Postpone. You will be moved again perhaps. Let us hope it will be back here. One thing I am certain of: we cannot do it from Hunsdon.'

I was not sure how disappointed I was. Now that I had lost my mother, I often thought I had lost my interest in life and my reason for living.

So the plan was set aside and in due course I came to my home at Hunsdon.

* * *

I had ceased to brood on what my fate would have been if the escape plot had proceeded, for events were moving very fast at Court. The rift between the King and Anne Boleyn was widening; his feelings for Jane Seymour were deepening; and people were rallying to the Seymour family as before they had to the Boleyns. Chapuys was excited. He believed that the marriage was about to be declared invalid, and he considered what that would mean to me. But if my father was enamoured of Jane Seymour, his desire would be to get a son from her; he could still do that if he divorced Anne, for now that my mother was dead he would be free to marry, even in the eyes of the Pope – though my father did not have to care for his opinions now. We all knew that he could without much difficulty cast off Anne Boleyn. He only had to trump up a charge against her. Adultery was the most likely for, according to reports, she was always surrounded by admiring young men, and her attitude was inclined to be flirtatious with them.

Chapuys was watching the situation closely, and his visits

to me were more frequent. He told me that my father had people looking into the possibility of a divorce.

'There seem to be some difficulties,' said the ambassador. 'All the proceedings were so closely linked to his marriage with your mother, and he does not want that brought out again. It will remind people of his quarrel with the Pope. He just wants to rid himself of Anne Boleyn as simply and speedily as possible.'

'What do you think he will do?'

'He might try charging her with adultery, which would have far-reaching effects. Treason to himself . . . foisting a bastard on the nation as the King's child . . . all good reasons for getting rid of her.'

It was long since I had thought of the child Elizabeth. How I had resented her when we were both at Hatfield and I was more or less a member of her household. Poor baby, it was no fault of hers. Yet I had hated her. That was just because I had been insulted by her taking precedence over me. Now I thought: Poor child, is she to be treated as I was? What will become of her?

The winter was over, and spring had come; and my father was still married to Anne Boleyn. I heard rumours of the quarrels between them, how she had discovered him with Jane Seymour behaving like lovers, how she had raged and ranted against him and had been told she must take what her betters had before her. So he remembered my mother and admitted the anguish he had caused her. And the proud, brazen Anne Boleyn, how would she take that?

Everyone knows what happened on that May Day, how they were together at the joust at Greenwich, how the King did not speak to Anne as she sat beside him in the royal lodge, how she took out a handkerchief, wiped her brow and allowed it to flutter to the ground, how one of the courtiers – Norris, I think – picked it up on his lance and held it to her with a bow, how the King suddenly turned away in anger and so the joust ended.

That was the beginning. My father must have staged it, for he had already set Cromwell to question those about her. He had decided that, as it would be difficult to arrange a divorce, he would accuse her of adultery. His love had been intense, and no doubt that made his hatred the more fierce. Greatly he had disliked my mother but never with the same venom that he turned on Anne Boleyn. He was going to accuse her of adultery, treason to the King, which carried the penalty of death.

Cromwell wrung a confession from Mark Smeaton, one of her musicians, through torture, most people thought; the young men closest to her – Norris, Francis Weston and William Brereton – were all arrested and sent to the Tower. Most shocking of all, her brother George was accused of incest with her, and there was even a suggestion that Elizabeth was his daughter.

I had always hated her, as she had hated me. We had been the bitterest of enemies; but when I thought of all the indignity and humiliation which had been heaped on my mother, and realized that Anne Boleyn was now the object of my father's fury, I could feel sorry for her.

She was found guilty with those who were accused with her. Of course she was. It was intended.

Norris, Weston and Brereton were taken out to Tower Hill and beheaded. George Boleyn and his sister would follow.

The day before her execution, Lady Kingston, in whose care Anne Boleyn had been placed in the Tower, came to me.

She said: 'The Queen has sent me to you, my lady.'

I was always a little taken aback to hear Anne Boleyn referred to as the Queen, even now, though Heaven knew I had heard that title used often enough to describe her. I was about to retort: You are referring to the concubine. But something restrained me. For all her sins, she was suffering acute anguish now.

'What would she want of me?' I asked.

'Forgiveness, my lady,' she replied. 'She made me sit in her chair . . . the Queen's chair . . . for they have not taken that away from her . . . and she knelt most humbly at my feet. She said to me, "Go to the Princess Mary and kneel to her as I kneel to you. My treatment of the Princess weighs heavily on my conscience. I was cruel to her and I regret that now. For everything else I can go to my Maker with a clear conscience, for I have committed no sin save in my conduct towards the Princess and her mother. I cannot ask forgiveness of Queen Katharine but I humbly beg the Princess to grant me hers. Let her know you come in my name and that it is I who kneel to her through you."'

I was astounded. I thought: Poor woman, she is indeed brought low.

But she remembered me in her darkest moments and she was now asking my forgiveness.

It was hard to forgive her, but an image of my mother rose in my mind and I knew what she would have me do.

I said: 'Tell her to rest in peace. I forgive her on behalf of myself and my mother.'

The next day she went to Tower Green and laid her head on the block.

The Betrayal

No sooner was Anne Boleyn dead than my father was betrothed to Jane Seymour. I am not sure how many days elapsed before he married. It could not have been more than ten. I heard that it had taken place on the 30th of May in the Queen's Closet at York Place. Anne Boleyn had died on the 19th.

I often wondered about my father and whether his nights were disturbed by the ghosts of those who had fallen foul of his will. For so many years Anne Boleyn had been the centre of his life. How could he have tired of her so quickly? I wondered about Jane Seymour. I had seen her on one or two occasions and found her gentle and unassuming. She had always been pleasant to me.

The story was that about a month before Anne's death my father had sent her a purse of sovereigns, telling her of his passion for her and hinting that she should become his mistress. Her reply had been that she could be no man's mistress, not even the King's. It was the familiar pattern. Anne Boleyn had started it. I wondered Jane Seymour did not have a few qualms about following her predecessor along such a dangerous path.

Of course she had ambitious brothers and, from what I heard of her, I imagined she would not be one to put up much resistance. In that of course she was the exact opposite of Anne. In fact, she seemed to be so in many ways. Perhaps that was why the King was attracted by her.

Elizabeth was at Hunsdon. She was now three, old enough to recognize the chilly change which was passing through the house and was to affect her.

She was no longer the pampered princess. Poor motherless little creature, I wondered how much she understood. She was a bright child with reddish hair almost exactly like her father's. She resembled him in many ways and had his fondness for her own way. Lady Bryan adored her. It was pleasant to be with my old friend again. I would always be grateful to her for her kindness to me when I was so alone.

Several of my old servants came to me . . . people I had not seen for several years. That was a joyous reunion. I was above all delighted to see Susan Clarencieux, who had been in my household when I was at Ludlow. I had always been especially fond of her.

I had thought that my circumstances would change with the departure of Anne Boleyn from the scene, and I was proved right.

Chapuys came to me. He was gleeful.

'You could very easily be received back at Court,' he said. 'That is what we must work for. The new Queen is ready to be your friend.'

'I do remember meeting her in the past.'

'She has sentimental feelings about the family. The King is amused by them and apt to be indulgent at the moment. I am sure she will speak to him with regard to bringing you to Court.'

'A change from her predecessor!'

'A great change indeed . . . in all ways. The point is . . . I wonder how long it will take the King to tire of this shy violet. However, I feel sure it will not be long before you are back at Court. There must be no hitch. It is imperative that you come out of your exile.'

'Do you think the King will admit now that he was truly married to my mother?'

'I think he has gone too far with that to retreat with ease.'

'Still, he now hates Anne Boleyn so much.'

'And blames her for all that has happened. He is saying that it was through witchcraft that he became enamoured of her and now that is removed he sees clearly. The people cheer you when you go out, do they not?'

'Yes, more so than ever now.'

'That is good. The King will have to respect the people's wish which is that you be reinstated. It might be advisable for you to write to him and ask his blessing and forgiveness.'

'Forgiveness . . . for what? For saying what is true . . . what I meant . . . for defending my mother?'

Chapuys raised his hand admonishingly. 'A little compromise might be necessary.'

'I shall never deny my mother's marriage. *She* never did and was incapable of lying.'

'We shall see . . . we shall see,' murmured Chapuys. 'The King is in a mellow mood just now. He has a new wife and she pleases him. He has convinced himself that Anne Boleyn was evil, a witch . . . so his conscience is at rest on that score.'

'Do you think he will return to Rome?'

'I fear not. He has come too far to turn back.'

'So we are doomed for ever.'

Chapuys looked at me slyly. 'It is unwise to talk of these matters, but it is not inconceivable that one day England will return to the true faith.'

'But if the King never would . . .'

He was looking at me intently. 'You are no longer a child. Princess Elizabeth is now proclaimed to be a bastard. Fitzroy might have presented a threat but he cannot live more than a few months. He has death written on him. And the King's fall affected him more than was realized.'

'You mean his fall from the horse just before my mother died?'

He nodded. 'He has not ridden in the joust since. He has aged considerably. I have heard that there is an ulcer on his leg which is very painful. There is a possibility . . . But perhaps I should say no more. Indeed, it might be unwise to . . .'

I knew what he meant. My father was ageing. He had not been spectacularly successful in begetting children. What if he could get no more? Then who would follow him? Elizabeth? She was out of favour now, judged a bastard, for the King did not accept his marriage with Anne Boleyn. Nor did he accept his marriage to my mother. So there were two of us. Young Richmond – Henry Fitzroy – could not be counted because he would not be here much longer. I was the elder, and I would find greater favour with the people than the daughter of Anne Boleyn.

Chapuys was pointing to a dazzling prospect. Queen of England! A queen with a mission, which was to bring England back to the Holy Catholic Church.

Something happened to me then. I was lifted out of my despondency. I had a reason for living.

God would smile on me, surely. He would approve. My father had sinned against the Church. If ever I were Queen of this realm, I would repair the damage he had done.

Everything had changed. I was a woman with a mission.

* * *

I must return to Court. I had been long enough in exile. I was not sure how my father felt about me, but I did know that he had been very angry about my loyalty to my mother. I had stood firmly for her against him and what had especially infuriated him was that the people were on my side. He would remember those cries of 'Long live the Princess Mary!' when he had declared that I was no princess. Even now they were shouting loyally for me, and he could not have liked that.

I dared not write to him direct. Instead I addressed myself to Cromwell.

I did humble myself. I hoped my mother would understand if she could look down and see what I was doing. If I continued to be obstinate, I should be in exile forever, always wondering when someone would consider it necessary to make an end of me. Chapuys had now endowed me with a new ambition. I would succeed. I must succeed. I should have Heaven on my side, for I should be the one to bring England back to the true religion.

And if to do so I must humble myself, then humble I must be.

So I wrote asking my father's forgiveness, and I said how sorry I was to have disobeyed his wishes.

I waited for some response. There was none.

I wrote to him again and, having written, my conscience smote me. How could I, even as I stepped towards that dazzling future, deny the legality of my mother's marriage? Whatever the result, I knew that could only give her pain; and she, with her Catholic Faith, her unswerving devotion to the Church of Rome, would never wish me to deny my faith . . . no matter what good it brought to England.

On impulse I wrote a separate note to Cromwell, telling him that, while I wished him to give my letter to the King, I feared I could not deny the validity of my mother's marriage and I could not agree with the severance from Rome.

In spite of this, Cromwell seemed determined to do all he could to bring me into favour with the King. He was fully aware that the people expected it and wanted it and that the King should do it for that reason. He must have been uneasy as to the effect my father's conduct was having on the people, who had clearly shown their support for us; true, they had hated Anne Boleyn when she was puffed up with pride, but people are apt to change their minds when those about them fall from grace. There was no cause now to envy Anne Boleyn, and envy is often at the roots of hatred.

Cromwell was first and foremost a politician and he would see that I must be received back at Court, which was the safest place for me to be . . . not for myself so much as

189

for him and the King. He wanted no supporters gathering round me, seeking to right my wrongs.

My father must have realized that it could be dangerous to refuse to bring me back. I was, after all, no longer a child, being twenty years old – old enough to be a figure-head, old enough for those who deplored the break with Rome to rally to me.

It may be that the wily Cromwell persuaded him but the fact was that the Duke of Norfolk and the Earl of Sussex headed a small party who came to visit me. They brought with them a document in which I was referred to as a monster – a daughter who had acted disobediently towards her father. It was only due to the generous and gracious nature of the King that I was still here to ask his forgiveness.

It was difficult for me. I kept thinking of my mother. How could I deny her? She had always been adamant, even though she had believed her enemies were trying to poison her and would possibly use other means to kill her. Always she had stood defiant against them. But Chapuys had shown me my mission.

Even so I could not bring myself to accept the verdict that my mother had never been truly married to my father, that I was a bastard and the Pope was not the Vicar of Christ but just another bishop.

I tried to keep that glittering future in mind. I prayed for guidance. If God meant to lead me to my destiny, He would help me.

But I could not do it. I said I would obey my father in all things save his denial of his marriage with my mother and his break with Rome.

They were very angry – in particular Norfolk, who was a violent man and not of very good character, as his Duchess could well confirm. Both he and Sussex were abusive. I was understanding more of people now and I guessed that they were afraid. They would have to go back to the King and tell him that I stood firm on the very two issues which had caused all the contention between us. He would have to face the fact that he had a rebellious daughter and that many of his subjects, who were already murmuring about the state of the Church, would agree with her. I could see that I was a danger and that my father wished to have me back in the fold. He wanted to ride out with me and the new Queen, showing the people that I was his beloved daughter – though illegitimate – and that all was well between us. And these men would have to go back and tell him that they had failed.

Messengers bringing ill news were never popular; and the King's moods were variable and could be terrible. He had changed with the failing of his health. 'Bluff King Hal' peeped out only occasionally now and then, when years ago this had been the face his courtiers saw most frequently.

Sussex shouted at me: 'Can it be that you are the King's daughter? I cannot believe this to be so. You are the most obstinate woman I ever knew. Surely no child of the King could be as wayward . . . as stubborn . . . and as foolish as you are.'

I looked at him sardonically. He might have known that what he called my stubbornness had been inherited directly from my father.

Norfolk was even more explicit.

'If you were my daughter, I should beat you.'

'I am sure you would attempt to, my lord,' I replied. 'I believe your conduct towards your wife, simply because she objected to your mistresses, has been especially brutal.'

His eyes narrowed and his face was scarlet. 'I would beat you . . . to death,' he muttered.

'I am of the opinion that, if you attempted to do so, the people in the streets would set upon you and you would suffer a worse fate.'

He knew there was truth in my words and he shouted: 'I

would dash your head against the wall until it was as soft as a baked apple!'

'Threats worthy of you, my lord. And they affect me not at all. You would not dare lay a hand on me. And I should be glad if you would remember to whom you speak.'

Lady Shelton had complained of my regal manners, so I suppose I possessed them; and now, with Chapuys' prophecy before me, perhaps they were even more apparent.

They slunk away, those irate commissioners, like dogs with their tails between their legs.

* * *

Chapuys came to see me.

He was very grave, although there was a hint of amusement in his gravity.

'The commissioners were ill received when they returned to the King. He is convinced that you are in touch with the rebels. There is a party forming in the North and murmurings throughout the country. Your name is often mentioned. The King is most uneasy. But you have seen how obstinate he is . . . and we must get you to Court. I fear he may take some drastic action against you on the spur of the moment. Do not forget, he is all-powerful in this country. Now that he has broken with Rome, the Church has no hold on him. Who would have believed this possible?'

'But we shall come back one day.'

'I beg of you, do not speak of it now.'

'But that is our eventual aim.'

'To be put away until the time is ripe. It is something to think about but never to be spoken of. If it were . . . your life would not be worth much. Remember. The Church relies on you. Your day will come. And until it does we must play this game as deviously as is demanded.'

'What do you mean?'

'I mean you cannot stay in exile. We have to do anything . . . simply anything . . . to get you to Court. Cromwell

192

goes in fear of his life because he first told the King that you would be ready to bow to his will. The King is in such a mood of anger that no one is safe. But this is good, for it shows the extent of his uneasiness. Queen Jane pleads for you with the King. She is simple and clearly does not know the man she has married. She was heard to say that it was natural that you should defend your mother and she thought it was a noble thing to do. She was abruptly told not to meddle in matters beyond her powers of understanding and to remember that her predecessor meddled and what happened to her. It is the first time the King has been heard talking to her thus, and it shows how anxious he is.'

'Then we should be pleased.'

'Not entirely. He is capable of drastic action when aroused to anger, and his anger has its roots in uncertainty. Those about the King, including Cromwell, have to act regarding you. They are preparing a document. It is headed "The Lady Mary's Submission". In it will be set down all that the King will require you to agree to.'

'That will include . . .'

He nodded. 'Your agreement that your parents were never legally married, that you are illegitimate and accept the King, your father, as Head of the Church in England.'

'I will never do it.'

'Have you thought of the alternative?'

'What do you mean?'

'You forget that Bishop Fisher and Sir Thomas More lost their heads because they would not sign the Oath? You are doing the same.'

'You mean that I should lose my head?'

'I mean that you could be tried for treason . . . and the punishment for treason is death.'

'My father would not dare.'

'He has dared a great deal. He fears a rising in your favour. But he is the most powerful man in the country. He could put down a revolt, and then what would happen to the Princess Mary? What of the plans for the future of England?'

I said: 'What must I do?'

'There is only one thing you can do. You sign.'

'Deny my mother's marriage! Deny Holy Church!'

'There could be a papal absolution which would relieve you from the sin of perjury,' said Chapuys. 'The Emperor and the Pope will know the reason why you signed. I advise you to do it. This is the only way. If you do not, I would not give much hope for the chances of your survival.'

'I would not do it for the fear of what would happen to me.'

'I am aware of that, as you are of your destiny. It would be folly now to refuse to sign.'

I knew he was right, but I had to quieten my conscience. My mother would understand. Those who cared for me, who knew that I had a duty to perform . . . they would all understand why I had to sign.

So, with a firm hand and a strong purpose in my heart, I put my name to the document.

* * *

Now that I had given way, my life changed. I was treated with the respect due to the King's daughter – though not a legitimate one. I enjoyed more freedom than I had known for years. I was no longer treated with suspicion. I could write to whom I pleased and receive visitors.

I was still grappling with my conscience. I had committed perjury. I had agreed to that which in my heart I abhorred. I prayed constantly. I talked to my mother as though she were with me.

'Understand, please, dear Mother. I did this because I believe that in time it will have been proved to be the right action to have taken at this time. They would have tried me for treason if I had refused. They would have trumped up some charge against me. If the King could kill his wife, why not his daughter? Chapuys knew it. I acted on his advice and one day, I swear on all that is sacred to me, that when the opportunity comes I shall bring England back to the Holy Church.'

That was the motive I kept my eyes on. And I began to believe fervently that what I had done – however much it had been against my principles – was the only way in which I could have acted.

Elizabeth was at Hunsdon, still under the charge of Margaret Bryan. I was with her a great deal. All my enmity towards her had gone. How could one dislike a three-year-old child? Her mother might be evil but what crime had the child committed? Lady Bryan never ceased to marvel at her. She was the most perfect child it had ever been her joy to know, she told me. She was so bright and eager to learn. 'Nose into everything,' said Margaret fondly. 'If it is there, she must know what and why. Questions . . . all through the day. And she remembers, too. To see her skip and dance . . . and hear her little voice singing . . . She can already handle a lute, you know.'

Then she would express her fury at the manner in which her little darling was being treated now.

'Look at this kirtle! I have darned and patched it. I need new clothes for her. I keep asking but none come. It is a shameful way to treat a princess.'

'Hush, Margaret,' I cautioned her. 'Do you want to be charged with treason?'

She shook her head sadly. 'I know not what we are coming to.'

I took her hand and pressed it.

'I know. I understand your feelings. It happened to me . . . just like this. At least Elizabeth is too young to understand.'

'There you are mistaken. That child is old for her years.'

'That is well. She will have need of her good sense, I doubt not.'

'My poor innocent lamb! I suppose I must go on with this patching. She asked for her mother. "When will she come to see me?" It breaks my heart. At least it seems a little brighter for you, my lady. Perhaps you can put in a word for your little sister.'

'I will . . . when I can.'

'Bless you. There has been such suffering, but none should hold that against this little one.'

'I do not,' I said. 'Nor would my mother.'

Margaret nodded. She was too moved for words.

There was a great deal of talk about what was happening throughout the country. During the previous year my father had set Thomas Cromwell to make a report on the conditions of the monasteries. This had sent a ripple of unease throughout the land. The monasteries were devoted to the Church of Rome, and everyone knew that this was no ordinary survey. It was a further gesture of defiance towards the Pope; and Cromwell was prepared to give my father what he wanted, knowing full well that he dared do nothing else.

The result was the Black Book in which were set down all the evils which were said to be practised within those walls. I could not believe it. There were sinners everywhere, I knew, but according to Cromwell the monasteries he visited were hotbeds of vice. We heard stories of orgies between monks and nuns, of riotous and lewd behaviour, of unwanted babies being strangled at birth and buried in the grounds.

It was time, said my father, in his most pious tones, that these matters were brought to light and given close examination.

There was a great deal of wealth in the monasteries, and the royal exchequer, which had been so well stocked by my shrewd and careful grandfather, had become much depleted during my father's extravagant reign. A great deal of money had been spent on his lavish entertainments, his splendid journeys, his magnificent jewels, and latterly on bribery all over Europe in the hope of getting agreement on his divorce. The exchequer needed bolstering up and the spoils from the monasteries could play a good part in doing that.

An Act had now been passed for the suppression of all monasteries whose incomes were less than £200 a year.

I wondered whether that was an experiment to see how the people reacted to it. The larger monasteries were left unmolested; but I could imagine that many an abbot was trembling in his sandals.

Then I was told that I was to meet the King, and everything else was banished from my mind.

My feelings were mixed. I wanted to see him. Part of me could not forget those days of my early childhood when he had loomed so large in my life – a god, all-powerful and gloriously benign. I had been so proud that he should be my father; and although I loved my mother more dearly than any living person, it was he who filled me with awe and admiration. His smile of approval had made me sublimely happy, and no matter how cruelly he behaved to me and those I loved, I still had the same special feeling for him which I was sure could never be entirely eradicated.

He would not come to Hunsdon; nor should I go to Court . . . yet. He wanted to see me first and he did not want too much noise about it. He must have felt a little uncertain about meeting a daughter who had for so many years defied him and had only just signed her submission most reluctantly.

I was to be taken at an appointed time to a country house where he would receive me.

I could not eat. I could not sleep. I hovered between excitement and apprehension. I prayed for guidance. I talked to my mother, begging her, once more, to understand why I had betrayed her in words, although in my heart I would always be true to her.

I talked to Susan Clarencieux of my fears.

She reassured me. 'My lady,' she said, 'you need have no fears. You are royal . . . as royal as the King.'

I put my finger to her lips. 'Hush, Susan. I do not want to lose you. Such things as you say could be construed as treason.'

'It is true.'

'Truth can sometimes be treason, Susan. There. I am worse than you. We must guard our tongues. Let's talk of other things. What am I going to wear?'

For so long I had had few clothes and what I had were mended; but recently new garments had been sent to me and now I believed I could dress so that I would not look too shabby for the occasion.

Command came that I was to leave the following morning. Margaret Bryan came to me on the night before. She sat by my bed and held my hand as she used to in those long-ago days when my trials were just beginning.

'Have no fear,' she said. 'All will be well. Remember, you are his daughter.'

'He forgot that once.'

'Nay. A man does not forget his daughter. He was plagued by other matters.'

'And I would not say what he wished me to. And now, I have, Margaret. God forgive me.'

'Hush, hush,' she said. 'Everything will be understood. Try to rest. Be yourself . . . and all will be well.'

At the door she paused and looked at me.

'Do not forget the child,' she said. 'She is only a baby. Speak for her . . . if there is a chance.'

I said: 'I will, Margaret. But I must go carefully. He is so full of hatred for her mother now . . . as once he was for mine.'

'They are both gone now, God rest their souls,' said Margaret. 'It is the poor children who remain.'

She then left me and I tried to compose myself and prepare for the next day's ordeal.

* * *

At dawn we set out and by mid-morning had reached our destination.

There I met the father whom I had not seen for five years. With him was his new Queen.

For a few moments we stood looking at each other. I wondered what he thought of me. When he had last seen me I had been a thin, spindly-legged girl of fifteen. Now I was a woman. I knew I had gained in dignity, especially so since I had been aware of my destiny. But I was so shocked by the change in him that I could think of little else.

When I had last seen him he had been the most handsome man I had ever known. He had stood taller than most men; he had always been recognized by his height and width at all those masques where he had delighted in trying to disguise himself. His complexion had been florid, but healthily so. Now it was purplish rather than pink. His weight had increased enormously. His was no longer an athletic figure. 'Corpulent' would be a more accurate way of describing it. But it was his face in which the greater change had taken place. In the past there had been an engaging aspect. Could I call it innocence? Hardly. Perhaps rather a boyish delight in the world and himself which at that time had seemed endearing. Even in those days we had dreaded to see his mood change, which it had done now and then, and the small mouth would become a thin, straight line and the little eyes points of light almost disappearing into his full face. Much of the old benignity had departed. New lines had appeared to rob him of that quality. To look at him now, so large in his surcoat with the puffed sleeves barred with strips of fur and built-up shoulders which increased his size and made him a figure of splendour, completely over-awed me. I felt very small and insignificant beside such a glittering figure and I knew that I could never do what I had thought during my journey here that I might, which was to throw myself at his feet and beg him not to ask me to deny my mother and the Church of Rome.

To see him there, powerful and formidable in the extreme, I knew that I should never do it even if I could.

And beside him was his new Queen – slender, pretty, looking frail beside his great girth, gentle, welcoming, a little hesitant, but endeavouring to tell me she was pleased to see me.

I went to him and knelt. He gave me his hand, which I kissed. Then he made a gesture for me to stand up, so I did so.

'At last,' he said. 'I rejoice to see you, daughter.'

I was trying to overcome my emotion and he sensed this. It pleased him. He saw me as the repentant daughter, asking for forgiveness because of her foolish behaviour which had caused him pain.

I would have knelt to the Queen but she had taken my hands. She must have been about the same age as Anne Boleyn . . . but she seemed younger and I felt older in experience.

There was nothing false about the greeting she gave me. She smiled tremulously. 'Oh welcome . . . welcome,' she said. 'I have so wanted this meeting.'

The King smiled at her indulgently.

'The Queen speaks for us both,' he said.

He dismissed everyone so that we should be alone together, he said, and talk as a family should.

So we were alone and he spoke of his sufferings, of how he had been mistreated, but now that he had his good Jane beside him, all that was behind us.

He sat in the chair which had been provided for him, and Jane brought up one for me so that I could sit beside him.

'Your Grace must not wait on me,' I said.

'But it is what I want,' she told me with her rather girlish smile. 'I am so happy. I have always wanted you to be at Court, and now you are going to be there.'

The King was evidently enamoured of her. She was so gentle and seemed to me guileless. She was as different from Anne Boleyn as one woman can be from another. Therein, I supposed, lay her attraction.

Jane sat close to the King, who from time to time patted her knee. I thought she was like a little kitten, and I could not suppress the question which rose in my mind: How long can he be content with her?

Meanwhile she was eager to show herself my friend.

'We shall arrange for you to come to Court . . . in time,' said the King.

'Yes,' added Jane, 'and it shall be soon.'

'I shall be leaving for the hunting season shortly,' said my father. 'Perhaps after that.'

'Thank you, Your Majesty,' I said. Recently he had given himself the title of 'Majesty' which was now generally used instead of the old 'Your Grace'. After all, dukes could be Graces, but only the King – and Queen – Majesties.

'You are uneasy, daughter,' he said. 'Do not be so. Now that you have confessed your faults, I forgive you freely. She who did you much harm has now reaped her just deserts. Witchcraft is a fearsome cult. It must be crushed wherever we find it. And now . . . if you will be my good child, I will be father to you.'

'You will be welcome at Court,' said Jane. 'We shall be friends . . . we shall be as sisters.'

The King laughed at her. I thought her charming in her rather simple way.

He asked about my household at Hunsdon. I said that of recent date it had begun to grow.

'You shall have the comforts you once enjoyed before you were misguided enough to oppose my will.'

'I thank Your Majesty.'

'Aye . . . and you will find there will be much for which to thank me.'

Jane laughed happily. I thought she was really a good creature and was genuinely rejoicing in my changed fortunes.

I wondered whether I could mention Elizabeth but the dark look which had come into his face when he had spoken of her mother made me hesitate. Not yet, I thought. I must tread very carefully.

'Yes,' my father went on. 'Be a good daughter and you will find me not ungenerous. I am giving you a thousand crowns so that you can indulge yourself. Get some little comforts, eh? I'll swear you could use them.'

'You are most gracious . . .'

His face had become soft and sentimental, as I remembered it from the past. 'Aye . . . and ready to be more so . . . as you will find, will she not, Jane?'

Jane smiled from me to him. 'The most generous King in the world,' she said ecstatically.

I thought how different she was from my mother as well as from Anne Boleyn. Could it be possible that this one could give him what he wanted? If she could provide a son, yes. And if not . . . I found myself looking at that white neck.

She had taken a diamond ring from her finger and held it out to me.

'It would make me very happy if you would wear this for me,' she said simply.

Then she took my hand and slipped the ring on my finger.

'You are so good to me,' I told her.

My father watched us, his eyes glazed with sentiment. How quickly his moods changed! I wished that I did not see him quite so clearly. Part of me wanted to go on believing in the image I had created in my childhood; but

I kept thinking of my mother. On whose order had the Welsh beer been produced? Had she been poisoned? I thought of Anne Boleyn, the one for whom he had sacrificed his religious beliefs and had run the risk of losing his crown; and yet there had come the day when she had been taken out to Tower Green and her head had been cut off with a sword specially sent from France. What could I think of such a man? How could I love him? And yet, in spite of all I knew of him, in a way I did.

Poor little Jane Seymour, what would become of her?

The mood passed. Jane, with her simple reasoning, had an effect on us. She saw this as a family reunion and she made us see it as such. I lost some of my qualms; my father forgot that he was King; in that brief moment we were father and daughter, and Jane's presence, with her simple faith in the goodness of human nature, had created this scene in her imagination and, briefly, we accepted it.

It was a pleasant half hour. There was laughter: I was delighted to be with my father, for after all he had done, he was still my father, and such was the aura which surrounded him that I could suppress my fears of him. Whether it was love, I do not know; but it was something akin to it. And while we were together, I forgot that I was deceiving him, that I had lied to him; and he seemed to forget the past when he had had it in his mind to poison me or take my life in some way.

Jane was there, rejoicing that the dissension in the family was over; and everything was as it should be; in the future we should all love each other.

Such is the power of innocence.

*　*　*

I did not see my father for some time. He went off with the Court for the hunting season. My household at Hunsdon was growing, as was customary for a person of my rank.

203

People were sending me gifts. Thomas Cromwell had taken me under his wing and had sent me a horse as a present.

The newly elevated brother of Jane Seymour was now Lord Beauchamp and Chamberlain. He wrote to ask me what clothes I needed.

I was delighted. I was able to ask for some materials which Margaret could make into clothes for Elizabeth. I was getting quite fond of my little half-sister. She was such an engaging child, and our friendship gave great pleasure to Margaret. My reconciliation with my father delighted her, and that helped to ease my conscience. She was fond of me but the darling of her heart was young Elizabeth, and she was so pleased because she thought I should be able to do something about the neglect from which the poor child was suffering.

Then there was trouble in the North which gave me some uneasiness for, in my vulnerable position, I could so easily be implicated.

The appearance of the Black Book, containing its accusations against monks and nuns, and the suppression of the smaller monasteries, had been the cause of this unrest. The first sign of trouble was in Lincolnshire but this was quickly suppressed by the Earl of Shrewsbury, who assured the objectors that everything that had happened had been sanctioned by Parliament.

It was not long before a more serious revolt broke out in Yorkshire. The people were against the break with Rome and they wanted the Supremacy of the Church to be in the hands of the Pope as it always had been. A man called Robert Aske led the people on what he called the Pilgrimage of Grace. They marched with banners depicting Christ on the cross on one side and on the other a chalice and wafer. They did not accept the King as Supreme Head of the Church. The Pope had been for them and their fathers Christ's Vicar on Earth and still was. No Acts of Parliament could change that. They wanted the true religion brought back to England.

The revolt quickly spread through the North. These men were ready to fight for the religion they wanted. But there were rumours. If they succeeded, the King, who had set himself up as Head of the Church, would naturally be deposed. He had in their eyes one legitimate heir, for they had always believed that my mother was the true Queen of England and legally married to the King. That heir was the Princess Mary; and although their main aim was to restore the true religion, it was hinted that it was also their plan to set me on the throne.

I was in acute danger. Chapuys was soon on the spot to advise me.

'Keep out of sight,' he warned me. 'Do not be seen in any public place. Keep to the house and the gardens. We will watch events closely.'

The King was very disturbed, as he always must be when some of his subjects were in revolt, and as it was an uprising of this size there was something to be really anxious about.

He sent an army up to the North. I was certain that the rebels would not be able to stand against it and there would be terrible slaughter. However, the rain was heavy and prolonged and the land became so water-logged that the two armies could not approach each other.

There were many who were ready to interpret this as a sign from God. He was working a miracle to save the rebels. My father was loth to go to war with his own subjects and after discussions with those close to him, he sent a message to say that he would pardon all rebels, and if they would prepare a list of their grievances he would study them carefully.

The insurgents, no doubt feeling they had made their point, returned to their homes. The King had suggested that their leader Robert Aske should come to London, where he would be received and differences discussed.

Just after this I was surprised to receive a visit from the King.

It was one morning when I returned from riding to find the household in a flutter of excitement. The King, out hunting, had called and was in the house. He was impatiently waiting to see me, and I had better go to him with all speed.

I found him pacing up and down in the salon. He was alone.

I went to him and knelt. He took my hands and kissed them with a show of tenderness.

'I trust I find Your Majesty in good health,' I said.

'Yes . . . yes . . . and you, daughter?'

I thanked him for his gracious enquiry and told him that I was well.

He shook his head impatiently. 'There has been trouble with these rebels in the North,' he said.

'I trust it is settled to Your Majesty's pleasure.'

'Yes . . . yes. That was soon put to rights. There'll be no more trouble from them. There were some who would have it that you were involved in it.'

'I swear I knew nothing about them.'

He lifted a hand. 'I know it. I know it. But when these fools start meddling in matters of which they know nothing . . . they will speak of you.'

'It is my earnest regret that they should do so.'

'You are a loyal subject then?'

'I am, Your Majesty. I do not forget that I am your daughter.'

He nodded. 'Methinks you speak truth. Do you know, there is one thing I abhor . . . and I will do all in my power to stamp it out. It is dishonesty.'

I was beginning to tremble.

'Myself . . . I am a stranger to that vice,' he went on.

'You may think that there are occasions when a king must speak what is an untruth . . . for the sake of diplomacy, eh?'

'I am an ignorant woman, Your Majesty. I know nothing of these matters.'

He grunted, suggesting approval of my attitude. 'I will not do that. Nay!' He began to shout. 'Even though I am told it is expedient and it is not dishonesty in the normal sense . . . "This is for the country," they may say, but no: I am an honest man.'

I lifted my eyes and tried to look admiring; but I could not stop thinking of all he had done and how he had talked of his conscience, how he had made it work for him, so that all his deeds were wrapped in a covering of righteousness. It was hard to hide my feelings when he talked of dishonesty – but I must.

This was one of those occasions when he believed himself, and he saw no reason why I should not believe him either.

'I want to be sure of your sincerity,' he said.

I felt my knees would not support me, and I was afraid he would see my hands trembling and would regard my fear as evidence of my guilt.

'You signed the Act of Submission,' he said. 'You agreed that my marriage to your mother was invalid, and you accepted me, as did my loyal subjects, as Head of the Church.'

'Yes,' I said faintly.

'Will you give me a truthful answer?'

'Yes, Your Majesty,' I said even more quietly.

'You had much to gain from signing, had you not?'

'I yearned for Your Majesty's favour.'

'Aye. Your fate depended on it, did it not? You would have been a fool not to sign, and I do not think you are a fool, daughter. Your mother would not give in. It would

207

have been easier for her if she had. But you are made of different stuff.'

Yes, I thought, common clay. I could never be the martyr she was. I lack her goodness, her saintliness.

'But tell me this,' he went on. 'Did you agree with your heart as well as your pen?'

I dared not hesitate. To do so would be fatal. I had my mission, my destiny.

I answered: 'Yes, Your Majesty.'

He gave me an expansive smile and took me in his arms.

'Then, daughter,' he said, 'we are in truth good friends. You have told me that you signed the submission in good faith, and that pleases me. There are some who would suggest that you were forced to do this. You and I, daughter, know that this is not so. But there are those doubters, and I would have them know the truth. You will help me to dispel their doubts, good daughter that you have now become. There are two of these doubters to whom I would have you address yourself. One is the Emperor Charles; the other is the Pope.'

I was appalled. Was it not enough that I had signed his document? Must I deny my love for my mother, my adherence to the Faith? Must I tell this to the whole world?

Refusal trembled on my lips. I saw myself languishing in the Tower, tried for treason, brought out to Tower Hill as his beloved, the ill-fated Anne Boleyn, had been.

Where was that shining dream? I must bring England back to the Faith.

I was not merely a devoted daughter: I was a woman fighting for her future, perhaps her life, but my life was of little importance beside what I must do for the Faith.

He was looking at me intently; his little eyes were benign at the moment, but I knew how quickly they could change.

I heard myself say: 'Yes, Your Majesty, I will write to them. I will tell them that I am in agreement with everything that has been done and will be done.'

He could be charming when pleased. I could see why men followed him. He was like the father I had known in my childhood. He seized me in his arms and held me against his jewel-encrusted jacket. I felt the stones pressing into my heart. I despised myself. I murmured apologies to my mother; but I knew this had to be done.

'Now,' he said, 'all is well, and this is a delight to me. I like it not when there is discord in families. From now on you are my dear daughter. You shall come to Court. All shall be as it should be between a father and his daughter.'

He was in an excellent mood, and I was fighting to hide my despondency. He would prepare drafts for me to send to the Emperor and the Pope. All I needed to do would be to sign them and the matter would be most happily settled from his point of view.

I was becoming devious. I was playing my own games as carefully as he played his; only perhaps I had more of the quality which he so much admired: honesty – and with myself. I despised myself and yet I knew that what I was doing was necessary. I could honestly say I was not doing it to preserve my life or to bring myself a comfortable style of living. Always I had the main object in mind; and it was for that I lied and dissembled.

I was thankful that I could see people freely now; and when Chapuys visited me I gave him an account of my interview with my father.

'You did what was right,' he told me.

'But I have lied. I have denied my legitimacy and dishonoured my mother.'

'Sometimes it is necessary to act against one's conscience if the matter is great enough.'

'I do not wish the Emperor to regard me as a weakling who has given way to save her life.'

'The Emperor knows well your purpose.'

'I wish to write to him personally to tell him that what I have officially sent to him is untrue.'

'Do so,' he said, 'and I will see that the letter reaches him.'

'If it did not and was discovered, that would be the end of my hopes . . . and of me.'

Chapuys nodded gravely. 'It shall not be discovered. All the hopes of the Church rest with you. I swear to you that your letter will be delivered safely into the Emperor's hands.'

'I must also write to the Pope.'

'Do that. They will be sure then that you are working for God and the Church.'

He smiled at me and went on: 'You are anxious. You fear that you have betrayed your mother. Rest assured that she understands. This country of England will have reason to thank you. You are going to bring it back to the Faith when the time comes.'

He took my letters. I had visions of their falling into the hands of my father. I dared not dwell on what my fate would be if they did. But I could trust Chapuys, and my cousin Charles would know that I was no traitor to the Faith.

Thus I was able to still my conscience.

The Arrival of Edward

I was summoned to join the Court at Richmond for the Christmas festivities. This meant that I was received back in favour. My letters to the Emperor and the Pope had sealed the matter.

Queen Jane, realizing that after my exile I might not have the clothes I would need and the means to come to Court, thoughtfully sent me money. 'A little gift,' she called it; and it came with a message that she was so much looking forward to greeting me.

The weather was bitterly cold, and I was glad of the fur-lined wrap which I had been able to acquire through her thoughtfulness.

It seemed strange, after so many years, to be back among the grandeur that was my father's Court. He had stamped his personality upon it, and it was glittering, splendid and outwardly merry, all laughter and song; and yet, I wondered, how many of those seemingly carefree courtiers lived in terror of offending him? I fell to thinking what it must have been like in my grandfather's day. How he would have deplored the extravagance as he watched the dwindling effect it must be having on the exchequer. But this was my father's day, and the perversity of men is such that they loved him more, with all his tantrums, extravagances and adventurous marital life, than they ever did my solemn, careful grandfather. Parsimonious, they had called him, when, if he were so, it was for their betterment.

It was Jane, the Queen, who helped me through those days. There was something very gentle about her. I wondered if she ever considered the perilous nature of her position. Did she ever give a thought to what had happened to Anne Boleyn, so passionately loved at one time and, not so long after their marriage, sent to the block? If she did think of her, she gave no sign of it. She did give a good deal of thought to the comfort of others; she was far from clever; indeed, she was something of a simpleton, but she was able to understand how I was feeling, and she did everything possible to put me at my ease.

Now that I had begun to live a double life, as it were, hiding my true motives under a cloak of deceit, I felt a little ashamed in the company of Jane, who was so straight-forward and guileless. But sometimes I asked myself whether she, too, was playing her own little game? How did it feel to be the third wife of a man who had destroyed the two who had gone before? Was Jane assuming the role of docile, loving wife? One might say: Why had she married? Poor girl, what chance had one of her tempera-ment against two ambitious brothers and a monarch who desired her?

However, she did help me over those first difficult days at Court.

My father was tender with her, liking her submissive-ness. What a contrast to Anne Boleyn! But I fancied there were times when I saw a little impatience creeping through, and I found myself guessing how long it would take him to tire of her.

I remember one occasion particularly. Jane was so eager to make our reconciliation complete and did everything to smooth things between us, and one day she remarked how pleased he must be to have me at Court: his own daughter, who was so beloved by the people and so important in their eyes.

He looked at her with faint contempt and said: 'You are a fool, Jane. You should be thinking of the sons you will have . . . and not seeking to bring forward others.' He touched her stomach and went on with a touch of coarse-ness: 'That is where your hopes should lie.'

Poor Jane looked abashed. Was she really beginning to suffer from that anxiety which had plagued the lives of both my mother and Anne Boleyn? Was it six months she had been married and no sign of pregnancy yet?

There were times when I gave myself up to the pleasures of being at Court. Jane saw that I had new gowns. I chose bright colours. I felt I needed to because, although I was not ill-favoured, I was not startling in any way. My once fresh-coloured complexion had grown pale – probably from the privation I had suffered. My features were regular. I suppose I should have been considered quite ordinary outside royal circles; but at least I was the King's daughter, and that set me apart – particularly as he had recognized me as such.

I encountered a certain amount of adulation and secret congratulations, for most knew that I had come through some hazardous times and still managed to survive.

I was twenty-one, so perhaps a little frivolity could be forgiven me. I danced – as I loved to – and I joined in the festivities with a gusto due to long abstinence. I was, in fact, delighted to be back at Court.

Jane noticed this, and it pleased her. 'We shall see that it is just as it used to be long ago,' she told me. 'I believe you were then the darling of the Court.'

'That was when I was a little girl . . . and all was well between my parents.'

Jane nodded and changed the subject. I noticed that she avoided any talk which might be controversial; so perhaps she was not quite so simple after all.

Secure in her friendship, I began to talk more freely.

I told her about my dear Lady Salisbury and how, since she had left me all those years ago, I had not seen her. I wished to hear of her and longed to see her.

Jane understood. 'She is well, I think,' she said. 'But she does not come to Court.'

'No. I suppose her friendship with me over all those years has debarred her.'

'The King is displeased with her son, Reginald Pole.'

'Yes, I know,' I said. 'Do you think that, now all is well between us, my father might allow me to see the Countess?'

She said she would see what could be done.

Poor Jane. Her endeavours brought down the wrath of the King on her head.

She came to me in some distress. 'He was quite angry. He shouted at me. Had he not warned me not to meddle? "No," he said. "The Countess of Salisbury may not come to Court. Her son is a traitor. I'd have had his head if he had not been skulking abroad spreading malice about me. As for the lady in question, she would do well to take care." He was really angry.'

I said: 'I am sorry you did it for me.'

She said: 'I know how one feels about the companions of our young days. They pass all too quickly, don't they, and then . . . one grows up.'

Poor Jane! She was striving so hard to be the docile wife, remembering no doubt the horrific fate of Anne Boleyn, perhaps giving a thought to the tribulations of my mother. She was in a position as dangerous as any in the country, without my mother's stern resolution and strong character and Anne Boleyn's fire and sharp wit to help her face the onslaught when it came.

Jane was already learning that – as with those two – everything depended on her ability to produce a son.

I was indeed sorry that she had aroused the King's anger through me.

I did remember, though, Margaret Bryan's concern for Elizabeth, and I talked to Jane about the little girl.

'She is bright, intelligent and very attractive,' I told her.

Jane nodded. She would have liked to bring Elizabeth to Court. I was there, and Elizabeth should be. Jane longed for a happy family atmosphere. The little one was not responsible for her mother's misdeeds. Jane's eyes filled with tears when I told her how the child was being neglected, no money being sent for her clothes, and how Lady Bryan was at her wits' end wondering if in a few months' time she would have any clothes at all.

'There is a very small allowance for her food,' I said. 'It is so sad. She is after all the King's daughter.'

Jane listened and sympathized.

'I shall bring her here,' she said. 'It will be possible later but just now the King is so angry at the mention of her mother's name that I dare not.'

I understood, of course. She had risked his displeasure when she had talked to him of the Countess. She could not do it again by mentioning Elizabeth.

'It will change,' she assured me. 'But as yet I dare not.'

I was liking her more every day.

She told me I must stay at Court. We had become such good friends that we should not be apart.

This was gratifying. Jane might be a mild creature but she was the Queen and might have a little influence on the King. It was an indication of how my character had changed that I could work out the advantages which could ensue from such a friendship. But on the other hand, I was fond of her. It was impossible not to be fond of Jane. I had a strong urge to protect her. She seemed to me like a lamb among wolves, unsuspicious of danger because, for the time being, they were not preparing to harm her.

So I did want her friendship and not only because of the advantages it might bring me. I even thought that at some stage I might be able to help her, for, one day, God knew, she might need any help she could get.

In the meantime she went on in her own sweet way and we were often together.

The King was pleased to see the friendship between us, though there were times when a tremor of fear ran through me because I thought I caught a gleam of suspicion in his eyes.

But Jane continued to delight in my company, and she confided to me that she very much wanted to bring Elizabeth to Court. 'In time,' she assured me, 'the King will forget her mother, and his attitude will change towards the child.'

I hoped so. But at the moment I must rejoice in my own return to favour.

All through that January I was with the Court. Jane whispered to me with great delight that she thought she was pregnant, and I rejoiced with her. By the beginning of March she was sure.

The King was absolutely delighted. At last he was going to get his son. When he did, he would know that Heaven approved of everything he had done to reach that happy state.

He talked continually of his son; he would pat Jane's stomach. 'Good girl,' he said. 'This is the first of many.'

Jane was happy and at the same time fearful. She must have been feeling what the others had in their turn.

Would she produce the all-important son? And if not, what would happen to her?

* * *

Soon after Christmas Robert Aske, the leader of the Pilgrimage of Grace, had come to London to see the King. My father received him and listened carefully to his complaints. They should have consideration, he told him, and shortly he would make a visit to Yorkshire and visit the city of York, where his Queen might be crowned.

Robert Aske must have felt the visit was a great success, and he returned to his native Yorkshire. But of course the King was not going to give up the supremacy of the Church in favour of the Pope; he was not going to accept the Pope's judgement on his first marriage and declare me his legitimate daughter. I supposed he was just trying to show his benign nature to the people and hoped the revolt would simmer down.

But the people of the North were serious, and no sooner had Aske returned than a new revolt broke out. Sir Francis Bigod led this. The King marched north, and this time there was no miracle to save the rebels. They had no chance against the King's army. The leaders were caught and hanged in the cities where they had raised the revolt. Robert Aske came to London. This time he was sent to the Tower.

My father was done with peaceful negotiations. He was going to show these northerners who was their master.

Robert Aske was taken to York and hanged in chains, where his body was left for the crows and that all might see what happened to those who opposed the King's will.

The Pilgrimage of Grace was over, and the people, he hoped, had learned their lesson.

* * *

It was an anxious time for me because now I knew that every time there was an insurrection I should be in danger. There would always be a hint that the King was to be deposed, and I was the one who would be put in his place.

It was, of course, what I was working for; but it must come about in a natural manner. I was only twenty-one. Time was on my side. I felt in my heart that one day I was going to be Queen of this country and, when I was, my first mission would be to bring it back to Rome.

I was not yet ready for the task. I was too young. I had lived too far from the Court for too long. I had much to learn, and I must prepare myself. I must worship as my mother had — wholeheartedly. Religion must come first with me as it had with her; and the only reason why I could think and plan as I did, with a good conscience, was if I made it my first concern, my whole reason for living. I could believe that I had been sent on Earth for this one purpose: to bring the Church of England back to the true Roman Catholic fold.

So I could watch the decline of my father's health with mixed feelings. I was fond of him – odd as it may seem – but it is difficult to describe that unique temperament. One could hate what he did but not entirely hate him. One was warmed by his smile, though it might be fleeting; and to bask in his approval, uncertain as it was, brought a glow of happiness, a gratification, a delight that one had earned it. I cannot explain his charismatic charm; I can only think that it was that which kept men faithful to him – even those against whom he had committed the most outrageous and often barbaric acts.

With the Pilgrimage of Grace over and Jane pregnant, he was a happy man during those waiting months.

I was at odds with myself. I had become so fond of Jane. She admitted once her fear that the child might be a girl; it seemed unfair that she should suffer such anxiety over a matter in which she had no choice. Life was so unfair. If, through no fault of her own, she produced a girl, she would be despised, dubbed no better than her predecessors, and perhaps it would be the beginning of the end for her; on the other hand, if the child were a boy, she would be praised and fêted . . . good Queen Jane.

And my own position? As I said, I was fond of the girl. I wanted her to be happy; yet if she produced the boy, what of my hopes of achieving my mission?

It was not that I coveted the crown for myself. I wanted it for God and the true religion. It was a crusade, and I was to lead it. I was to bring this country back to the true Faith, which surely must find favour with God.

Now, long after, when I look back on all that happened, I can see why I did the things I did later. I had lived so much of my life on a precipice from which at any moment

I could be hurled to disaster. That has an effect on people. Human life can seem of little value; it is the cause that is important. Yes, perhaps that is why I acted as I did. Am I trying to find excuses? Perhaps. But excuses there are, for our characters are surely formed by the events in our early years.

At this time I was fêted at Court, the dear friend of the Queen; and I had my father's favour – but how transient that favour could be everyone knew. The Pilgrimage of Grace had brought that home to me. Men's bodies were now rotting in the great cities of the North, reminding the King's subjects of what happened to them if they disobeyed him. I was his subject, and whenever there were risings of any sort, my name would be bandied about. They had known of my mother's unswerving faith, and they would believe that her daughter shared it. There would always be suspicions. I was not safe. At any moment the King's wrath could be turned on me.

I walked a dangerous path and, looking back, I see that it was even more perilous than I realized at the time.

The Pilgrimage of Grace and its outcome, the suppression of the monasteries . . . these matters hung over me, for I could not be free of them. In spite of the Queen's friendship and the King's newly discovered affection for his daughter, I lived in fear during those days when the Pilgrimage of Grace was remembered.

I travelled with the Court to Greenwich and back to Richmond and then to various other houses as the Court moved round for sweetening and visiting. And all the time my friendship with Jane was growing. I had not mentioned the Countess of Salisbury again, but I did talk to Jane now and then of Elizabeth; but, with the memory of the Pilgrimage of Grace still in his mind, the King was in no mood for listening to the plight of his young daughter.

The months passed. The Queen's pregnancy was becoming obvious, and never was there a more welcome sight.

The King was tender towards her, certain that she bore the son he wanted. Seers prophesied the sex of the child to please him; they would have to make themselves scarce if they were proved wrong.

I was torn between my desire for Jane's happiness and my own need to accomplish my mission, for the two were incompatible. I told myself that, if it were God's will that Jane should bear a son who would be the future King and, on account of his age and mine, my plans would be frustrated, I must not complain.

I was ready and waiting if wanted. I could leave this in God's hands.

Jane was so eager that Elizabeth should be brought to Court that she plucked up courage and mentioned this to the King, and he, eager to pamper her and perhaps fearing what adverse effect there might be on her child if she were crossed, agreed that Elizabeth might come; but he did imply that he did not wish to see her.

I knew how delighted Lady Bryan would be if there was some recognition of her darling, and I wanted to take the news to them and help the child prepare. So I left the Court at the end of summer and went to Hunsdon.

There was a great welcome for me. Margaret was delighted to see me. As for Elizabeth, when she heard she was going to see Queen Jane, she was overjoyed.

Her face was alight with pleasure and anticipation, her red curls bobbed up and down as she jumped, for she found it difficult to keep still, and Margaret was always admonishing her about this. She was four years old but her manner and way of speech were more fitting to a child of eight or nine. She was exceptionally bright and very forward. Margaret said she had never seen a child so full of vitality and yet so eager to study her books. I only half believed Margaret, for I knew her darling was perfect in her eyes. But it was true that Elizabeth was a most unusual child – the sort that one might have expected the King and

Anne Boleyn to produce between them. It was over a year now since the little one had lost her mother. I wondered if she still thought of her.

Margaret was anxious about the child's clothes. She could not go in patched shifts, she declared. I was no longer poor. Gifts had been showered on me since my reinstatement, and I had an income and money from both the King and Queen. So between us we were able to equip the child for Court.

Her delight was infectious. I forgot to wonder what would be the outcome of my mission. I was caught up in the excitement of taking Elizabeth to Court.

* * *

It was September. The birth was expected during the following month. There were no more appearances in public for Queen Jane. She was to have a month of quietness at Hampton Court. It is, I suppose, with its courtyards and towers, one of the most magnificent buildings in England. I could never be in it without thinking of Thomas Wolsey. There he must have experienced great anguish when he realized that he, who had risen so high, was soon to fall. How had he felt when he had handed this palace over to the King? My father had questioned whether it was right that a subject should live in greater splendour than his king, and Wolsey, with that immediate perception which had brought him to his elevated position, had remarked that a subject should only have it that he might present it to his king. With that remark he may have given himself a few weeks' grace, but it had lost him his palace.

And now here we were, while Jane awaited the birth of her child.

She was, as I had known she would be, enchanted by Elizabeth. Bright-eyed, with reddish curls and that amazing vitality, she possessed that charisma which I had never seen in any other person except my father in his youth. She must have inherited it from him. How could any of her mother's enemies suggest for a moment that she was not his child? He was there in her gestures, in her very zest for life. I thought, if he would only allow himself to see her, he would be completely beguiled.

But he did not see her. He did receive me. He told me that he had heard from Dr Butts that I was well and that if I would not get over-excited I would cease to be tormented by my headaches.

'You should live more peacefully,' he told me, giving me one of those suspicious looks as though to ask: What are your aspirations? What is it that over-excites you? You are only a bastard, remember.

I shall never forget Jane during those weeks before her confinement. I wondered if she had a premonition of what was to come. It was only natural that she must have been overcome with dread – not only because of the ordeal of childbirth but by what the outcome might be if she gave birth to a stillborn child or one of the despised sex. There were dismal examples of what had happened to others, and I guessed she could not dismiss them from her mind.

I can see her now, standing with me in the great banqueting hall which had only just been completed. She had gazed at the entwined initials – her own and those of the King: J and H. It was a custom of his to have his initials entwined with those of the wife who happened to please him at the moment. They were all decorated with lovers' knots and cast in stone, which was ironical because it was so much more enduring than his emotions, and so remained long after his passion had passed away.

Jane was looking pale and by no means well. I thought a little fresh air would be good for her, such as a quiet walk in the gardens or to sit awhile under one of the trees and enjoy the autumn sunshine. But it was forbidden. The King feared there might be some minor accident which would bring about a premature birth. She was reminded at every turn that she carried the country's – and the King's – hopes for a male heir.

Elizabeth was with us, and she created a diversion. There was no doubt that Jane found pleasure in her company. Elizabeth was completely sure of herself and did not seem in the least concerned because her father would not see her. I was sure she believed that when he did he would fall victim to her charm, as almost everyone else did. I thought it was strange that she, who wanted an explanation of everything she saw or heard, never mentioned her mother. It seemed to me that it was an indication that she knew what had happened to her. Margaret would never have told her, but the sharp ears would be constantly alert for information; and I felt she knew. What would a child of four think of a father who had murdered her mother? What did I think, for he had as good as murdered mine? It says a good deal for his personality that neither of us hated him. It may have been largely due to the aura of kingship which was so much a part of him. But it was more than that. He had something in his nature which enabled him to act most cruelly – barbarously, in fact – and still people would forgive him and seek his approval.

At last the day arrived. The Queen's pains had started. There was a hushed expectancy about the palace. All were afraid to approach the King. The next few hours would be decisive. Either we should have a happy monarch or a furious, raging tyrant to contend with.

We were all in a state of tension. 'A boy!' prayed the King and all those about him. Not surprisingly I was unsure of what I wanted. A boy would mean the end of all hope for me. I should lose that great chance which I had believed Heaven was holding out for me if the child were a boy. And yet . . . a boy would make life easier for us all. Suspicion would shift from me. No one could doubt that the King's marriage to Jane was legal, for both his previous wives had been dead at the time he married. A boy in any case would come before me . . . and Elizabeth.

I should be praying for a girl . . . or, more to my advantage, a stillborn child. But how could I? I could not bear to think of the troubles which had beset my own mother falling on Jane.

I said to myself: 'God moves in a mysterious way. If it is His will that the task of bringing England back to the true Faith shall be mine, then it will be so.' And I believed that.

The vigil was long. I was in the ante-room with those in high places who must be present at the birth. The time was passing. No child yet . . . The anxiety was growing. Was something wrong? Was it possible that the King could not get healthy children?

The doctors came out. They must see the King at once. It was clear that the birth was not going as it should.

It seemed possible that both the child and the mother could not live. There might have to be a choice. The King must make the decision.

I was glad that Jane was too ill to know his reply, to realize how deeply he desired a son, how frail was his love for her.

His reply was typical of him – brusque and revealing. 'Save my son. Wives are easily found.'

My poor, poor Jane!

It was Friday the 12th of October of that year 1537 when the child was born. It was the longed-for boy.

The King's delight was unbounded. At last he had that for which he had so long prayed.

His own son, and meek little Jane had given it to him.

* * *

The boy was received with such acclaim that little thought was given to Jane. She was exhausted and very ill but she still lived.

I talked to Margaret about it.

'Poor lady,' she said. 'Her ordeal was terrible and she was never strong. Keeping her shut up like that . . . it was all wrong. I said it from the first. Fresh air would have done her the world of good.'

'But she did it, Margaret. She has produced the son. Both my mother and Anne Boleyn would have given everything they had to do that.'

Margaret nodded. 'What she needs now is rest . . . not all this coming and going.'

'She is happy now, Margaret. She has been so worried.'

'I can believe that! Well now, she must have a good rest . . . rest and quiet and no more children for a long time.'

'The King's appetite is whetted. She has given him a son. He will want more.'

'He will have to wait. He's got one. Let him be satisfied with that.'

There must be no delay. The baby must be baptized. He was to be called Edward. The King was in a mood of exuberance. He carried the boy in his arms and had to be restrained from bouncing him up and down in his excitement. He smiled good-humouredly at the nurse who stopped him. The baby was very precious.

It was a Friday when he was born and he was to be baptized on the Monday night.

'Too soon for the Queen,' commented Margaret.

'She will be in her bed.'

'There'll be too much fuss round her.'

'I think she must be very happy, Margaret.'

But Margaret looked grim. She bore a great grudge against the King; she could never forget what he had done to her darling's mother and all the subterfuge she had had to practise to keep it from the child.

The baptism of little Edward was to take place in Hampton Court Chapel, and I was to play an important part in the ceremony. My father would feel less anxious about my position now for he had a true heir to replace me.

225

He was therefore inclined to bring me forward a little. Perhaps this was why I was chosen to present the baby at the font.

The procession would begin in the Queen's chamber. Jane, of course, could not rise from her bed; she was far too weak. It was this which angered Margaret so much. She thought rules and customs should be set aside if people were not well enough to partake in them. These men did not realize what it was like, giving birth to a child, she said; it was a pity some of them didn't have to do it sometimes, then they would have some idea of what it was like. Even if everything had gone smoothly, the Queen would have needed rest at such a time.

However, Jane, in accordance with custom, was to be removed from her bed to a state pallet, a type of couch. This was very grand, being decorated with crowns and the arms of England worked in gold thread. The counterpane was of scarlet velvet lined with ermine.

As they lifted her from the bed, Jane was hardly aware of what was happening. She did not seem to see us as we crowded into the chamber and the trumpets blared forth.

In his benign mood, the King had decided that Elizabeth might be present. She had been brought from her bed and put into ceremonial robes. She was to carry the chrisom and, as she was just four years old, this would have been too big a task for her, so Edward Seymour, one of the Queen's ambitious brothers, carried her in his arms.

How she loved the ceremony! It was nearly midnight but she was wide awake, smiling at everyone, so happy to be a part of the procession.

I saw her grandfather, Thomas Boleyn, Earl of Wiltshire, in the chapel; he had a towel about his neck and was carrying a wax taper. I felt a wave of revulsion towards the man. How could he take part in a ceremony which could never have come about but for the murder of his daughter?

226

I supposed his head was more important to him than his principles.

The sight of the man brought home to me a reminder of the perilous times in which we were living and that, because of my position, I was more vulnerable than most.

The baby was carried by the Marchioness of Exeter, under a canopy borne by four noblemen, to a small corner of the chapel, and there he was baptized.

'God, in His almighty and infinite grace, grant good life and long to the right high, the right excellent and noble Prince Edward, Duke of Cornwall and Earl of Chester, most dear and entirely beloved son of our dread and gracious lord, Henry VIII.'

The trumpets rang out. Elizabeth took my hand, and together we walked in the procession back to our stepmother's bedchamber.

It was midnight, and the ceremony had lasted three hours.

The King was beside himself with joy; he smiled on all. He was certain that God had shown His approval for the match with Jane. I wondered if he felt a twinge of conscience, for what he had done to his once-loved Anne. He would be assuring himself: She was a witch. She set a spell on me, and I was not to blame.

God was confirming this. Had He not given him a son!

* * *

The next day Jane was very ill. The ceremony had completely exhausted her.

Her priests were at her bedside. She rallied a little but she had caught a bad chill on the night of the baptism and she could not recover from this, so weak was her state.

The King was to go to Esher. He always avoided being near the sick. Illness reminded him that he was not immune. He had never been the same since his fall, and the ulcer in his leg would not heal. It gave him great pain, and the doctors were reticent about it, as though they feared it might be a symptom of something else; so it must not be mentioned.

He was a little irritated. It was absurd that Jane, who had given the nation – and him – the most important gift of a son, should now be too ill to enjoy all the honours he had prepared for the occasion. She must make an effort to get well, he said.

Poor Jane was beyond making efforts. She grew worse, and the King finally decided that he must wait a while before leaving for Esher. He was now expressing concern for the Queen's health as she grew steadily worse.

On the 24th of October, twelve days after she had given birth to Edward, she became very gravely ill. Her confessor was with her. He administered Extreme Unction and at midnight she died.

So the rejoicing for the birth of a son was turned into mourning for the death of the Queen.

* * *

The day after Jane's death they embalmed her, and in her chamber Mass was said every day until they took her away. Tapers burned all through the night and ladies kept a watch. I was chief mourner, so I was present, and as I sat with others at the side of her dead body, I thought of her youth, her simplicity and her fears . . . Jane, who was the tool of ambitious men. I wondered if my father would ever have noticed her if her brothers had not thrust her forward. I was angry that women should be treated so . . . angry for my mother and myself . . . and yes, even Anne Boleyn.

And the nights passed thus in meditation and, in spite of the birth of the child, the feeling was strong within me that God had chosen me to work for Holy Church in my country.

It was on the 12th of November when we set out from Hampton for Windsor. In the hearse was Jane's coffin, and on it was a statue of her in wax, so lifelike that one could believe she was really there. The hair fell loose about the shoulders, and there was a crown on the head.

She was buried in St George's Chapel.

* * *

I fell ill that winter. I suffered from acute headaches and dizziness and could not rise from my bed. My ladies rallied round me and served me well, and my father sent Dr Butts to me. I recovered sufficiently to spend Christmas at Court. It was dismal. How could there be the usual feasting with the Queen so recently dead. My father wore black – a great concession. He had not worn it for his two previous wives. He was not his exuberant self, and I began to wonder whether he had cared for Jane. But I soon discovered that he was already putting out feelers to replace her.

His greatest joy was in his son. He would send for the child to be brought to him and hold him gently in his arms. He would look at him with wonder and talk to him. 'You must get strong and big, my son. You have a realm to govern one day. A long time yet . . . but one day.' He would turn to those standing by. 'See how he looks at me? He understands. Oh, he is a wonderful boy, this. He is the son I always wanted.'

He was almost boyish in his enthusiasm. Perhaps that was at the root of his charm. He seemed to be saying: 'I did this . . . I murdered my wives . . . I have caused grievous suffering to monks . . . I have killed those who were my best servants . . . Wolsey . . . Sir Thomas More . . . Fisher . . . but I am only a boy really. My heart is warm and loving, and those barbarous acts . . . well, they were for the good of the country.'

And they seemed to believe him. I half did so myself.

And while he was making a show of mourning for Jane, he was looking for her successor.

He would regard me cryptically. Twenty-two years of

229

age. That was mature for a princess . . . or should I say a king's daughter, for he would not allow me that title.

I had my household now. I was comfortable. But I did often feel a longing for children. There was Elizabeth. I could have wished she was my daughter; and there was now Edward. What would I have given for such a boy!

And here I was – a spinster, a virgin, to wither on the branch, unloved, unfulfilled – and all because I was branded with the taint of illegitimacy.

But it was a good life compared with what I had known. I had good friends; my servants were loyal to me; they were more than servants; they cared for me; they all believed that I should be proclaimed princess. I was never frivolous. I tried to lead a good life. They all knew I was deeply religious because I was my mother's daughter. My house was open to all the needy. We never turned any away. I had my income from the Court, and a great deal of it was spent on charity. I liked to walk about three miles a day, and it was pleasant to be able to go where I chose; and I always had pennies in my purse to give to those who, I thought, needed it.

The people were fond of me. They always called a loyal greeting when I passed.

I had my books, my music and now beautiful garments to wear. I was well educated. I could talk to any diplomats who came to Court. I was a good musician – excellent with the lute and the virginals.

But I was a woman, and I felt that I was missing the greatest blessing in life. I wanted a child.

Yet the days continued pleasant. I lived the life of a royal person in my own household. My father had even sent me a fool. She had always been a favourite of his. In fact, I think Will Somers was a little jealous of her. It was rare to have a woman as a fool, but Jane was good. Her very appearance set one laughing before she came out with her merry quips. She would dress exactly like a court lady but her hair was shaved off, and the result was ludicrous. She could sing well, and she had a repertoire of comic songs and a host of tricks with which to divert us. Evenings with Jane the Fool amused us all and were very welcome indeed.

So there was little of which to complain, but I wanted the normal life the poorest woman might expect – that I should be allowed to justify my purpose and help replenish the Earth.

There had been one or two propositions. My father would never have let me go abroad before the birth of Edward. That would be asking for some ambitious man, married to the daughter of the King of England, to set about claiming the throne. But now there was a male heir perhaps it would be different.

There were feelers from both France and the Hapsburgs . . . each eager to form an alliance against the other. There was Charles of Orleans, the son of François, King of France, and Dom Luiz, the Infante of Portugal, who was put forward by the Emperor.

For a few weeks I lived in a state of excitement. I was assured that either of these gentlemen would make a perfect husband. They were both handsome, charming princes. It was just a matter of which it should be.

Then came the stumbling block which had not, as I had hoped it would be, been removed because of the favour my father was showing me.

The King of France intimated that there was no one he would rather have for his son than myself. Yet there was the stain of illegitimacy. If that could be removed . . . well, then he would welcome none with the same ardour which he would bestow on me.

It was the same with the Portuguese. Yes, the match would be very desirable but there was, of course, this little matter.

The King was furious. He would not give way. To do so would be to undermine the supremacy of the Church – a matter which was already causing him a great deal of trouble.

So these matches were abandoned.

There was a certain rumour which gave me pleasure. I remembered how my mother, since I could not marry the Emperor Charles, had expressed a desire that I should marry Reginald Pole.

In the quietness of my room I talked with Susan Clarencieux, who had become one of my dearest friends. I could talk to her of my dreams and aspirations more openly than anyone else.

She understood my desire for marriage.

She said: 'I saw your fondness for the little Elizabeth, although for a while you seemed to fight against it.'

'I hated her mother. She ruined mine. And I am afraid at first I passed my hatred on to the child. That is something one should never do . . . to blame the children for their parents' sins of which they are entirely innocent. It was cruel and wicked.'

'And the young Elizabeth is such an enchanting creature.'

'I often wonder what will become of her. I fear she will take everything she wishes or, failing to, bring herself to some terrible end.'

'I have a feeling that she will somehow survive.'

'Her position is even worse than mine. The King at least acknowledges me. Sometimes I think he tries to tell himself that she is not his daughter.'

'Could he look at her and doubt it?'

'Perhaps that is why he does not wish to look at her.'

'I have heard certain rumours lately. I believe that at one time you were very fond of him.'

'Of whom do you speak?'

'Of Reginald Pole.'

'Oh.' I was smiling. Memories were coming back. How young I had been, and he had seemed so wonderful . . . so much older than I was . . . so much wiser . . . and yet I had loved him and believed he loved me.

'What did they say of him?' I asked.

'That he has only taken deacon's orders . . . not those of a priest . . . so that, when the time comes . . . he will not be debarred from taking a wife. You and he could be married.'

'Do you think there is any truth in this?'

'It is what some people would like.'

'You mean . . . those whom the King would call his enemies?'

'Yes.'

'But Reginald is a cardinal now.'

'He remains free to marry.'

'Oh, Susan, I wonder if it could ever be . . .'

She lifted her shoulders. 'The King hates him now, you know. He regards him as an enemy who can do him a great deal of harm on the Continent.'

'Yes, I do know. Oh, Susan, why are things never as they should be?'

She smiled at me fondly. 'You would welcome a marriage with him,' she said, more as a statement than a question.

I nodded. 'It would be suitable in every way. He is a Plantagenet. Our rival houses would be joined. Besides, I know him well.'

'It is long since you saw him.'

'But he is not a man to change. Susan, there is no one I should rather have for my husband.'

And so we talked.

But I was no nearer to marriage for all that. Sometimes I thought I never should be.

Two Wives

Ever since the death of Jane, my father had been looking
for a new bride. He was obsessed by the idea. Why he did
not take a mistress, I cannot imagine. There might have
been several prepared to accept that honour. But marriage?
Any woman would look askance at that. The whole world
knew what had happened to his first two wives. And the
third? Had she escaped a similar fate by dying?

He had his eyes on several women at the French Court.
The Duke of Guise had three daughters, François Premier
one. All were eligible. My father wrote enthusiastically to
François. Perhaps the ladies could be sent to England and
he would promise to choose one of them to be the next
Queen of England.

François' retort was typical of him. 'Our ladies are not
mares to be paraded for selection,' he said.

The fact was that none of the ladies was eager for
marriage. Perhaps my father had forgotten that he was no
longer the eligible bridegroom he had once been. He was
ageing. His handsome looks were no more; he had grown
fat; his once-dazzling complexion had turned purple. Since
his fall he walked with a limp, and there was a fistula on his
leg which refused to heal. There were times when it was so
painful that he could not speak, and his face would grow
black in his efforts to prevent himself calling out loud.
There were some who said it was an incurable ulcer, others
– though only a few bold ones said this – that it was the
outward sign of some horrible disease. In addition to all
this, it was remembered what had happened to his first two
wives.

He was restive and angry; he flew into rages. On one

hand fate had sent him his longed-for son and on the other it had turned life sour for him.

He wanted to be young again; he wanted to be in love, as he had been with Anne and Jane – and perhaps in the early days with my mother.

There was a spate of killings. Anyone who spoke against the King's supremacy in the Church was found guilty of treason. Many monks were butchered in the most barbarous way. Hanging was not enough. They were submitted to the most horrifying of all deaths, cut down from the gallows while they still lived; their bodies slit open and their intestines burned before their eyes; the object being to keep them alive as long as possible so that they might suffer the greater pain.

The more opposition there was to my father's rule, the more despotic he became.

He was reaping great wealth from the monasteries, and for some time he had had his eyes on that shrine which was perhaps the most splendid of them all. He must have known that to touch it would arouse great indignation, for the whole country revered Thomas à Becket. Ever since the death of the martyr, people had brought precious jewels to lay on his shrine while they prayed for him to intercede for them in Heaven. My father asked why there should be such worship for a man who had been the enemy of his king? He did not care for traitors, and that was what Becket had been. There should be an end to this idolatry. Becket had been a traitor. He should have been despised rather than idolized.

Becket's bones were burned and, as the belongings of traitors were forfeit to the King, my father took all that was in the shrine at Canterbury. He even wore Becket's ring on his own finger as a gesture of defiance to all those who questioned his behaviour.

A tremor of horror seemed to run through the country. I was sure many were waiting for the wrath of Heaven to strike the King dead. For three years the threat of excommunication had hung over him. Not that he took any notice of it. Now the Pope signed the sentence. My father laughed. Who was the Bishop of Rome to tell him what to do? Foreign bishops had nothing to do with the Church of England over which the King was now Supreme Head.

But I think he must have been a little shaken and perhaps in his secret thoughts had a few qualms about his bold actions. He would not fear the wrath of God. My father always made his own peace with God, who was a part of his conscience; he would have already given God his very good reasons for acting as he did. The Church of Rome was corrupt. It extorted bribes. He was a religious man and would see that his subjects were too. God could have no quarrel with him.

But there were other forces. For instance there were signs of growing friendship between Charles and François; and what if they, with the Pope, looked for someone to replace him?

The Tudors' hold on the throne had not existed for very long, and there were still those who boasted of their Plantagenet blood. I knew that he often thought of Reginald, who had done the King's cause no good from the moment he had left the country.

It was on the Poles that my father turned his anger.

The Poles were troublemakers, he said. He could not touch Reginald because he kept out of his way, and he was the real enemy. However, there were other members of the family, and they were within range of his displeasure.

I was horrified when I heard that Sir Geoffry Pole had been arrested and sent to the Tower. Geoffry was the youngest of the Pole brothers and the most vulnerable. He was accused of being in correspondence with his brother the Cardinal, and he had been heard to make remarks in which he showed his disapproval of the King.

I was extremely anxious. My friendship with the family

was well known. The Countess of Salisbury, mother of Geoffry, had been my dearest friend. As she and my mother had often talked of the desirability of a marriage between Reginald and myself, she might still be hoping for it. It was strange that that ardent churchman, the Cardinal, had kept himself in a position to marry.

I could see danger creeping close to me, ready to catch up with me. Of course my father was anxious. There were murmurings in the Court against him. The spoliation of the shrine of Canterbury, the dissolution of the monasteries to the great profit of the King and his friends, the severance from the Pope whom they had looked upon as the Vicar of Christ all their lives . . . this could turn many against him.

And now the Pope had excommunicated him. Reginald Pole was circulating evil gossip about him. He was without a wife and the ladies of France were not eager to marry him; even though he might offer them the crown of England, they did not want it since they had to take him with it. The pain in his leg was cruel; the wretched ulcer seemed to get better and then would flare up again. My father was an angry man.

He gave orders that Sir Geoffry was to implicate his brothers and his friends. At any cost this must be achieved.

As my father must have guessed, Sir Geoffry was not able to stand out against the rigorous questioning and as a result broke down and said all that was required of him.

As a result his eldest brother, Lord Montague, and Henry Courtenay, Marquis of Exeter, among others, were arrested and put in the Tower.

My father now had in his power the Plantagenet Poles and Courtenay whose mother was the youngest daughter of Edward IV and therefore in the Plantagenet line. If he could have arrested Reginald at the same time, he would have been overjoyed. As it was, he must leave it to him to wreak his mischief abroad. But he would see that the others did not continue to plague him.

It was tragic. There could not have been a family in the country who had been more ready to support the King when he had first come to the throne; but they were a devout Catholic family; they could not accept first the divorce from my mother and secondly the break with Rome. It was revealed that they and the Marquis of Exeter had expressed approval for what Reginald was doing abroad. They had been in communication with him, and Montague had said there would be civil war in the country because of outraged public opinion on what was being done; and if the King were to die suddenly, it would be certain.

My father could never bear talk of death – and he had always considered mention of his own treasonable.

Lord Chancellor Audley and the jury of peers knew what verdict my father wanted and they gave it.

I was deeply distressed. My thoughts were for the Countess. What anguish she must have suffered. Her sons on trial for their lives, and in the present climate facing certain death.

For some reason Geoffry was pardoned. Perhaps the King was too contemptuous of him to demand the full penalty and possibly believed that more information might be extracted from him. But on the 9th of December Lord Montague and the Marquis of Exeter were beheaded on Tower Hill.

They went bravely to their deaths. Geoffry was released; his wife had pointed out that he was so ill that he was nearly dead. Poor Geoffry – his, I suppose, was the greater tragedy. How did a man feel when he had betrayed his family and friends whom he loved? Desperately unhappy, I know, because a few days after he was released he tried to kill himself. He did not succeed and lived on miserably.

All I could think of was the Countess. How I longed to see her, but I guessed that, in view of the suspicions under which her family now lived, that would never be allowed.

Then, to my horror, I learned that the Earl of Southampton and the Bishop of Ely had been sent to her home to question her and as a result she was taken to Southampton's house at Cowdray and kept a prisoner there. What was my father trying to prove? It was years since the Countess had been snatched from me, but I wondered if he were trying to implicate me.

He was in a vicious mood. Many people were against him, and that was something he could not endure. I heard, too, that his leg, far from improving, was growing more painful. He had always been watchful of those of royal blood. I waited for news in trepidation.

An attainder was passed by Parliament against Reginald and the Countess, among others, including Montague and Exeter who were already dead. Southampton had found a tunic in the Countess's house which had been decorated with the arms of England – the prerogative of royalty.

She was taken to the Tower.

I could not stop thinking of her plight. I knew how bitterly cold it could be within those stone walls when one had no comforts at all, no heat, no warm clothing; and she must be in her late sixties. How could she endure it?

I wanted to go to my father. I wanted to ask him what harm an old lady like that could do.

It was not so much that I feared to face his wrath but that if I attempted to plead for her I would not only arouse his suspicions against myself but make things worse for her. But if I could have helped her, I would have done anything. I found I did not greatly care what became of me, but my instinct told me that to plead for her would only increase his anger against her. He had destroyed Montague and Exeter . . . royal both of them. Geoffry Pole was too weak to be a menace; Reginald, whom he regarded as the arch conspirator, was out of reach. And, apart from that, the Countess was the last of the Plantagenet line. But how could he really believe that she would harm him?

How precariously we all lived!

Chapuys came to see me.

'You must act with the utmost caution,' he said.

I replied that I was worried about my very dear friend who had been as a mother to me.

He shrugged his shoulders. 'The Countess will remain in the Tower, whatever you do.'

'It is ridiculous to say that she is a traitor. She would never harm the King. She is guilty of no crime.'

'She is guilty, Princess, of being a Plantagenet.'

I turned away impatiently.

'Listen,' he said. 'The King is fearful of revolt. Those who would take up arms against the King look for a figurehead. He is pursuing a perilous path. I cannot believe he fully understood what he was doing when he proclaimed himself Head of the Church of England.'

'He is determined to remain so.'

Chapuys looked over his shoulder and whispered: 'It could cost him his throne. And little Edward is too young. A baby cannot rule a country.' He looked at me steadily. 'The King greatly fears the influence of Cardinal Pole. He has hired assassins and sent them to Italy to kill him.'

'Oh no!' I cried. 'Will this nightmare never end?'

'In time it will. Have no fear. We are aware of what is happening. The Cardinal will take care. He believes it is his duty to live, to play his part in righting this wrong. He always travels in disguise. None could recognize him as the Cardinal.'

'What are his plans?'

'Perhaps to gather together the foreign princes and force England back to Rome.'

'You mean war?'

'The King will never admit that he is at fault. He will never come back to Rome. It would have to be a new king . . . or queen . . .'

I caught my breath.

240

Chapuys lifted his shoulders. 'We can only wait. But for the state of affairs in Europe this would have been done long ago. But . . . François is unreliable, and my master has many commitments.'

'The times are dangerous.'

'It would be well, my lady Princess, if you remembered that. Lie low. Say nothing that could have any bearing on what is going on.'

'But I am so wretchedly unhappy about the Countess.'

'Curb your grief. Remember . . . silence. It could be your greatest friend at this time.'

* * *

Meanwhile my father was becoming restive. He had been a widower far too long and he wanted a wife. He had been very set on the beautiful Mary of Guise and was furious when she was promised to his nephew James V of Scotland. He raged and demanded what they thought they were doing, sending the woman to that impoverished, barbarous land when she could have come to England?

No one said that the lady might be remembering that the King of England had had three wives – one who was discarded and might have been poisoned; another who was blatantly beheaded; and the third who had died in childbirth; and that he had been heard to say when her life was in danger: 'Save the child. Wives are easily found.'

Now, it seemed, not so easily.

Thomas Cromwell, always looking for political advantage, had turned his eyes to the German princes. They were Protestant – a point in their favour; moreover François and the Emperor were now behaving in a friendly fashion towards each other. So . . . Protestant Germany seemed to offer a possible solution.

The Duke of Cleves had recently died and his son, William, had succeeded him. Alliance with England and the possibility of his sister Anne becoming Queen of England would be a great honour for his little dukedom.

My father was very eager to have a young and beautiful girl for his wife. He remained furious with Mary of Guise who was going to Scotland. It was a slight hard to forgive, and he needed to be soothed by a bride younger and more beautiful than Mary of Guise.

He was interested in Cromwell's schemes for the new alliance: it would give him particular satisfaction to snap his fingers at those two old adversaries, Charles and François; alliance with the Germans would give them some anxious qualms. He could attain two desires at one blow – disconcert them and get a beautiful bride for himself.

But she must be young, she must be beautiful, and she must match Anne and Jane in physical attraction and at the same time be docile, loving and adoring . . . everything he would ask for in a wife.

He sent Hans Holbein to Cleves to make an accurate portrait, and when the artist came back with an exquisite miniature, my father was entranced. The contract was signed at Düsseldorf and with great impatience he awaited the arrival of his bride.

Cromwell had learned his lessons from Wolsey, who had always sought to strengthen alliances through marriages; and now Cromwell concerned himself with mine. Perhaps he should have paused to remember poor Wolsey's humiliating end and that some of the easiest projects to disappoint were these proposed marriages. At first he decided that the brother of Anne of Cleves would be just right for me, but before the plan could be put into action, he had discovered a man who, he felt, would be a more powerful ally than William of Cleves. He would have the alliance with Cleves through the duke's sister Anne, so why not strike out in another direction? The aim would still be among the German princes. Philip of Bavaria was a nephew of Lewis

V, the Elector Palatine, so by this alliance we could have allies in two places instead of one.

Moreover Philip of Bavaria would be coming to England with the embassy which was to arrive for the wedding of the King and his new wife.

For so long I had been the victim of frustration. I had reached the age of twenty-two, which is old for a princess to remain unmarried; and when I came to think of all the prospective bridegrooms I had had, I had come to believe that there would never be a marriage for me.

And now . . . Philip of Bavaria was here and I was to meet him and, as Cromwell was anxious to forge the bonds between our country and his, it really did seem as though my marriage might be imminent.

I shall never forget that meeting. My heart leaped with pleasure at the sight of him. I could hardly believe what I saw. He was tall and fair, with Nordic good looks; his manners were easy and pleasant; he was a very attractive man.

He took my hand and kissed it and raised his blue eyes to my face. They were such kind blue eyes. I warmed towards him, and I felt he did towards me.

The manners of the Court of Bavaria were different from those of ours, and I was taken by surprise when he leaned forward suddenly and kissed my lips.

I had no German and he no English, so we must speak in Latin.

He told me how great was his pleasure in beholding me, and I replied that I was glad I pleased him.

I wondered how truthful he was. I knew I was not one of the beauties of the Court; I was small and thin and in spite of this I was lacking in that very desirable quality of femininity, for I had a rather deep voice. People often said that when I spoke I reminded them of my father; but I do admit that he had a rather high voice for a man, while mine was somewhat low for a woman.

243

I must regret – as I always would – that my prospective bridegroom was not Reginald; but I was growing old, and it was long since I had seen him. My father would never consent to *that* match, and Philip of Bavaria was an exceptionally attractive man.

I enjoyed our conversation. It was somewhat stilted, being in Latin, and very often caused us to smile; but I was gratified and content when he told me that he was falling in love with me.

He presented me with a diamond cross on a chain which he said I must wear for his sake.

Such an adventure was a novelty to me, and I enjoyed it without giving a great deal of thought to what a match with Bavaria might entail.

Chapuys came to see me. He was most disturbed about the Cleves betrothal but far more so with the proposed marriage of myself and Philip of Bavaria.

'You will be expected to embrace the Protestant Faith,' he said.

I stared at him.

'Had that not occurred to you?' he asked in a shocked tone.

What a fool I had been! I might have known nothing could go smoothly for me. How could I expect to have the joy of a perfect marriage? I liked Philip. When I considered the kind of bridegrooms who were presented to some princesses, I had reason to rejoice. If only that were all. He was handsome, charming, a man whom I could like. But, of course, he was a heretic.

Chapuys was regarding my horror with some satisfaction.

'You could never marry a heretic,' he said.

'Never,' I agreed. 'And yet . . . my father has allowed Cromwell to arrange this marriage.'

'My master will be greatly displeased.'

I might have pointed out that his master had done little to help in a practical way, being always too immersed in his own political schemes. They did not seem to realize that I was a poor desolate young woman with little power to act in the way she wanted, even though she might have the inclination.

'This marriage will be disastrous.'

'What of the King's?'

'The King's is not good. But you are the hope . . .' He did not finish but his words made me tremble. I was the hope of the Catholic world. Mine was the task to bring this country back to the true Faith.

How could I have been so blind as to rejoice because Philip of Bavaria was a young and presentable man . . . when he was a heretic?

I could not marry him. Yet it might be that I must. I prayed. I called on my mother in Heaven to help me. But what could I do? If my father – and Cromwell – desired this marriage, I was powerless to prevent it.

My dream of possible happiness was fading away. I was weak. I was helpless – and I was about to be married to a heretic. I did think about him a good deal. I had wanted this marriage . . . I was tired of spinsterhood. I had dreams of converting him to the true Faith. I encouraged that dream because I wanted to marry, and it was only with such a project in mind that I could do so with a good conscience.

* * *

On the 27th of December Anne of Cleves left Calais to sail for England. When she landed at Deal, she was taken to Walmer Castle and, after a rest there, she proceeded to Dover Castle where, because the weather was bitterly cold and the winds were of gale force, she stayed for three days. Then she set out for Canterbury, where she was met by a company of the greatest nobles in the land, including the Duke of Norfolk. She must have been gratified by the warmth of her welcome and perhaps looked forward with

245

great pleasure to meeting the man who was to be her husband.

Poor Anne! When I grew to know her, I felt sorry for her; and I often pondered on the unhappiness my father brought to all the women who were close to him.

He forgot that he was ageing, that he was no longer the romantic lover. He was excited. Pretending to be young again, going forth to meet the lady of Holbein's miniature and to sweep her off her feet with his passionate courtship. He had brought a gift for his bride: the finest sables in the kingdom to be made into a muff or a tippet.

It was at Rochester where they met. Unable to curb his impatience any longer, my father rode out to meet her cavalcade. He sent his Master of Horse, Anthony Browne, on ahead to tell Anne that he was there and wanted to give her a New Year's present.

I wished that I had seen that first meeting. I will say this in his favour. He did not convey to her immediately his complete and utter disappointment. He curbed his anger and made a show of courtesy. But she must have known. She was never a fool.

I did hear that, when he left her, he gave vent to his anger. There were plenty who heard it and were ready to report it. He was utterly shocked. The woman he saw was not in the least like Holbein's miniature, he complained. Where was that rose-tinted skin? Hers was pitted with smallpox scars. She was big, and he did not like big women. She was supposed to be twenty-four, but she looked more like thirty. Her features were heavy, and she was without that alluring femininity which so appealed to his nature.

He did not stay long with her. It would have been too much to keep up the pretence of welcome when all the time he wanted to shout out his disappointment.

Lord Russell, who witnessed the scene, said he had never seen anyone so astonished and abashed. As soon as he left her, his face turned purple with rage and he mumbled that he had never seen a lady so unlike what had been represented to him. 'I see nothing . . . nothing of what has been shown to me in her picture. I am ashamed that I have been so deceived and I love her not.'

He could not bring himself to give her the sables personally but, as he had mentioned a New Year's gift, he sent Sir Anthony Browne to give them to her.

Meanwhile he raged against all those who had deceived him. She was ugly; her very talk grated on his ears. He would never speak Dutch – and she had no English. They had brought him a great Flanders mare.

I wondered what she thought of him. His manners might have been courtly enough during that brief meeting; his voice was musical, though of a high pitch. But he was now overweight, lame and ageing; though he still had a certain charm; and he would always retain that aura of royal dignity.

It is well known now how my father tried to extricate himself, how he sought to prove that Anne had a pre-contract with the Duke of Lorraine and was therefore not free to marry.

Nothing could be proved. Anne swore that there had been no pre-contract. Glaring at Cromwell as though he would like to kill him, the King said: 'Is there none other remedy that I needs must, against my will, put my neck in this yoke?'

A few days after Anne's arrival, my father invested Philip of Bavaria with the Order of the Garter. It was a moving ceremony, and Philip looked very handsome and dignified. I was proud of him. People commented on his good looks and his reputation for bravery. I was learning more about him. He was called 'Philip the Warlike' because he had defended his country some years before against the Turk and scored a great victory. And . . . I was liking him more every day.

There were many opportunities of meeting him, and

Margaret Bryan said I was fortunate. It was not many royal princesses who had the blessing to fall in love with their husband before their marriage.

Margaret was now looking after Edward and, as she had Elizabeth with her, she was happy. Moreover, my position had improved so considerably that she no longer felt the anxieties she once had with her charges.

How I wished that the Countess could be with me! I should have loved to visit her in the Tower and take some comforts to her, but that of course was out of the question. I could not get news of her, much as I tried. She was constantly in my thoughts though.

Young Edward's household was at this time at Havering-atte-Bower. He was quite a serious little boy, already showing an interest in books. He adored Elizabeth, who was so different from himself. Full of vitality, she was so merry and constantly dancing; she was imperious and demanded Edward's attention, which he gave willingly.

'You should see his little face light up when his sister comes in,' said Margaret fondly.

I did see what she meant. There was that quality about Elizabeth.

I was happy to be part of this family, scattered as it was, and living, as I often thought, on the edge of disaster. Neither Elizabeth nor I knew when we would be in or out of favour.

The New Year was a pleasant one, apart from those recurring memories of the Countess and a slight apprehension about my prospective bridegroom and his heresy . . . though I had to admit that, so charming was he, I was lulling myself into an acceptance of that. I would convert him to the true Faith, I promised myself, which helped me indulge in daydreams of what marriage with him would be like.

I enjoyed being with the family that Christmas and New Year.

Elizabeth was always short of clothes, and Margaret was in a state of resentment about this; she was constantly asking for garments for her and grew very angry when there was no response. So, for a New Year's gift, I gave the child a yellow satin kirtle. It had been rather costly but I was glad I had not stinted in any way when I saw how delighted she was. I have never known anyone express her feelings so openly as Elizabeth did. Her joy was spontaneous. She held the kirtle up to her small body and danced round the room with it. Edward watched her and clapped his hands; and Margaret fell into a chair laughing.

For Edward I had a crimson satin coat, embroidered with gold thread and pearls. He was just past two at this time and a rather solemn child, completely overpowered by Elizabeth. Elizabeth declared the coat was magnificent. She made him put it on and, taking his hands, danced with him round the chamber.

Margaret watched with some apprehension. Everyone was perpetually worried that Edward might exert himself too much. If he had a slight cold they were all in a panic. They feared the King's wrath if anything should happen to this precious child.

Elizabeth was very interested to hear about the new Queen.

'I want to meet her,' she said. 'She is, after all, my stepmother, is she not? I should meet her.'

I often wondered how much she knew. She was only a child – not seven years old yet; but there was something very mature beneath the gaiety – watchful almost. She was certainly no ordinary six-year-old.

When I was alone with Margaret, she told me that Elizabeth had begged her to ask her father's permission to see the new Queen. The King had replied that the Queen was so different from her own mother that she ought not to wish to see her; but she might write to Her Majesty.

And had she done this? I asked Margaret.

'She never misses an opportunity. I have the letter here but I have not sent it yet. I suppose it is all right to send it as she has the King's permission; but I should like you to see it and consider that it is the work of a child not yet seven years old.'

She produced the letter.

'Madam,' Elizabeth had written, 'I am struggling between two contending wishes – one, my impatient desire to see Your Majesty, the other that of rendering the obedience I owe to the King, my father, which prevents me from leaving my house until he has given me permission to do so. But I hope that I shall shortly be able to gratify both these desires. In the meantime, I entreat Your Majesty to permit me to show, by this billet, the zeal with which I devote my respect to you as my Queen, and my entire obedience to you as my mother. I am too young and too feeble to have power to do more than felicitate you with all my heart in this commencement of your marriage. I hope that Your Majesty will have as much good will for me as I have zeal for your service . . .'

It was hard to believe that one so young could have written such a letter.

'Surely someone helped her,' I said.

'No . . . no . . . it is not so. She would be too impatient. She thinks she knows best.'

I marvelled with Lady Bryan but she told me that she had ceased to be surprised at Elizabeth's cleverness.

Later, when they did meet, Anne was completely charmed. I daresay she had been eager to meet the six-year-old writer of that letter. Her affection for the child was immediate, and she told me that if the Princess Elizabeth had been her daughter, it would have given her greater happiness than being Queen. Of course, being Queen brought her little happiness, but she did mean that she had a very special feeling for Elizabeth, and as soon as she was acknowledged as my father's wife she had the girl seated opposite her at table and accompanying her at all the entertainments.

It was decreed that I should spend some time with her. I was to talk to her in English and try to instruct her in that language. I should acquaint her with our customs. This I did and came to know her very well; I grew fond of her and, during that time when she was wondering what would become of her, because it was quite clear that she did not please the King, having suffered myself, I could sympathize with her.

I was wondering whether my father would actually marry her. But there was no way out. It had been proved that Anne had entered into no contract with any man and therefore was perfectly free. My father's three previous wives were all dead. There was no impediment.

My father must have been the most reluctant bridegroom in the world. He said to Cromwell just before the ceremony: 'My lord, if it were not to satisfy the world and my realm, I would not do what I have to do this day for any earthly thing.'

Words which boded no good to Cromwell, who had been responsible for getting him into this situation – nor to his poor Queen, who was the victim of it.

I was present at the wedding. My father looked splendid in his satin coat, puffed and embroidered and with its clasp of enormous diamonds; and he had a jewelled collar about his neck. But even the jewels could not distract from his gloomy countenance.

Anne was equally splendid in cloth of gold embroidered with pearls; her long flaxen hair was loose about her shoulders.

And so the marriage was celebrated.

There was feasting afterwards. I soon learned that the marriage had not been consummated. It was common knowledge, for the King made no secret of it. In his own words, he had no heart for it, and he was already looking for means of ridding himself of Anne.

Because I was close to her at that time, I knew of her anxieties. The King was no longer trying to hide the revulsion she aroused in him. She was quite different from all his other wives. She was not learned like my mother; she was not witty and clever like Anne; she was not pretty and docile like Jane.

I sensed the speculation in the air. What did he do with wives when he wanted to be rid of them? Would he dare submit her to the axe? On what pretext? He was adept at finding reasons for his actions. Was her brother, the Duke of Cleves, powerful enough to protect her? Hardly, when the Emperor Charles had not been able to save his aunt.

I knew what it felt like to live under the threat of the axe. I myself had done so for a number of years. We were none of us safe in these times.

When we sat together over our needlework, she would ask me questions about the King's previous wives. I talked to her a little about my mother, and it was amazing to me that there could be such sympathy between us, because she was a Lutheran; yet this made little difference to our friendship.

I think she was most interested in my mother and Anne Boleyn – the two discarded wives. Jane had not reigned long enough for her to meet disaster; and she had been the only one to produce a son. I knew what was in her mind. The King wanted to be rid of her, and we had examples of what he did with unwanted wives.

At times there was a placidity about her, as though she were prepared for some fearful fate and would accept it stoically; at others I glimpsed terror.

There was something else I noticed. It was at table. There was a young girl there – very pretty, with laughing eyes and a certain provocative way with her, and the King often had his eyes on her.

I asked one of the women who she was.

'She's the old Duchess of Norfolk's granddaughter, Catharine Howard.'

'She is very attractive.'

'Yes . . . in a way,' said the other.

I thought if she was related to the Howards she must be a connection of Anne Boleyn. There was something about these Howard women.

I put the matter out of my mind. After all, the King had always had an eye for a certain type of woman.

I did not realize then how great was my father's passion for this girl. She was small, young and childlike – very pretty in a sensuous way, with doe-like eyes and masses of curly hair. There was a look of expectancy about her, a certain promise, which I understood later when I learned something of what her life had been.

As for Anne of Cleves, she had none of that quality about her at all; she was pleasant-looking; she was tall, of course, and perhaps a little ungainly; her features were a trifle heavy, but her eyes were a beautiful brown, and I thought her flaxen hair charming.

However, my father would have none of her, and his growing passion for Catharine Howard made him determined to be rid of her.

They were uneasy days. Philip had gone back to Bavaria after taking a loving farewell and telling me we should soon be together. I was sorry to see him go. I had liked to have him near me. I had had so little of that attention he bestowed on me, and it made me feel attractive and desirable like other women; and as one day I planned to convert him back to the true Faith, I was able to still my conscience about his religious views.

Cromwell was created Earl of Essex in April. I wondered why, for my father was blaming him more and more for his marriage.

Politics were changing, too. Chapuys told me with some

amusement that my father's interest in the German princes was waning, and he was veering now towards the Emperor. My cousin was a man of whom my father was afraid more than of anyone else – and with good reason, too. Charles was proving himself to be the most astute monarch in Europe; his power was increasing, and it was not good to be on bad terms with him. My mother being dead meant that there was no great reason for contention between them. I was being treated with a certain respect, so there was no quarrel on that score. Of course, the Emperor would not approve of my betrothal to Philip of Bavaria any more than he had liked the alliance with Cleves, but my father did not like it either – so he and the Emperor were in agreement about that.

Who had forged the German alliance? Cromwell. Who had brought the King a bride he disliked? The same.

The King had never liked Cromwell, and, like Wolsey's, Cromwell's swift rise from humble origins had angered many at Court; moreover, Cromwell's enemies were as numerous as those who had helped Wolsey to his fall.

There were two things my father ardently desired: to rid himself first of all of his wife, and secondly of Cromwell. And those who looked for favours would help him to attain both those ends.

The alliance with the petty German princes had been a mistake; and Cromwell had made that mistake. He had, it was said, received bribes; he had given out commissions without the King's knowledge; he had trafficked in heretical books. There was rumour that he had considered marrying me and setting himself up as king, an idea which shocked me considerably, even though I did not, for one moment, believe it.

He was tried, and as all those present knew what verdict the King wanted, they gave it.

I was horrified. Whatever else Cromwell had done, he had worked well for the King. It appalled me that he could have come to this. I knew that Cromwell's vital mistake was to have arranged the marriage with Anne of Cleves. But was it his fault that her physical appearance did not please the King?

I felt sorry for the man . . . to have risen so high and to fall so low. There was only one to say a good word for him and that was Cranmer. Cranmer, though, was not a bold man. He asked the King for leniency but was abruptly told to be silent, and immediately he obeyed.

Cromwell languished in prison, not knowing whether he would be beheaded or burned at the stake. He did implore the King to have mercy, but my father was intent on one thing, and that was to bring his marriage to Anne of Cleves to an end.

Norfolk was sent to visit Cromwell in the Tower, and there Cromwell revealed to him the content of several conversations he had had with the King disclosing intimate details of the latter's relationship with Anne of Cleves which made it clear that the marriage had not been consummated.

As a result it was declared null and void.

I was with Anne at Richmond when the deputation arrived. She went to the window and saw Norfolk at the head of it. She turned very pale.

'They have come for me,' she said. 'They have come as they came for Anne Boleyn.'

I stood beside her, watching the deputation disembark at the stairs and come towards the palace.

'You should leave me,' she said.

I took her hand and pressed it firmly. 'I will stay with you,' I told her.

'No, no. It is better not. They would not allow it . . . Better to leave me.'

I knew her thoughts. She was seeing herself walking out to Tower Green as her namesake had done before her. She

255

must have thought during the last months of this possibility, and she had considered it with a certain calm, but when it was close . . . seeming almost inevitable, she felt, I believe, that she was looking death straight in the face.

I could see that my presence distracted her. So I kissed her gently and left.

I learned that when the deputation was presented to her, she fainted.

* * *

They had gone.

I went to her apartments. I had already heard of the faint and was surprised when she greeted me with exuberance.

'I am thanking God,' she said.

'But you were ill . . .'

'I am well now. I am no longer the Queen.'

I stared at her, as she began to laugh. 'I . . .' she spluttered. 'I am the King's sister!'

I could see that she needed to recover from the shock she had suffered when the deputation had arrived, for she had been sure they had come to conduct her to the Tower. But no . . . they had come to tell her that she was no longer the King's wife. In future she would be known as his sister.

'How can this be?' I asked.

'With the King,' she said, still hovering between laughter and tears, 'they do anything he wishes. I was his queen and now he has made me his sister. How can that be? you ask me. It can be because he says it is so.'

'And you . . . you are safe.'

She gripped my hands, and I knew how great her fear had been.

'I am no longer the King's wife,' she said soberly. 'And that is something to be very happy about. Ah, I must be careful. They would call that treason. But you will not betray me, dear Mary.'

'Be calm, Anne,' I said. 'You have been so wonderfully calm till now.'

'It is the relief,' she replied. 'I did not know how much I wanted to live. Think of it! I am free. I do not have to try to please him. I wear what I like. I am myself. I am his sister. He is no longer my husband. Can you imagine what that is like?'

'Yes,' I told her. 'I believe I can.'

'That poor woman . . . think of her . . . in her prison in the Tower, waiting for the summons . . . waiting for death . . . she was Anne . . . as I am. I know what it is like.'

'I understand, too.'

'Then you rejoice with me.'

'I rejoice,' I told her.

'I am to have a residence of my own and £3,000 a year. Think of that.'

'And he has agreed to this?'

'Yes . . . yes . . . to be rid of me. If only he knew how I longed for him to be rid of me. Three thousand a year to live my own life. Oh, I am drunk on happiness. He is no longer my husband. There is a condition. I am not to leave England.' She laughed loudly. 'Well if I tell you the truth, my dear Mary, it is that I do not want to leave England.'

'Shall you be content to stay here always?'

'I think so.'

'He does not want you to go out of England for fear you marry some foreign prince who will say you are Queen of England and have a right to the throne.'

She laughed again. 'I am happy here. I have my little family . . . my sweet Elizabeth and you, dear Mary. To be a mother to you, Elizabeth and the little boy . . . that is to me greater happiness than to be a queen.'

I never saw a woman so content to be rid of a husband as Anne of Cleves was. My father was at first delighted by her mild acceptance of her state, but later he began to feel a little piqued at her enjoyment of her new role. However, by this time he was so enamoured of Catharine Howard that he could not give much thought to Anne of Cleves.

The alliance with the German princes was at an end; and that meant that there was no question of a betrothal to Philip of Bavaria.

* * *

The year 1540 was a terrible one for death. My father was filled with rage against those who defied him. He was probably worried now and then about the enormity of what he had done; it was not only that he had denied the Pope's supremacy and set himself up in his place in England; he had suppressed the monasteries and taken their wealth. His rule became more despotic and those about him obeyed without question, anticipated his desires and did everything possible to avoid offending him. But it was different with the people; and when those men who called themselves holy had the effrontery to deny him and to suggest that he was not the head of his own country's Church, his rage overflowed.

He wanted vengeance and would have it. Respected men were submitted to humiliating and barbarous torture on the scaffold, men who, the people knew, had led blameless lives, like Robert Barnes the divine and Thomas Abell, were submitted to this horrible death with many others.

I thought of these things and shuddered. My father had indeed changed. Where was the merry monarch now? He was irritable, and the pain in his leg sometimes sent him into maddened rages.

When I heard that Dr Featherstone had been treated in the same manner, I was deeply distressed and I was glad that my mother was not alive, for she would have been very distressed if she knew what was happening to her old chaplain. He had taught me when I was a child, and I could well remember his quiet kindliness and his pleasure when I learned my lessons. I could not bear to think of such a man being submitted to that torture. And all because he had refused to take the Oath of Supremacy. How I admired those brave men, and how I deplored the fact that it was my father who murdered them.

People were burned at the stake in such numbers that in the streets of London one could not escape from the smell of martyrs' flesh and the sight of martyrs' bodies hanging in chains to feed the carrion crows.

Rebellion was at the heart of it. My father had broken with Rome but that did not mean he was no longer a Catholic. The old religion remained; the only difference was that he was head of the Church instead of the Pope. He wanted no Lutheran doctrines introduced into England. People must watch their steps . . . particularly those in vulnerable positions. I was one of those.

Cromwell lost his head on the very day my father married Catharine Howard; that changed him for a while. How he doted on the child . . . she was little more. They looked incongruous side by side – this ageing man with the purple complexion and the bloodshot eyes, fleshy and irascible, biting his lips till the blood came when the fistula in his leg pained him. And she . . . that dainty little creature with her wide-eyed innocence which seemed somehow knowledgeable, with her curls springing and feet dancing, a child in her teens . . . and yet not a child, a creature of overwhelming allure for an ageing, disappointed man.

But he was disappointed no longer; he was rejuvenated; he had regained something of his old physical energy: he was dotingly, besottedly in love.

I felt sickened by it. I remembered his treatment of my mother and Anne of Cleves; to those two worthy women he had behaved with the utmost cruelty, and yet, here he was, like a young lover, unable to take his eyes from this pretty, frivolous little creature whose doe's eyes had secrets behind them.

A horrifying incident happened that year. I shall never

forget my feelings when I heard. Susan, whom, happily, I had been able to keep with me, came to me one day. I guessed she had something terrible to tell me and was hesitating as to whether it would be better to do so or keep me in the dark.

I prevailed on her to tell me. I think I knew beforehand whom it must concern because she looked so tragic.

'My lady,' she said when I insisted, 'you must prepare yourself for a shock.' She looked at me with great compassion.

I stared at her, and then my lips formed the words: 'The . . . Countess . . . what of the Countess?'

She was silent. I tried to calm myself.

She said: 'It had to come. It is a wonder it did not come before.'

'Tell me,' I begged. 'She is dead . . . is she not?'

'She had been suffering all these months in the Tower. She was wretched there. It is best for her. Cold, miserable, lacking comfort. Heartbroken . . . grieving for her sons . . .'

'If only I could have gone to her.'

Susan shook her head. 'There was nothing you could have done.'

'Only pray for her,' I said.

'And that you did.'

'I always mentioned her in my prayers. Why . . . why? What had she done? She was innocent of treason.'

'That insurrection of Sir John Neville . . . such things upset the King.'

'I know. He wants the people to love him.'

'Love must be earned,' said Susan quietly.

I went on: 'But there have been so many deaths . . . so much slaughter . . . fearful, dreadful deaths. And the Countess . . . what had she done?'

'She was a Plantagenet . . .'

I covered my face with my hands as though to shut out

260

the sight of her. I could see her clearly, walking out of her cell to East Smithfield Green, which is just within the Tower precincts.

'She was very brave, I know,' I said.

'She did not die easily,' Susan told me.

'I would I had been with her.'

'You would never have borne it.'

'And she died with great courage. She . . . who had done no harm to any. She who had had the misfortune to be born royal.'

'Hush,' said Susan. 'People listen at times like this.'

'Times like these, Susan. Terrible . . . wicked times. Did she mention me?'

'She was thinking of you at the end. You were as a daughter to her.'

'She wanted me to be her daughter in truth . . . through Reginald.'

'Hush, my lady,' said Susan again, glancing over her shoulder.

I wanted to cry out: I care not. Let them take me. Let them try *me* for treason. They have come near enough to it before now.

'She did mention you. She asked all those watching to pray for the King and Queen, Prince Edward . . . and she wanted her god-daughter, the Princess Mary, to be specially commended.'

'So she was thinking of me right to the end.'

'You can be sure of it.'

'How did my dear Countess die?'

Susan was silent.

'Please tell me,' I begged. 'I want to hear of it from you. I shall learn of it later.'

'The block was too low, and the executioner was unaccustomed to wielding the axe.'

'Oh . . . no!'

'Do not grieve. It is over now, but several blows were needed before the final one.'

'Oh, my beloved Countess. She was my second mother, the one who shared my sorrows and my little triumphs during those early years. Always she had been there, comforting me, wise and kind . . .'

I could not bear the thought of her dear body being slaughtered by a man who did not know how to wield an axe.

All through the years I had not seen her I had promised myself that we should meet one day.

The realization that we never should again on Earth filled me with great sorrow and a dreadful foreboding. How close to death we all were.

* * *

My father was in a merry mood those days. He was delighted with his fifth wife. He watched her every movement, and he did not like her to be out of his sight. He took a great delight in her merry chatter. I thought she was rather silly.

When I remembered my father's turning from my mother, from Anne of Cleves, even from Anne Boleyn, I marvelled. All of them were endowed with qualities which this silly little girl completely lacked. Yet it was on her that his doting eyes turned again and again.

Queen of England she might be, but I could not treat her with respect. To me she was just a frivolous girl. It could only have been her youth which appealed to him. He was fifty and she was about seventeen; and he was desperately trying to share in the radiant youth which was hers.

I was five years older than she was. I wonder now why it was that I disliked her so much. She was mild enough, and I daresay if I had shown some affection she would have returned it. She was stupid; her education had been neglected, although she was the daughter of Sir Edmund

Howard, a younger son of the Duke of Norfolk. He had been the hero of Flodden Field but his services to his country had never been recognized and consequently he was desperately poor. There were ten children and it was a strain on his resources to care for such a large family and he was constantly trying to elude his creditors. He was, therefore, glad to send young Catharine off to her grandmother to be brought up in that rather disreputable household – which was what set her on the road to disaster.

But that was to come. At this time, there she was . . . the uneducated little girl who had suddenly found herself the King's petted consort, his little Queen.

It was not that she gave herself airs. She certainly did not. She was just overwhelmed by all that had happened to her. She behaved like a child but she was quite experienced in certain ways of the world, as was to be revealed. I realized – only, I must admit, later, when I knew something of her past – that she was a girl of lusty sexual appetites and even if her good sense – of which she had very little – had warned her that she must not act in a certain way, she would have been unable to resist doing so.

I suppose she was just the girl to appeal to the jaded senses of an ageing man who had been bitterly disillusioned in his hopes of a beautiful bride.

I was surprised that she was aware of my dislike. I should have thought she was not intelligent enough to sense it. It was not a habit of hers to complain, but she did about my attitude to her, so she must have felt it deeply.

My father was annoyed that I had offended his little darling.

He said of me: 'It is those women about her. She has too many of those whispering cronies. There is too much chatter in those apartments . . . too much brooding on this and that and rights and wrongs. She shall be taught a lesson.'

The lesson was to rob me of two of my women.

I was angry. I was fond of the women about me, and ours was a very happy household. I needed all the friends I could get. Fortunately Susan remained with some others of my closest comrades, but I did miss those two who were sent away.

I was about to protest when Chapuys came to see me.

'You must patch up this quarrel with the Queen,' he said.

'That stupid little creature!'

He laughed. 'She pleases the King.' He gave a little smirk. 'They say he has never been so pleased since he set eyes on the girl's cousin all those years ago. There must be a similarity to Anne Boleyn there.'

'Anne Boleyn was a clever woman,' I said. 'This one is a fool.'

'None the less, one must beware of fools if they have power.'

'This one has power?'

'Through her devoted lover, of course. You are not entirely out of favour with the Court. Don't forget. You are next . . . after Edward.'

'Edward is so young.'

Chapuys looked at me slyly. 'Who can say?' he murmured. 'However, there must be no further estrangement between you and your father, and there will be if you continue to offend the Queen.'

'I did not think to offend her.'

'Yet you have shown disrespect for her in some way.'

'She is so silly.'

'Silly to you, but delectable to His Majesty, and it is His Majesty who has the power over us, remember. Find some means of making up the quarrel. The breach between you must not widen.'

I saw his point. There was always sound thinking behind Chapuys' words.

It was not difficult. When I was next in her presence, I

264

admired her gown. She flashed her smile at me. She was really very pretty, and she had been so unused to having beautiful clothes that she was childishly delighted with her wardrobe. I admired her beautiful curls.

A few days after I had spoken to her, I made some progress. I learned that, while the Countess was in the Tower, Catharine had sent some clothes to her; and because his wife had wished it so ardently, the King had allowed her to do this.

I think that helped matters a great deal between us.

I mentioned to her that I knew she had done this, and I wanted to thank her for it.

'I heard that she was to die,' she said, 'and it seemed terrible in that cold place. I hate the cold. It was cold in my grandmother's house in winter . . . and we were so poor, I hadn't any warm clothes . . . and I thought of the poor Countess . . .'

I said with feeling: 'It was so good of you. I wanted to thank you for what you did . . .'

She gave me her dazzling smile.

'I sent her a nightgown of worsted, furred and lined . . . and I sent her some hose and shoes.'

'It was so kind . . . so very kind . . .'

'You loved her dearly,' said the Queen softly.

I nodded, too moved for words.

'She took the place of your mother. I had my grandmother . . . but she never took much notice of me.'

'Thank you, Your Majesty,' I said. 'Thank you from the bottom of my heart for what you did for the Countess.'

It was the first time I had brought myself to call her 'Your Majesty'. There were tears in her eyes; she was easily moved. I could not really like her or feel close to her as I had to Jane and Anne, but I knew she was goodhearted and generous, and if she was a little stupid, it was not for me to be annoyed because she had wormed her way into my father's affections.

After my speaking to her of the Countess, we were on better terms and I felt my relationship with her should no longer cause Chapuys any anxiety.

The King might be in a state of euphoria now that he had found the perfect wife, but the country was still in turmoil. It was when Sir John Neville had headed a revolt in the North that my father had decided that the Countess must die. The country was now more or less split into two. There were those who wanted to cling to Rome and those who saw the advantage of a break; there were those for the King and those against him. But the issue was not as clear cut as that. The Protestant Church had begun to grow, and there were some in England who were ready to embrace it. The King was not one of these. The break with Rome did not mean a break with the old religion; all the King wanted was to give the Church in England a new head. That was all he sought. It was due to the rival factions that the King had his great power, for neither was big enough to overcome the other, and the King stood apart from them and yet remained the great despotic ruler. It seemed strange that there had been two living Queens, Katharine and Anne; and now we were left with two different queens with similar names. There would be many people in the country who believed that, since the King had gone through a ceremony of marriage with Anne of Cleves, his marriage with Catharine Howard was no true marriage – just as in the days when my mother was alive, some had believed he could not be married to Anne Boleyn.

The tangle of his matrimonial affairs would be discussed for many a year, and I suspected there would always be different opinions. He was aware of this, and it irritated him . . . just as did the conflict in his realm which had in so many ways resulted from his involvement with his wives.

My father was infuriated by rebellion. He wanted his people to love him and when they showed signs of not doing so, he was more hurt than alarmed.

The John Neville rebellion had enraged him. He uttered threats against Reginald Pole – that devilish mischief-maker, as he called him – roaming the Continent stirring up trouble. He gnashed his teeth because he could not lay his hands on him and do to him what he had done to other members of his family.

He decided to go to Yorkshire to settle matters for himself. The Council he left in London to take care of affairs was well chosen – Cranmer, Audley and one of Jane Seymour's brothers – all men who accepted the King's supremacy in the Church and enemies of Rome.

Seymour had gained a good deal of power; not only was he the brother of the King's late wife – the only one not to be discarded – but also the uncle of Edward, the future King. I think the Howards were casting suspicious eyes on the Seymours, as undoubtedly the Seymours were on the Howards. The Howards were at the moment in the ascendancy, having just provided the delectable Catharine for the King's pleasure.

Chapuys had said we must be watchful of the growing power of the Seymours and the Howards.

Everywhere on his travels the King was received with acclaim. How much of it was genuine, I did not know. The people had seen so many dead men hanging in chains; they had caught a whiff of the smell of burning flesh. They would be careful how they acted towards this powerful monarch.

Meanwhile my father became more and more enamoured of his Queen. He was an uxorious, adoring husband; she soothed him and pleased him in every way. If only his people would stop being contentious, he remarked, he could be a very contented man.

It is strange how one does not recognize important events when they occur. The Court was at Pontefract Castle when Catharine admitted a new secretary into her household.

This was a good-looking young man of rather dashing appearance. His name was Francis Dereham.

Poor Catharine! She would have been quite unaware of the storms which were blowing up around her. She would know nothing of the intrigues which were commonplace in the life of the Court. She was the adored Queen of an ageing King; she would not have believed that any harm could come to her.

She did not know that there were men watching the King's besotted attitude towards her; she did not know that the Catholic Howards were rubbing their hands with glee; she did not guess that the ambitious Protestant Seymour brothers were furiously noticing the King's devotion to the Howard Queen. The Seymours had risen from obscurity because their sister had married the King; now it was the turn of the Norfolk Howards.

It could not go on.

By the time the Court returned to Windsor, the plot was in progress. From Windsor the Court went to Hampton Court, and it was there that the storm broke.

I joined my brother's household at Sion, where Elizabeth was also. It was ironic but the day we arrived – it was the 30th of October, I remember – the King and Queen went to church to receive the sacrament, and my father made a declaration in the church. There were many to hear it, and it expressed his utter contentment with the Queen.

'I render, O Lord, thanks to Thee,' he announced in ringing tones at the altar, 'that after so many strange accidents that have befallen my marriages, Thou hast been pleased to give me a wife so entirely conformed to my inclination as her that I have now.'

How many wives had received such public acclamation of their virtues? She stood beside him, smiling with pleasure, acting in just the way he wished her to. He was a man of some intellect, a man of foresight, and of all the clever women who surrounded him it was this nonentity who pleased him!

Of course, he had always been one to deceive himself. Therein lay his weakness. He had a conscience but that conscience worked according to his will, so he was completely in control of it. He saw everything in the light of what good it could bring to Henry Tudor. And this little girl who said 'Yes, my lord,' 'Yes, my lord', all the time, who titillated his ageing senses and aroused in him the desire of a young man pleased him because he drew on her dazzling youth and felt young again.

How deeply he must have felt about her for, having made that public declaration at the altar, he asked the Bishop of Lincoln to prepare a public ceremony. It would be a thanksgiving to Almighty God for having at last blessed him with a loving, dutiful and virtuous wife.

Fate is ironic. It was the very next day when the blow was delivered.

Susan told me about it.

'The King was in the chapel, my lady. The Queen was not with him. It may be that that was why Cranmer chose that moment. He handed a paper to the King and begged him to read it when he was alone.'

'Why? What was in this paper?'

'They say that it is accusing the Queen of lewd behaviour before her marriage.'

I was astounded, yet I suddenly realized what it was about her that I had noticed. It was wrapped up in the fascination she had for the King. Of course, she was pretty – but so were others; there was something more than that about Mistress Catharine Howard. She was lusty, and lustiness such as she had, accompanied by fresh, youthful, dainty prettiness was irresistible. Before anything was proved, I guessed the accusations against her were true.

'What do they say?' I asked.

'That she had lovers.'

269

'They will never prove it. The King won't believe it.'

'The King, they say, is very unhappy.'

'Then if he does not want to believe it, he will not.'

'It may not be as easy as that. There are strong men surrounding him . . . determined men.'

'So you think it is a matter of politics?'

'Is that not generally the case?'

I had to agree.

We waited for news. These cunning men had collected evidence against her. They could produce her lovers; they had an account of what her life had been like in the household of the Dowager Duchess of Norfolk. There were young people . . . all sleeping together in one large room, living intimately. The Dowager Duchess herself was too old or too lazy to care what was happening to her wayward granddaughter. A girl like Catharine Howard, brought up in such a household, could hardly be expected to emerge as an innocent maiden.

I had not liked her and I had thought my father had demeaned himself by doting on her so blatantly. Perhaps I was angry because he had treated my own mother so shamefully, humiliating a great princess of Spain and becoming so foolishly enslaved by this ill-bred little girl. But when I heard the state the poor child was in and how she had taken the news, I felt an overwhelming pity for her.

She had almost gone into a frenzy. She had seen the axe hanging over her head. It was what all my father's wives must have felt when they offended him. The ghost of Anne Boleyn would haunt them all as long as they lived.

And this one was really only a child, in spite of her knowledge of the needs of men. She would not know how to defend herself. She would only think of what had happened to her own beautiful, clever cousin who had found herself in a position similar to that which now confronted her. The difference might be that Anne Boleyn had been innocent; but was Catharine Howard? On the other hand, the King had wished to be rid of Anne that he might marry Jane Seymour. He certainly did not wish to be rid of Catharine Howard.

The shadow of the axe would hang over every bride of my father's from the day of her wedding. Catharine must have felt secure in his love – so petted, so pampered, she was the pretty little thing who knew so well how to please. Had it never occurred to him that she might have learned her tricks through practice?

They told me about her, how she had babbled in her anguish, how she had worked herself up to a frenzy and to such an extent that they feared for her sanity.

How could she help it? Poor girl, she was so young, so full of life. She enjoyed life to such an extent that she could not bear the thought of having it snatched from her.

She believed, naturally, that if she could speak to the King, if she could cajole him, if she could, by her presence, remind him of the happiness she had brought him and still could . . . he would save her. He would cherish her still. But the wicked men would not allow her to see him. They would keep them apart because they knew that, if she could but speak to him for a moment, this nightmare for her would be over.

They said that when she heard he was in the Hampton Court chapel she ran along the gallery calling his name. But they stopped her before she reached him. They dragged her back to her chamber and set guards on her so that the King should not be aware of her terrible distress. They must have believed, as she did, that if he saw her, he would forgive her.

Susan and I discussed the matter. I suppose everyone was discussing it.

We learned many things about the life Catharine Howard had lived before the King set eyes on her and made her his Queen. We heard details of the establishment of the

Dowager Duchess of Norfolk, of the young people who had been under her care . . . only there was no care.

It was a sordid little story. I could picture it all . . . the long dormitory, those high-spirited young people. For a girl of Catharine's temperament there would be temptations, and she was not a girl to resist them. Therein lay her great attraction. There would have been many to enjoy what had so pleased the King.

I remembered that she had taken Francis Dereham into her household at Pontefract. What a little fool she was to do so. She was foolish not to see the danger which would have been obvious to a more worldly person. Her knowledge of sexual adventuring might be great but she had no understanding of human nature. It would never occur to her that, for some to see the little Catharine Howard – the poor girl who had scarcely been able to clothe herself – now revelling in the silks and satins which she loved, would arouse great envy, and envy is a most destructive passion.

It all came out . . . the flirtations with Manox, the musician, the familiarities she allowed Francis Dereham, who wanted to marry her and claimed her as his wife. It had been as though they were married. And she, as Queen, had brought this man, the lover of her humbler self, into her household!

How easy it must have been to build up evidence against her!

There was one other case which was even more damning. Her cousin, Thomas Culpepper, was in the King's household, and many had noticed the soft looks which had passed between him and the Queen. It was soon discovered that there had been interviews between them when they had been alone in a room together.

Lady Rochford's name was mentioned as one who had helped arrange the meetings with Culpepper and to make sure that the pair were not disturbed during them.

I had never liked Lady Rochford. The fact was that I

had never liked anyone connected with the Boleyn family overmuch. I had seen Anne Boleyn as the one who had killed my mother. I was not sure that she had plotted to poison her, but I felt she had killed her all the same; but for Anne Boleyn, my father would have remained married to my mother, and I believe she would have been alive still.

Lady Rochford had been the wife of George Boleyn, and it was she who had given credence to the story that he and Anne were lovers. I had never believed that, much as I hated them, and I had always wondered how a wife could give such evidence against her own husband. And now she was accused of helping to further an intrigue between the Queen and Thomas Culpepper. I believed that such a mischievous and unprincipled woman could do just that.

I wished I could go to my father and comfort him. Of course, I could never have done so.

I wondered how deep his affection went and whether it would be strong enough to save her. She had pleased him so much. He had recently given thanks to God for providing him with a wife whom he could love. Surely he would not want to lose her, merely because she had had a lover – or two . . . or three – before her marriage to him? I sometimes felt an anger against men who, far from chaste themselves, expect absolute purity in their wives. If Catharine had not had some experience before her marriage, how could she have been the mistress of those arts which seemed to please him so much?

I wondered what he would do. I did not talk of this to Susan. I feared I would be too frank about him. He was my father and he was the King. I thought about him a great deal. I had seen him in his moods, when he was preoccupied with his conscience. I had judged him in my mind but I could not do that before others. So I said nothing of these intimate matters.

Susan said one day: 'They have arrested Dereham.'

So, I thought, it has started. He will not save her. His

273

pride will have been too hurt. He did not love her more than his own pride.

'On what charge?' I asked.

'Piracy,' she replied. 'He was involved in that in Ireland where he had gone to make his fortune, some say, that he might come back and marry Catharine Howard.'

I nodded. I knew what would happen. They would question him, and he would be persuaded to answer them. Persuaded? In what way? How strong was he? I had thought him a dashing fellow – but one can never tell who can stand up against the rack.

We heard later that he confessed that, when they were together in the Duchess's household, the Queen had promised to marry him. They had thought of themselves as husband and wife, and others had considered them as such; they had exchanged love-tokens. They had lived together in the Duchess's household as husband and wife.

They tried to force him to admit that when he returned and was taken into the Queen's household the relationship between them had been that which they had enjoyed in the Duchess's. This he stoutly denied. There had never been the slightest intimacy between him and Catharine since her marriage to the King.

We heard that the King shut himself in his apartments, that he had burst into tears, that he had raged against fate for ruining his marriage. There was great speculation. Would the King waive her early misdemeanours and take her back?

Even I, who knew him so well, was unsure of what he would do. I wished that I could have seen him, talked to him. I could imagine his tortured mind. He wanted to believe her innocent and on the other hand he wished to know the worst.

I think he might have relented. He could usually be relied on to adjust what he considered right with what he wanted; and he wanted Catharine Howard. There was no doubt of

274

that. I think he would have taken her back if it had not been for Culpepper.

It is not easy for people in high places to act and no one know what they are doing. Catharine had received Culpepper in her chamber, and Lady Rochford had helped her arrange the meetings.

It was all coming out. There were men like Thomas Wriothesley who were determined to ruin the Queen and make reconciliation with the King impossible.

How I hated that man! There was cruelty in him. He sought all the time to bring advantage to himself, and he cared not how he came by it.

All those connected with the early life of Catharine Howard were now in the Tower – even the poor Duchess of Norfolk, sick and ailing, and a very frightened old woman.

My father must have tortured himself. He could not believe that his dear little Queen, his 'rose without a thorn', could possibly have had a lover when she was his wife. That was something he found it hard to forgive. That was the charge he had brought against Anne Boleyn, but I think he never believed it. It was treason for a Queen to take a lover, for it meant that a bastard could be foisted on the nation. And the thought of that charming, passionate little creature going off to her lover – perhaps laughing at the King because he was no longer so young and lusty as Master Culpepper . . . was more than my father could bear.

He summoned Cranmer. 'Go to the Queen,' he said. 'Tell her that if she will acknowledge her transgression . . . even though her life might be forfeit to the law, I would extend to her my most gracious mercy.'

I understood his feelings. He had to know . . . though he did not want to.

Poor Catharine! I heard that when his message came to her she was almost out of her mind with fear. She was so terrified that the fate which her cousin had suffered would be hers. She was too distraught to speak; words would not come. Cranmer believed that if he questioned her she would go into a frenzy, so he said he would leave her with the King's gracious promise and when she had composed herself he would come back and hear her confession.

It was some time before she was ready to do that. Every time she was approached she was ready to fall into what they called a frenzy. They feared she was losing her senses. But in the end she was ready to talk.

She did admit that she had believed at one time that she was going to marry Francis Dereham. They had kissed many times.

She broke down and it was impossible to get any more information from her; when they attempted to, she became frenzied and was overcome with such terrible weeping that they feared she would do herself an injury.

Culpepper was the son of her uncle, and they had known each other since they were children; they had always been very friendly.

There were those who were ready to give evidence against her. They wanted to prove that she had been guilty of adultery. She had been reckless, indiscreet, there was no doubt of that.

A certain Katharine Tilney of her household told how she and another maid had wondered why the Queen sent strange, enigmatic messages to Lady Rochford and why sometimes they were dismissed before the Queen had retired. They reported secret whisperings with Lady Rochford and the fact that sometimes the Queen would not retire until two of the morning. Thomas Culpepper was seen in her apartments and Lady Rochford kept watch.

It was all very incriminating.

There was a hush over Sion House. Elizabeth, who was now nearly nine years old, was very concerned about what was happening. Could she be remembering how similar was the fate of this Queen to that of her mother? She had only been three years old when Anne Boleyn had been beheaded, but she had always been ahead of her years.

Edward was aware, too. He was always susceptible to Elizabeth's moods. There was a puzzled look on his face.

Elizabeth sought me out when I was alone and asked me what was happening to the Queen.

I said: 'She is in the Tower.'

'What are they going to do to her?'

'I don't know.'

'Will they kill her as they did . . .?' I looked at her steadily. She blinked and went on: 'As they did my mother?'

It was rarely that I heard her speak of her mother. What happened to Anne Boleyn was something she kept to herself and brooded on. Not even Margaret Bryan knew how she felt about her mother. Whether she remembered her and mourned her, I do not know. It was always difficult to tell with Elizabeth. Anne Boleyn was not a person who could be easily forgotten, and she was Elizabeth's mother.

'I like her,' she said. 'She is a sort of cousin to me.'

'Yes, I know.'

'She is very pretty.'

I nodded.

'My father loved her dearly.' She frowned. 'Why does he no longer do so? And what will happen to her now?'

I could only fall back on those often-repeated words: 'We shall have to wait and see.'

Edward came in. 'What are you talking about?' he asked.

'The Queen,' Elizabeth replied.

'Why don't we see her now? She is in disgrace, is she not?'

'She is in prison,' Elizabeth told him. 'In the Tower.'

'In the Tower. That is for wicked people.'

'The King puts his wives there when he doesn't like them any more,' said Elizabeth, and she turned away abruptly

277

and ran from the room. I think she was going to cry and did not want us to see her do so.

I thought: She does remember her mother. Perhaps also she was crying for Catharine. Elizabeth was resolute and strong and she had already come to terms with an uncertain existence such as we all must who relied on the favour of the King.

* * *

They were bringing Catharine to Sion House, and we had orders to move. We were going to Havering-atte-Bower. I was sad. I should have liked to be near the Queen. So would Elizabeth. We might have comforted her a little.

How sordid this was! How dreary! Why did they pursue it? It was clear that Catharine had behaved freely with certain men. They were tortured, but Dereham would admit only that he had loved Catharine as his wife because he had once regarded her as such. Was that a sin, for there was no question then of her marrying the King? He was a brave man, this Dereham; they tortured him cruelly and tried to make him admit that there had been impropriety between him and the Queen since her marriage, but he would not do so.

Catharine had denied any sexual involvement at first but after a while she broke down and confessed to it.

I know my father was suffering in his way. There was no proof that she had committed adultery in the case of Culpepper. I daresay she had flirted a little with him. It was in her nature to flirt with men – particularly those who admired her – and most did.

I went on wondering whether the King's obsession with her would override his pride. I think it might have done – and if it did, men like Sir Thomas Wriothesley and perhaps Cranmer would find themselves out of favour.

They had seen what happened to Thomas Cromwell over Anne of Cleves. He had died, it would seem, more because

278

he had provided the King with a bride he did not like than for the foreign policy he had pursued with the German princes and the charges which had been brought against him.

So there were powerful men who would find a reconciliation an embarrassment to themselves, and they made sure that the story of Catharine's misdemeanours was circulated abroad. François, King of France, for ever mischievous, wrote his condolences to his brother of England. That was the deciding factor. My father could not take back a wife who had humiliated him, however much he wanted her.

I wished that I could have gone to her. Elizabeth did, too. The child was deeply upset. She had been fond of Jane Seymour; she was even closer to Anne of Cleves; and now Catharine Howard was to die.

She became very thoughtful. I guessed she was thinking of the precarious lives we all led.

How brave they were, those two men. Neither Dereham nor Culpepper would implicate Catharine; and surely what had happened before her marriage could not be construed as treason. But the verdict had already been decided. Norfolk turned against his kinswoman just as he had against Anne Boleyn. He had wanted to make the most of the advantages which came from their being in favour, but as soon as they lost that favour he became their most bitter enemy. I despised such men – just as I had Thomas Boleyn for meekly presiding at the baptism of Edward. Self-seekers, all. They had no feeling, no heart. They made me despair of human nature.

That December Dereham and Culpepper were condemned to death. The court judged them traitors. The sentence was to be carried out with that barbarous method of execution which had been seen too frequently in these last years.

How did they feel when they – surely for no crime which could have been proved against them – were condemned to die? How did the Queen feel . . . if she knew? Poor girl. They said she was in such a state that she was hardly aware of what was happening about her.

Culpepper was of noble birth, and therefore the horrendous sentence would be commuted to beheading. So he, poor man, was merely to lose his head for a crime he had not committed. It was different with Dereham, whose birth did not entitle him to such a privilege. He must suffer the dreadful fate of hanging, drawing and quartering.

He petitioned against it, and the petition was taken to my father. He must have been enraged at the thought of someone's enjoying Catharine's charms before him. He should have known that she was not the girl to have come through her early life without some amatory adventures. If he had wanted an entirely chaste woman, he should have stayed with Anne of Cleves. He wanted everything to be perfect, and if it were not, those who denied it to him must pay with their lives.

So at Tyburn the terrible sentence was carried out on Dereham. He died protesting his innocence, as did Culpepper, who was beheaded at the same time.

The heads of both men were placed on London Bridge – a terrible warning to those who offended the King. People might ask how Dereham could possibly have known he was offending the King. Was no man to love a woman or to speak of marriage to her . . . for fear the King might fancy her?

Perhaps people were asking themselves a good many questions during those terrible times.

* * *

It was a miserable Christmas. I was glad I was not at Court. I could not imagine how my father could celebrate it. It would be a mockery. Catharine was still at Sion House. I wondered if she still thought the King would pardon her. The uncertainty must be terrible. I expect she had been fond of Dereham once; I believe she still was of Culpepper; and she would know that these two had died because of her. Doubtless she would have heard how they stood up to torture and had tried to defend her to the end.

February came – a dreary, desolate month. There was mist over the land until the cold, biting winds drove it away. They brought the Queen from Sion House to the Tower. I guessed that meant her death was inevitable.

I heard she was a little calmer now. She seemed to have accepted the fact that she was to die. Lady Rochford was in the Tower, condemned with her. She was accused of contriving meetings between Catharine and Culpepper; she was therefore guilty of treason.

I kept thinking of Catharine's youth. Such a short time she had been on Earth, and she had been such a merry creature, relishing life in the Duchess's household, revelling in that sexuality which pleased the men. And then the King's devotion, which, they said, she believed to the end would save her.

Susan and I talked of her. We could think of nothing else. I supposed the whole nation was talking of her. She would be the second of my father's wives to be beheaded – but that had not yet become commonplace.

It was the thirteenth day of February when she was taken out to die. Young, so pretty, her crime being that she had been too free with her favours before the ill-fated choice had fallen on her.

At Havering we heard that she had died with dignity. When she knew there was no hope and that the King, who had professed his love for her, was going to leave her to her fate, she accepted it meekly.

What seemed to worry her more than anything was that she might not know what she had to do on the scaffold, and she asked for a block, which would be exactly like the one on which she would have to lay her head, to be brought to her so that she might practise on it. She did not want to stumble on the day of her death. This was done. Later she went out bravely, and before she died she declared that she would rather have been the wife of Thomas Culpepper than a queen.

Lady Rochford died with her. I felt no compassion for that woman. In spite of my hatred for the Boleyn clan, I could not believe in the incest between Anne and her brother, and I thought how depraved she must be to have accused them.

Her last words were reputed to be that she deserved to die for her false accusation of her husband and sister-in-law and not for anything she had done against the King; for she was guiltless of that.

So perished the King's fifth wife, Catharine Howard, on that same spot where his second, Anne Boleyn, had died before her.

The Queen in Danger

The King came to visit us at Havering — or perhaps not to visit us especially, but it happened to be on the route he was taking to somewhere else.

Edward was always uneasy when the King was under the same roof as he was.

'I am not the son he wants,' he told me, his pale face anxious, his blue eyes a little strained, as Margaret said, from too much reading.

I told him he was wrong. 'You are everything he wants,' I assured him. 'Elizabeth and I . . . we are only girls and a great disappointment to him. You are the son for whom he has longed for many years. Of course you are what he wants.'

'He would like someone big like himself.'

'You have a long way to grow as yet.'

'He said when he was my age he was twice as big as I am.'

'Big people are not always the best.'

'But they can ride and hunt without getting tired.'

I studied him carefully. He was a delicate child; his attendants had always fussed over him, terrified that something would happen and they be blamed for it.

'I would like to be able to dance and jump and run like Elizabeth,' he said.

'Oh, there is only one Elizabeth.'

He laughed. He agreed with me. He was completely in her thrall.

When the King arrived, we all had to make our respectful bows and curtsies, and when he looked at his son, I could see he did not like the boy's pale looks; he tried to stop

283

himself looking at Elizabeth but she had a way of pushing herself forward, even in the royal presence, and at times I saw him giving her a furtive glance. She looked more than a little like him. If he would have allowed himself, he could have been very pleased with her. She was the one among us most like him.

To my surprise, shortly after his arrival he sent for me, and when I entered his presence I found that he was alone.

'Come and sit beside me, daughter,' he said.

I was amazed at such condescension and obeyed with some apprehension.

He saw this, and it seemed to please him. 'There, there,' he said. 'Do not be afraid. I wish to talk to you. You are no longer a child . . . far from it.'

'Yes, Your Majesty.'

'How long is it since you were born?'

'Twenty-six years, Your Majesty.'

'And no husband! Well, these have been tragic times for me. I have been disappointed in my wives . . . though Jane was a good wife to me. It would seem that there is some curse upon me. Why has God seen fit to punish *me* thus?'

I felt myself growing stiff with anger, as I always did when anyone said a word against my mother. I wanted to shout at him: You had the best wife in the world and you cast her off for Anne Boleyn.

I think he sensed my feelings and, as he was favouring me at the moment and meant to continue to do so, he was mildly placating.

'I was under the spell of witchcraft,' he said. 'I was bewitched.'

I did not answer. His eyes had grown glazed. He was seeing her, I imagined, the black-eyed witch with all her enchantments, seducing him . . . turning him from a virtuous wife and the Church of Rome. It was necessary to see her thus now. It was the only excuse for murder.

'And Jane,' he went on. 'She died . . .'

'Giving Your Majesty your son,' I reminded him.

'How is the boy? Does he seem weak to you, Mary?'

'He is not strong like Elizabeth, but Lady Bryan says that delicate children often become stronger as they grow older.'

'*I* did not have to grow out of weakness.'

'Your Majesty cannot expect another to have your strength and blooming health, not even your own son.'

'I do expect it, daughter, and methinks I do not expect too much . . . only what is due to me. I am too trusting. You see how I am treated. I believed that girl was sweet and innocent . . .'

I thought: Then you can have had little experience of women. It was strange to be with him like this – answering in asides remarks which I dared not say aloud.

He made a self-pitying gesture, and I tried to look sympathetic, but I kept seeing that poor child running along the gallery at Hampton Court. I kept thinking of her terror as she realized that the axe which was poised above her head was about to fall on her as the executioner's sword from France had on her cousin – his second wife.

'Daughter,' he was saying, 'I want you to be beside me. I have no Queen now. I need someone beside me . . . someone who can play the Queen. We will have a banquet and a ball. We will set aside our gloom. We must, for the sake of our subjects. They like not this sadness. The people must be amused. So . . . you will come to Court. You will be beside me.'

He was beaming at me, expecting me to express my joy.

I was uncertain of my feelings. I was finding life dull and monotonous. I wanted to be at Court. I wanted to know what was happening, to *see* events at first hand, not learn of them through hearsay.

And here was a chance.

Yet to be near the King was dangerous. Well, I had lived with danger for most of my life.

He was looking at me steadily.

'I see the idea pleases you,' he said.

He leaned over and patted my hand in a fatherly gesture.

Not since I was a very little girl had he shown me such affection.

* * *

My position had changed. I was now in high favour. The King would have me beside him. He made it clear that he recognized me as his daughter.

The loss of Catharine Howard had had its effect on him. He looked much older; even he could no longer deceive himself that he was a young man. His legs were swollen and very painful; his appetite had not diminished, and now that he had less exercise he was beginning to grow very fat. His glinting eyes and his petulant mouth often seemed almost to disappear in the folds of flesh about them. He was melancholy and irascible. People feared him more than ever. I was amazed at his gentle attitude towards me. His health was clearly not good. That running sore on his leg was an outward sign of the state of his body; for some time he had tried to conceal it, but now it was impossible.

Naturally there were spies about the Court whose intention was to report everything that happened, and it was soon known throughout Europe that the King was not in good health, that Edward was frail – and at that only five years old; and it would seem significant that my father had brought me to Court and was treating me with more affection than he had shown towards me since he had decided to discard my mother.

It was not long before King François of France was putting out feelers. His son Charles of Orleans was in need of a bride, and there was none he would welcome as he would the Lady Mary.

I was not very pleased. I had almost become reconciled to being a spinster, to living on the fringe of the Court;

after all, there was a great deal to be said for a certain obscurity. One did not have to suffer those alarms every time trouble with which one could be connected sprang up somewhere.

I had settled into a routine, where I could read, write to my friends, occasionally receive them, walk a good deal – I was fond of fresh air – be with my ladies in the evenings by the fire or perhaps, in summer, sit out of doors with dear old Jane the Fool to enliven the hours. It might be a little dull and unadventurous but it was not without its pleasure, and peace of mind was something to treasure when one had had little of it.

How should I know what would be waiting for me at the French Court? Moreover, Chapuys would be against it. If there was to be a union – and I could not have Reginald; that seemed impossible now for he was getting quite old – I would have liked it to bring me closer to the Emperor.

In fact, I found the whole matter rather distasteful, particularly when I discovered that French spies had been questioning my bedchamber women. It was well known that throughout my life I had had bouts of severe illness, and these spies asked delicate and embarrassing questions. They wanted to assure themselves that I was capable of bearing children. They would be considering the many miscarriages my mother had had; my father's children – apart from Elizabeth – were not strong. The Duke of Richmond had died young; Edward was fragile, and I was plagued with illness from time to time. Did that mean that I might not be capable of bearing children?

How serious the negotiations were, I am not sure. The political situation on the Continent was never stable for long; friends became enemies overnight, and that had its effect on proposed marriages. It might have been that it was never intended that there should be a marriage.

The fact that there was a great deal of squabbling over the dowry suggested to me – now experienced in these matters after so many proposals which had come to nothing – that the proposed marriage was a gesture to give the Emperor some apprehension, as the last thing he would want would be an alliance between France and England. My father offered a dowry of 200,000 crowns and François demanded 250,000. Charles of Orleans was only a second son, it was pointed out; I do not know what the response was, but it might have been that the doubts of my legitimacy were referred to.

As the haggling went on, I guessed nothing would come of it, but I was in a state of uncertainty. I had so wanted to marry happily and most of all to have children. I thought this must be the greatest joy on Earth. How wonderful to have a child who would be to me as I had been to my mother! The longing for such a life was with me always.

I think it was due to this uncertainty – another proposed marriage which was to end in nothing – that made me ill. There were some doctors who thought my illnesses were due not so much to an affliction of the body as one of the mind. Not that I was in any way unbalanced; but I was often melancholy; and I had suffered so much in my youth, living as I had on the edge of death, that it had affected my health. I was different from my sister Elizabeth. She, too, was in a precarious position, but she seemed to thrive on it. But she was not in such danger as I was, for throughout the country I was seen as the figurehead for those people who wished to deny the King's supremacy in the Church and to lead them back to Rome.

I was very ill this time. Every time I lifted my head from the pillow, I suffered such dizziness that I could not leave my bed. My head ached and I was seized with trembling fits.

I believe those about me thought I would die.

My father visited me. He was most concerned.

'You must get well,' he said. 'You shall come to Court.

You shall take the place beside me which the Queen would have. You shall be my right hand.'

I smiled wanly. I was too tired and listless to care whether he favoured me or not.

He sent Dr Butts to attend to me – a sign of his favour; Dr Butts was the only one who seemed to understand my illness and with his care I began to recover.

Susan told me that he thought that if I were happily married and had children I should cease to be tormented by these bouts of illness.

'The Lady Mary has nothing wrong with her body,' he told her. 'If she could live in peace and ease . . . live naturally . . . I would be ready to wager that she would gradually cast off these periodic bouts of illness.'

He appeared to know how to treat me, and the very presence of Dr Butts in the household had an effect on me.

My health was improving.

The King came to see me and said I must come to Court as soon as possible, where I could be sure of a welcome.

I always seemed to recover quickly after my illnesses, and I took a week or so to get completely well – taking walks, playing the virginals, chatting with my ladies and laughing at Jane the Fool.

Then I was ready to return to Court.

My father had been right when he said I should be welcomed. As I rode into the city with my household, the people came into the streets to cheer me. They had always been my friends. I did wonder whether the attention I was receiving now was partly to placate them. But as, recently, he had often acted in a manner to make himself unpopular, perhaps it was not that. It might be that he really did feel the need to have his family about him and wanted to have a happy relationship with his daughter.

The cheers of the people were always music in my ears.

It was Christmas, which was being celebrated at Hampton Court.

My father himself took me to the apartments which had been specially prepared for me and my ladies. They were splendid.

There was a happy smile on his face as he watched me examine them; he looked almost young, so delighted was he in my pleasure.

'You shall take the place of a queen,' he said. 'I need a queen to be beside me.'

Ominous words, but they passed over my head at that time. I thought it was just his way of welcoming me.

I was courted now and treated with the utmost respect by those who had previously thought me unworthy of notice. It amused me; but it pleased me also.

I felt better than I had for a long time. I wanted to be at Court; I wanted to see at first hand what was happening. There was something extremely exciting in it, and I began to think that Dr Butts might well be right that my illness grew out of melancholy and boredom.

My father never did anything half heartedly. His affection for me, which hitherto had not seemed to exist, now overflowed. There were jewels for me; fine clothes were sent for me to choose from. He expressed his delight to see me looking better. He treated me more like a mistress than a daughter. I think perhaps he did not know how to be a father.

In any case, I was delighted.

Chapuys was rubbing his hands with glee. Then I understood. We were once more in conflict with the French, and my father was seeking the friendship of the Emperor.

Nothing would please my cousin more than to see me brought back into favour. He would be well aware of my father's state of health and the frailty of Edward. The outcome seemed obvious. My dream did not now seem impossible, and it might well be that I was destined to bring England back to Rome. I must not betray for one moment that this was in my mind. It would be treason in the extreme; but one cannot help one's thoughts; and the need for friendship with the Emperor did explain to some extent my sudden rise to favour.

My father had cast off his gloom. He seemed better. He was at the centre of the revels. He could not dance as he once did, but no one called attention to this; everyone behaved as though he were the handsome King he had once been – standing head and shoulders above all other men; it had never been difficult to deceive him in matters like that.

He was happy. He was keeping his enemies and friends on the Continent guessing which way he would turn – secretly jeering at François who had haggled over 50,000 crowns. Perhaps he wished he had not been so parsimonious now! The King of England would not have wanted to go to war with the family into which his daughter had married; and now war seemed imminent and the King of England stood with the Emperor.

I was still the tool of their political schemes; but on the other hand my father did seem fond of me.

He talked to me now and then, and there was real affection between us. My father had acted in a manner which had seemed very shocking to me; his actions had been responsible for my mother's sufferings; yet such was his nature that I could forget that while I was with him, and be happy because he seemed fond of me. He had great charm when he cared to exert it; I had seen the effect he had on people, and I think it was not entirely due to his power and that aura of royalty. It was something in his personality. My sister Elizabeth had inherited it, and I sometimes saw it in her.

He said: 'I am happy now, daughter, that all is well between us. We have been the victims of evil influences . . . both of us. They have contrived to keep us apart. But now, praise God, right has prevailed.'

It was yet another facet of his personality that I almost

believed him when I listened to him. I suppose I *wanted* to shut my eyes to the truth which should have been clear enough and to accept the verdict which was his alone. It was no use reasoning with such a man. He saw only one viewpoint – that which was made to fit his ideal of himself in order to keep that conscience of his in the chains he had forged for it to keep it in restraint.

He said to me one day: 'Methinks I owe it to my people to marry again.'

I was alarmed. So he was contemplating taking another wife.

He nodded regretfully. 'It is a duty, you know, daughter. A king should have many sons. I have Edward . . . and I have my good daughter . . .' He patted my knee affectionately. '. . . but I should give my people more sons.'

I could see that the cosy period was over. There would be another woman led to the sacrificial altar. I could tremble for her. Who would be brave enough to be the next?

'I am no longer young, Mary,' he went on. 'This leg . . . this devil of a leg . . . you have no idea what I suffer.'

'I have, Your Majesty,' I replied. 'And I am deeply sorry for the pain it causes you.'

He pressed my knee again. 'I know, I know. It is a trial. I need a good woman . . .'

I was silent, fearing to speak lest I chose the wrong words.

'I need someone who will not plague me . . . someone not too young . . .' Thinking no doubt of that fresh, sensuous face of the girl who had been no coy virgin and had doubtless pleased him because of that for which she had been taken away from him – though I never believed that it was his will that she had been. Left to himself, he would have found some means to reinstate her, but her enemies had been astute enough to get the story circulated abroad. He could not have endured to think of François

laughing at the poor old cuckolded King of England. 'Yes,'
he went on, 'a mature woman . . . of good looks . . .
experienced of life. No doll . . . a woman of some intellect
. . . tender and loving . . . to be a comfort to me.'

'Where could such a woman be found, Your Majesty?'

'Ah, there you speak wisely. And mayhap I shall never
find her.'

I guessed then that it would not be long before we had a
new Queen.

* * *

The news circulated round the Court. The King was
looking for a wife. This time, it was whispered, he would
not have some foreign bride who was sent to him to
strengthen a treaty, someone he had never seen before. He
would choose her himself and by so doing make sure that
he was not plagued further in his mature years.

I went to visit Anne. She was deeply disturbed.

'My brother is hoping that the King will take me back,'
she said.

I stared at her. Could that be possible? In spite of the
King's original revulsion for her, she was quite a good-
looking woman. She no longer wore the hideous Dutch
fashions which she had arrived in, and in our softer clothes
she was almost handsome. Moreover the peaceful life she
had been living agreed with her.

The King visited her now and then. He had made her
his dear sister, and since she had ceased to be his wife he
had grown quite fond of her.

Yes, I thought, she has reason to be afraid.

'I could not bear it,' she said to me. 'I like so much my
life here. I have my home . . . my income . . . my friends.
I see Edward, and he is glad to see me . . . and my dear
Elizabeth. To be with her makes me happy. I am not
denied their company. I see you, my dear Mary. You are
my friend. I have this family I have inherited. I do not
want to go back to Cleves. I want to go on living here in

my nice house with my nice servants . . . and my dear family close. I want no change.'

'Do you really think he might want to take you back as his wife?'

She looked alarmed and then, as though she were trying to convince herself, she said: 'No . . . he did not like me when I came . . . Surely he cannot have changed. But I do know he likes to talk to me. He respects my views. He is fond of his dear sister. There is just a fear . . .' She put her hand to her heart. 'A little fear in here. But I could not bear it, Mary. Sooner or later . . .'

She put her hand to her throat.

'I understand,' I said. 'Oh, my dear Anne, I hope it never comes to that.'

'Sometimes I wake in the night. I think they have come for me. I am not sure what I dreamed. Have they come to take me to the Palace or to the Tower? I think of that young girl . . . who followed me. I remember how enamoured he was of her . . . and yet that did not save her.'

I said: 'I cannot believe he will want to take you back. Not after all that has gone before.'

'But my brother wishes it.'

'Anne, try not to think of it. I am certain it will not come to that.'

'No,' she said slowly. 'He did not like me when I came. He did not like me at all. He could not want me like that . . . now.'

'I am sure that is so,' I reassured her.

But I could well understand her terror; and it would be so with any woman he chose to be his wife.

* * *

It seemed to me that my father expected his ideal woman to emerge from all the banquets and balls which were now taking place at Court.

294

I noticed him watching and assessing them. It was interesting to see that any woman who caught his eye on her would seek to efface herself. One thing was certain: no woman at Court – or in any foreign Court – was eager to become the King's sixth wife.

I marvelled that he was not aware of this. It did not seem to occur to him that the fact that he had beheaded two wives would be held against him. Those two wives, he would have told himself, had been traitors, and death was the penalty for that crime. Anne of Cleves had been honourably treated. As he was not pleased with her as a wife, he had made her his sister. My mother . . . well, that was a matter between him and his Maker. It was no fault of his that he had made a marriage which was no marriage and he had had to set her aside – reluctantly, he would assure himself.

I congratulated myself that I was outside the range of his choice, but I could well understand the apprehension of those within it.

I had made the acquaintance of Lady Latimer; she had had two elderly husbands and was now a widow. She was good-looking in a rather unspectacular way, wealthy, kindly and of an intellectual turn of mind. Her conversation was rather erudite, and it was a pleasure to join in discussions with her.

She was the daughter of Sir Thomas Parr who had at one time been Comptroller of my father's household. I never knew him. He had died a year after I was born, leaving a son and two daughters, one of whom was Katharine.

Katharine had married Lord Borough of Gainsborough when she was little more than a child. I do not know what difference there was in their ages, but I did know that Lord Borough's son's wife was fourteen years older than Katharine, so I should imagine she was quite a little girl.

On the death of Lord Borough, she was given to another old man. This was John Neville, Lord Latimer, who had taken part in the Pilgrimage of Grace. After his original foray into danger, from which he was lucky enough to emerge with his head still on his shoulders, Katharine, who was always wise and far-seeing, had persuaded him to have nothing to do with rebellion and to keep himself clear of trouble.

He had recently died, and there was Katharine, about thirty years of age, good-looking, clever and wealthy. She was her own mistress now. She had been the wife of two old husbands; if she wished to marry again, the choice should be hers.

I thought I knew on whom her choice would fall. I had noticed the looks which passed between her and Thomas Seymour. He was a dashing figure at Court – a great favourite of the King. He was just the type to appeal: flamboyant, adventurous, good-looking – and of course he was the King's brother-in-law and uncle of young Edward who adored him. He was the little boy's favourite uncle. He was about four years older than Katharine – a man in his prime – overambitious, I should say, like his brother Edward. It was these two brothers who had determined that their sister Jane should be Queen of England. Jane would never have done it on her own. Naturally the Seymours had received great favours since the marriage of their sister. The Duke of Norfolk had tried to ally himself with them through marriage, but Norfolk's son, Thomas, Earl of Surrey, had been so opposed to an alliance between the two families that the matter had been dropped.

Now it seemed that Seymour had his eyes on Lady Latimer, and she was more than willing to encourage him.

Then, to my horror – and certainly to hers – I noticed that the King's eyes rested on her often.

I heard him say one day: 'Come and sit beside me, Lady Latimer. I overheard your discussions on Erasmus. I should like to hear your views on the Dutch scholar. You must tell me what you think of *In Praise of Folly*.'

At first she was not alarmed. She talked brightly and amusingly, and from time to time the King smiled.

The next day he looked for her, and when he did not see her he asked where she was and said that when she was found she must come to him.

'I enjoy her discourse,' he said. 'She is a lady of firm views.'

That was a beginning.

He watched her as she danced, which she did gracefully enough, but she was not outstanding. She was perhaps not as beautiful as some of the younger ladies; but beautiful young women would remind him of Catharine Howard. He was looking for a sixth wife, and he wanted no mistakes this time.

* * *

I missed Lady Latimer at Court, and when I enquired after her I was told she was unwell and had taken to her bed for a few days.

I visited her, and found her melancholy.

'You are ill, Lady Latimer,' I said.

She nodded. Then she said: 'The King has asked me to be his wife.'

I wanted to comfort her, to tell her that I was her friend; but I was never very good at showing my feelings. So I just looked at her with sympathy and understanding in my eyes.

'I am not young,' she went on piteously. 'I am not beautiful. Why should he choose me?'

'I guess that he likes your company.'

'But I never thought . . .' Her eyes were appealing. I read in them that which she dared not utter. She was remembering that I was his daughter; how could she tell me she was afraid that to marry the King would be to put her life in danger?

I said: 'You have agreed to become his wife?'

She replied: 'I told him that I would prefer to be his mistress rather than his wife.'

I stared at her. 'That was bold of you.'

'He thought so. It angered him. It shocked him. He said he did not understand my meaning. Then he smiled and said: "You are overcome by the honour, Kate. No need to be. I choose you and that is enough." I could see how angry he would be if I refused. He went on: "Then the matter is settled. You shall be my Queen. I have had my eyes on you for many a day, and I know that there is happiness ahead for us two."'

'And so,' I said, 'the matter is settled.'

'When the King commands, one obeys.' She looked at me piteously. 'I have had two old husbands. I have been a nurse rather than a wife.'

I thought of his leg. I had never seen beneath the bandages but I believed it was not a pretty sight. Those in attendance on him must bathe it, apply the prescribed ointments and endure his fury when the pain was great.

It seemed that her fate was to act as nurse to old men. And there was Thomas Seymour, good-looking and romantic, cast by nature in the role of lover, waiting for her.

'If you are ill . . .' I said. 'My father cannot bear illness. He never has.'

'But I am not ill. I am just . . . afraid.'

'Perhaps you could tell him you are already betrothed.'

She looked over her shoulder. I understood. We were speaking too frankly.

We had come to the conclusion that there was no way out for her.

'You will be our stepmother,' I said gently. 'If I could have chosen, there would be none I would rather have.'

Then she embraced me, clinging to me for comfort.

I tried to give it to her. I wished I was able to convey more firmly my understanding and my sympathy; but it was not easy for me to give way to my emotions, and I am afraid I could not help her much. In any case, what help could I give her?

* * *

My father sent for me. He was beaming; he was clearly happy and looking younger. He smiled at me affectionately.

'Good news, daughter. The best of news. I am to have a wife. This will be a good marriage. It is Lady Latimer.'

I fell to my knees and kissed his hand.

'I am happy for Your Majesty.'

'Yes, yes . . . get up. We shall be married soon. There will be no point in delay. I have been long enough without a wife.'

Long enough! It was a year since Catharine Howard had walked out to Tower Green; it was scarcely six since Edward had been born, and there had been two wives since then. But he said he had been a long time without a wife, so that was what we must accept.

'It will not be a grand marriage. I want no delays. A family affair. You will attend on the new Queen.'

'And Elizabeth?' I asked.

He hesitated, then he said: 'Yes. Let the girl be there. This is a family occasion. You should prepare her.'

I said I would, although I did not think she would need much preparation. Did she not revel in royal occasions and constantly endeavour to be included in them?

He dismissed me, and I left him happier than he had been for a long time.

Edward was at Hampton Court, and I knew that I should find Elizabeth with him. Those two were constantly together. They shared a love of learning. In fact, Edward could scarcely be parted from his books, and as soon as he rose in the morning he wanted to be reading. He was quick and clever, rather as Elizabeth was.

I had been something of a scholar myself but I was never as avid for learning as those two were. In Edward's case I believe it was partly due to the fact that physical exercise tired him; lessons never did; and as he excelled at them, his enthusiasm was great. But Elizabeth, though she loved to dance and ride, was as eager as he was to learn. It made a great bond between them.

I guessed that if I went to his apartments I should find Elizabeth there.

I was right; and I was not really surprised to see Thomas Seymour there, for I knew he was a frequent visitor.

I heard sounds of merriment as I approached the apartments but when I entered the schoolroom there was silence. The atmosphere had changed suddenly. Seymour bowed low and, coming to me, took my hand and kissed it humbly, raising his eyes to my face as he did so; there was nothing humble in the look he gave me. His eyes were admiring, his respect was flattering; but that was Seymour's way with women and it did not impress me.

Edward was slightly flushed; Elizabeth looked a little sly. I felt I had intruded on an intimacy which had been very enjoyable to the company.

I went to Edward. He held out his hand to me, and I kissed it.

He was aware of his position – second to the King – and he remembered it on occasions like this, though I imagined where Elizabeth was concerned much formality was dispensed with, for she was certainly in command.

Whenever I was in her company I was always very much aware of her. She seemed watchful. She was not yet ten years old and exceptionally clever – and not only in book-learning; she had a shrewdness, a maturity, a secretive air as though she harboured thoughts which would not bear the light of day. She was not pretty, but her startling vitality called immediate attention to her. Her green gown accentuated the red of her hair; her white skin was clear and radiant. She had more than beauty.

There was Seymour, too, who was of particular interest

to me because of what I had just heard from Lady Latimer who was in love with this man and he – so she thought – with her. I wondered how far his love would carry him. Would he take her away . . . snatch her from under the King's nose and fly with her? Fly where? Leave the country? Seek refuge with the King of France or the Emperor? Would he dare? He looked daring but I fancied he would be concerned with himself. Heads rolled so easily, and his was far too handsome for him to wish to part with it.

I said: 'I trust you are well, my Prince, my sister, Lord Seymour?'

Characteristically, I imagined, Seymour answered for them all.

'We are well, are we not? And we trust the Lady Mary is in the same happy state.'

I assured him that I was.

'I seem to have interrupted some frolic,' I said.

'There is always frolic when my Lord Seymour visits us,' said Elizabeth. 'Is there not, brother?'

Edward lifted his shoulders and giggled. He looked younger – more like an ordinary little boy than I had ever seen him before.

'The Prince is always gracious to his poor uncle,' said Seymour.

'He calls him his favourite uncle,' added Elizabeth.

'Which gives me great delight, but I fear he flatters me.'

'He does not. He does not,' cried Elizabeth. 'And you know it, Lord Seymour. You *are* his favourite uncle.'

I thought: How fond Edward is of him . . . and Elizabeth, too. It was understandable. He had charm and good looks, and they went well with his somewhat flamboyant manner.

'It is a great honour for our sister to visit us,' said Elizabeth demurely.

'Even when she interrupts a merry game?' I asked.

'But you are most welcome,' said Elizabeth. 'Is she not, Edward? Tell her she is welcome.'

What presumption! I thought. She is telling the heir to the throne how to behave . . . she, who, though she may be recognized as the King's daughter, is his acknowledged bastard. Yet Edward seemed to like it, and Seymour was amused.

'I have brought news for you,' I said. 'Though you may have heard it. It is not really unexpected. Perhaps my Lord Seymour has been imparting it to you and that is the cause of your merriment?'

They were looking at me expectantly.

'You are to have a new stepmother.'

Silence. Consternation. Edward's face puckered. He had known two stepmothers already – although never his own mother. Anne he liked very much, and he still visited her; Catharine Howard's beauty and easy manners had won his heart; he had been very sad to lose her. And now there was to be another!

Elizabeth was alert; and so was Seymour. Did he guess? I wondered. How much did he care for Lady Latimer? Not as much as she cared for him, I speculated.

'Who is it who will be our new stepmother?' asked Elizabeth impatiently.

'It is Lady Latimer.'

My eyes went to Seymour's face. I saw it pale slightly, and for a moment the mask of high spirits and favourite uncle slipped. He was disturbed.

'Lady Latimer!' said Edward. 'She is a lovely lady.'

'I like her well,' added Elizabeth, as though that in itself was good enough reason for the marriage.

Seymour said nothing.

I looked at him and said: 'For some time the King has been showing his interest in this lady, but I think she was

302

as surprised as you are that he has asked her to be his Queen.'

He still did not speak. Elizabeth and Edward chattered about Lady Latimer and how they would welcome her as their new stepmother. I was sure they were both remembering Catharine Howard, for it was such a short time ago that she had held that unenviable position.

Seymour then said quietly: 'My Lady Mary, you are sure of this?'

'I have had it from both Lady Latimer and the King himself.'

'Then it is so,' he said.

'The marriage will take place shortly. You are to be in attendance, Elizabeth.'

'Oh!' She clasped her hands together in ecstasy. There was little she liked better than to be present at royal functions. Showing herself to the people, Susan called it. Susan shared Margaret Bryan's view that Elizabeth would come to either great triumph or absolute disaster. There would be no half measures with Elizabeth. 'When will it be?' she demanded.

'Very soon. The King wants no delay.'

She was smiling secretly. She turned to Seymour. 'You hear that, my lord? I am to be present at the ceremony.'

Her look was almost defiant. I wondered how much she knew of the love between Seymour and Lady Latimer; she was teasing him in some way; he gave her a strange look, too. He seemed to be recovering fast from the effect of the first blow and it was something in Elizabeth which made him do so, I fancied. It was almost as though there was some secret understanding between them.

I said to her: 'You will have to be prepared.'

'Yes. What shall I wear? What am I to do?'

'You will just be there. You will do nothing. It is just a gesture . . . to show this is a family matter.'

She clasped her hands and looked ecstatic. Edward was

smiling, well pleased. I could not fathom Seymour's expression; but I felt sure that he must be very unhappy to have lost his bride.

* * *

My father was determined that there should be no delay. On the 10th of July of that year 1543 Archbishop Cranmer granted a licence for the marriage, and two days later it took place.

Elizabeth and I were present, and with us was our cousin, Lady Margaret Douglas. The ceremony took place in the Queen's Closet at Hampton Court and was presided over by Gardiner, the Bishop of Winchester.

The King was attended by that other Seymour, Edward, now Lord Hertford. Thomas had tactfully retired from Court. I wondered whether it was because he could not bear to see the one he loved married to someone else, or that he feared the King might have discovered his feelings for the lady. In any case it would be discreet for him to banish himself. Over the years I had learned something of men, and I was almost certain that Thomas Seymour's feelings might not go as deep as he would charmingly indicate they did. Men such as he charm effortlessly. He did it automatically, and such men should not be taken seriously. Perhaps Lady Latimer had done just that. I was desperately sorry for her. How did she feel as the nuptial ring was put on her finger? Surely her thoughts must be with her predecessors?

I greatly admired my new stepmother. She was a woman of remarkable courage, and it was sad to think that she, who had been a nurse to two husbands, should have a similar task awaiting her . . . but with an alarming difference. This last marriage could take her by a few steps to the scaffold; and that was a thought which must always be with her.

Yet after she had overcome her initial fear she gave no

304

sign that it haunted her. As for the King, he was delighted. Most people thought that here was a wife who was personable enough to please him and of a temperament to soothe him; and in any case they might hope for a more peaceful life ahead.

We were of an age to be friends, and I felt this could be a happy state of affairs between us.

On the day of her marriage she gave me a gold bracelet set with rubies. I exclaimed at their beauty.

'I want you to think of me when you wear it,' she told me. 'It is a very special wish of mine that we shall be friends.'

I was touched and replied that it was what I hoped for.

'You must not think of me as a mother,' she said. 'How could you? I know how dearly you loved your own mother. But perhaps we could be as sisters. I shall regard you and dear Edward and Elizabeth as my own . . . that is, if they will allow me to.'

'They will be pleased to. Both of them have lacked a mother.'

She nodded. 'I want you to accept this money,' she went on. 'I know that it is sometimes difficult for you to meet your expenses.'

'Oh please . . . you are too kind to me.'

'There must be no reluctance to help each other. That is how it is with sisters . . . is it not? Or it should be.'

She gave me £25, which was quite a princely sum to me.

She went on: 'I want to make things happy . . . between you all and your father. You are at Court now . . . but Elizabeth shall come, too.'

'That is what she wants more than anything.'

'It is her right, and I shall do my best.'

'She will love you for it.'

'And for other things besides, I hope.'

I said earnestly: 'I believe this is a happy day for us all now that you have become the Queen.'

'I pray so,' she said very seriously. 'I hope so. You are to come with us on our journey. It is the King's wish.'

'Yes, he has changed towards me of late. Since he was . . . alone . . . he has sought my company. Perhaps now he will not want me there.'

She shook her head. 'No, there will be no change. You are the King's daughter, and if it is in my power I shall remind him of this . . . if by some chance he should forget.'

'You must walk carefully,' I said before I could stop myself.

'Never fear,' she replied. 'I shall take every step with care.'

* * *

Before the royal party could leave Hampton on what I supposed was to be a honeymoon, there was trouble over a group of reformers at Windsor.

The teachings of Martin Luther were taking a hold in some parts of the Continent and there were people who were working hard to bring them to England. Stephen Gardiner, Bishop of Winchester, was a firm Catholic, though he wholeheartedly supported the King's supremacy of the Church, but it was the Catholic Church and the only difference from the old religion was that the King was Head of the Church and not the Pope as before.

This was how the King preferred it to be. It was not the religion he objected to – only the power of the Pope to dictate to him. So, Gardiner was favoured by him.

He was, however, watchful of those who wanted change, and as a result Anthony Pearsons, a priest, and three others, Robert Testwood, Henry Filmer and John Marbeck, were arrested. John Marbeck was a chorister at Court whose singing had particularly pleased the King.

Books favouring the new religion had been found in their apartments which was enough to condemn them all to the flames.

The Queen asked me to come to her, and when I arrived I found her in deep distress.

She dismissed all her attendants and we were alone.

'What ails Your Majesty?' I asked.

She looked over her shoulder nervously.

I said: 'None can hear us.'

'It is these men,' she said. 'They will be burned at the stake.'

'They are heretics,' I reminded her.

'They are thinkers,' she replied.

'It is forbidden to have books such as they have had in their possession.'

'How can that be a crime?'

'It is a crime because it is against the law.'

'If men are not allowed to think . . . if they are not allowed to have opinions, how will the world ever advance?'

'They may have opinions if they coincide with what is the law of the country.'

She covered her face with her hands. 'I cannot bear this intolerance.'

'Tell me,' I said. 'Why does this affect you so deeply?'

'Because these men will be burned for their opinions.'

'A foretaste of what they will suffer in Hell.'

'Do you think God would be as cruel as men?'

'We are taught that Hell awaits the wicked.'

'All these men have done is read books and talk of religion.'

I stared at her. I was horrified . . . not so much because of her faith – which was diametrically opposed to my own – but because of what this could lead her to. Here she was, a few weeks married to my father, already confessing that she was as guilty as those men. She was leaning towards heresy. Yet such was my affection for her that I could only think of the danger she was in.

'Your Majesty . . . my lady . . .'

She held her head high. 'I shall always uphold the right

of men and women to act according to their consciences,' she said.

'Please . . . *please* do not mention this to anyone.'

Suddenly she put her arms round me, and I forgot my reserve sufficiently to cling to her. Already I loved the woman, and I wanted to protect her. My thoughts were all for her safety.

'You must never, never talk like that to anyone,' I said.

'Not yet . . .' she answered.

'You think . . .'

'There may come a time. Life is changing. Opinions change. The truth will shine through in the end.'

'You mean . . . the reformed Church?'

'I mean that whatever is right must prevail.'

'My lady . . . my dear stepmother, I want you to be here to see it.'

'How fortunate I am to have you as my friend!'

'I want our friendship to last. I do not want it to be cut short. I have lived through some dangerous years . . .'

'My poor, poor Mary.'

'I have not always said what I believe to be true. I have prevaricated . . . I think on more than one occasion I have saved my life by being less than frank.'

'I know what you mean.'

'Promise me you will do the same. If you believe . . . it is better to live and help that belief . . . rather than die . . . however nobly.'

'I want to live. God knows I want to live.'

'Then watch for Gardiner. He will be your enemy.'

'It is at his instigation that these men have been arrested. Mary, I must try to save them.'

'How can you do that?'

'I thought to plead for them with the King.'

'Oh, take care. If Gardiner knew of these . . . tendencies in you . . . he would not hesitate. He would do his best to . . . remove you as others have been removed.'

308

'I know.'

'You could be in acute danger.'

'For a while the King is pleased.'

'He was pleased with others . . . for a while. Please be very careful.'

'I will. But I must plead for these men.'

'If you ask for them all to be freed, you will betray yourself.'

'If I say that it is unseemly that men should be burned at the stake while we are celebrating our marriage . . .'

'You would be suspect. Plead for one. Plead for Marbeck. He was a favourite of the King. It would seem as though you liked his music.'

'I did. But it is for his views . . .'

'I have told you. *I* have been in danger. My views are as strong as yours. But I know how to preserve my life. There may be work for me to do . . . work for you . . . Take care. Please listen to me. Plead for Marbeck. Save his life if you can . . . then perhaps that might help the others.'

She looked at me steadily. 'I believe you may be right,' she said.

I left her. I was absolutely astounded by what she had betrayed to me. She leaned towards the Reformed Faith. I could not believe she understood what acute danger she was placing herself in.

* * *

Chapuys visited me and told me what had happened.

He said: 'Marbeck is to go free. It is a special favour to the Queen. She asked for the freedom of all four heretics, and the King has compromised by giving her Marbeck. It is whispered that he intended to pardon him in any case, for he did not want to lose one of his best choristers.'

'But the other three?'

'They go to the stake.'

309

'If she had asked for one of the others, it might have been better then.'

'Who knows? The King is in an uxorious mood at the moment, having been so shortly married. He must have been rather pleased that she asked for Marbeck because he was able to gratify her wish and please himself at the same time – though I am of the opinion that he would not have freed one of the others. A law has been passed to suppress what they call the New Learning, and it is forbidden to be in possession of translations like Tyndale's. It is against the law, and those men have broken the law. I am inclined to think that this is a beginning, and Gardiner will soon have more in the cells awaiting the fiery death.'

He looked at me steadily for a few moments, pausing before he went on: 'The Queen is an erudite woman. Gardiner will have his eyes on her . . . after her pleas for Marbeck. It may be that he will think that it is not only on account of his singing voice that she wants him free.'

'What other reason could there be?'

He smiled at me and said quietly: 'Gardiner will be watchful.'

I thought: I could not bear it if she went the way of the others . . . not good, kind Katharine who had married the King so reluctantly. It would be too cruel of fate. I could not stop thinking of Anne Boleyn in the Tower awaiting her end . . . of little Catharine Howard, running screaming along the gallery at Hampton Court. Not this kind stepmother who had never done anyone an injury in the whole of her life.

I must impress on her more strongly the need for caution.

She was delighted, of course, that Marbeck had been spared.

'But the others,' she said. 'I dream of them . . . I can hear the crackle of the flames . . . I can feel the scorching of their limbs . . .'

'But your intercession saved Marbeck.'

'I tried for the others. I tried so hard . . . but he began to get irritable, and I was afraid that I might lose Marbeck if I persisted.'

'You were wise to desist. My lady . . . Katharine . . . they must never know. Gardiner must never guess . . . about your views.'

'I know,' she said. 'He would have me at the stake if he did.'

'Please . . . please take care.'

She said she would, and I believed I had impressed on her the danger she was in.

* * *

The reformers had perished at the stake, and we were leaving on a journey through the country to celebrate the King's marriage. We were to go to Woodstock, Grafton and Dunstable – there would be hunting on the way – and we should stay at the grand houses of noblemen who would be expected to put on grand entertainments for us. I know these royal progresses were a source of great anxiety to those who had to entertain us, for they could become bankrupt in the process. But the King would have been put out if an inadequate welcome was given to him; and those who failed to treat him royally would soon find they were out of favour at Court – and it was always feared what that might lead to.

We had not gone far when one of my attacks came on. I tried hard to fight it but it was no use.

My father was always irritated by illness, and it was thought best to send me off in a litter. We were not far from Ampthill, which had at one time housed my mother, and to this place I was sent.

I do not think it helped being in her old house. Memories of her came back, and I was plunged into melancholy. Dr

Butts was sent to me, and he thought the best thing was to move me to a house which was not full of shadows for me.

Edward was at Ashridge – Elizabeth with him – and it was decided that I should go there to recuperate.

I was feeling very tired, listless and far from well, so it was pleasant to be in the country away from the activities of the Court. I did enjoy seeing the children occasionally – after all, they were my own sister and brother.

Little Jane Grey was with them at this time. She was an attractive child, just about Edward's age – very pretty, dainty and quite learned. Edward was devoted to her. I was amused once more to see how Elizabeth dominated them. She was, after all, four years older, and she had the nature of a leader. The other two looked up to her and in a way protected each other against her.

There was no doubt that, much as Edward admired his sister, he was very pleased to have Jane as an ally.

Mrs Sybil Penn, who had looked after him since he was a baby, said: 'Lady Jane is such a dear little playmate for him. His sister, the Lady Elizabeth, is inclined to bully . . . much as he adores her. But Lady Jane . . . she is just sweet and gentle. To see them at their books together . . . well, it just amazes me that there should be such learning in those two little heads.'

Jane was a sort of cousin. She was the daughter of Henry Grey, Marquis of Dorset, who had married Frances, daughter of Charles Brandon, Duke of Suffolk, and my namesake, Mary Tudor, my father's sister. Jane herself was the eldest of three sisters.

Mrs Penn was fierce in her defence of Edward. She reminded me of Lady Bryan. I often thought what a lot we owed to those women who were mothers to us in our babyhood. They would fight our battles with the King himself if need be. Thus it was with Mrs Penn.

She was angry about the treatment little Jane received in her home. 'Poor little mite,' she said. 'They are very severe

312

with her. They think nothing of beating her and locking her up in her room and keeping her without food. I've seen marks on her little body from the whip. I'd turn it on them, I would . . . dukes or marquises, whatever they be . . . to treat a child like that and her such a sweet little thing. She's happy here, and my prince is happy to have her with him. I hope we can keep her for a while. Perhaps you would speak for that, my lady.'

I said I would, and then the motherly soul turned her attention to me. She said I needed looking after. She would like to see a little colour in my cheeks.

So it was rather pleasant to watch the children together – to note the tender affection of Edward and Jane; and Elizabeth watching them, making sure that she lost none of her influence over the pair.

I was recovering – and in due course I returned to Court.

The Queen was determined to persuade the King to give full recognition to his daughters and, emboldened by her success over Marbeck and knowing that the King was pleased with her, she attempted to do so.

Having nursed two husbands already, Katharine was experienced in the art. She had gentle hands which could be firm when necessary; she could dress his leg more quickly and less painfully than anyone else; he would often sit resting the leg on her lap, and that seemed to ease it considerably. He liked to talk to her of literature, music and theology; and provided she chose her words carefully he found the discourse to his liking.

He was happier than he had been for a long time. He was sure he had chosen wisely, and most would have agreed with him on that point.

In February of that year following his marriage, I was reinstated to my old position at Court. I was even included in the line of succession, but after Edward would come any daughter my father might have by the Queen or – ominous

313

phrase – any succeeding wives. It was a great step forward – and Elizabeth was to come after me.

Elizabeth was full of high spirits during this time.

We owed a great deal to Katharine – but perhaps not all as far as I was concerned, for my father was eagerly seeking to renew his friendship with the Emperor, and it might well have been for this reason that he was treating me as he was.

But that would not account for Elizabeth's recognition, so I suppose we did owe a great deal to the Queen.

It was impossible not to be fond of her. She was determined to be a mother to us and took an especial interest in Edward and Elizabeth, on account of their youth, I think; and they both loved her. They were fond of Anne of Cleves too, and they had liked pretty Catharine Howard, but none had been the mother to them that the present Queen was proving to be. I think that Katharine had always longed for children of her own; it was sad that she had only stepchildren on whom to lavish her affection; and that she did with abandon. She really was a mother to those children – including Jane Grey, who was touchingly devoted to her.

She believed that my weakness and debility were due to a lack of interest in life. Like many people, she thought that I should have married. Perhaps she was right. I seemed to have withered. I had longed for children so much but I had come to the conclusion that I should never have them.

To give me an interest, Katharine suggested that I make a translation of Erasmus' Latin Paraphrase of St John. It was a task which appealed to me, and I set about it with zest and found myself waking each morning with the urge to get on working at it.

When I had finished it, Katharine was loud in her praises; she said I must have it printed so that many could read it.

I was reluctant at first, wondering whether it was beneath

314

the dignity of a princess – now recognized as such and in line for the throne – but Katharine said she would not rest until she had persuaded me.

Meanwhile I was becoming aware of danger.

Katharine and the King had been married for a year, and there was no sign of pregnancy. Was he beginning to be restless? The fact was that under her skilful hands he suffered less pain; indeed there were times when he was quite without it. It was ironic that Katharine, who had been the one who had brought about this relief, should be the one to suffer for it. It might have been my imagination, but did I see his eyes linger on some of the beauties of the Court? I had also seen a glimmer of anxiety when he looked at Edward. One son was all he had; he was feeling better; I could imagine him telling himself that he was still full of vigour. There were some tempting beauties at Court, and it must be Katharine's fault that there was no child.

It was amazing how those about him were aware of his feelings.

Then came what many believed was a definite sign that the Queen was losing her place in his affections.

Hans Holbein had been out of favour since he had brought back that deceiving picture of Anne of Cleves, representing her as a beauty and completely ignoring the fact that her skin was faintly pock-marked.

'But the fellow is a good painter,' said the King, 'and I pay him a retainer of £30 a year, so he may as well earn it.'

He wanted a portrait of the family – with his son and daughters and his Queen beside him.

Elizabeth was delighted to be included. She would have liked to be in the forefront of the picture; but this was not the King's intention.

He would be in the centre, with Edward beside him and on the far left should be one of his daughters and the other on the far right. Still, we were in the picture. But the crux of the matter was that, when Katharine prepared to take

315

her place beside the King, she was brusquely told that her presence would not be needed. My father wanted the artist to make a picture of Edward's mother, Jane Seymour, the only wife who had given him a son, and she should take the place of honour beside him.

The insult to Katharine was too marked to go unnoticed. She had been deeply hurt – and, more than that, she must have been overcome with alarm.

It was the sign for her enemies to prick up their ears, to ask themselves if the familiar pattern was emerging again? No sons . . . a barren wife . . . and so on. Even though he now had one son and two daughters, we did not give him great delight. Edward was too delicate, and Elizabeth and I were only girls.

Gardiner was waiting to step in. He already suspected Katharine of leaning towards the new religion; he was right in that. I had warned her to be careful, and she had been, but it was not easy for one who was constantly on the stage to keep out of danger.

It was not only the Queen they had their eyes on. Wolsey had fallen through Anne Boleyn, Cromwell through Anne of Cleves; they had decided that Cranmer should go with Katharine.

Very soon after that portrait had been painted, several people of the Queen's household were arrested and taken to the Tower.

Katharine was in a state of great anxiety, but fate was kind to her on this occasion for the King's ulcer was worse and nobody could dress it like the Queen. She managed to soothe it with her gentle fingers; he was pleased with her and turned angrily on those who were preparing to trap her.

He wanted to know what all this was about – arresting people in the Queen's household. What did it mean?

It meant, they told him, that writings had been found in

the possession of these people, and they had been overheard to make certain remarks.

The King made it clear that he wanted no implications about the Queen, and by arresting people in her household they had cast a slur on her. The whole thing was a fabrication to annoy him, he declared, and he wanted to get at the truth of the matter.

The truth actually was that evidence had been forged. It would have been perfectly acceptable if – as they had calculated – the King wished to rid himself of his wife. But he certainly did not at this time. He grumbled that he was surrounded by clumsy oafs who handled him roughly. Only the Queen had gentleness in her hands.

Gardiner was berated as a fool who should have taken more care before flinging accusations at his betters.

Gardiner pleaded that his servants were over-zealous in their service to the King, but he was sent away with the King's abuse ringing in his ears.

But Katharine was left uneasy. She had escaped this time, but would she again? It had just been good luck that he had happened to need her attentions more than usual and that had made him realize her value to him; he was still hankering after another son, and there were several younger and very pretty women at the Court.

Hostilities proved a diversion. Relations with Scotland were never good; now they were verging on disaster, and it seemed that we should soon be at war not only with that country but with France also.

Norfolk was sent north with an army, and at the Battle of Solway Moss James V was killed, leaving his infant daughter, Mary, Queen of Scotland.

My father now had the idea of preventing trouble in Scotland by uniting the two countries through a marriage between Edward and little Mary of Scotland. He wanted Mary to be sent to England to be brought up at his Court. The Scots blankly refused.

317

My father was now ready to conclude a treaty with the Emperor Charles; and we were at war with both France and Scotland.

Edward Seymour was sent to Scotland with an army, and Thomas Seymour to France. Then my father decided that he would accompany the army for, with the Emperor as his ally, he must have contemplated an early victory and naturally he wanted to be there for the triumph.

He must leave a regent in England and as, years ago, my mother had filled that role, it was now Katharine's turn. She would have Cranmer to help her.

My father set out for Calais, leaving her in charge not only of the country but of Edward.

I think the latter must have caused her the greater anxiety. Edward's health had been a matter of concern since his birth. It was not only Mrs Penn who watched him so anxiously. Mrs Penn did so from love of the child whom she regarded as her own, others out of fear of what their fate would be if anything should happen to the heir of England and they be held responsible.

Since her marriage Katharine had lived in a state of perpetual anxiety. I wondered she was as well as she was.

Naturally I was present when my father took his farewells of the family, and I heard him say to Katharine that she must take care of his son, for it seemed God had denied him the blessing of others. That was a veiled threat – well, at least a reproach – which must have made her shiver. I was so sorry for her. So unwillingly had she gone into that marriage, and rarely could a crown have sat so heavily on any head.

My friendship would have been deeper with her had it not been for her leanings towards the reformed religion. It put a barrier between us. My dream of bringing England back to Rome was stronger than ever, for I could not believe that Edward had a long life before him. I was approaching thirty, and I was the next in line. I was sure that my father would never get a healthy child. It was significant that the Duke of Richmond had died so young. It seemed that only the girls could cling firmly enough to life to sustain it. Elizabeth was an example of this, and I had managed to survive so far in spite of my recurring illnesses.

I suspected that the Queen was interesting Edward in the New Learning. She was with him and Elizabeth and Jane a great deal. Edward and Jane were almost fanatically devoted to her, and I was sure they would believe all she told them. I was not certain of Elizabeth. When I was present, these matters were only lightly touched on. The Queen knew that I was a devoted Catholic. My mother had been one, and I should never change. She knew in her heart that I did not accept my father as Supreme Head of the Church, but she never mentioned this because to do so would put me in acute danger.

I tried to discover from Elizabeth how far this indoctrination of Edward had gone, but Elizabeth was non-committal. She herself would never be totally immersed in religion. She was like so many in high places. Her religion would depend on what was most expedient to her own welfare.

While the King was away, Anne Askew arrived at the Court. I did not realize at the time how significant this was.

I heard about it from Susan.

She said: 'The Queen is so kind to those in distress. Poor Anne Askew is indeed in trouble. Some people's lives are so sad . . . particularly women who are shuffled about to please their families. Anne should never have married. She is a reformer really. She is deeply religious . . . one of those people to whom religion means more than anything on Earth.'

'Tell me about her. Why is she here?'

'She was Anne Kyme and forced into marriage in spite of having no taste for it. Her elder sister was betrothed to

Mr Kyme of Kelsey. It meant a joining together of estates – those of Mr Kyme and Sir William Askew. The elder sister died before the marriage could take place, and Anne was served up as the bride.'

'Poor girl. As you say, we are treated like clauses in a treaty. I should be well aware of this. How many times has it happened to me?'

'You, my lady, had the good fortune to escape.'

'I often wonder whether it was always good fortune.'

'Philip of Bavaria was a very charming man. Perhaps . . . who knows . . . ?'

I shook my head. 'Tell me more of this Anne.'

'She had two children, but her faith meant more to her than anything else. There are people like that.'

I thought of my mother, and I was aware that I had failed. I had saved my life with a lie. I had agreed to the King's supremacy. Well, Chapuys had advised me to do so and I had to think of my mission.

'In what way did her faith mean more to her than her children?' I asked.

'She would insist on proclaiming it. Now she has lost her home. Her husband has turned her out. It is said that there will be a divorce and she will lose her home and her children for her faith.'

'What will happen to her?'

'The Queen will help her. Doubtless give her a place in her household.'

'She will find her discourse interesting, I doubt not.'

Susan nodded but said nothing. We were on dangerous ground.

I saw Anne Askew on one or two occasions. She was very good-looking and clearly a woman of purpose. There was something rather awe-inspiring about her.

I forgot about her in the next few days. The weather had become exceptionally hot, and almost as soon as we had moved into a new house we had to leave it for sweetening.

One could not escape the stench of decaying rubbish in the streets; there were flies everywhere.

At such times an outbreak of plague was almost inevitable.

Susan came to me and told me breathlessly that the body of a man had been found in Gray's Inn Lane. He had collapsed and died and the spots on his face indicated that he was a victim of the plague. That was the first case. Others came fast and in increasing numbers.

The Court was in London, and the Queen was full of anxiety.

She came to me and said: 'Should we leave, do you think?'

I was unsure.

She went on: 'Edward is not well at the moment. He is coughing and having his headaches rather frequently. We should have to pass through the streets on our way. He would be very susceptible to infection. On the other hand, to leave him here . . .'

I could not give her an opinion. If she allowed Edward to stay here, and he caught the plague, she would be blamed for leaving him in danger; so would she be if she took him through the streets of London and he caught it. There was no way out of her dilemma.

She loved the boy; but also her own life was in danger. If Edward died, some charge would surely be brought against her.

She was in a state of nervous tension. There was no one who could advise her. None dared. They wanted no hand in this decision.

At length she made up her mind.

The sultry heat was continuing; the plague was growing worse.

She gave orders that the household was to prepare to leave London.

* * *

In the clean country air Edward's cough improved and Katharine gave thanks to God for one more deliverance. Her head was safe on her shoulders until the next alarm came.

The Regency had been successful, and the King was coming home. He had taken Boulogne so he could return as a conqueror, a role which pleased him mightily.

His friendship with the Emperor – never on very firm ground – had waned and, although they claimed themselves to be allies, they were fighting with different objects in view. Each was concerned with his own interests: my father to subdue Scotland forever and to bring it under the control of England and the Emperor to force François to give up Milan.

But he was home, and Edward was safe. However, the campaign had not improved the condition of his leg. The sores were spreading, and the other leg was infected now.

'The clumsy oafs did not know how to dress it,' he said. 'The bandages were either too loose or too tight. By God's Life, Kate, I missed you. There is none that has the way with a bandage you have.'

So her task of nursing began again. She was appalled by the condition of his legs, which were indeed growing worse. He was in great pain at times and would shout abuse at any who came near him.

Only the Queen was allowed to dress the sores.

Chapuys said to me: 'The King has the worst legs in the world, and the Queen should thank God for them.'

I looked at him questioningly and he gave me his sly smile. He was implying that it was the King's bad legs which kept the Queen's head on her shoulders.

* * *

Under Katharine's soothing hands and the new ointments she had discovered, the King's legs improved. But instead of being grateful to her, his eyes strayed to others.

Perhaps in his heart he believed that a miracle could happen – his legs would be well again; this excessive flesh would drop from him and he would be a young and agile man again. Perhaps he thought back to the days of his glorious youth when one ambassador had said that he was the most handsome man in Christendom. If one has been handsome, it is hard to forget it; and I suppose people see themselves not as they are but as they once were. I think that was how it was with my father; and in these moods he would ask himself: What am I doing with such a wife . . . a barren wife? Her only claim to his affections was that she knew how to tie a bandage.

There were beautiful women at Court. There was Lady Mary Howard for one, the widow of his son, the Duke of Richmond – a very lovely girl, with the Howard looks which, in the case of Anne Boleyn and Catharine Howard, had enchanted him.

Charles Brandon had now died and the young and beautiful wife was now an attractive widow. So there were two beautiful young women, either of them capable of bearing sons; and watching men, waiting to snatch at an opportunity, were aware of the King's thoughts.

Gardiner and Wriothesley wanted to be rid of the Queen – and with her, Cranmer. The Queen's leanings were well known. They had already come near to destroying her. If the King's legs had been better instead of worse, they might have achieved it. But this time they would act more carefully.

They were interested in the arrival at Court of Anne Askew. They regarded her closely. The woman was blatant in her conduct; she made no effort to disguise her views, and placing a few spies round her was an easy matter; in a short time she had said enough to give them reason to arrest her.

I was with the Queen when news was brought to her that

Anne Askew had been walking in the gardens when two guards had come to take her away.

Katharine turned pale and dropped the piece of embroidery on which she was working.

'Anne . . . in the Tower,' she whispered.

Jane Grey, who was seated at her feet working on another part of the embroidered altar cloth, picked it up and looked appealingly at the Queen: I could see by the child's expression that she knew why Anne had been arrested and how deeply it disturbed the Queen.

'On . . . what grounds?' asked Katharine slowly.

'For heresy, Your Majesty.'

'They will question her,' said the Queen. 'But Anne will be strong.'

A gloom had settled over the Queen's apartments. Everyone knew how fond she had been of Anne Askew.

Once I came into the schoolroom where Jane and Edward sat together. There were books on the table, and they were talking. Jane was saying that terrible things were happening in Spain, and under the Inquisition people were burned at the stake for their beliefs.

'They die for their faith, Edward.'

'Yes,' said Edward. 'They are martyrs. They die for the true faith.'

When they saw me, they stopped talking. So, at their age, they were aware of the dangers regarding the old and the new religions. Could it be that, under the Queen's guidance, they were leaning towards the new?

I was anxious about the Queen. I wondered what trouble she was storing up for herself. On the other hand, I believed wholeheartedly in the old ways. It was my mission to bring England back to Rome, if ever I had the chance. I was fond of Katharine. I knew she was a good woman; yet we were in opposing camps.

All the same, I wanted no harm to come to her.

* * *

They had taken Anne Askew to the Tower for questioning. Questioning! That dreaded word! It sounded mild enough – just a few queries to answer; but everyone knew what methods could be used to get the answers, and unless they were the answers the questioners wanted, the prisoner could be maimed for life . . . if any life was left to him or to her.

Susan said: 'She will stand up to it. They will never wring anything from her.'

'What could they want to know?' I asked. 'She will state her beliefs. She always has. They are said to be treason . . . but she has never made any secret of them.'

'They know that. I fear it is not for her that they go to such lengths. They are angling for bigger fish.'

I knew what she meant by this, and I trembled for the Queen.

Anne Askew's arrest and subsequent incarceration in the Tower set people whispering. There was so much persecution now. Those whom the King called traitors to the Crown fell into two groups: the Lutherans and the Papists. All the King asked was that people should worship in the old way, the only difference being that he was head of the Church instead of the Pope. It seemed simple enough to him; but there were those who had to follow this wretched Martin Luther, and others who traitorously declared that the Pope was still head of the Church of England. Both must be eliminated.

The triumphs abroad had lost some of their glory. The Scots were putting up a great fight and having some success. The French had made an attempt to recapture Boulogne. They had not done so, but they had attempted to land in England and had come as far as the Solent.

At such times my father was at his best. He was a great king and, in spite of everything he had done, the people recognized this quality in him. When he was concerned with the affairs of the country, he showed his powers of leadership. He did not spare himself; and although people were heavily taxed to deal with the emergency, he himself gave all he could. The common people had never suffered at his hands as those close to him had. The murdered wives were represented to the people as guilty of loose living in the case of Catharine Howard and of witchcraft with Anne Boleyn. Those who had suffered for their religion were mostly in high places, rarely those of humble origins. The people would always remember him as the glittering sovereign of their youth; even now, in his old age, he carried that aura of royalty with him wherever he went, and it could win them to his side.

Disease was his ally, for it worked for him against the French. The sailors in those French ships which had attempted an invasion of England were so stricken that there was nothing for them to do but turn back, and François was forced to make peace. Boulogne was to remain in my father's hands for eight years, then its fate would be reconsidered. The war with France was over.

True, there was still trouble in the north, but there was often trouble in the north, and my father was able to turn his full attention in that direction since he was not being harassed on another front.

Meanwhile there was news of Anne Askew.

Susan was alarmed. 'She has been most grievously racked,' she said. 'There are few who can withstand that pain.'

'What do you fear?' I asked.

'The others will be implicated.'

'Why . . . why should they be?'

'Because they share her opinions . . . because they have sent comforts to her in the Tower perhaps.'

I knew the Queen had sent warm clothing to her, and I felt sick with fear.

I learned later that the Lord Chancellor Wriothesley and Sir Richard Rich, exasperated with Anne because she would not implicate the Queen, had worked the rack most ferociously with their own hands in order to inflict greater pain.

Poor Anne Askew! There are some made to be martyrs, and she was one. Firmly she refused to betray anyone; nor would she deny her faith; and she was condemned to be burned at the stake.

The Queen was in a state of grief and panic. I do not know how she lived through those days. She must be with the King, talk to him, dress his legs, pretend to be merry . . . and all the time she must have been wondering when it would be her turn.

There came the day when Anne Askew was taken to the stake. The Lord Chancellor sent her a letter telling her that even now, at this late stage, if she would recant, she would have the King's pardon.

Anne proudly shook her head.

'I have not come here to deny my Master,' she said.

So her poor broken body was bound to the stake, and they lighted the faggots at her feet.

* * *

There was a subdued atmosphere – not only in the Court but in the streets. A pall of smoke hung over Smithfield. People were whispering about Anne Askew – young, beautiful and brave. She had died for her faith. She had done no harm to any. All she had done was read books which were forbidden – that, and cling to her opinions.

People did not like it.

They were inclined to think the King was misled by his ministers. It amazed me how they always made excuses for him. They had made of him the strong leader, and that was how they wanted him to remain. Weakness was the greatest sin; he had never been guilty of that. Sensual he was; oh yes, fond of the pleasures of the flesh; but he always partook of them under a cloak of morality. Other kings sported with countless mistresses; the King had wives, albeit he either divorced or murdered them; but still he clung to the morality of the marriage vows; he might be a callous murderer but he was deeply sentimental; and his old friend – that adaptable conscience – was never far away. And somehow, in spite of all that had happened, he managed to keep his popularity.

He was faintly irritated with those who had arrested Anne Askew and taken her to the Tower. There had been too much noise about the matter because she was young, fair and a woman. He was displeased. Moreover, Boulogne was proving expensive to maintain and, although taking it from the French had been a great pleasure, he was beginning to find it a burden.

But he had driven off the French and had only the Scots to contend with, and they had never worried him very much; he had come to expect periodic warfare on the border, and the lords of the north were capable of dealing with that.

In the old days he would have found great pleasure in the hunt but that was denied him now. Long hours in the saddle tired him. Growing old was unpleasant, and he did not like it.

Edward was sickly. There was no denying it. And what had he besides? Two daughters! I could read his thoughts when his eyes rested on us.

I was very much aware of the tension, although the Queen did not take me into her confidence as much as I am sure she would have done had it not been for the divergence in our beliefs.

I had long become aware of the methods of men like Gardiner and Wriothesley; and I knew they were waiting to pounce. While Wriothesley had worked the rack so fiercely on Anne Askew, his aim had been to implicate the Queen. Previously he would have fabricated evidence, but in view of his last endeavours he dared not be proved at fault again.

He must have known, though, that in time the opportunity would come. And it did.

We were seated in the garden. The King had been wheeled out. That in itself was enough to put him in a testy mood; his leg was so painful that he could not put it to the ground without suffering acute agony.

Gardiner was with him, and the Queen was beside him. He had lifted his leg and placed it on her lap. The Earl of Surrey was present and one or two others.

Surrey was rather a mischievous young man. I guessed that one day he would be in trouble; but he was a good poet and he gave himself airs. I am sure he thought he was more royal than the Tudors.

He mentioned Anne Askew.

From my corner I watched the immediate effect on the Queen. Gardiner was aware of it, too. He said something about the books which were being smuggled into the country, and he added that there was no doubt that people like Anne Askew saw that they were circulated.

He looked directly at the Queen and said: 'Your Majesty must be aware of this.'

'To which books do you refer, my lord Bishop?' she asked.

'Forbidden books, Your Majesty.'

'Forbidden?' she asked. 'By you, my lord Bishop? Would you seek to instruct us on what books we must read?'

I was afraid for her. She was being reckless. She had suffered so much at the time of Anne Askew's death. She had lived for so long in fear of what might happen that she must be near breaking-point.

'Only, Your Majesty, if the books were those which the law forbids being circulated throughout the country.'

The King was growing impatient. He said: 'We now permit our subjects to read the Holy Scriptures in our native tongue; and I have made it known that this is done so only to inform them and their children and not to make scripture a railing and a taunting stock. It grieves me that this precious jewel, the Word of God, is disputed and rhymed, sung and jangled in every alehouse and tavern, contrary to the true meaning and doctrine of the same.'

Katharine should have been wise enough to let the matter rest there but, as I said, she was in a reckless mood.

'When Your Majesty says to dispute,' she said, 'you cannot mean that it is unlawful for people to discuss the interpretation of the Gospel.'

He frowned at her. 'Would you question our decision?'

'Indeed not, Your Majesty, but I would ask Your Grace if you might cease to forbid the use of books which . . .'

The King's leg seemed to twitch. He shouted: 'Madam, when I say it is forbidden, it is forbidden!'

'Yes, Your Majesty,' she said. 'But when people have a translation which they understand and they wish to talk . . .'

'No more,' said the King. 'Come, I would go in.' He signed impatiently to the two men who stood by his chair. Then he muttered so that all could hear: 'A good hearing it is when women become such clerks – and much to my comfort in my old age to be taught by my wife!'

His chair was wheeled away. The others followed, leaving Katharine standing there mortified.

I had seen the glint in Gardiner's eyes.

* * *

It was not until later that I learned the true story. I just knew that the Queen was in such a state of health that those about her feared for her sanity.

I guessed what had happened. We had expected it must come some time. She had been fortunate so far, but she had been as near disaster as any wife of his must be on occasions, and everything depended on the chance of the moment whether it was the end or she went on to await the next alarm.

Looking back, I tell myself that Katharine must have had a special guardian angel.

She was surrounded by women who were completely devoted to her which was inevitable with a woman of her nature. She had always been kind to all, and however humble any servant of hers was, she was treated with consideration. When Katharine had changed from Lady Latimer to Queen, she herself had not changed with it; she still remained the kindly, motherly woman who always had time to listen to and condole with another's troubles. Hence the devotion which she now enjoyed.

Gardiner and Wriothesley determined to lose no time. The Queen was in disgrace. She had argued with the King once too often, and this in the presence of others. She had been reprimanded in front of them. She must be very low in the King's estimation at this moment; so therefore the time was ripe for her removal.

I could imagine Wriothesley and Gardiner closing in after that scene in the garden. Would the King be tutored by his wife? Indeed he would not. He was clearly piqued by her learning. But she was not clever enough to know when she should be quiet. The King did not want a clever woman; he wanted a Catharine Howard without her blemishes with the nature of Katharine Parr – or a Katharine Parr with the body and sensuality of Catharine Howard.

Now was the time to strike at the Queen, for she clearly leaned towards the Reformed Faith which the King had forbidden. Thus she was giving her enemies the opportunity they needed. She was questioning the King's right to supremacy. His Majesty would never endure such behaviour from a woman. Anne Askew had been such another – saucy, defiant, acting in utter disobedience to the King's orders and the laws of the country.

Surely there must have been intervention from Heaven.

It happened like this: one of the Queen's women was hurrying across the courtyard when she saw the Lord Chancellor Wriothesley passing through, carrying a batch of papers. He was a man whom none – great or humble – wished to come face to face with unexpectedly, for it could not be known whether one might offend him – and he was not the man to take an offence lightly.

So the woman drew back to the shelter of a pillar, and as she did so, she saw him drop one of the papers. He obviously did not notice, for he did not stop to retrieve it. She ran from her hiding-place and picked it up, meaning to give it to him, but by that time he had disappeared into the Palace. Some impulse made the woman look at the scroll, and she saw at once what it was. It was a mandate for the Queen's arrest.

She stood for a moment staring at it, unsure how to act. If she took it to the Chancellor, the Queen would be in the Tower very shortly. But if the paper were lost, he would have to get another. That would take time, and time was all-important on such occasions.

Tucking the scroll under her arm, she made her way in great haste to the apartments of the Queen's sister.

Lady Herbert almost swooned when she saw what it was. She had been expecting trouble and had, I believe, on many occasions warned her sister, to whom she was devoted; when she actually saw a warrant for the Queen's arrest, she must have thought the end was near.

She decided what she must do. Her sister must be prepared. She went to her immediately and showed her what the woman had brought to her.

It was then that Katharine sank into such melancholy that they feared for her life.

She wept piteously, Lady Herbert herself told me afterwards. They did not know what to do. They had seen the mandate, and there would be some delay, but it would come. The King had approved this. His signature was on the document. So there was no hope.

Katharine could think of nothing to do. She was a very religious woman but she was afraid of death. The shadow which had hung over her since that fearful day when she had been told the King wished to marry her, was now upon her – a shadow no more: a reality.

The fact that she had had this on her mind and had lived so long with fear did not help her. It would come soon: the walk to the block, the gory death while people looked on and would say: 'That is the end of the sixth wife.'

'And who will be the seventh?' she said hysterically. 'The Duchess of Richmond . . . the Duchess of Suffolk? And how long for them?'

Lady Herbert tried to console her but there was no consolation.

'The King put a ring of doom about me when he put the ring on my finger,' she said. 'I knew it at the time. I am no martyr. I am no Anne Askew. She went willingly to her death for her faith. I am merely a woman who does not please her husband.'

Anne Herbert was afraid for her sanity. Her eyes were wide and tragic . . . she saw herself taking those last steps to the scaffold.

Her sister called me, and I went to see Katharine. We tried to soothe her. Her eyes were glazed and she began to sob. Then she called out that she did not want to die. She was too young to die. She had never lived the life she had wanted. She had been nothing but a nurse to old men, and now she was to die.

We tried to calm her but a fearful hysteria had taken possession of her. She was laughing and crying at the same time. It was heartbreaking to hear her.

I really think she would have lost her senses, but God saw fit to save her.

She was the most fortunate of the King's wives, which

333

was due to the fact that he was now old. His fancy for the Duchesses of Richmond and Suffolk waned according to his health. The state of his diseased body was Katharine's salvation; she was such a good nurse.

He had signed the mandate that she should be taken to the Tower and questioned about her religious beliefs; no doubt it had been presented to him when he was smouldering with anger against her because he thought she was daring to contradict him. The rumblings of discontent which had followed Anne Askew's death were not far behind. They had aroused his rage, and to think that there was dissension in his own household must have infuriated him.

So in a flush of resentment he had signed the document.

With Katharine indisposed, one of his gentlemen had to dress his leg – and that was when he missed her.

Katharine was certainly lucky. I often thought of poor little Catharine Howard, who had not had a chance. I had always believed that, if she could have reached him, pleaded with him, he, who had been so enamoured of her at that time, would have forgiven her and turned against all those who had attempted to destroy her, and she would have been alive today. But she had not had the luck of Katharine Parr.

He asked where she was. She was sick unto death in her apartments, he was told.

'Then I must go to her,' he said.

He could not walk. His accursed leg would not allow it. He must be wheeled to her. This was done. I wondered how he felt when he heard her sobbing. Did he feel a twinge from that well-ordered conscience? I doubted it. That conscience was as well disciplined as he expected his loyal subjects to be.

I only know what I heard later of that interview. Katharine herself told Lady Herbert, who told others, and so it came to my ears.

I wondered what the Queen had felt, seeing before her the man who had signed the mandate for her arrest. At that time, Lady Herbert said, Katharine despaired of saving her life and thought she was looking Death straight in the face.

He must have had a little pity for her. He was a sentimental man at times. He could change in a few minutes. Here was the Queen, of whom, shortly before, he was planning to rid himself, now lying helpless, frightened, believing that she was going the way of her predecessors. He must have remembered her gentleness, her kindness to his children, how she had made a home for them such as they had never had before. She was a woman of some learning: that was where the trouble had arisen; but he had enjoyed her discourse, and she had such gentle hands.

He must have made up his mind that, if her beauty did not set him afire with desire, if she failed to give him sons, he was getting too old for amorous adventures; he needed a good nurse rather than a voluptuous wife. So he came to her in a conciliatory mood.

He said that he disliked to see her in such a state, and he would do a great deal to restore her to health.

It must gradually have dawned on her that he had changed his mind about ridding himself of her. But she was too far gone in melancholy to rejoice. No doubt she thought that, if she were saved today, what would her fate be tomorrow? In those first moments she must have been far too bemused to remember what was said, and he, being aware of her state and the reason for it, realized how important she was to him.

This much she did remember. He became thoughtful. He said that they were well matched. He was no longer young; he was looking for peace, and she brought him that. He had been deceived by those he had loved; his marriages had failed when all he had sought was a loving and happy family. All he had wanted from a wife was fidelity, love . . . and obedience.

It was the last word which was significant. It was where Katharine had failed.

At this stage her hysteria was fading. Death was receding. There is an urge in all of us to cling to life, and Katharine must have realized that here was a chance to save hers. She had to forget that bold signature on the mandate. She must remember how quickly his moods changed.

He then raised a theological point concerning the scriptures. She believed that more should be translated into English so that many people could understand them. He wanted her to tell him if there was still disagreement with him. Here was the crux of the matter. He was swaying towards her, giving her a chance to save herself in a way which would be easy for him.

'Your Majesty,' she said, 'it is not for a woman to have an opinion. Such matters should be passed to the wisdom of her husband.'

I could imagine his little eyes watching her shrewdly. He would know of the state to which she had been reduced. He would want to make absolutely sure that this was a mood of true repentance and not merely a desperate, frightened woman fighting for her life.

He replied: 'Not so, by Mary. You are become a doctor, Kate, to instruct as we take it, not to be instructed by us.'

She assured him that he had mistaken her intentions. She had taken a different view now and then only to amuse him, to divert him, to take his mind from the terrible pain he suffered. She had believed he found their talk entertaining, and she had sometimes taken a view opposed to his own, for if she had not, there would have been nothing to discuss. That had been her sole intention – to divert, to amuse, to entertain. Moreover, she wanted to profit from his learned discourse. She wanted to hear him express his views with more vehemence than he would, perhaps, if she agreed with him.

The words were wisely chosen. He was placated. After

all, he had intended to be. He needed her. She was the best possible nurse, and there was no one who could replace her.

He had said: 'Is that so, sweetheart? Then we are the best of friends.'

The battle for her life was over. But she must have asked herself: For how long?

* * *

The sequel was amusing. She had returned to his apartments with him, removed the clumsily applied bandages in her skilful way, dressed his leg and talked to him.

The next morning they were in the garden together, and it was there that Sir Thomas Wriothesley came with his guards to arrest her.

There were several to witness this scene, so I had an accurate report of what happened.

'What means this?' demanded the King.

Wriothesley replied that he came with forty halberdiers on the King's orders. 'We have come to take the Queen to the Tower, Your Majesty. My barge is at the privy steps.'

One would have thought my father would have felt some embarrassment. He may have done but he let it erupt in anger against Wriothesley.

'Make sure it is not you who are sent to the Tower,' he growled.

'Your Grace . . . Your Majesty . . .' stammered Wriothesley. 'The mandate . . . Your Majesty has forgotten . . . the Queen was to be arrested at this hour . . .'

'The Queen is where she belongs . . . with the King!' shouted my father.

'The order was to arrest her wherever she might be, Your Majesty.'

My father lifted his stick and would have struck Wriothesley if the man had not quickly dodged out of the way.

'Get you gone!' he shouted.

Katharine must have been in a state of terror. The King's mood might have changed. He might have remembered the order and decided to carry it out after all. She had only to say one thing of which he did not approve and which might have sounded to him like arrogance, making a doctor of herself to instruct him . . .

The King turned to Katharine.

'The knave,' he grumbled.

'Methinks he believed he was obeying Your Majesty's orders.'

'Don't defend him, Kate. Poor soul, you do not know how little he deserves grace at your hands.'

So for this time she was saved. She had seen death very close, and now there was a reprieve. But still there must be the eternal question: For how long?

* * *

It seemed clear to everyone except the King that his end could not be far off. His legs were now in such a state of decay that they could scarcely support him. He needed constant attention, and the Queen was essential to his comfort. We did not say it, but it was in everyone's mind that she was the luckiest woman on Earth, for it seemed possible that she was going to outlive him. He was beyond sexual desire now – another point in her favour.

Yes, said the Court – and, I have no doubt, the country – Katharine Parr is a very fortunate woman.

He was irritable in the extreme and his anger could boil up in an instant, so it was still very necessary to take care. As for Katharine she looked blooming, younger than she had for some time; she could see the end in sight.

Intrigue was rife. There would be a young King, and he was already in the hands of his Seymour uncles, who were supporters of the Reformed Faith. This was not at all to the liking of the Howards, who must have cursed fate which gave the heir to the Seymours and not the Howards, who had had two chances, one with Anne Boleyn and one with Catharine Howard.

The more feeble the King grew, the greater was the arrogance of the Seymours. Young Edward doted on them, and in particular on the younger uncle, Thomas; and everyone knew that the Seymour brothers were the two most ambitious men in the country.

The Duke of Norfolk and his son, the Earl of Surrey, stood on one side, and the Seymours on the other. I watched with interest. They were like carrion crows, fighting over the carcase before it was dead, while the King, who had always hated even to talk of death, went on pretending to himself that he had years before him.

It was certainly an anxious time. Edward would be King, and he was not ten years old. No wonder the uncles were rubbing their hands with glee. The government of the country – by grace of their sister Jane – would be in their hands.

Surrey was one of the most reckless men I have ever known. He was extremely handsome, proud, arrogant, a poet of some ability, a scion of a family which considered itself the highest in the land – so great, he implied, that the Tudors were upstarts in comparison.

On the other hand there were the Seymours, and Edward Seymour was, without doubt, one of the cleverest men at Court. I could not say the same for Thomas. Like Surrey, he was exceptionally attractive – and well aware of it. He had charmed Edward and, I fancy, little Jane Grey and even Elizabeth. He was very ambitious but a little lacking in wisdom, I always thought.

The younger Seymour was often in my thoughts, because I knew that the Queen was in love with him. Poor lady, had the King's eyes not alighted on her, she might have been Thomas Seymour's wife by now. I fancied I had seen his eyes on Elizabeth. I could not believe that he fancied her as a possible wife for himself. She was, after all, the daughter of the King, and she would be Protestant or Catholic, whichever the people desired. Seymour would recognize her qualities, and her position could be considered promising.

Uneasy days they were, with all eyes on the King. Serious-minded people willed him to live until his son was just a little older. It was not good for a country to be left with a minor for a king and a divided people.

Edward Seymour, Lord Hertford, with John Dudley, Lord Lisle, and Cranmer were preparing to rule through the new King. They – with the help of the Queen – had managed to instil in him a fondness for the New Learning. On the other hand there was Norfolk, with Surrey, and the Catholic supporters such as Gardiner and Wriothesley who might even attempt to return to papal authority.

It was an interesting situation, which it was feared, if the King were to die, might lead to civil conflict.

I wondered how Katharine felt when she saw death coming nearer and nearer to my father. Did she dream of days without the threat of death hanging over her? Did she dream of the marriage with Thomas Seymour which had been stopped by the King's preference for her? Was married bliss with the man of her choice to prove to be just a postponement?

That was how it was as my father's health deteriorated and it became obvious to all that his days on Earth were limited.

Surrey became more reckless. There were times when it seemed that his contempt for the Seymour brothers would bring about open warfare between them.

He referred to them as a low family which had been brought up solely because one of its women had happened to please the King.

The Seymours retaliated by demanding: What of the Howards? Had they not used their women to further their own ends?

The quarrel between the Howards and Seymours went on during the whole of the winter. Everyone knew that it could not be long before it flared into open warfare. The Howards were foolish and no match for the wily Hertford, who saw himself lord of all England when his nephew became King; and he was determined to rid himself of his enemies.

It was not difficult to bring a case against the Howards. They might have blue blood but they had very little common sense to go with it.

Edward Seymour was soon accusing them before the King. They were in communication with Cardinal Pole, the King was told, and there was little that aroused his fury more than the very mention of that name. He had regarded Reginald as his friend, and there was greater enmity in his heart for one whom he had trusted in years gone by and who had, as he said, turned traitor. Moreover the Howards had planned to make Mary Howard, Duchess of Richmond, who was, of course, Surrey's sister, the King's mistress so that she could influence him.

To tell the King that someone was going to influence him was the quickest way to arouse his fury.

Then there was the final outrage. Surrey had had the leopards of England emblazoned on one of the walls of his mansion at Kenninghall. Thus he proclaimed himself royal. He boasted that he had Plantagenet blood in his veins besides being descended from Charlemagne.

This was too much to be borne. Norfolk and his son, Surrey, were sent to the Tower.

* * *

It was a bitterly cold Christmas. The King was growing feeble. He was the only one who would not admit it.

In the January Surrey lost his head – a lesson to all. He had died from his own vanity. Was the setting up of the royal arms on a wall worth his life, for it was that which had really been responsible for his death?

Crowds had gathered to see Surrey die. There was silence as his head fell. It was such a handsome head and he such a proud man. He was so young to die, son of a noble house and one of the finest poets at Court; but a man of little sense, to barter his life for the sake of a witty quip, for the sake of parading his claim to royalty.

And his father was in the Tower. Norfolk was not much loved. He had been a meddler in affairs all his life. He had been callous to his poor, sad kinswomen; he had applauded them when they became Queens of England and turned against them as soon as they fell out of favour. When those two women had been condemned to death, they had not had a greater enemy than their noble kinsman – apart from Anne Boleyn, whose enemy was her own husband.

There had been a scandal when Norfolk left his wife for the laundress Bess Holland. Yet he had been loud in his condemnation of what he called his lewd and immoral kinswomen. I think everyone hates a hypocrite – so Norfolk was certainly not popular.

How bleak it must be in the Tower with the January winds buffeting the walls, seeping through every crack and crevice to make his prison more uncomfortable than it had been before. How did he feel, I wondered, knowing his son had lost his head . . . believing perhaps that in a few days he would be led out to meet the same fate?

Everyone about the King knew that he was dying. Wriothesley had said the King was rotting to death. Fortunately for him, not in the King's hearing. But it was an apt phrase. His legs were a mass of putrefying sores. The end could not be far off.

To my surprise he sent for me. I had heard how ill he was but I must confess to surprise – I might say horror – when I saw him. He lay in his bed, his eyes scarcely visible in the folds of unhealthy-looking flesh. Some of his colour had gone now but I could see the network of veins where it had been; his mouth looked slack; his beard and hair were white. I would hardly have known him for the King; and the contrast with that grand and handsome figure of my childhood was tragic indeed.

His lips formed my name. 'Mary . . . my daughter.'

'Your Majesty, I heard you wished to see me, and I came with all speed.'

'All speed,' he murmured. 'That was well. Daughter, come closer, I cannot see you. You seem far away.'

'I am here, Your Majesty.'

'Fortune has not gone well with you. I have not given you in marriage . . . as I desired to. It was the Will of God. Daughter, the Will of God . . . perhaps the state of my affairs . . . your ill luck . . . Understand . . . it was the Will of God.'

'It was the Will of God,' I repeated.

'And now . . . you are no longer young . . . and there is not much time left to me. There is your brother. He is little yet. Take care of your brother . . . a little helpless child . . . be a mother to him. Be a mother . . .'

'I will, Your Majesty, I will . . . Father . . .'

He nodded slightly.

One of the doctors came and laid a hand on my arm. He led me to a corner of the chamber.

'His Majesty is failing fast,' he said.

Royalty cannot die in peace. Death is like birth. The important men of the day must be sent for to see it happen.

So they were coming to see the King die. Members of the Council. I recognized the Seymours . . . Lord Lisle, Wriothesley, Sir Anthony Denny. The Queen was not present.

My father half rose in his bed and with a cry fell back on the pillows.

'What news?' he growled. 'Why do you stand there? What do you say? My legs are on fire. What do you? Will you let

343

me burn?' Then he said a strange thing. 'Monks . . . who are these monks? They cry to me. Why do they cry? They look at me with their wild eyes. I like not those black-cowled monks. What news, eh? What news, Denny?'

Denny came to the bedside. He said: 'Your Majesty, there is nothing more that can be done. Your doctors can do no more. You should prepare to meet God. You should review your past life and seek God's mercy through Christ.'

There was a look of disbelief on his face. Death . . . so close. All his life he had refused to think of death; he had hated sickness; he always wanted to shut himself away from it; now here he was, face to face with death and there was no running away this time.

'Review your past life!' Did I detect a note of triumph in the words? 'You, who have had great power, of whom we all went in fear and trembling, must now face One greater, more powerful than yourself. How does it feel, Sir King?'

Oh no! Denny's face was a mask of sympathy. But the King had made them all tremble for their lives at times.

They told him he must see his divines, but he started up and said he would see no one but Cranmer.

Cranmer was at Croydon, and they sent for him to come right away.

We wondered whether he would arrive in time, for the King was in delirium. He seemed not to know where he was and why so many people had crowded into his bed-chamber. It was uncanny. He was seeing ghosts, and through his eyes one saw those figures from the past who were there to watch him as he died, to mock him for the power he had once had over them, to remind him that he had none now nor ever would again.

'Anne . . .' His lips formed her name. I could almost see her, her black hair loose, her flashing eyes, that quick tongue that cared nothing for any . . . not even him. 'Witch,' he murmured. 'Anne, you're a witch. Had to be . . . Sons for England . . .'

344

So even at the end he was making excuses.

'Cardinal . . . what do you, sitting there? Why do you regard me so? I like not your look, Cardinal. Too clever . . . knew too much. You died. I was sad to see you die, Thomas. Can you see her there? Tell her to take those black eyes from me. Witch . . . sorceress. Blood . . . blood everywhere. The monks are there. Monks . . . monks. Monks.' His voice rose to a scream.

One of the doctors gave him a soothing drink.

'Ah,' he murmured. 'Better . . . better. Who is that by the door? Tell her to go away. Who is that screaming? Catharine. She is young . . . very young. Led astray. Stop her screaming. Where is the Queen? Kate. Kate. Such gentle hands. There she is . . . that one. She is coming closer. Her hands are about her neck . . . I can see the blood there . . . and she is laughing . . . mocking. Send those monks away. I like them not. What time is it?'

'Two of the clock,' said Wriothesley.

'Shall I live through the day?'

No one answered. None believed he would.

'The boy is young yet . . . Take care of him. Watch over him. He will be your King. Such a little boy . . . not yet ten years old . . . not strong . . .'

'Your Majesty should have no fears,' he was told. 'Your ministers will do all that has to be done.'

By the time Cranmer came, the King could not speak. He placed his hand in that of the Archbishop. Then he closed his eyes.

The King was dead.

* * *

He lay in state for twelve days in the chapel of Whitehall. A wax figure had been set up beside the coffin. It was uncannily like him, dressed as it was in jewelled robes of great magnificence. The body was to be taken to Windsor for burial and placed beside that of Jane Seymour, the mother of his son.

The procession was four miles long, and the wax effigy was put into a chariot and rode beside the coffin. At Sion House they rested awhile, and the coffin was placed in the chapel there.

It was at Sion House, where Catharine Howard had spent some of her most tortured hours while she was waiting to be taken to the Tower, that a most gruesome event was supposed to have taken place.

It was said that, when the coffin was removed, beneath it was seen blood on the stone flags of the chapel, and it could only be assumed that it had seeped through the wood of the coffin. Then some man said he saw a little dog come in and lick up the blood.

Whether this was true or not I cannot say. But if it was not, it was an indication of what was in people's minds. They would remember those two murdered wives; one might say three, for my mother's death had been hastened by his treatment of her. Katharine Parr had come near to losing her head, and barbarous torture had been inflicted on the monks. People would remember handsome Surrey. Norfolk, by sheer good luck for him, was still in the Tower, the King having died before he could sign his death warrant.

It was remembered that Friar Peto had likened the King to Ahab and had prophesied that the dogs in like manner would lick his blood.

Perhaps it was this prophecy which had prompted the man to imagine he had seen the dog in the chapel. One could not tell. But it did show that the people were aware of the blood which had been shed, and there could not have been one man in the country who would have liked to take on the burden of guilt which must be the King's.

And so to Windsor, where the coffin was buried next to Jane's under the floor of the chapel. After it was lowered by means of a vice, sixteen Yeomen of the Guard of his household broke their staves of office over their heads and threw them down onto the coffin.

De Profundis was said, and Garter's voice rang out to tell everyone present that there was a new king.

'Edward the Sixth, by Grace of God, King of England, France and Ireland, Defender of the Faith and Sovereign of the most noble Order of the Garter.'

Gardiner caught my eyes. There was speculation in his. He must be feeling very uneasy.

He knew that the new King had leanings towards the Reformed Faith and that he would be in the hands of his uncles – and Gardiner was a staunch Catholic.

I knew what he was thinking as he looked at me. I was no longer young. I was thirty-one years of age . . . old for marriage, but when the crown was considered, youth was not such a desirable asset. There was Edward, for example, whose youth was greatly deplored. No, I was a good age for a ruler and would be so for another ten years or more. The King was not ten years old and was delicate.

I read hope in Gardiner's eyes; and I felt my mission was coming very close.

The Planned Escape

It soon became clear to me that my brother was fanatically devoted to the Reformed Faith. I had, of course, known he leaned that way, for he had been instructed by Katharine Parr and his uncles, and they were the people who had most affected him.

He was a strange little boy, and being aware of how important he had become had its effect upon him. He had been affectionate enough as a little child. He had loved Mrs Penn dearly and also the Queen; he had been devoted to Jane Grey; he had been fond of me and had adored Elizabeth.

It was a great misfortune that the crown should be thrust on him when he was so young. He must have felt the need to preserve his dignity, being in the centre of so much ceremony, surrounded by so many ambitious men, all trying to guide him – for their own benefit, of course. He was very serious; his delicate health had made him turn to his books rather than indulge in the outdoor life. He was wise for his years, but of course not wise enough to deal with the intrigue, scheming and machinations which must necessarily go on around him.

His uncle, Edward, Earl of Hertford, was the one who had chief control. My father had ordered this in his will, in which he had pronounced Edward as his sole heir and named eighteen executors to act as a Council of Regency during Edward's minority. The two chief among them were the Earl of Hertford and Viscount Lisle.

On his father's death Edward was brought with Elizabeth from Enfield, and from there the new King was taken to the Tower to prepare for his coronation. There he created his uncle Edward Duke of Somerset, and Lord Lisle became the Earl of Warwick and Thomas Seymour Lord Seymour of Sudley and Lord High Admiral of the Fleet.

The coronation was a sumptuous occasion much enjoyed by the people; there was little they found so touching as to see a child crowned King of the Realm. It did not occur to them that such a state of affairs could be highly dangerous.

He was acknowledged Supreme Head of the Church.

I was fully aware that my position was as precarious as it had ever been. Moreover I had lost my good friend Chapuys. His health had been failing for some time, and he had now retired. In his place as the imperial ambassador was François van der Delft. I trusted him, for I was sure the Emperor would not have sent him if I could not do so.

The Emperor had always been for me the rock on which I could rest if need be, although there had been times when he appeared to be a little indifferent to my plight. But I always convinced myself that he was a man of great power and many commitments and that, if anyone could help me, he would be the one. But I knew I was going to miss the special relationship I had had with Chapuys.

I was now first in line to the throne. I represented the Catholic party, and if, as I believed, the religion of the country was now to be changed, there would certainly be many who disagreed with what was done; and those people would look to me as a leader.

On the advice of van der Delft, I retired from Court. I made the excuse of mourning my father, and my own ill health. I went from Havering to Wanstead House, Newhall and Framlingham Castle. I was not poor now, for I had an income from Newhall, Beaulieu and Hunsdon, and I had just acquired Kenninghall, which had come to me with the fall of the Howards.

Norfolk still remained in the Tower, and because my father had not signed his death warrant, he was allowed to languish there.

I guessed I should remain in obscurity until I saw more clearly what was going to happen.

My sister Elizabeth was to live with the Queen, and I was sure Katharine would be pleased about that. She had always been the good stepmother. Life had changed for Elizabeth, too. She was no longer merely the bastard daughter of the King, not to be received at Court; she was second in the line of succession, coming after me; and she had her income of £3,000 a year, just as I did. So I could imagine she was not displeased with life. She had always been on friendly terms with Edward; and if I knew her, now that he was King, she would not allow that friendship to diminish. She was now a very knowledgeable fourteen.

I had given up all thought of marriage for myself. To have been betrothed so many times and for it all to have come to nothing had had its effect on me. I knew there was concern about my health. It seems one's body is not one's own if one is royal. It was known that I suffered periodic pains and difficulties – there were spies among my bed-chamber women – and this caused a certain amount of speculation as to whether I should be able to bear children. I knew the state of my health had been discussed in all the Courts of Europe. It may have been one reason why my proposed marriages had come to nothing.

Now there was another hint of marriage . . . from Thomas Seymour! I was amazed and appalled. Was there no end to the aspirations of that family! Their sister Jane had happened to please the King, and she had done that which none of the others had been able to – bear the heir to the throne who was now the King; and because of this the obscure family from Wiltshire had royal ambitions. So Thomas Seymour, now Lord Seymour and High Admiral, had the temerity to hint that there might be a marriage between us. I guessed he thought that Edward would not have long to reign, and then glory for me . . . and Thomas

Seymour saw himself as Queen's consort ruling the land. I wondered what his brother Edward thought of that project.

I had not had time to answer the proposal with the scorn it warranted before I heard another rumour. He had offered marriage to Elizabeth! How did my fourteen-year-old sister feel about that? I had seen her eyes sparkle when she looked at him; he was a very handsome man, and even at her age she was already susceptible to such as he was. What had her answer been? That was if he had truly made the offer. One could never trust rumour.

There was yet another. This time Anne of Cleves was named. I could scarcely believe that. What would Anne of Cleves have to offer an ambitious man? An ex-queen could not possibly compare with a woman who might have the crown.

Then came the whispers that Seymour was already married . . . not to any of those mentioned in the recent rumours, but to his one-time sweetheart, Katharine Parr.

I could not believe it at first. Could the Queen really have married so soon after the death of the King? It was most unseemly. But having seen the manner in which that man could attract women, I believed he might have succeeded in persuading her. After all, she had been in love with him before the King chose her – and she had certainly hoped to marry Seymour then. So I did believe there might be some truth in this rumour.

I was amazed to receive a letter from the Admiral in which he asked my opinion of the proposed marriage to the Queen, and asking me to give my sanction to it.

I was flattered to be asked, yet if the rumour were true and he was already married, why ask my sanction? I wrote back, primly I suppose, saying that I was the last one of whom he should ask such advice, as I knew nothing of these matters; but as it was scarcely six months since Katharine had become a widow, I thought it might be too soon for her to be contemplating matrimony.

351

And as it turned out, he was at the time actually married. What a reckless man he was! That was to become more and more apparent as time passed.

It was not long before the new King's love of the Reformed Faith was apparent. Somerset and most of the councillors were of his way of thinking; and it seemed that the new religion had come to England.

Reformers from all over Europe were arriving in England. They sang the new King's praises.

When Gardiner preached at Winchester some five months after Edward's accession, it was expected that he, as a Roman Catholic, would attack the new doctrines and find himself in trouble. But Gardiner was a wise man; he skirted the difficult ground and proclaimed the King Supreme Head of the Church. I was sure this disappointed his enemies.

I lived very quietly throughout that year. Seymour's marriage to the Queen had caused a great deal of disapproval, but he shrugged that aside and Katharine was supremely happy. I was pleased for her, though I thought she had shown a lamentable lack of discretion in marrying so soon. I supposed she feared to lose him if she delayed. I wondered if she knew he had looked around for a match which might have been more advantageous to his ambitions. However, I was glad she was getting some of the happiness she deserved. I did fear though that she might be building on shifting sands with such a man.

I spent Christmas at Court. Edward was very conscious of his position. Naturally he would be. A great burden had been placed on his young shoulders. I hoped he would not be overwhelmed by all the adulation which came his way. He was beautiful, said the flatterers, witty and amiable; he was gentle and grave; he was already the father of his people, and if this was how he was at ten years old, how great and wise he would become with the passing of the years.

He was very gracious to me, telling me how tenderly he regarded me and that, although he called me sister, he thought of me as mother, so good had I been to him in his young years.

He was devoted to religion. I knew he always had been, but it was more apparent now. And, of course, that devotion was for the Reformed Church. I did not discuss religion with him because I felt it would be dangerous. Gentle as he was, he could be dogmatic, and when people felt as deeply as he did, intolerance was apt to creep in.

I was not sorry to leave Court. I was deeply aware of the new influences and felt it was no place for me. I went back to Hunsdon. I had my pleasant manors, my friends about me, my books, my music, and I was free to take long walks in the fresh air. I should be foolish to seek anything else at this stage.

It was during the next year that I heard of the scandal concerning my sister and Thomas Seymour. I must say it did not surprise me – knowing them both.

I was sorry for Katharine. It seemed she was doomed never to be happy. Her husbands had brought her little joy. Nurse to two of them, and with the third she had been subjected to great terror, and when she thought she had at last entered into a happy union, she found she had married a philanderer.

There were many who might have told her that this was what she would find in Thomas Seymour, but that the Princess Elizabeth should be the one involved with him was quite unexpected.

I knew there had always been an attraction between those two. My sister had been born with a shrewd nature or she might have accepted him in marriage. She would see, though, that that would have been the utmost folly. All the same, she had had a fancy for him.

Had Katharine not been aware of the flirtatious behaviour between her husband and Elizabeth? Or had she shut her eyes to that which she did not want to see? Had she made the mistake of regarding Elizabeth as a child?

The story came out. There were always servants to tattle. What had they thought when the Admiral made a habit of teasing the girl, kissing her, even coming into her bedroom when she was in bed and tickling her? It was unseemly, even though sometimes the Queen had joined in the game.

There was a great deal of talk about that occasion when the Princess came into the garden wearing a black dress which Seymour said he did not like because not only was it unbecoming but it was too old for her. She should remember she was only fourteen . . . or was it fifteen? In any case he would not allow her to wear such a gown. Of course, it was all supposed to be fun – another of those games which the Admiral and the Princess so enjoyed and in which the Queen often joined. But the Admiral had taken a knife and slit up the skirt so that the Princess's petticoats were visible; the game had grown wilder until the gown was slit in many places and the Princess was there in the garden in her petticoats.

'My Lord Admiral,' she had cried, 'you have ruined my dress. You must buy me another.' And he had replied: 'Most willingly.'

It was clear that the Lady Elizabeth and the Admiral had greatly enjoyed the romp.

Jane Grey was with them, for on the King's death she had joined Katharine's household. Katharine was delighted to have her; she would be easier to understand than Elizabeth; she was such a docile, gentle creature, and Elizabeth was so unpredictable. I often wondered what Jane thought of all the rompings in that household.

It was certain to come to an end sooner or later.

Meanwhile Katharine was having trouble with Anne Stanhope, Somerset's wife. The trouble was over a matter of precedence. Anne, as wife of the elder brother, thought her place should be before that of her husband's younger brother's wife, for, Anne said, Katharine was no longer in the position of Queen, particularly as she had married so hastily after the King's death.

I was amazed at Anne. I had always been friendly with her and had quite liked her, for I had always found her reasonable. Katharine was not a woman to give herself airs, and I was sure she did not greatly care about a matter of precedence. But I thought it was rather sad that there should be this conflict.

Katharine became pregnant about the same time as Anne Stanhope did, and I believe Anne had grand ideas for her child. She was already scheming for her daughter Jane, whom she wanted to marry to Edward. My brother had been meant for Mary of Scotland, but after Somerset had beaten the Scots at Pinkie Cleugh, Mary had been carried off to France, which put an end to that project. No doubt they would get him married as soon as they could; but he had a little way to go yet before he could produce an heir.

The quarrel between Somerset's wife and the Dowager Queen flourished, but then the scandal concerning Elizabeth and the Admiral came to such a stage that it could not be ignored.

Katharine was now several months pregnant. They say that is a time when husbands often stray. That would not apply to Seymour. He would be ready to stray at any time. But it so happened that the Admiral was not careful enough, and one day the Queen opened the door of a room and found Elizabeth in the arms of her husband; and this was no game. It was obvious that they either were, or wanted to be, lovers.

I felt so sorry for Katharine. Elizabeth had been foolish, but she was only fifteen years old and Seymour was a rogue. Even Katharine could not deceive herself any longer. She must realize that her husband was a philanderer and Elizabeth a wanton. Here she was, for the first time in her life, about to taste the joys of motherhood for which she had longed all her life; and they had turned it sour for her.

I cannot imagine what happened during the scene which followed, but I did know that Elizabeth's sojourn under her roof was over. It would have been quite impossible for the child to stay after that. She would have to go.

She was sent away with her governess, Mrs Katharine Ashley, to Cheston, and afterwards to Hatfield and Ashridge.

There was a fearful state of unrest throughout the country. People never take religion calmly, and I suppose one could not expect them to slip from Catholic to Protestant without an upheaval. My father had always supported the Catholic Faith, the only difference being that he was Head of the Church of England. But Edward believed in the reformed religion and most of those about him did also; and they were determined to make England Protestant.

According to the converts, everything about the old religion was evil; saints were reviled; priests were mocked; and the Pope to them was the Devil incarnate.

Nor was this confined to words. Churches were violated, beautiful stained-glass windows smashed, altars desecrated, and there was public contempt for the old religious practices.

On the advice of François van der Delft, I remained in obscurity – though I did not need him to tell me to do that. Of course, there would be those who rose in anger against the new ideas; and I was next in succession; it was well known that I was an ardent Catholic. True, I had accepted my father's supremacy in the Church, but that was to save my life, and in my heart I had never agreed with it. Those who deplored the way the country was going would look to me.

It was an alarming time. It is always a dangerous situation when the king of a country is a minor, but when there is religious conflict – and one of such magnitude – the times are indeed perilous.

There was, of course, the Emperor. But for his powerful presence I should have been despatched long ago. I was his cousin, so there was the family tie; and, more important, I was next in succession and I should be the upholder of the Catholic Faith. In England, good Catholics must be hoping that Edward would not long survive; they would certainly pray that he would never marry and have offspring, for then it would be my turn, and this period of aberration, this straying from the fold, would be over. Triumphantly, I would bring England back to that fold, which she should never have left.

So I remained away from Court, and it was conveyed to me discreetly that there would be no interference for the time being in the manner in which religious observances were carried out in my household.

So, in the seclusion of my manors, I lived quietly, seeing François van der Delft whenever possible and learning all I could about what was going on in the country.

I often thought of Katharine and wondered what she was feeling. She would have her child, and I believed that would give her great comfort. Poor, sad lady! Indeed, I might apply this to myself. Life was harsh to some of us.

I thought a great deal about Elizabeth and wondered how she liked being sent away in disgrace. She would make excuses for herself – she would be like our father in that. How deep had her feeling for Seymour been? What a situation! As a princess second in line for the throne, she was old enough to realize that her cavortings with Seymour might have had results.

Anne Stanhope, Duchess of Somerset, gave birth to a boy. I hoped Katharine would be lucky. But when had she ever been lucky? I could imagine her . . . brought to bed . . . longing for her child, and all the time nursing her resentment against her husband. I hoped Elizabeth felt some qualms of conscience. How could she have behaved so in her own stepmother's house! It was hard for me to understand . . . not so much that she should have a fancy for the man, but that she could so far forget her honour, her *destiny*. I was well aware that Elizabeth had her eyes on the crown. There was a certain sparkle which appeared in them every time it was mentioned. She was healthy; she was young; how could she have risked throwing it all away for a philanderer like Seymour? Perhaps she thought she could have both. She was greedy, my sister.

Katharine gave birth to a little girl. I wished her well. Seymour would have preferred a boy. Do not all men? But Katharine, I knew, would be content with the child, whatever its sex.

Then came the sad news. Katharine had fallen into a fever soon after the child was delivered. One of my women heard afterwards from Lady Tyrwhit, who was attending her, what had happened.

'Poor soul,' Lady Tyrwhit had said. 'She told me she knew she would not leave her bed. The Admiral was there. He seemed to be overcome with grief. He tried to comfort her but she turned away from him, and spoke not to him but to me. She said, "I am most unhappy, Lady Tyrwhit. Those I love have cared not for me. They mock me. They laugh at my love. They wait for my death so that they may be with others." It was pathetic to hear the poor lady. The Admiral tried to soothe her but she would not listen. He said he would never harm her, and she answered that she thought he did not speak the truth. He begged her to remember that they loved each other and how they had wanted to be together more than anything else. She said to him coldly . . . oh, so coldly: "You have given me some shrewd taunts." Then she turned to me and said, "I do not think I shall live. I do not want to live." He wanted to lie beside her on the bed and hold her hand and tell her he loved her, to beg her to live, but she turned from him, and I told him he must go for he disturbed her rest.'

Lady Tyrwhit had wept when she told this, and when I heard it I myself felt near to tears. Very soon after that Katharine Parr passed away – such a good woman, who had never done harm to any. Life had been cruel to her.

There was change all about us, and no one knew from one day to another what would come next.

* * *

Thomas Seymour was one of the most reckless men I ever heard of. It was certain that he must sooner or later come to disaster. He should never have risen to such a high place – nor would he but for the charms of his sister. He lacked the good sense of his brother Edward. His were the handsome looks, the dashing personality, the ability to attract people to him; but without good sense such attributes can be dangerous.

They certainly were in his case. He had sought to charm the King and become his favourite uncle, and this he had done. That was when Edward was a child, but having had kingship thrust upon him, he had now come to a certain maturity. Frail he might be, but he was learned beyond his years; he had the pride – and, yes, the arrogance of a Tudor; although attracted by good looks he was not entirely bemused by them.

After the death of Katharine, Seymour appeared to have his feet firmly set on the slippery path to disaster.

He should have been content with his spectacular rise. His brother Edward had become the Protector of the Realm and was therefore the most important man in the country; and he himself had received great honours. But, as I said, the man was a fool and like most fools he estimated himself too highly.

He had begun his reckless acts by his marriage before the King was cold. It had been said that, if the marriage had been productive from the start, there might possibly have been a doubt as to the paternity of the child, and that could have been a very grave matter. However, that did not arise. But Seymour was a man who made wild plans and acted on them before he had had time to consider them. He had resented his brother's supremacy and had tried to win Edward's affection for himself alone. All his misdemeanours were revealed after he had gone too far and was under restraint.

Before the death of my father, Thomas Seymour had been a constant visitor to Edward's apartments; he had supplied the boy with pocket money and treated him with mingling respect and affection in a manner which had won the boy's affection and rendered Thomas the favourite uncle. When Edward was King and Somerset Protector, Thomas had talked slightingly of his brother and had tried to persuade the young King to take the government into his own hands. He, Thomas, would be beside him to help in the task. Edward listened, but he was not the simple boy Thomas evidently believed him to be.

Thomas had thought it would be a good idea if Edward married Lady Jane Grey, who was being brought up in his household. Naturally it occurred to him that, with two such children, whose affection he had won, the government of the country would be in his hands.

As soon as his wife was dead, he renewed his courtship of Elizabeth. Thomas Seymour's greatest weakness was in underestimating the intelligence of others.

How I wished I could have talked with my sister at this time. How I should have loved to know what was in her devious mind! Marry Seymour? No. That was not for Elizabeth. She had flirted with him in her stepmother's house because she was attracted by the man – most women were, and Elizabeth was not immune from masculine charm – but that had been a game to her. The practised seducer had not understood that he was not in command of the situation.

My sister Elizabeth was one who learned her lessons, and learned them well. She had no intention of making the same mistake twice.

Scheming against his brother, trying to win the confidence of the young King, trying to persuade Elizabeth into marriage, Seymour was a menace and a traitor to authority.

There was something else against him. He had used his position as Lord High Admiral to amass a fortune. A year or so previously he had set out to capture a certain pirate known as Thomessin who used the Scilly Isles as a base when he intercepted and robbed ships of all nations. The pirate could not stand out against Seymour's superior forces and was quickly captured; but when Thomessin explained to Seymour the profitability of privateering, the Lord High Admiral agreed to turn a blind eye to these activities in exchange for a share of the profits.

Somerset had offended certain of the landowners throughout the country, and Thomas sought the friendship of these people. He then had the idea of building up a force of his own, and for this purpose he indulged in devious practices with Sir William Sherrington, a rogue such as himself, who was vice-treasurer of the Mint at Bristol. This man had made a fortune by clipping coins and other nefarious actions. Seymour, conniving at this, obtained control of the Mint and was therefore able to build up a store of ammunition. His boast was that, in addition to this store, he had 10,000 men who would spring to arms at his command.

Even the most indulgent of brothers could not have allowed this to pass, and Somerset was certainly not that. He sent for Thomas, saying he wished to talk to him. Guessing what that conversation would be about, Seymour did not appear. There was only one action to take, and

Somerset took it. Thomas was arrested and imprisoned in the Tower.

That was when the story of his misdemeanours was brought to light, and very soon Sherrington, with Elizabeth's servants, Kate Ashley and Thomas Parry, were also in the formidable fortress.

Sherrington, Ashley and Parry were released but the arrest of her close servants must have been a shock to Elizabeth. Seymour was found guilty of treason; counterfeiting coins and his dealings with pirates and those whom he believed to be the King's enemies could all be called treason.

The end was inevitable. On the 20th of March he was taken out to Tower Hill and the handsome head which had charmed so many was severed from his body.

My thoughts were with Elizabeth. How much had she cared for him? I was very anxious to hear how she had received the news of his execution.

I did hear, for several had been present when she was told. She had shown no emotion. All she said was: 'He was a man of much wit and very little judgement.'

Yes, she was one who learned her lessons quickly and well. I doubted she would ever again come so close to disaster through a man.

* * *

There was a new king in France, for shortly after my father died, François Premier had followed him to the grave. In his place was Henri Deux – a very different man from his father. If he lacked François's culture, he possessed immense physical energy. Soon we were at war with him.

The Protector had concentrated his efforts on the war with Scotland, and France and Scotland were allies. The little Queen of Scots was now being brought up in the Court of France as the bride of the Dauphin, and our possessions in France were being attacked. Hence our involvement in an unpopular war.

The people were in rebellion. Many objected to having a new religion forced on them. There were risings in Essex, Norfolk and Oxfordshire. In Cornwall churchgoers insisted on priests bringing back the Mass. I heard that rebels were massing in Devonshire and were ready to march.

Cardinal Pole's name was mentioned. 'Bring him back!' was the cry.

I was getting worried. So was François van der Delft. Although it was comforting to know that so many people regretted the passing of the old religion and wanted it brought back, the more vociferous people became in its defence, the more dangerous was my position.

I knew that I was closely watched; they had not forbidden me to worship as I pleased, but that was only due to my powerful relation, the Emperor. I was certain that, but for him, I should have lost my head long ago.

There was trouble about matters other than religion. The country was in a state of upheaval. Food was not plentiful, and what there was of it was highly priced. There were great grievances over the enclosure of land which previously had been common land and open to everyone. In some places it was being fenced off by the lords of the manors; but those who had been grazing their cattle on it for years declared it belonged to the people.

It was in this connection that I first heard the name of Robert Kett. He held the manor of Wymondham in Norfolk from John Dudley, the Earl of Warwick. When men in his neighbourhood pulled down the fences which had been set up by those who would enclose the common lands, Kett joined them. He was a man of some standing and soon became their leader.

He marched on Norwich, and by the time he reached that town he had a force of 16,000, so this was not just a small rebellion. It was a rising of which the government had to take some notice.

Kett set up his camp at Mousehold Heath, and a list of grievances was drawn up. The demands were not great; they wanted the power of the lords of the manors to enclose their lands to be restricted, and men to be free to fish in all rivers and set up their dovecots.

A herald arrived in the King's name offering pardon if the rebels would go back to their homes, to which Kett replied that the King should pardon the wicked, not innocent and just men.

Fighting then broke out between Kett's army and the King's men. The result was that John Dudley, Earl of Warwick, came to Norwich with an army. The rebels were no match for trained soldiers and were soon defeated, Kett being taken prisoner.

The rebellion was over. Kett was found guilty of treason and taken back to Norwich, and his body was hung in chains for all to see what happened to those who set themselves against the King and his government.

The rising had nothing to do with religion but it was an example of the general unrest throughout the country.

I knew that Somerset and Dudley were uneasy about me. If they had dared, they would have found some way of getting rid of me; but if they did so, that could arouse the wrath of the Emperor, and he might even have been induced to invade the country. There was a possibility that the Catholic population, which must be large, might have risen. It was gratifying to me, but highly dangerous.

Wherever I went, there were people to cheer me. I had made up my mind now that never again would I deny my faith. I would die rather. I saw my mission coming nearer and nearer. Edward's health did not improve . . . and after him, it would be my turn. I was sure many would rally to my banner. The state into which my father had led the country after his break with Rome would be at an end. I should lead England back to the fold. There were many about me . . . the unseen watchers . . . the faithful who would emerge as soon as I was there. It could happen . . . soon.

In the meantime I must keep myself alive. If I did not, the crown would go to Elizabeth. And what would she do . . . this calculating, scheming girl woman? She would do what she considered best for Elizabeth. That should not be my way. I would dedicate my life to the service of God, and that meant bringing my country back to Rome.

The Act of Uniformity had been passed in January of that year. It ordered that the Book of Common Prayer be used by all ministers. Failure to use it would mean that they forfeited their stipends, and there would be heavier – and indeed severe – punishments for second and third offences.

I received a call from Chancellor Rich, who informed me that the Act of Uniformity must be obeyed by all, and there could be no exceptions. I told him that I would worship in my own way, and I knew from his response that he would be afraid to take drastic action against me. Once more I thanked my cousin, the Emperor.

I was told that my Comptroller, Sir Robert Rochester, and my chaplain, Hopton, were to return with Rich and his men that they might answer certain questions which the Council wished to put to them.

I felt defiant, for I sensed in Rich a desire not to offend me. The times were uncertain. Edward did not look as though he would live to maturity. I was after all the next in succession. It was true that there were many powerful men who would try to prevent my coming to the throne, but who could say what would happen? So . . . Rich was determined not to upset me too much.

I said: 'I am afraid my Comptroller is much too busy to leave the household at present; as for my chaplain, he has been sick and is not yet recovered.'

I was amazed at his meekness. He and his party accepted my word and left.

But that was not the end of the matter. There was a further summons, this time from the Protector himself. Rochester's and Hopton's presence was requested by the Council.

I realized that I could not refuse to send them, for if I did their next move would be to come and take them away; it was better for them to go of their own accord rather than as prisoners.

I wondered whether they would be put into the Tower. There would be an outcry if they were. I myself would protest, and I would make sure that it was known that I did. The trouble all over the country must have made them pause for thought, for Sir Robert Rochester and Hopton returned shortly. They were to try to persuade me to forsake my old ways in religion and consider the enlightened form.

Van der Delft was very alarmed when he heard my servants had been taken for questioning. He went to see Somerset and told him his master would be dismayed if he came to the conclusion that I was being forced to act contrary to my beliefs.

The ambassador came to me to tell me the result of that meeting.

'The Protector has said that you may continue as you wish providing you make no great noise about it. In private, there is no objection. "She may hear Mass privately in her own apartments," he said.'

It was a reprieve.

* * *

Life was not running smoothly for Protector Somerset. The exchequer was low, and there was no money to pay the German mercenaries who were fighting for him on the Scottish border. Consequently the Scots had gained one or

366

two important victories, and the French were taking advantage of the situation. There was rebellion throughout the country on religious grounds, on account of the depreciation of the currency and the enclosure laws. Landowners were against him no less than the common people.

Warwick's star was rising, and Warwick was a very ambitious man who wanted to rule alone. Wriothesley, who had become Earl of Southampton, had never been a friend. He was at heart a follower of the old religion, though that was something he did not stress at this time. Warwick had scored a military success when he had put down the rising in Norfolk and was regarded as the better man by many people. Somerset, they said, had become Protector merely because he was the King's uncle. Warwick was organizing secret meetings, the object being to turn men against Somerset.

Realizing what was happening, the Protector sought to rally his friends and to his dismay found that few were loyal to him, and when the City of London turned against him he knew there was little he could do to save himself.

It was not long before he found himself in the Tower.

My brother Edward surprised me. He was supposed to be fond of his uncle but he made no move to speak for him. He accepted the imprisonment of his Uncle Edward as he had the death of Uncle Thomas – his favourite, I remembered.

Somerset put up little fight to defend himself. He had come to understand that governing a country was not as easy as he had thought. His listlessness suggested that he was eager to give up the thankless task, for he accepted all the complaints against himself, admitted failure and threw himself on the mercy of the Council.

The result was that he was deprived of his protectorate and of lands to the value of £2,000. Then he was given a free pardon. How lucky he must have felt himself to be, to have escaped with his head. Perhaps this had come about through his meekness, but I believe that his enemies might have feared the effect his death would have on the people. In any case, he was freed, admitted to the Privy Council and made a gentleman of the King's bedchamber.

Warwick clearly did not want open warfare between them at that stage and, to prove that there was no enmity between them, shortly afterwards Somerset's eldest daughter married Warwick's eldest son, Viscount Lisle.

This seemed very amicable. I wondered if it occurred to Somerset that things are sometimes not what they seem.

I did not feel very easy in my mind at the thought.

* * *

Elizabeth was now at Court. I heard that she was made much of there. I had not been invited. I should have been a little worried if I had been, but it was not difficult to understand what this new favour to Elizabeth was all about.

I was not sure what her religious views were, but I guessed they would be trimmed to the order of the day. She had said, 'What does it matter how one worships God, as long as He is worshipped? Do you think He minds?'

That seemed utter blasphemy to me; and it was said with an innocence of which I did not think my sister capable.

The King was a Protestant and, the laws of the country being in favour of that religion, Elizabeth would be a Protestant. That was what the Council liked. Edward's health was deteriorating. Who next? they were asking. Mary, to plunge us back to Rome? Or Elizabeth, who will be quite accommodating?

Clearly it must be Elizabeth.

The King, I heard, was devoted to her. She would know how to sweeten him. She was brazen. Most young girls would have hidden themselves away after what had happened with Seymour. But now Seymour was dead and it might be that soon his brother would be, too. I would not trust Warwick. Elizabeth would behave as though she had never been involved in that unsavoury scandal and would doubtless have everyone believing that she was an innocent and simple girl. Not so innocent. Never simple. I could imagine her, smug and content, attracting attention with her bright reddish hair and witty manner. The King would be entranced and she was in her element.

But I could not be forgotten. What did they plan for me?

I had not disliked Somerset. He was at heart a good man, I believed. He had been overcome by ambition and had seen his fortunes change when Jane pleased the King; but now they were changing again, for he had reckoned without the wily Warwick. One could never know what Warwick was planning.

I was now certain that, if my brother Edward was near to death, they would seek to remove me. Should I suddenly awake one night to find myself ill after eating something . . . drinking some wine?

I was an encumbrance. They knew my mind, I had made that clear. I was not of their faith. They knew I would seek to bring back the old religion and return England to Rome; and if I succeeded, what would become of these men who had followed my father and gone on to what he had never intended?

I became very much afraid. I was constantly reminding myself of the task which had been given to me. I had to save my country, and these men would do everything in their power to thwart me; and the only way to be sure of doing this would be to remove me.

I became obsessed with the notion that they were planning my death. I would wake in the night trembling, imagining hired assassins creeping into my bedchamber. I remembered the little princes in the Tower. They had been sleeping in their beds, it was said, when men crept in and placed pillows over their faces. I would start at every footfall; when messengers came, I would think they brought a warrant for my arrest. I remembered so well

369

those terrible days when Catharine Howard had feared her death was imminent. I understood how she had suffered.

I had my mission. I must save myself if possible, and each day I was believing myself to be in more and more acute danger.

To whom could I look for help? There was only one who could save me, whose influence had been a beneficial source to me all my life; my cousin, the Emperor.

I recalled those days when I had thought I was to be his bride. I had never forgotten standing at the stairs with my mother, while the barge carrying him, with my father, came in. He was arriving to claim his bride, and that bride was myself. I could see him now, a pale, serious young man in black velvet and a gold chain, looking serene and dignified beside my glittering father. He had taken my hands and smiled kindly. I was in love with him; or I believed I was because my women told me so.

He had wanted to take me back to Spain, but my parents would not allow that. If I had gone, I might have been his wife these many years.

He had given me a ring as a token, saying the ring was a sign of his regard for me. If ever I was in distress and apart from him and sent him the ring, he would do all in his power to help me.

I still had that ring. I took it out and an idea came to me. Now was the time to send it.

I wrote to François van der Delft and asked him to come to me.

Before he could reach me, I received an invitation to go to Court for Christmas. My brother wished me to join the family. Elizabeth would be there, and I should be, too.

A fit of trembling seized me. I knew what this meant. There would be religious ceremonies, and I should be forced to observe the new ways. I should be deprived of the Mass. I was being asked not because I was a member

ll follow a

the Cr

use they wanted to show me I must

elf. 'I will not deny my faith.'

I told them that my state of

s well aware of them

dangerous.

about him. His

a persistent

He said: 'The King. health does not improve. He su d a persistent cough, and he has grown very thin.'

'Somerset is without power,' I said. 'It is all in the hands of Warwick.'

Van der Delft nodded.

'They have asked me to go to Court for Christmas,' I told him.

I saw the alarm come into his eyes.

'You know why, I see,' I said. 'It is to make me conform to their way of worship. I will not, Ambassador. I will not.'

'No. So you will not go. You will plead ill health.'

'It is the only way.'

'I like it not.'

'That is why I have asked you to come and see me. I have been thinking a great deal about my position here. I am sure I am most unsafe. I do not sleep well. I am disturbed by dreams. The slightest noise and I awake in terror.'

'It is not good,' he said.

'What shall I do?'

He said, looking over his shoulder and speaking quietly: 'If the King dies, which he could well do, you are the next in succession.'

'Do you think they will ever let me come to the throne?'

'They would have to. There are thousands in the country who would stand beside you.'

'They are trying to promote Elizabeth.'

371

'I know.'

'She will go whichev...

faith that leads her to...

want Elizabeth. The...

back to Rome. The...

before . . . the Kin...

He was silent. The...

man; he suffere... been a comfort to me, but he was not

was kindly and...

like Chapuys whom I missed very much. Van der Delft

...ouncil

...the country

...al to be rid of me

...m intently. He was an old

...e gout and he was not well. He

was nervous. He had been sent to serve my interests. The
Emperor relied on him to keep me safe for the great project
which, with Edward's health in its present state, could not
be long delayed. The testing time was close.

I said: 'I must get out of the country. I must have a
refuge where I can live in safety until the time when I can
claim my throne and do my duty to God and my country.'

'You mean escape . . . leave England?'

'It is what I have decided. I firmly believe that if I stay
here they will find some way of ridding themselves of me.'

'They would never let you go.'

'Indeed they would not. So I must go in secret.'

He looked alarmed. 'It would be a great undertaking.'

'Nevertheless, I am of the opinion that it is the only way.
I have a premonition that they are plotting to be rid of me.
I must foil them in that. To stay here . . . their easy victim
. . . is to play into their hands. You know my health is not
good. Even now I am telling them that it will not allow me
to go to Court. It will be easy for them. "Poor Mary," they
will say. "She was never very strong. It was inevitable." I
can see it all so clearly. You must help me, Ambassador.'

'I will do everything I can.'

'Very well. Get in touch with the Emperor. Tell him
what we have discussed. Send this ring to him. He will
remember it, for he himself gave it to me long ago. When

he sees it, he will know how dire my need is, for otherwise I should not have sent the ring to him.'

Van der Delft was silent for a few moments. Then he said: 'I will write to the Emperor at once, and I will send a trusted messenger with the ring. There must be absolute silence on this matter. I beg of you, do not speak of it to anyone.'

I readily agreed with him.

I felt a good deal better after van der Delft left. I put my trust in the Emperor.

* * *

Eagerly I waited for some reply. I felt better. I must live until the rescue came.

After weeks of my waiting, watching the roads, finding the frustration almost unendurable, van der Delft came with a reply from the Emperor.

He was hesitant so I guessed before he told me that the Emperor was not over-enthusiastic about the scheme.

'What does he say?' I commanded. 'Please tell me. Hold nothing back.'

'The Emperor feels it would be a hazardous undertaking. The task of getting you out of the kingdom could be almost insuperable.'

'I know it will be difficult but surely with careful planning . . .'

Van der Delft nodded. He was wary. He did not tell me what I discovered later, that the Emperor had raised the point of who would support me when I arrived in his realm. I was glad I did not know that, for it would have wounded me deeply. It had not occurred to me at the time that a princess must have her household, and a cousin of the Emperor could not live like a pauper, and if I left England I would be thrown on his bounty. But van der Delft had the tact and courtesy to keep that from me. I should have remembered that, during the difficult times through which my mother had passed, the Emperor had always been too deeply involved with his dominions to give more than moral support. I should have been more realistic. I should have understood that, to the Emperor, the trials of his relations and even the break with Rome were not major concerns. He was the most successful and most powerful ruler in Europe and could not be diverted in the smallest way from the immense task of remaining so. He would help me only if that did not disturb him too much and if no sacrifices were demanded.

That was why he was not enthusiastic about my plan to leave the country. Instead he thought of a more traditional way out of my troubles. Marriage.

If I married, I could leave the country with dignity and so escape from danger.

I said: 'And when the time comes for me to claim the throne?'

'The Emperor says you would have a husband to help you.'

'But I should not be here.'

'The Emperor thinks it is a good plan, and you would not be here if you escaped.'

'And whom does he suggest?'

'Dom Luiz, brother of the King of Portugal.'

'No,' I said. 'No.'

'The Emperor feels it is the best solution.'

Was that a hint? If I did not agree, I could not rely on his help?

Van der Delft was putting forward his master's point of view. He reiterated: 'If you escaped as you suggest, you would not be here. A husband would help you gain your throne.'

It did occur to me then that the Emperor was thinking that, if I married, I should not be his responsibility, but there was something in the suggestion that if I had to fight for my inheritance I would need help.

374

I began to see that my plan to leave the country was fraught with difficulties, not only in putting it into practice but in what might follow.

I felt depressed after van der Delft's visit. But I need not have worried about the proposed marriage. It was merely a proposition put forward by the Emperor and the Portuguese were as lukewarm about it as I was.

Dom Luiz gracefully extricated himself by stating that he could not agree to the marriage until there was a religious change in England, which, of course, meant that the Council refused to go further. In any case, I should have needed a dowry, and I understood the exchequer was extremely impoverished so the marriage would have been ruled out on that aspect alone.

Christmas had come. I had spent mine in retirement, pleading illness. It was a good excuse. I had had many illnesses and people believed I was not strong. Edward was not in good health either; the only one of my father's children who seemed to have escaped the weakness was Elizabeth.

I was still in a terrible state of disquiet, wondering what schemes were being concocted against me. The situation had changed little. Elizabeth was still at Court, being treated, some said, like the heiress presumptive. I might not have existed.

My Comptroller of the Household, Sir Robert Rochester, came to me one day and told me he had disquieting news.

I waited in some dismay for his revelation.

'Of course, it is only gossip, Princess, but these things sometimes hold a few grains of truth. It is said that there are changes to be made in your household and that its members are now to be prevented from hearing Mass.'

'You mean some of the members of my household . . .'

'No, my lady Princess, you too.'

I said: 'I think I must see the ambassador without delay.'

Van der Delft arrived and I told him what I had heard. He, too, had heard the rumour and had already imparted it to the Emperor.

He had already received the Emperor's reply and was preparing to come to me when my message had arrived.

'The Emperor,' he said, 'is considering the escape.'

My spirits rose. I had to face the danger of leaving England, but when one has lived in fear of death for many months, action is desirable.

Van der Delft said we should need the co-operation of people whom we could trust. I understood that. I told him that Sir Robert Rochester had always been a good friend to me, that he was a staunch Catholic and I would trust him with my life.

Van der Delft had the same opinion of Sir Robert, and we called him in to tell him of the plan.

He said he had feared for my safety for some time and was glad that I was to be taken away. He would do anything he could to help. He had a friend who had a boat. The boat could sail up the River Blackwater as far as Malden, which was close by Woodham Water, the house in which I was at this time staying. The boat could carry me out to a Flemish ship which would be waiting at sea.

'Can we trust this man?' asked van der Delft.

'Yes. And he would not know it was the Princess he was taking. He would just see a figure in a concealing cloak. I would imply to him that I am the one who is fleeing the country.'

Van der Delft continued to look very worried. I think he felt that the project went beyond the duties expected of an ambassador. He was in poor health, and I am sure he would have given a great deal not to be involved in such an adventure.

I wondered how my staunch old Chapuys would have reacted. With a little more enthusiasm, I should imagine.

I believe that in his heart he was uneasy because of the

Emperor's reluctance. My cousin had agreed to the project only as a last resort. The plan was full of weaknesses as far as he was concerned and I am sure it was only because he felt my life to be in danger that he agreed to it. After all, I should be out of the country at the crucial moment; but it was no use having me *in* the country . . . *dead*. I supposed the Emperor thought this was the lesser of two evils and that was the sole reason why he agreed to it.

Van der Delft told me that he would write to the Emperor telling him of Rochester's suggestion, and when he had his master's approval, the plan would be put into action.

Shortly afterwards I received a further communication from van der Delft. He was being recalled and in his place would be Jehan Scheyfve. I was horrified. To exchange ambassadors in the middle of such a project seemed extraordinary to me. I began to suspect that van der Delft had asked for the exchange.

He told me that Scheyfve would shortly be calling on me, which I presumed meant that he himself was saying goodbye.

Robert Rochester came to me with an alarming piece of news. Summer was coming on, and it was in summer that tempers ran high and people's grievances were uppermost in their minds. The Council did not want a repeat of rebellions, so they were making a careful watch of the roads this summer, and people who might not be about their ordinary business would be stopped and questioned. It was the duty of every householder to take part in this watch; any who did not do so might find himself in trouble with the Council. It was for the protection of all, and they must do their duty.

'It means,' said Rochester, 'that the roads will be watched and, if you are seen riding to Malden, which you almost certainly would be, the alarm would be given. Moreover, this friend of mine has taken alarm and will not be involved in this.'

I was in a quandary. Van der Delft, who had been working on the plan, was now going, and this new man was in his place. What did he know of it? I wondered.

I sent an urgent message to van der Delft. He must come and say goodbye to me . . . in person, I insisted.

I hoped he would understand by the wording of my message that it was imperative that I see him.

When he arrived, I was appalled by his appearance. The man looked really ill, and he was decidedly worried. I told him Rochester's news without delay.

'Then,' he said, 'we have to plan again.'

'But you are going away.'

He was silent and I went on: 'What of this new man?'

'It has been decided that Scheyfve should know nothing of the plan.'

'But you will not be here . . . and if this man knows nothing of it . . . what can we do?'

'Scheyfve cannot know of this. Imagine what would happen. Suppose the plot failed and he were involved . . . and if it succeeds and it were known that he was aware of it . . . he would be discredited.'

'Is that why you are being withdrawn?'

'It is that . . . and for reasons of health.'

I felt bewildered and very much alone. I could see that no one wished to be involved in my dangerous existence.

I was wrong. Van der Delft was a good man; he was genuinely sorry for me, and he was going to do everything he could to help.

He said to me: 'If this plan is undertaken, it must succeed.'

'How can we be sure that it will?'

'We must not attempt it until we are sure.'

'I will trust in God,' I said.

He lifted his shoulders. He looked so terribly ill, poor

man. I knew his gout was very painful. But still he wanted to help. He had a good secretary whom he could trust, a certain Jean Dubois; and his idea was that, disguised as a merchant, Dubois should come in a ship bringing grain for the household.

That would not be considered unusual, for grain was now and then brought to the household. When the grain was delivered, I should be smuggled out. We should be away before I was missed, and I should very soon be in Flushing.

I said: 'Will you come too, Ambassador?'

He looked helpless.

'You must come,' I said. 'I shall need you.'

'Dubois is a trusty servant.'

'But you must come. I must have your promise.'

He smiled at me almost tenderly. 'I give it,' he said. 'I shall come as a grain merchant, and we shall have you out of harm's way . . . in no time at all.'

* * *

I began to wonder if everything must go wrong for me.

When I heard the news I was astounded and stricken with grief, for, though I had compared van der Delft with Chapuys to his disadvantage, I had grown fond of him and I had relied upon him. He had been with me through a dangerous time and he had been my only link with the Emperor, whom, in spite of everything, I still regarded as my saviour.

On arriving in the Netherlands, van der Delft wrote to the Emperor an account of what had happened, and as soon as he had finished he took to his bed. He had fallen into a fever and was delirious.

It was apparent that he was on his deathbed. He was suffering from gout, but it seemed that the plots for my escape had so preyed on his mind that he had become further enfeebled.

The poor man went into raving delirium and talked of the boat which was to take me away from England; he had rambled about the watch on the roads, and the dangers of getting me to the boat. There must have been many who heard it.

I received a note from the Emperor. It came sealed by way of the ambassador who, of course, knew nothing of its contents. It was very disconcerting to have an ambassador in whom I could not confide. Chapuys had been my great comfort, and after him van der Delft . . . and now, when I most needed help, there was no one to give it to me.

The Emperor did not want to drop the plan in spite of all the difficulties which had arisen, but he thought it must be put aside for a few weeks while his spies informed him what effect the ravings of van der Delft had had. He would send men into the markets to drink with the merchants and there discover if anything had leaked out.

In due course I heard from him again. Apparently there had been no mention of the plot, and it seemed that all was safe.

Now we were free to go ahead.

I was overcome with melancholy and great trepidation. Van der Delft was replaced by a man I did not know. A stranger was coming, disguised as a grain merchant, and I was to escape with him . . . to the unknown. It was a frightening proposition.

There would be ships lying off the coast, and a small grain ship would sail up the river. Grain would be delivered, and then I should be taken out to safety. It was a dangerous operation but it had the sanction of the Emperor, and Dubois was eager to carry it out with distinction.

We received a message that the merchants had arrived and would bring a sample of corn for the comptroller to see. The next step would be for Dubois to bring the corn into the house.

I had decided which ladies were going with me. I had packed my jewels. I was ready.

We heard that people were watching on the roads. They would be there on the route along which I had to pass to reach the river. It would be a great feat for any of those people to capture me; and, moreover, they would be in trouble if it were discovered that they had allowed me to slip through.

Sir Robert Rochester came to me and said that he had something on his mind and wished to speak to me. I bade him continue.

'My lady Princess,' he said. 'There is a rumour that the King is in a very delicate state of health. He cannot marry. He will never produce an heir. It could be that, in a very short time, you will be the rightful queen of this country.'

'I know it,' I said. 'The thought is constantly with me.'

'You are the hope of the country, Princess. Many people are waiting for you to return them to God's Church.'

I nodded and was silent.

'If you were not here,' went on Sir Robert, 'it would be the Lady Elizabeth.'

'I should have to come back to claim my right.'

'It is never easy to come back, my lady.'

'Sir Robert, what are you suggesting?'

He was silent for a few seconds, and then he said slowly: 'This is a desperate operation. If you are discovered, what will happen?'

'I shall be taken to the Tower. I shall be judged a traitor. I have been in communication with a foreign power. You know what that means, Sir Robert.'

'They would seize upon it. It would give them the opportunity for which they have been waiting.'

'You are telling me that it is unwise for me to go.'

'I believe, Princess, that if you go . . . even if the escape is successful and you reach Flanders, you will have lost a kingdom.'

381

I saw the reasoning behind this.

I said: 'I am in fear of losing my life here.'

'That is true, but we will be watchful, and you have many friends. I believe your enemies are aware of this, and they would not dare to harm you.'

'They might by subtle means.'

'There is a possibility. But your servants love you and guard you well. They pray, Princess, for the time when you mount the throne and sweep away this evil which has taken possession of the land.'

'You are telling me I must stay.'

'It is your decision, Princess.'

'Dubois will be here soon,' I reminded him.

'You could tell him you were not prepared to go . . . just yet.'

'After all the preparations!'

'The Emperor will try again if he is really in favour of your escape.'

'You think he is not entirely so?'

It was then I learned that the Emperor had hesitated because he feared he would have to provide me with a household and that I should be a drain on his exchequer.

I said: 'The Emperor was ever a careful man. It is the reason why he is the richest and most powerful man in the world.'

'That may be so, Princess. But would you wish to be a burden . . . one he might shoulder reluctantly?'

'What then, Sir Robert? Are we to tell Dubois when he comes with his grain that I will not go?'

'That is for you to say, my lady Princess. The decision is entirely yours. If you decide to go, rest assured that I will do all I can to assure your safety. It is for you to say whether you will risk staying here in order to gain your kingdom, or whether you will take an equal risk and give it away to those who would destroy it in the eyes of God.'

I wanted to be alone to think. He had reduced me to a terrible state of indecision.

I spent a restless night. I did not sleep at all. Rochester was right, I told myself. I would be throwing away my heritage if I left. I had soothed my conscience by telling myself I would return and win my kingdom when it was mine by right. But how could I do that? With the Emperor's help? Had the Emperor come to save my mother when she was in dire distress? Would not his continuing commitments demand all his attention, all his forces? That was how it had been in the past. Would it change? The Emperor would certainly wish to see the true faith returned to England, but how far would he be prepared to risk his forces to bring it about?

I had to be realistic. I had to rely entirely on my own judgement. I was in danger here. I was in constant fear that one day or night some assassin would make an end of me. I would continue to live in fear. But should I be safe in Flanders? Had not my father sent assassins abroad to try to kill Reginald Pole? They had not succeeded but they might have done so.

Let me look truth in the face. God had put me in this position. I could perform a great mission if I lived. My life was in God's hands. If he wished me to succeed in this great task, I needed His help. I needed His guidance. To go or to stay? Rochester had made me see clearly that if I went I might save my own life but in doing so lose my kingdom.

I prayed, passionately asking for guidance.

I felt the presence of God beside me, and in the morning I knew what I should do.

* * *

Sir Robert had received a letter from Dubois.

He had arrived with the corn, and he and his men had made it known in the town that they were there. That night the water would be high in the river, and that would enable the boat to come right in. It would not be so easy after this night. Because of the tide, it would be reasonable for the boat to be in the most convenient spot at two o'clock. I should not bring too many women with me, for that would arouse suspicion.

Rochester sent a note to Dubois asking him to meet him in the churchyard. If they were seen together, there would be no cause for suspicion as it would be thought they were discussing the consignment of corn.

I saw Rochester before he went.

I said to him: 'I have been questioning myself all the night.'

'I know it, Princess, and you have come to the right conclusion. You are too good a Catholic to have come to any other.'

'I have a duty,' I said. 'I can do nothing else.'

He took my hand and kissed it. 'It cannot be long,' he said, 'before I shall fall on my knees and call you Her Majesty the Queen.'

'There is much danger to be lived through first.'

'But with God's help, my lady . . .'

'Yes,' I answered, 'with God's help.'

We were silent for a moment. I was thinking of what we had said. If overheard, if could cost us our lives. I was certain of Sir Robert's loyalty to me, and I was exultant in the midst of my fear, for I knew I had chosen rightly.

I said: 'You will go to the churchyard and tell Dubois.'

'I must break it gently,' he replied. 'If I say bluntly that you are not going after all this preparation, I cannot answer for his reaction. I think it better to hint at a postponement.'

'But he says it is tonight or never.'

'Well, my lady, it is not going to be tonight.'

He went to his tryst with Dubois, and when he returned he came straight to me and said that he had told Dubois that there was no chance of my going this night. The watch

384

on the roads had been doubled and I should certainly be stopped. 'The Emperor must understand how dangerous it is,' he had said, 'and when he does he will realize the necessity for postponement. The escape could have a better chance of success in the winter.'

Dubois had been deflated. He had said brusquely that he was only acting on orders and it was not for him to make decisions. He could not believe that the Princess, after all her entreaties for help, had, now the moment had come to put the plan into action, decided not to carry it out.

'He is very disappointed in us,' I said.

'He said he had had his instructions from the Emperor, my lady, and he would need letters from you discharging him from his duties.'

'He shall have them,' I promised. 'It shall be known that no blame is attached to him.'

'I told him,' said Rochester, 'that I would give a great deal to see you safely out of the country, and indeed I had been the first to suggest it. I impressed on him that it was not that you did not wish to go but that you felt this was not the moment, for it is very unsafe to do so and the chances of being caught, due to this watch on the roads, have been multiplied. In the winter it could be considered again. He said that to him it was just a question of to go or to stay. He merely wanted a Yes or No.'

Later Dubois came to see me. By this time I was completely convinced that I must not go.

The man was irritated. He had been sent out to perform a mission, and he would return with it unfulfilled. He needed my written word that it had failed through no fault of his and that it was entirely my decision that at the last moment I would stay.

He left us and was soon on his way to Flanders.

I do not know how the rumours got about. It is always difficult to say. A careless word here and there is taken up and exaggerated. However, rumours were circulating that

I had escaped. There was talk of visits to the house at Woodham Water and of grain ships sent by the Emperor to convey me out of the country. People were intrigued by the thought of men disguising themselves as grain merchants and coming to the aid of a princess.

The Council was aware of what had happened and had all ports manned with soldiers; all ships coming in were subjected to special examination.

I was not surprised when messengers came from Court. I was asked in such a way which made it a command either to move inland or to go to Court.

My reply was my usual one. My health was not good enough to allow me to move.

I knew that I was in more acute danger than ever.

At Last – The Queen

Somerset had fallen into trouble again. I was sorry to hear this, for he had, in his way, been good to me. I think it was due to him that I had been allowed to hear Mass unmolested all this time.

He seemed to be gaining support in the country, and Warwick losing popularity. Somerset planned to replace him but Warwick was a wily man, and he wanted more and more power. He had ennobled himself and was now the Duke of Northumberland.

Before long he declared he had uncovered a plot hatched by Somerset to murder him, Northumberland, and seize power. Somerset was commanded to come to the Council and was arrested and put into the Tower, accused of plotting to secure the crown for his heirs.

There was proof that he had planned to replace Northumberland, but that in itself was no crime. However, Northumberland was determined on his destruction and, as he was the most powerful man in the country, Somerset was found guilty and condemned to lose his head.

He met his death with dignity and was buried in St Peter's Chapel, between Anne Boleyn and Catharine Howard.

With unscrupulous Northumberland in command and my brother turning more and more to the Reformed Religion, I was becoming very uneasy indeed.

To my dismay, a letter arrived from the Council and another from the King. I was very distressed when I read them, although I was prepared for some drastic action after it became known that I had contemplated escape.

So far, I had been allowed to worship as I pleased, but that was to be so no longer, it seemed.

My brother demanded that I conform to the new religion, which was that of the country. I had misunderstood if I thought I might do that which was forbidden to others. Was it not scandalous, he wrote, that so high a personage as myself should deny his sovereignty? I saw what he meant. In disobeying the laws laid down by the present regime, I was disobeying *him*. It was unnatural, he went on, that his own sister should behave so. I must be reminded that further disobedience was unacceptable to him and could incur penalties which were applied to heretics.

What did he mean? Burned at the stake? Hanged, drawn and quartered? Perhaps as I was royal he would be satisfied with my head.

He finished by adding that he would say no more, for if he did, he might be even harsher. But he would tell me this: He would not see his laws disobeyed, and those who broke them must beware.

If ever I heard a threat, I did then, and I was saddened to realize that my once gentle brother was the tool of those men who ruled us, for Northumberland was to all intents King of this realm, and Edward was just a figurehead.

I could not believe that, if I were face to face with my brother, he would speak to me as he had written, for I had no doubt that that letter had been dictated by Northumberland.

Of one thing I was certain: I would not deny the Mass. I was not like my sister Elizabeth, adopting whatever guise she thought would be to her advantage. I must stand firm now. It could be that at any moment the day would come when my mission would be clear before me. I believed that all over the country people were waiting for me . . . looking to me . . . I must not betray them.

I decided I would visit my brother and see for myself whether he would be so harsh to my face.

On a cool March day I rode into London. It was a bold thing to do but I thought the occasion warranted it. I took with me a certain number of my household so that I could come in style. My reception along the road amazed me. It was wonderful to see the people coming out of their homes to cry: 'Long live the Princess Mary.'

Many of them joined my party, and to my intense joy I saw that a number of them were wearing rosaries. This proclaimed them true Catholics. Clearly they wished me to know that their beliefs were the same as mine.

It was heartwarming. I had been dreading the meeting with my brother but those good people gave me courage. That journey taught me that there were more with me than I had dared hope. I believed then that in truth a large number of people all over the country were waiting for me, praying for the time when I should come and wipe out heresy. I had been right not to escape. My place was here among the people who relied on me.

When I arrived at the gates of the city, though I had set out with a company of fifty, my ranks were swollen to 400, and it was difficult to make our way through the streets, so crowded were they. I wondered what my brother would think of my reception by the people; but he would think what Northumberland told him to.

I felt bold by this time. I had to face the Council but I was deeply shocked by the sight of my brother. He was much more feeble than when I had last seen him, and he was plagued by an irritating cough. I felt great pity for him and with it a return of the love I had felt for him when he was a little boy. He looked so frail – fragile almost – too young to have such a burden thrust upon him. It was pathetic the way he tried to take a kingly stance and cast stern looks in my direction.

He told me that in defying the Council I was disobeying the will of our father.

'Your Majesty,' I said, 'a promise was given to the Emperor's ambassador, François van der Delft, that I should not be forced to deny the Mass.'

My brother replied that he had made no promise to van der Delft and added rather naïvely that he had been sharing in affairs for only a year.

I said quickly that he had not then drawn up the ordinances for the new religion and therefore, in not obeying them, I was not disobeying him.

He looked bewildered, and I went on to ask him how he could expect me to forsake what I had been taught from my earliest days?

'Your father's will stated that you must obey the Council. Northumberland told me.'

'Only where my possible marriage was concerned,' I retorted. 'I believe the King, our father, ordered Masses for his soul each day, and this has not been done, so it would appear that it is Your Majesty and others who are not obeying the King's wishes.'

So the talk went back and forth for two hours, and we arrived nowhere, for I was determined not to give way; and my reception as I had ridden to London and that of the citizens of the capital had shown these men quite clearly that if they harmed me there would be an outcry from the people.

I turned to my brother and said that all that mattered to me was that my soul was God's. As to my body, they might use it as they pleased. They could take my life if they must . . . but my soul was God's, and it should remain so.

I could see the exasperation in the men who had hoped to break my spirit. But in truth I seemed now not afraid of death. Others had died for their faith. I thought of brave Anne Askew who had been tortured and burned at the stake. I thought of those noble monks who had suffered the most barbarous and humiliating of all deaths. They had undergone that dire penalty but they would be in Heaven now . . . glorified . . . saints who had died for their religion.

No, I can say that I was not afraid any more, and a lack of fear frustrates an enemy who is at heart cowardly.

I went on, looking at Edward: 'Do not believe those who speak evil of me. I always have been and always will be Your Majesty's obedient and loving sister.'

I remained at Court, wondering what effect this meeting would have. I believed that it had disconcerted Northumberland and bothered my brother.

Scheyfve came to see me a few days later. He told me he had sent a report of the meeting to his master and was waiting to hear the result. He had told the Emperor of my reception by the people and the manner in which I had stood for my religion.

'They must have come to the conclusion that I will not be moved,' I said. 'I will remain true to my faith no matter what the consequences.'

Scheyfve nodded approvingly.

'I believe that it would be disastrous for you to change now,' he said. 'The effect on the people would be great. There were so many wearing rosaries, and it is my belief that they are waiting . . . waiting for the day. They are all true Catholics at heart, and they want to be led back to the true faith. It would not do for the one they look to as leader to show weakness now.'

'I will show no weakness,' I said. 'I know what I have to do.'

It was as when I was on the verge of the flight that I suddenly knew that I must stay. And now I knew what I had to do.

It was a week or so later when Scheyfve called again. He had heard from the Emperor, who had sent a letter to the

Council. In it he had threatened war with England if the right to worship as I pleased was denied to me.

I was exultant. I was sure that I was going in the right direction.

* * *

It was Christmas of that year 1552. I was not at Court but a few days after the festival I decided to call on my brother to wish him well. I had felt sorry for him when we had met in the Council for I knew that he was acting as Northumberland bade him and that his harsh words had given him as much pain as they had me.

In any case, the object of the meeting had been to stop my worshipping in the way I always had; and that had failed. Scheyfve said it was due to the Emperor's threat, and this was in some measure true; but I did believe that my reception by the people had some part in it; Northumberland must remember that, in accordance with my father's will, I was next in the line of succession.

I felt sure he would do all in his power to prevent my coming to the throne. I could see nothing short of death, for he knew that as soon as I had the power my first act would be to bring the country back to Rome.

I prayed for guidance. I must be careful now. Northumberland, the most powerful man in the country, dared not let me come to the throne.

When I arrived at Court, it was to learn that my brother was too ill to see anyone. This was not an excuse to avoid me. He had caught a chill and, in addition to his other ailments, this could be dangerous.

I was greeted with some respect by the Court. I saw speculation in the eyes of many. The King was ill. Moreover, he was suffering from several diseases. How could he possibly recover, and then . . .?

My sister Elizabeth was being very subdued. I guessed she was thinking that certain powerful men would never accept me as Queen. How cold they were, all those men who had done everything they could to turn me from my religion, to browbeat me, to force me to deny the Mass. They would take her, she was thinking. They *must* take her. She was wily; she was clever; but she could not hide the ambition in her eyes.

The King's health did not improve. All through that winter he was hardly ever out of his bed. I heard horrifying reports of his illnesses, and I feared some of them were true. He coughed blood; his body was a mass of ulcers similar to those which had plagued the late King. He was on the point of death. No one was able to see him except his ministers. Parliament came to Whitehall because the King could not go to Westminster. It cannot be long, was being said all over the country, and then . . . what?

Lady Jane Grey came to see me at Newhall. She must have been about fifteen or sixteen years old at that time. She had a certain quiet charm but she was a clever girl of firm opinions. She was very sad at this time because of Edward's illness.

She talked about him a great deal. They had always been such good friends, and the happiest times of her life, she said, had been when they were together.

'Can it really be that he is dying?' she asked.

I replied that I could not say. Sometimes delicate people surprised everyone. They were often stronger than people thought and everyone was so intent on keeping them alive that they sometimes succeeded.

'We were so much together . . .'

'I know. He loved you as a sister.'

She nodded sadly.

I thought she was rather pathetic. She had had a sad childhood. Her parents had treated her with the utmost severity, I had heard. I remembered Mrs Penn's indignantly saying that there were marks of physical punishment on her body. She had an air of frailty, but I guessed she would have a will of her own.

During that brief stay, she told me that her parents were proposing to marry her to Lord Guilford Dudley.

'Northumberland's son!'

She nodded. 'He is the Duke's fourth son. It had to be he. The others are already married.'

I was aghast. It was clear that Northumberland wanted Jane in his family because she had royal blood through her mother, who was the daughter of Mary Tudor and Charles Brandon.

Jane was frightened at the idea. She did not want marriage yet, and she was in great awe of her prospective father-in-law. I wondered whether she would speak to my brother and ask him to intervene on her behalf. Of course, he was very much under Northumberland's influence, but on the other hand he was very fond of Jane.

I tried to soothe her by telling her of all the marriages which had been arranged for me, none of which had come to fruition.

She smiled wanly. 'I think the Duke of Northumberland is very determined,' she said.

I was full of sympathy for the poor child but felt less so later when Lady Wharton, one of my ladies, told me what had happened in the chapel.

'I was passing through with Lady Jane,' she said. 'There was no service in progress. As I passed the Host, I curtsied, as we always do.'

'Yes?' I asked, as she had paused. 'And the lady Jane . . .? What was it she did?'

'She said to me, "Is the lady Mary here, that you curtsy? I did not see her." I was amazed. I said, "But I curtsy to Him that made me." Oh, my lady, I hesitate to say . . .'

'Please go on,' I said.

'She replied as though in all innocence, "But did not the

394

baker make Him?" My lady, she was referring to the bread and wine . . .'

'I know to what she was referring. It is what she has been brought up to, Lady Wharton. Perhaps we should not blame her.'

'But such sacrilege, my lady . . . and in a holy place . . .'

'She was brought up with my brother,' I said. 'It is the way they would have things throughout the country now.'

Lady Wharton looked at me earnestly: 'Mayhap it will not always be so.'

'Hush,' I warned her. 'You should not say such things . . . even here . . . even to me.'

We were silent but I could see she was asking herself the same question that I was asking myself.

What will happen next? We could not know. But we knew something must happen soon.

* * *

I heard news of Lady Jane. I was sorry for her. She was little more than a child. She had no wish for marriage, and she seemed to be as much in fear of her future father-in-law as she was of her own parents. The girl had some spirit. Perhaps she drew that from her religion, for after that outburst in the chapel I tried to discover more about her convictions and learned they were very strong. She and my brother were alike in that; and misguided though she was in her faith, it might have helped her endure her hard life.

Susan told me she had heard how the girl resisted, declaring she would not marry, and how she had been beaten, starved and locked away until they feared for her health, for she would be no use to their schemes if she were dead.

All the same, the marriage took place in May, and at the same time Jane's sister Catharine – who was younger than she – was married to Lord Herbert, the Earl of Pembroke's son; and Northumberland's daughter, another Catharine, was married to Lord Hastings, son of the Earl of Huntingdon.

There was, of course, a method in these marriages. They were bringing together the most powerful families whose thoughts must be running in one direction. Edward's death was imminent, and they planned some drastic action. I could guess that action meant disaster for me, and I could think of only one solution which would bring them what they wanted; and that was my death.

I must be careful. If ever I was going to achieve my mission, everything would depend on how I acted now.

I wished that I could have seen my brother. I knew that the reports of his illness were not exaggerated; he must have been very sick indeed at that time. I had been so fond of him when he was younger and before religion had become such an impassable barrier to our friendship. I wanted to explain to him that I could not give up my faith any more than he could give up his. I thought I might have made him understand. He had a logical brain; he was extremely learned; but people were obdurate concerning religion. Perhaps I was myself. It was just that one *knew* one was right. It was a fusion of something divine . . . difficult to explain. No doubt he believed he had that divine guidance as I did.

But at least we could have talked.

He wanted to be a good king. He cared deeply about the poor and those in distress. He had decided that his palace at Bridewell should be given as a resort for those poor people who had no means of making a living for themselves. He had thought of poor children who, though they might be clever enough, received no education because their parents were too poor to give it to them. The monasteries had been suppressed, and that of Grey Friars was empty. Why should it not be used as a school for poor scholars? It was called Christ's Hospital. I heard it gave my brother great pleasure that he had done these things. Then there were the sick. He would set up a hospital at St Thomas's where the poor could be treated free. He was sure the people of London would willingly help him to keep these charitable institutions in existence.

He cared for the people. He was good at heart – but oh so sick and weary of life, I knew. And he was in the hands of ambitious men.

I was frustrated. I was sure the rumours of his failing health were true; and that was of vital importance to me.

If only Chapuys had been here to advise me, or even the worthy François van der Delft; Scheyfve tried hard but his English was poor, and consequently he did not always understand what was going on.

Antoine de Noailles, the French ambassador, was a shrewd man, more of a spy, I fancied, than an ambassador; and as I was never sure on whose side the French would be, I felt alone and afraid.

Northumberland was expressing friendship towards me now. He sent me details of the King's illness – not that I always believed them; but his motive was to let me know that he was my friend. Did he mean he thought I should soon be his sovereign? When and if I were, he must have known I should never trust him. When he wrote to me, he addressed me with the full title which had not been accorded to me since my father put my mother from him: Princess of England. But how sincere was he?

Susan had heard a disquieting rumour that the Attorney General, Lord Chief Justice Montague, was at odds with Northumberland concerning a delicate issue.

'It is monstrous,' said Susan, 'and I cannot believe it is true.'

She was hesitating, trying to put off telling me because she feared it would be a great shock to me. But at length it came.

'The King has decided to leave the crown not to his

sisters, because they are children of marriages whose validity is in question . . . but to the heirs of the Lady Mary Tudor, sister to his father.'

I stared at Susan in disbelief. 'That's impossible!' I cried.

She looked at me steadily. 'The crown is to go to Lady Jane Dudley.'

'I . . . see. This is Northumberland's doing. He will make Jane Queen and Guilford Dudley King. And that means Northumberland will rule over us.'

'Montague says he will alter the succession . . . and that is treason. But then Northumberland replied that the late King did it.'

'That is not true,' I cried. 'The crown passed to Edward after him, and Edward is his son and rightful heir. I am next and after me Elizabeth. That is what my father ordered.'

'So says Montague.'

'Then . . .'

She looked at me solemnly. 'Montague has been browbeaten. He is a poor sick old man, and such do not wish to be embroiled in these matters. They do not want to spend their last days in the Tower. They want peace, which can come only with acquiescence.'

'It can never be.'

'So think I. The people will not have it.'

'What then?'

'My lady, it will not be for you to choose . . . but for the people to do that when the time comes.'

'They will seek to destroy me before that.'

'I think we should make plans to get as far from London as possible.'

'But they will proclaim Jane!'

'The people will not have her.'

'She stands for the Protestants.'

'There are many who want to return to the old way of worshipping. Everything will depend on that.'

398

'Northumberland is determined. He has gone so far he cannot now turn back. It may be that his ambitions will destroy him.'

'We must see that they do before he destroys you.'

I was very sad that my brother could be led so far from his duty as to proclaim Jane heiress to the throne. She was little more than a child but he knew she would uphold the faith which he so fanatically supported. And he was completely under the influence of Northumberland.

My poor little brother! I must not blame him. He was like a poor feeble old man who has never been young. I sometimes thought it would be a happier state to be born poor and humble than under the shadow of the crown.

* * *

I was at Hunsdon awaiting news. I heard that rumours persisted in the streets of London and that people were put in the pillory for saying the King was dead.

If he were not dead, he was close to death.

I waited in fearful trepidation.

I was relieved when I heard that the Emperor was sending a new ambassador to England. This was Simon Renard, a man of high diplomatic reputation in whom he had great confidence. I was sure that the good and honest Scheyfve would not be competent to deal with events which seemed imminent. The Emperor would want a man to be a match for Antoine de Noailles, the French ambassador, who had recently arrived on the scene.

At last there came a communication from Northumberland. He thought it would be wise for me to come to Court; a similar summons was sent to my sister Elizabeth. I wondered what she would do. She was not in the acute danger which I was in, but nevertheless her position could be precarious.

I left Hunsdon with a small company and moved south, but at Hoddesdon I waited, uncertain how to act.

If my brother died, I should be on the spot. Yet, on the other hand, Northumberland would be there, and I could be in danger.

While I was wondering which way to turn, Susan came to me to tell me that a man had arrived; he had obviously ridden some way and was exhausted, but he made it clear that he must see me without delay.

I had him brought to me, and I recognized him as a London goldsmith who had done some work for me on one or two occasions.

He knelt to me.

'My lady,' he said, 'the King is dead, although it is not yet known. I came with all speed to tell you this.'

'Someone sent you?' I asked.

'Sir Nicholas Throckmorton, my lady. He bade me tell you that, although the King is dead, the news will be kept secret for some days . . . and it would be inadvisable for you to come to Court.'

Sir Nicholas Throckmorton! I knew of him. He was a firm upholder of the Reformed Faith. He had been a close friend of my brother; and I remembered that at the time of Anne Askew's execution he had been one of those who were present when she died; he had gone to give her his support.

Why had he sent this man to warn me? He would not want me to be proclaimed Queen, for he would know that when I came to power my first act would be to return the Church to Rome.

If only it had been one of my old friends, a Catholic like Gardiner, I could have believed him. But Gardiner was a prisoner in the Tower. It would have been to *his* advantage to see me crowned Queen. But Throckmorton . . . Why did he warn me? It might be that he knew Northumberland was planning to kill me. There were some who would never connive at murder, even of those of a different faith.

I saw that the goldsmith was given refreshment, and I thanked him.

Whatever Throckmorton's motives, I knew I must not walk into Northumberland's trap. I sent a message to Scheyfve and to Simon Renard, to tell them that I was going to Kenninghall in Norfolk because sickness had broken out in my household. They would know that was a diplomatic excuse.

It might well be that the King was not yet dead and that this was some trap laid for me; but if it had been so, would they have sent the message from one who was known to me to be of the Reformed Faith? It was all very mysterious, but something within me told me that my brother was indeed dead.

I set out with a small party, choosing unfrequented roads for fear we should meet horsemen from London, as I could guess what orders they would have been given if Northumberland really intended to take my life. I would be close to the coast and then, if need be, I could take a ship to the Netherlands.

I very soon learned that I had done the right thing. Soon after I left Hunsdon, one of Northumberland's sons had arrived with 300 horse to escort me back to London. I should have been a prisoner, and that would have meant that my end was imminent.

From Kenninghall I wrote to the Council. I reminded them that my father had made me successor to my now deceased brother Edward and so I was the Queen of this realm. I knew they had worked against me, but by proclaiming me Queen without delay there should be an amnesty and I should bear no grudge against them for the malice I had in the past received at their hands.

They had no respect for me. To them I was a woman merely, and one who did not enjoy good health at that. I had no one to help me, they thought, except a cousin in another country who was too immersed in his own affairs to come to my aid.

They proclaimed Jane Queen, and they wrote to me

telling me that I was a bastard and had been named as such by my father in his will I was now citing; and if I were wise I would accept the new regime and my position in it.

'Never!' I cried to Susan. 'Now I see the way ahead. I will fight for what is mine and if necessary die in the attempt to seize it.'

'But we must not stay here.'

'No,' I agreed. 'Indeed we shall not. I intend to ride on to Framlingham.'

Framlingham Castle is a strong fortress. It belonged to the Howards, and when the Duke of Norfolk had been sent to the Tower – where he still was, because my father had died before signing his death warrant – his goods had been seized and with them this castle, which my brother had given to me.

It was in an ideal position, being close to the coast, which was another point in its favour, for it might be necessary for me to take flight. It had an inner and outer moat running close to the walls except on the west side where a great expanse of lake gave enough protection. The walls were thick and looked impregnable. It would be a formidable fortress, and I was fortunate to have it in my possession.

All along the road people followed me. They had heard the news that the King was dead, and they could not believe that Jane Grey had been proclaimed Queen. They had never heard of her, yet they had all known the Princess Mary since she was a child, and many of them had been indignant at the manner in which her mother had been treated, on account of her being disowned by her husband. I was indeed well known throughout the country and I had always had the sympathy of the people wherever I went.

And I was never more welcome than now. They clustered round me, calling my name: 'Long live Queen Mary!'

By the time I reached the castle, several thousands were

following me. It was comforting to see them camped outside the castle walls.

My standard was flown over the castle, and I felt my spirits lifting, especially when I was told there were some 13,000 encamped round the castle, swearing to protect me from the false Queen and the man who had set her up. Although my hopes were high, I felt I must not be too optimistic. Those people had only their loyalty and, although that was wonderful, it could not stand up against trained men of an army.

Northumberland had the control of the best in the land, and now he was calling me rebel and uttering threats against me. If he captured me, he could call me traitor: he could have me sent to the Tower and out to Tower Green, where my blood would mingle with that of those who had suffered before me.

In all my euphoria I never lost sight of that possibility.

We were moving fast towards a climax. I thought: The next few days will decide. Northumberland was setting out on the march. He was coming to take me himself. When I looked at my good and faithful followers, I wondered if I had done right. I had not run away when I had been tempted to; and if I failed now, it would be the will of God. I had done all in my power to succeed.

I was resigned. I could not see how my forces could triumph over Northumberland's trained men. I thought of David and Goliath and of Daniel in the lions' den. Men had overcome great odds before, and because God had been with them they had prevailed.

I prayed that God would stand beside me. I *must* succeed. If I did not, I should have lived and suffered in vain. It would all be so pointless. But if I could do this wonderful thing, if I could succeed in what all Catholics were willing me to, then everything that had gone before would have been worthwhile.

Then it was like a miracle, and after this I believed that

God was with me and in my heart I was going to fulfil my destiny.

I was blessed with some loyal followers, and one of the most trusted of these was Sir Henry Jerningham, who had been the first to come to me at Kenninghall, bringing with him his tenants who, he assured me, were ready to fight to the death for me.

He had followed me to Framlingham, but he did not stay there. He went on to Yarmouth to guard the coast and to raise men as he went.

Northumberland had just taken action to prevent my leaving the country and had sent to Yarmouth a squadron of six ships to intercept me if I should attempt to leave. There had been some fierce gales along the coast, and the ships lay at anchor in the harbour. When Sir Henry arrived at Yarmouth, the captains were ashore; and Sir Henry had an idea that, though they might be Northumberland's men, the crew members might not necessarily be so. He decided to find out in which direction the crew's sympathies lay, so he rowed out to the ships with some of his men and talked to the sailors.

He told me later what he had said. It was: 'The King is dead. The rightful heiress to the throne is the Princess Mary but Northumberland is setting Lady Jane Grey on the throne.'

They had never heard of Jane Grey but they all knew who I was. I was the King's daughter, next in succession to the throne after my brother Edward was dead. Then I was the rightful Queen. Did they agree? They did, to a man.

'Then,' said Sir Henry, 'will you fight for Queen Mary?'

'Aye, that we will,' they replied.

'But your captains, who are the tools of Northumberland, will command you to stand for Jane Grey.'

'Never,' they cried. 'We are for Mary, our rightful Queen.'

'Then come ashore and join the Queen's men,' said Sir Henry.

So they did, and Sir Henry was able to confront the captains with their decision. They could join us or be his prisoners, he told them. They chose to join us.

Not only had the astute Sir Henry brought the seamen to my aid, but with them all the ordnance which was on the ships. It was a great victory.

Sir Henry returned to Framlingham filled with enthusiasm.

'This is a sign,' he said. 'God is with us.'

'We shall have to fight,' I said. 'Can we do it?'

'We will, Your Majesty,' he said.

'Northumberland has his army with him.'

'There will be many loth to turn a hand against the Queen.'

'But they will do so because he has the might.'

'We shall have the might, Your Grace. We will have stout hearts, and it is God's will that will prevail. The men will feel more loyal if they see you. You must come out and review your troops. I think you will be pleased with them.'

So I rode out and, as Sir Henry had said, I was amazed at the numbers who had mustered to my aid.

As I rode along the lines, they called: 'Long live good Queen Mary!' My heart was lightened and I thanked God that I had been strong so far, and I prayed for His help and guidance that I might work His will and succeed in the task which I was sure now He had laid down for me.

There was comforting news. I had always known Sir Henry Bedingfield was loyal to me, so I was not greatly surprised when he arrived with his followers. But I was delighted to see that Lord Thomas Howard, whose grandfather, Norfolk, was still in the Tower, and all the chivalry of Suffolk, were flocking to my banner.

Northumberland was universally disliked. He had removed Somerset, who, although not liked by the people, was preferred to himself; he had forced Lady Jane Grey to marry his son Guilford and had had the temerity to set her up as Queen. He had gone too far.

His mistake was not to realize the power of the people; and those who had worked with him were now weary of his despotism; people were envious of his power. He himself was confident of victory and rode at the head of his army. But no sooner had he left London than the citizens noisily stated their true feelings.

They wanted no Queen Jane. A granddaughter of King Henry's sister she might be, but there were King Henry's own daughters to come before her. They had always shown affection for me, for I had been the ill-treated one, and they remembered my mother's sufferings.

'Long live Queen Mary, our rightful Queen!' they shouted.

I am not sure when Northumberland realized that he had gone too far and that defeat stared him in the face. He had risked a good deal for he had scored such successes in the past that he believed he could not fail. Now his friends were turning against him, and he had made his fatal miscalculation in reckoning without the people.

I was being proclaimed Queen all over the country.

There came a messenger from London. On the morning of the 16th a placard had been placed on Queenhithe Church stating that I was Queen of England, France and Ireland.

The Earls of Sussex and Bath were among those on their way with their forces to Framlingham . . . not to oppose me but to pay homage to me as their Queen.

I could not believe this. It was a miracle. The Council was declaring for me. Pembroke, so recently allied with Northumberland through marriage, had taken over command of the Tower and the Army – and he was for me. All over the land men were turning to me; even those who had been against me were now proclaiming me Queen. They might have stood with Northumberland so far, but when he had set up Jane Grey as Queen he had tampered with the line of succession, and they were with him no longer.

I wished that I could have been present when they brought the news to Northumberland. He was at Cambridge and could not then have realized how utterly he was defeated. He had known that the battle had not been the easy conquest he had anticipated, for he had despatched a messenger to France to plead for troops to be sent to his aid. How did he feel – the powerful man, the greatest statesman of the day, some said, son of that Dudley who had gone to the block to placate the people because of the taxes my grandfather had levied in his reign – how did the great Northumberland feel to be brought so low?

He had staked everything to gain the greatest power a man could have – to rule the country. Jane and Guilford were to have been his puppets. But, like so many of his kind who failed, he had reckoned without the people, the ordinary people, living their obscure lives, who en masse were the most formidable force in the world. What a mistake to discount them! And he had tried to foist on them a young and innocent girl as their queen. I doubted Jane had had any say in the matter. Northumberland had intended to rule through her, and he had failed miserably.

He must have come to a quick decision when he saw his ambitions crumbling about him and his dream evaporating. He went into the market square. He mounted the steps to the high spot where he could be seen by all, and he lifted his hat in the air and shouted: 'Long live Queen Mary!'

It was his admission of defeat, and he took it bravely. And as he mounted those steps calling my name, he must have seen himself mounting the block and laying his head upon it, as he had seen so many do – mainly his enemies and due to his command.

And now they were with me! Henry Grey, Jane's father,

had himself torn down her banner at the Tower; he was shouting for Queen Mary.

How I despised these men. I remembered Anne Boleyn's father, assisting at the christening of young Edward. They turned their coats to meet the prevailing wind with no sense of shame.

And young Jane . . . what of her? She would be my prisoner now. How could I blame her and her young husband? They were the innocent victims of other people's ambitions. Northumberland had forced them to do what they did, and now he was calling for Queen Mary!

News was brought to me that Northumberland had been arrested. My greatest enemy was now my prisoner.

* * *

My capital was waiting to receive me. I would never have believed that victory could come so easily, and I chided myself for my lack of faith. This was what I had been born and preserved for, and the will of God had worked through the will of the people.

My first duty was to have the crucifix set up in Framlingham Church. It would show the people I would lead them back to God through the true religion.

We must make our way out of London.

I set out with a mighty company. How different from when I had left Hunsdon such a short time ago in such stealth.

I rested at Wanstead, and while I was there I was visited by a distraught Duchess of Suffolk. I was amazed to see this proud and imperious lady so frightened and beside herself with grief. I thought it must be on account of her daughter, Jane, that poor innocent child who had been used by her ambitious family.

She prostrated herself at my feet, which in itself was amusing, for she had been one of those who had proclaimed

408

my birth not to be legitimate, King's daughter though she had had to accept me to be.

But I was sorry for her. She was a mother and she must be suffering deep remorse now that her daughter was in the Tower.

I said: 'Rise, Lady Suffolk. I know what you must be suffering. Your daughter is so young, and I know that she was forced to do this wicked thing by others.'

'Oh, my daughter,' she cried. 'She has sinned beyond redemption. I could not ask Your Majesty to forgive her. Her sin is too great. I plead for the Duke, my husband. He is ill, Your Majesty. I fear for his life if he remains in that cold cell. They have kept him there for three days . . . and I fear that he can endure little more.'

I felt anger rising within me. I could understand a mother's love for her child, but I remembered what Jane had said about the harsh treatment of her parents, and Mrs Penn's indignation at the violent marks on her body.

I said: 'Your husband is a traitor. He was partly responsible for setting your daughter on the throne. It is not Lady Jane who is to blame. She merely did what she was forced to. And you complain because your husband has spent three days in the Tower!'

'He has acted wrongly, Your Majesty, but he was led into doing evil acts. Your Majesty, I beg of you . . . he will die. Let him be sent to me. Let him remain your prisoner but let me nurse him. I beg of you. It is a matter of life or death.'

Life or death! That was how it was for most of us. She was weeping bitterly, this proud woman, and there was no doubt that her grief was genuine.

How could I refuse her? I did not admire her as a mother, but there was no doubt that the woman loved her husband.

I thought: What harm can it do? She is crying for mercy, and I must be merciful. He will die in the Tower. He will die in any case. He is a traitor, but I do not want his death on my hands.

I said: 'He shall be taken from the Tower to be nursed by you.'

She fell on her knees once more; she kissed my hand and blessed me.

* * *

When it was known what I had done, there was consternation.

Sir Henry Jerningham pointed out to me that the man I had freed was the father of Jane, and he had helped to set her up in my place. He had worked close to Northumberland, and they had planned to rule the country together through those two young people. Had I forgotten that?

'I have sent him out of the Tower to be nursed by his wife,' I said. 'He is a very sick man.'

'Sick with fear, Your Majesty, to see his wicked plans frustrated.'

'I wish to be a merciful Queen,' I told him. 'Grey shall not escape. Justice will be done.'

They shook their heads, and they trembled for me.

It was the same with Simon Renard. I heard later that he had reported to the Emperor that I should never be able to hold the crown for I was too governed by feminine sentiments.

I did not care. I knew Suffolk was ill, and I had been moved by his wife's pleading.

I prayed to God that night. 'You taught me to be merciful, O Lord, and I believe that is how You would wish me to act.'

* * *

I set out on my ride into London. I was thirty-seven years old – no longer young, but not too old for a Queen. I had some experience of life behind me. I was no beauty, but I was not ill favoured either. I was thinnish and of low stature. I wished that I had been taller – but I looked well enough on a horse; I had my father's reddish hair, and my complexion was as fresh as his had been in his youth, but mine had not coarsened as his had – I presumed because I had lived more abstemiously. Dressed in purple velvet, I looked quite regal, I believed, seated on my horse and surrounded by my ladies.

My sister had come to Wanstead to meet me. She was to ride into London beside me. I was sorry for this in a way, and yet I could not forbid it. She was so much younger and in such blooming health. She was much taller and about twenty years old – in her prime, one might say. The people cheered her and she did everything she could to win their approval, waving her hands and holding them up in acknowledgement of their greeting. She had very beautiful hands, and I had often noticed how she used every opportunity to bring them into prominence.

These people had shown their affection for me; they had proclaimed me as their Queen, and I believed that meant that they wanted the old faith restored. Had they forgotten that Elizabeth had refused to attend Mass? Were these Protestants who were cheering her? Or was she so popular because she was young and attractive to look at and showed such pleasure in their applause? Of one thing I was certain: wherever she was, she would bring a certain lack of ease to me, a certain puzzlement, for I should never understand the workings of her mind.

I kissed all her ladies to give an impression that I was pleased to see her but, as we rode along, I was thinking that I should have been happier if she had stayed away.

As we approached Aldgate, I saw streamers hanging from the houses; children had been assembled to sing songs of welcome. It was a heartwarming sight. The streets had been freshly swept, and members of the city crafts had gathered there, clad in their traditional dress. They looked very smart, and they were smiling and waving their banners with enthusiasm.

We were met by the Mayor. Lord Arundel was present, holding the sword of state. They joined the procession with a thousand men – and so they led me to the Tower.

This was London's welcome and meant that the city regarded me as the rightful Queen.

And there was the Tower, so often a symbol of fear, and now offering me hospitality and welcome.

I was greeted by Sir Thomas Cheyney, who was in charge at that time. The custom was that I should rest here until after my brother's funeral.

The King was dead: Long live the Queen! That was what this meant.

I shall never forget coming to the Tower that day. All the state prisoners had been brought from their cells and were assembled on the green before the church of St Peter ad Vincula.

There was the old Duke of Norfolk, who had been arrested shortly before my father's death and would certainly have lost his head as his son Surrey had done, had the King not died before he could sign the death warrant. He had aged since I had last seen him, which was not surprising, after six years' incarceration in that grim place. Stephen Gardiner was also there; but the one who stood out among all the others was Edward Courtenay, son of the Marquis of Exeter and Earl of Devonshire, who had been in the Tower since 1538, when he was about twelve years old, and had known no other dwelling for fifteen years. He looked bright and healthy in spite of this. I was deeply touched, not only by him but by all those people kneeling there, particularly when it was pointed out to me who they were.

I dismounted and, going to them, spoke to each one in turn. I kissed them and bade them no longer kneel.

I said to them emotionally: 'You are my prisoners now.'

412

The Duke of Norfolk was in tears, and so was I, as I embraced him. Gardiner took my hands, and we were too moved to speak for a few moments. I told him he should be sworn into the Privy Council at once. 'And you, my lord Norfolk, you go from here a free man and your estates shall be restored to you.'

I turned to the young man whose handsome face had attracted me from the moment I saw him. 'Lord Courtenay, is it not?' I said. 'Your estates will also be returned to you. You leave the Tower when you are ready to go, my lord Earl of Devonshire.'

I do not believe that any present could have been unmoved by the sight of so much joy. It was a happy augury for my reign, I thought. I was delighted to be able to show my people right from the beginning that, although I was a woman and they might think a man would be more suitable to rule them, I had a heart full of sympathy for my subjects and I would be a gentle and loving sovereign.

A cheer went up as I made my way into the Tower.

There I remained quietly until my brother was buried, when I ordered that there should be a requiem for his soul in the Tower chapel.

* * *

During the days in the Tower, while I was awaiting the burial of my brother, I gave myself up to meditation.

Now that that for which I had yearned and vaguely feared was upon me, I felt a little lost and bewildered. I was fully aware of the task ahead of me and that I must have good counsellors.

I must marry now. It was my duty. A sovereign should give the country heirs. That was what my father had always maintained, and the need to do so had governed his life and was responsible for so many of the actions he had taken. Thirty-seven was not an ideal age for childbearing, but it was not quite too old.

I would concern myself with marriage without delay.

Ever since I had known him, I had nourished tender feelings towards Reginald Pole. Why not? He was royal. My mother had thought fondly of a match between us. I remembered how she and my dear Countess of Salisbury had plotted together about it. Reginald was a good deal older than I, of course, but he had never married. One would not have expected a man of the Church to marry, but he had never stepped into that position which would have made it impossible for him to do so.

I wondered what public reaction would be if the suggestion were made known. He had been very popular at one time, but he had been abroad for so long. Perhaps now that I was Queen he would return to England; he would have nothing to fear from me; he would have encouragement and affection. I could do nothing yet, but I often thought of Reginald.

Jane Grey and her young husband were constantly on my mind. I knew that pressure would be brought on me to send them to the block, and I felt very reluctant to do this. Northumberland should have his just deserts, and I felt no qualms about this; but I should feel very uneasy if I were asked to sign the death warrants of those two young people.

But there was so much to occupy my thoughts during those days; there would be my coronation, which would need so much preparation that it could not take place before October.

On the 18th of August, Northumberland and his fellow conspirators were brought to trial.

There could be only one result for Northumberland, but when it came to the point I was reluctant to sign his death warrant. He was an extremely clever man – I think one of the cleverest of his day. He could have been a good servant to me; and I wished that it could have been different. There were eleven people convicted with him but only three went to the scaffold on the 22nd of August.

Jane's father, Henry Grey, Duke of Suffolk, had proclaimed me Queen at the gates of the Tower. I could not bear to think that my coming to the throne had resulted in numerous deaths, and I persuaded the Council that, on payment of a fine, Suffolk should go free. He was a weak man who had been the tool of Northumberland. I was not sure about his religious views, but I fancied he was a Protestant; but at this stage we were not prosecuting people for their religion. I recalled Frances Grey's pleas for her husband, and I could not bring myself to agree to his execution, so at length it was agreed that he should pay his fine and go free.

Although Northumberland had been the chief conspirator, the Council believed that Lady Jane and her husband should be despatched without delay. I pointed out to them that she was merely the figurehead. Figureheads had to be eliminated with all speed, they reiterated. Lady Jane should be brought to trial at once.

I could not bear that and I sought refuge in delay.

'Later,' I said. 'Later.'

Simon Renard came to me. He was an impressive man. He was no van der Delft or Scheyfve. He was another Chapuys, only, it occurred to me, more wily. I could understand why the Emperor had sent him, for now that I was Queen, I was of greater importance to him.

Renard was very respectful but nevertheless he had come to advise me, and I felt the great Emperor spoke through him.

'It is an odd thing, Your Majesty,' he said, 'that the chief conspirator in the plot against you still lives.'

'Northumberland has lost his head,' I replied.

'The imposter Queen still lives.'

'The girl was merely used, Ambassador.'

'She allowed herself to be used.'

'She had no choice.'

415

He lifted his shoulders. 'She has dared proclaim herself Queen.'

'She was acclaimed by others.'

'She wore the crown.'

'My lord Ambassador, I know this girl. She is my kinswoman. She is young and innocent . . . scarcely out of the schoolroom. I could not have her innocent blood on my hands.'

'Your Majesty prefers to have yours on hers?'

'There is no question . . .'

'While she lives, you are unsafe.'

'I believe the people have chosen me.'

'The people? The people will go which way they are made to.'

'This is a matter for my conscience.'

He was clearly dismayed. I saw the contempt in his eyes, and I could imagine the letter he would write to the Emperor. I should never make him understand. But I knew Jane, and I understood how she had been forced into this . . . and as long as I could, I would refuse to have her blood on my hands.

I must not free her, of course. That would be folly. She would be an immediate rallying point. I would have to be careful; and there was my sister, Elizabeth, another who would stand as a symbol for the Reformed Faith. Oh yes, I should be very careful. But as long as Jane was in the Tower, no decisions need be made.

I said: 'I intend to keep her prisoner for the time being. Then we shall see.'

Simon Renard left me. He gave me the impression that I was being a soft and sentimental woman and had no idea how to rule a country.

Shortly after that interview with Renard, I received a letter from Jane, and on reading it I felt more sorry for her and in a greater dilemma than ever.

She wanted me to know that the terrible sin she had

416

committed in allowing herself to be forced to pose as Queen was no fault of hers.

'I did not want it,' she wrote, 'and when my parents and my parents-in-law, the Duke and Duchess of Northumberland, came to me and told me that the King was dead, I was wretchedly unhappy, for you know how I loved him. When they added that I was heiress to the crown, I could not believe them, and when I understood that they were serious, I fainted. It was as though a sense of doom overcame me. I knew it was wrong. I knew it was wicked, even though Edward had named me. They did homage to me, and at the same time they were angry with me because I would not rejoice with them and was filled with this terrible foreboding.

'They took me to the Tower as Queen, and the Marquis of Winchester brought the crown for me to try on. I did not ask him to do this. It was the last thing I wanted. I wanted more than anything to go back to my studies. I knew that I should have resisted, but I dared not.'

No, I thought, she dared not. I remembered how they had beaten her in her childhood. I felt a grim amusement to think of those harsh parents doing homage to their daughter whom they had so ill-treated.

'I did not want to put it on,' she continued. 'I was afraid of it. They said they would have another made for my husband, for it was the Duke's wish that he should be crowned with me. I could not allow this. I did not want the crown myself, but at least I had some claim to it through my birth. But that they should crown Guilford because they had made me marry him . . . I would not have it. I said that if they made me Queen I must have some authority. They were so angry with me. They forgot for a time that they had made me Queen. They maltreated me . . .

'Your Majesty, you should know that I am ready to die

417

for what I did, for that deserves death. But, dear Majesty, it was not of my doing.'

I read this with tears in my eyes. It was true. I thought of her unhappy life. The happiest hours she had known must have been with Edward when they pored over their books and enjoyed a friendly rivalry as to who could learn their lessons the more quickly. And now, here she was, a prisoner in the Tower, awaiting death.

How could I ever bring myself to harm her?

* * *

My thoughts were preoccupied with marriage; and Reginald Pole was in the forefront of them. I wondered what he looked like after all these years. He was sixteen years older than I, and that would make him fifty-three years of age. Hardly an age for marrying.

I was excited to receive a letter from him. I opened it with eagerness, wondering if it would contain a reference to a marriage between us. I was not sure how I should feel about that; but I reminded myself that, if it did come to pass, it would have the blessing of my mother and the Countess if they were watching in Heaven, for it would be the fulfilment of their dearest wish.

He congratulated me on my accession to the throne. But his greatest pleasure was in the fact that he hoped to be receiving from me directions as to how we should set about restoring papal authority to England. There was one sentence in his letter which indicated clearly that marriage had been far from his mind, for he advised me not to marry. There would be plans for me but I was no longer young, and it would be better to remain single so that I should have full authority to bring about the necessary religious reforms.

It was hardly the letter of a lover.

There was also a letter from Friar Peto who, when he had escaped from England after he had so offended my

418

father, had lived with Reginald ever since. I remember how Peto had angered my father from the pulpit when he had openly criticized him for deserting my mother. He it was who had said that, as had happened with Ahab, the dogs would lick his blood after his death. The prophecy had come true. There was no doubt that Peto was a brave and holy man.

'Do not marry,' he wrote to me. 'If you do you will be the slave of a young husband. Besides, at your age, the chances of bringing heirs to the throne are doubtful and, moreover, would be dangerous.'

I felt depressed after reading these letters. The truth was stressed by the blunt Peto, and I had to face the facts. I was too old for childbearing. But it had been one of the dearest wishes of my life to have a child, and in my heart I would never really give up the hope. It was doubly necessary for me to have a child now. I should give birth to an heir. If not . . . Elizabeth would follow me, and who could tell what Elizabeth would do?

She was being very cautious now. She was in a difficult and highly dangerous position and none would recognize that more clearly than Elizabeth. I who knew her well could read the alertness in her eyes. She was taking each step with the utmost care.

I *must* have a child.

I would not listen to Peto or Reginald. They had been too long out of England. They had probably heard of my bouts of ill health. No doubt they had been exaggerated. I did believe they had been in some measure due to my insecure position. When I think of all the years I had lived close to the axe . . . surely that could have accounted for my delicate state of health?

But I had come through. God had shown clearly that He had chosen me to fulfil this mission.

I had to succeed . . . and I would. I would have an heir. And for that reason I must marry quickly.

Ever since his release from the Tower, I had seen a great deal of Edward Courtenay. I had made his mother, Gertrude, who was the Marchioness of Exeter, a lady of my bedchamber; and it seemed that Edward was constantly at my side. I did not complain of this. He was a most attractive young man. I was amazed that he, who had lived the greater part of his life in the Tower, could be so knowledgeable about the world, and so charming.

He owed a great deal to his good looks, which were outstanding. I noticed my sister Elizabeth's eyes on him. She had always had a liking for handsome men, as she had shown in the case of Thomas Seymour. She was flirtatious by nature, and when I saw Edward Courtenay paying attention to her, I told myself he could hardly do anything else. She so blatantly asked for admiration.

So I considered Edward Courtenay. He had so much to recommend him. Charm, good looks, vitality, but perhaps most important of all, his father's mother had been Princess Catharine, the youngest daughter of Edward IV, so he was of the blood royal.

He was about ten years younger than I. Was that important? My thoughts had turned to marriage, as they must do before it was too late. There might just be time if I married quickly; and I was more likely to become pregnant if my husband was a young man rather than an old one.

I had had such ill luck with my proposed marriages, but that was because of what they called my dubious birth. The constant question had been, was I or was I not illegitimate? Now that was all over. I was the acknowledged Queen of England, and there would be many eager to marry me.

The more I saw of Edward Courtenay, the more I liked the idea.

He was very merry and kept us amused. He talked of his years in the Tower, but there was nothing morbid in his conversation; he was one of those people who find life amusing; he made a joke of the smallest things which were truly no joke, but while one was with him one accepted them as such. One laughed with the laughter of happiness rather than amusement. I felt younger in his presence than I ever had in my life.

I began to ask myself if I were in love.

I wondered what the people would think of such a marriage. They would be delighted, I was sure. In the first place they would approve of my sharing my throne with an Englishman. Foreigners were always suspect. A young man who had been imprisoned by my father and set free by me . . . a young man with whom I had fallen in love and he with me . . . it was so romantic. The people loved romance.

They would approve, but what of the Council? There would be opposition from them; they never liked to see one of their own set above them. But what of that? Was I not the Queen? Was it not for me to decide the question of my marriage? I should certainly have my own way.

Simon Renard came to see me again. I was sure his all-seeing eyes had already detected the growing friendship between myself and Edward Courtenay.

As soon as he talked to me, I began to see that I had been living in a foolish, romantic dream.

'There should be as little delay as possible in your marriage,' he said. 'The Emperor has always had a fondness for you. He would marry you, but he is much too old.'

I felt emotional at the thought of marrying the Emperor. Ever since that day when my mother had presented me to him at Greenwich, and he had made much of me, he had been a leading figure in my imagination. He was the greatest and most powerful figure in Europe, and I had always convinced myself that he was my saviour. In fact, it had been his diplomatic presence that had done that rather than any act of his. In any case I had kept my awe of him.

'But,' Renard was saying, 'he has a son, Philip. He is as devout a Catholic as ever was. He is the Emperor's beloved son, and the Emperor is of the opinion that there should be a match between you. It is a suggestion. I bring it to you before I take it to the Council.'

When he left me, I was in deep thought. Philip, son of the Emperor. He was my second cousin, I supposed, since the Emperor was my cousin. A devout Catholic – one who would help me bring England back to Rome. He would be younger than I by eleven years. But it seemed I was destined to have a husband either my senior or my junior by a good many years.

Renard had said: 'Think of it. I am sure such a great marriage would bring you great joy.'

I was not sure. I had been thinking too much of Edward Courtenay. But queens have other matters with which to occupy themselves than romantic dreams.

* * *

The coronation was fixed for the 1st of October.

On the previous day I left the Tower in a litter drawn by six white horses. I was dressed in blue velvet decorated with ermine, and over my head was a caul netted in gold and decorated with precious stones. I found it rather heavy and looked forward to having it replaced with the crown. As I passed along, followed by my ladies, all in crimson velvet, I was immensely gratified by the cheers of the crowd.

There were also cheers for Elizabeth, who followed me in an open carriage shared with Anne of Cleves. They were identically dressed in blue velvet gowns with the long hanging sleeves made fashionable by Elizabeth's mother. All members of the household were there in the green and white Tudor colours; and my dear Sir Henry Jerningham, who was now the Captain of the Royal Guard, brought up the rear.

The citizens of London had shown themselves to be wholehearted in the matter of welcoming me. There was music everywhere, and I was met by giants and angels; and what delighted the people was that the conduits ran with wine. And, passing these splendid displays, we came at length to Whitehall.

I was so tired that I slept well that night in spite of the ordeal which lay before me the following day.

I felt a great exultation, a belief in myself. I felt the presence of God within me. He had chosen me for this mission, and I was convinced now that He had brought me to it in His way. The sufferings of my youth had been necessary to strengthen my character. I had a great task before me, and I must perform it well; and so should I, with God's help. So, after praying on my knees, I went to bed and knew no more until they awakened me in the morning.

October of the year 1553. It is a day I shall never forget – the day when I truly became the Queen of England, for no monarch is truly King or Queen until he or she has been anointed.

With my party I went by barge to the private stairs of Westminster Palace. It was a shell now after the great fire which had happened during my father's time. The Parliament Chamber was, however, still standing, and there I was taken to put on my robes and be made ready for the procession to the Abbey.

It was eleven o'clock when we set out. In my crimson robes, I walked under the canopy, which was, according to custom, carried by the wardens of the Cinque Ports. I was aware of Elizabeth immediately behind me. Her presence there seemed symbolic. I was glad Anne of Cleves was still beside her.

The ceremony should have been performed by the Archbishop of Canterbury, but this was Thomas Cranmer, who was, at this time, in the Tower. He had been involved in the plot to set Jane Grey on the throne, although he had tried to persuade Edward against changing the succession; but Edward himself had asked him to sign his will and, with a hint of a threat, my brother had said that he hoped he was not going to be more refractory than the rest of the household. I could see the dilemma Cranmer was in. He did not agree that the King should change the succession, but at the same time he was a strong supporter of the Reformed Faith and he knew that when I came to the throne I would regard it as my duty to turn the country back to Rome. He was committed to the Protestant cause; and therefore, when the people had shown so clearly that I was the Queen they wanted, he was sent to the Tower and was there awaiting judgement.

So it was out of the question for him to perform the ceremony; and in his place was my good friend Stephen Gardiner, Bishop of Winchester, accompanied by ten others – an impressive sight, with their copes of gold cloth and their mitres and crosses.

I was led to St Edward's Chair, and as I sat there Gardiner declared: 'Here present is Mary, rightful and undoubted inheritrix by the laws of God and man to the crown and royal dignity of the realms of England, France and Ireland. Will you serve at this time and give your wills and assent to the same consecration, unction and coronation?'

How thrilling it was to hear their response. 'Yes! Yes! Yes! God save Queen Mary!'

Then I was led to the high chair by the altar, where I took my coronation oath.

The ceremony of the anointing was carried out, and afterwards I was robed in purple velvet trimmed with ermine; the sword was placed in my hands, and the Duke of Norfolk brought the three crowns – St Edward's, the imperial crown and the one made for me. Each in turn was set on my head while the trumpets sounded.

It was a wonderful moment when I sat with the imperial crown on my head, the sceptre in my right hand and the orb in my left, and received the homage of the nobles of the realm, in which each promised to be my liege man for life . . . to live and to die with me against all others.

Through the chamber the cry rang out: 'God save Queen Mary!'

I was indeed their Queen.

Rebellion

It was four days after my coronation when I opened my first Parliament. It was a splendid occasion. People lined the streets to see me ride by, and everyone who could be there was present.

I realize now that I was guileless. I did not know how to dissimulate. How unlike Elizabeth I was! Innocently, I expected everyone to be as I was. It took me a little time to learn that they were not.

The people had chosen me for their Queen. I thought that meant they they were ready to turn back to the Catholic Church and that it would be just as it was before my father broke with Rome.

When it was learned that I intended to return to papal authority, there was dismay in all quarters . . . even where I had least expected it.

I can see now that few people cared as strongly about religion as I did. There were many who were ready enough to go back to the way it had been during the last years of my father's reign. The religion itself had not changed then. All that had happened was that the monarch was the head of the Church instead of the Pope.

There was another point. Almost every nobleman in the land had profited from the dissolution of the monasteries and acquired Church land, and they would be in no mood to give that up.

All the ambassadors were a little shocked – even Renard, who, I had thought, would be entirely with me.

'You are moving too fast,' he said.

I could not believe that I had heard aright.

'But this is what I have always intended,' I protested.

'The people know it. It is why they have made me their Queen.'

'There will be trouble throughout the country, and Your Majesty is not secure enough to withstand trouble.'

'What do you mean? Did they not proclaim me? Have you not heard how they shout for me in the streets?'

'They shouted for you because they see you as the true heir to the throne, and the people did not like the succession to be meddled with. But have a care. There are many Protestants in this country. They might accept a return to the Catholic Faith, but to take the Church back to Rome at one stroke . . . it would be too much . . . too soon.'

'But it is my mission . . . my purpose.'

'I know . . . and a worthy one. But go slowly . . . feel your way. Leave things as they are at the moment.'

'But I will have Mass heard in the churches.'

'That . . . yes. But do not press for a return to Rome . . . not yet.'

He was not the only one to warn me. De Noailles, the French ambassador, called. I did not trust him. He was a very wily man. I had known for some time that he was more of a spy than an ambassador. Most of them were, of course, but de Noailles more than any. I knew he hated the thought of my closeness to Spain. Simon Renard, as my cousin's emissary, was a confidant as well as an ambassador. De Noailles knew this, and I believe he wanted to drive a wedge between us, for France and Spain were perennial enemies. If the French had heard of a possible match between myself and Philip of Spain, they would do everything they could to prevent it.

But this time he was in agreement with Simon Renard. France, like Spain, wished to see England back under the papal authority; but they could foresee revolt in England if it came too suddenly. They had just seen Jane Grey made Queen – albeit for only nine days – and they realized how dangerous the situation was and how uncertain my grip on the crown. There was my half-sister Elizabeth waiting to seize her chance.

I was warned not to be too fervent a papist.

Gardiner was one of the few who supported me, but I remembered that he had made no protest when my father had declared himself Head of the Church; and now that there was a new sovereign who believed that the country should return to Rome, he was in agreement with that. Protestants, who must be deploring his release from the Tower, called him Turncoat and Doctor Doubleface.

At the opening of Parliament Gardiner was the one who announced that it was my intention to return to Rome. That was all, but the views of so many which I received afterwards influenced me, and I understood that I must not act too quickly; and nothing more was done about the matter at that time.

In the same Parliament I wanted it known that the harsh laws which my father had set up were to be relaxed. A great many people had suffered under my father's rule; I wanted mine to be more merciful.

I found a certain relief in writing to Reginald because I was sure that, from the Continent, he would be watching events in England with great concern.

'I had thought it would be simple,' I wrote to him. 'I thought it could be changed at once. But I have been warned. The Emperor's ambassador has warned me. I must not be too hasty. The people are not yet prepared. But I trust you do not think me dilatory. Please do not think for a moment I am failing in my purpose. But I dare not yet show the people my intent.'

He would understand, I felt sure.

How I wished he were younger – and with me. I felt uneasy about the proposed match with Philip. I wondered a great deal about him. I had heard that he lacked the astuteness of his father. Well, that was to be expected as the Emperor Charles was known as the wisest ruler of the age.

Philip, I was told, was deeply religious. On the other hand, he had led rather a wild life, some said. I had heard that he was sensuous and fond of women. That was what alarmed me. He had been married before, to Isabella of Portugal, who had died three years later giving birth to a son, Don Carlos, who must be about six years old. If Philip was looking for passionate excitement in a marriage, I was not the wife for him to choose. But he was the son of the Emperor and I was the Queen of England, so the match was highly suitable on that score. But was it? The people would not wish me to marry a foreigner. They would have liked me to take Edward Courtenay. Moreover, I could not leave my country to go to Spain, and Philip could not leave his and come here. We should see each other rarely, it seemed to me. I began to think that this marriage with Spain would go the way of all the others.

But Reginald I had known and loved in my childhood. Did it matter that he was older than I? Did it matter that we should be unlikely to have children?

What I looked for was loving companionship, someone to be beside me, to care for me, to cherish me.

Simon Renard was the nearest I had to that, but in my heart I knew that his loyalties lay not with me but with his master, as a good ambassador's should. I tried to assure myself that the Emperor's interests were mine and that we stood together . . . as we always had.

Now that the Mass was being said in churches, there were bound to be protests. There were rumours of restlessness in several of the counties. From Kent, Leicestershire and Norfolk there were complaints.

My sister Elizabeth was a source of anxiety. She would not attend Mass, and Renard believed that those who wished to keep the Protestant way of worship were looking to her as a figurehead.

'She is very dangerous,' he said.

The Council sent a message to her telling her that she must conform. She did not appear at the ceremony at which the title of Earl was bestowed on Edward Courtenay, using the often employed excuse of sickness.

Renard came to me in some consternation.

'What is this sister of yours planning? She is trying to please the Protestants. While she behaves as she does she is fomenting danger. People will look to her – and believe me, there are many. She should be sent to the Tower.'

'How could I send my own sister to the Tower?'

'Merely by giving the order. I doubt not that, if there was an investigation, something could be proved against her.'

'De Noailles is showing friendship towards her.'

'She will get no good from him. His one aim is to get Mary of Scotland on the throne.'

'Mary of Scotland! How could he believe that possible?'

Renard looked at me with a hint of pity for my shortsightedness.

'Mary of Scotland is the daughter-in-law of the King of France. De Noailles is his servant. The King sees England coming to France with Mary Queen and young François King. But depend upon it, de Noailles will use Elizabeth to try to bring this about.'

'Is there no one to be trusted?'

Renard shook his head. 'No one but my master, who is your friend and always will be. When you are married to Philip, you will have an even stronger hold on his affections, and you will have a man beside you. But in the meantime we have to deal with Elizabeth. We have to stop these Protestants looking to her as their new Queen.'

'It is treason.'

'Your Majesty speaks truth. So . . . let us begin to flout these treasonable schemes by turning our attention to your sister.'

'I cannot imprison her.'

'Not until she is implicated. But let us be watchful and begin by preventing her setting up this image to staunch Protestants. She must attend the Mass.'

'I will have her told that she must obey.'

'That will be the first step,' agreed Renard.

Before I could send the order to her, a messenger came from her with a letter begging me to grant her an interview. I did this.

As soon as she approached me, she fell on her knees.

I said: 'You may rise and tell me what it is you have to say to me. I see that you have recovered from the sickness which prevented your attending Courtenay's ceremony. You appear to be in rude health.'

'Thank you, Your Majesty. I have recovered. May I say I hope Your Majesty is in good health.'

There was a look of concern on her face which told me I looked ill. She did not say I did, for she knew that would annoy me, but she implied it with a glance of compassion which made me immediately aware of the contrast between us – she so young, so vital, so full of good health, and myself ageing, pale, several inches shorter than she was, so that when we stood, she looked down on me.

I told her I was well. I repeated: 'What is it you wish to say to me?'

'Your Majesty, I am deeply grieved.'

'Why is that?'

'I fear Your Majesty has lost her love for me. This makes me sad indeed. You have ever been a good sister to me, and I am desolate to think I may have done something to offend you. I know of nothing . . . except this matter of religion.'

I said: 'You have been told many times to attend Mass, and you stubbornly refuse to do so.'

'Your Majesty, I have not had your advantage. I was

brought up in the Reformed Faith, and I have heard no other.'

'There is no excuse. There are many who would instruct you.'

'Then Your Majesty has relieved me greatly. I must have instruction. Perhaps some learned man could be appointed for me. I will willingly learn. Your Majesty will understand that, having been instructed in one form of religion, it stays with one, and it is hard to change.'

I never knew whether to believe her or not. But for Renard's warning, I would have embraced her and told her that she should have tuition at once and we should be good sisters again. But I did hesitate. I knew Renard was right when he said she was wily and she must be watched. But seeing her before me, her eyes alight with enthusiasm, the look of humility in her face, the obvious eagerness to be taken back into my affections, I almost believed her.

I said: 'You will attend Mass on the 8th of September. It is the day the Church of Rome celebrates the nativity of the Virgin.'

She looked a little taken aback. I tried to read her thoughts. She could not refuse. She knew that there were spies about her, all waiting for her to make some slip. Renard would be happy to see her in the Tower, considering her safer there. De Noailles would want her out of the way too. He wanted us both out of the way, to make the road clear for Mary of Scotland. On the other hand, Elizabeth was next in succession, and she only had to wait for my death.

The thought made me shiver. But I could not believe this fresh-faced young girl would be foolish enough to become involved in a plot which, if it did not succeed, could cost her the crown and possibly her head.

I kissed her. 'We are sisters,' I said. 'Let us be friends.'

She smiled radiantly, and I warmed to her. I knew she had been deeply hurt because, when I had been acclaimed legitimate, that could only mean that she was not. When we had both been called bastards, there had been a bond between us. As Queen I had to be proclaimed legitimate, and deeply I had desired this . . . not only for myself but for the sake of my mother. But I did feel for Elizabeth. It was bad enough to be the daughter of Anne Boleyn who, many believed, had been a witch.

It pleased me to be lenient with her. I would help her. It might well be that all she needed was instruction.

But I was adamant that she must attend Mass on the occasion I had mentioned.

She did appear. She came, looking pale and wan.

How did she manage it? I asked myself. I only half-believed in her illnesses. She recovered a little too quickly for them to be genuine.

She was surrounded by her ladies. They almost carried her into the chapel. When they arrived, she asked them to rub her stomach in the hope of bringing her some relief.

It was a good piece of acting – if acting it was. People would say, 'Poor Princess! She was forced to attend Mass, but it was easy to see how reluctant she was. It made her quite ill.'

And it seemed to me that she had scored again.

* * *

Renard was incensed by the manner in which Elizabeth had behaved. Far from upsetting the Protestants with her little bit of playacting, she had strengthened her position.

'I shall never be happy while she remains free,' he grumbled.

He thought I was a fool. I had been taken in by my sister's wiles. I kept Jane Grey alive in the Tower. Again and again he tried to impress on me that these two women represented rallying-points. The country could break into revolt at any time. Did I not see that Elizabeth and Jane,

433

as Protestants, could be at the very centre of plots against me?

I replied that the people were with me. They had chosen me.

'They could choose Elizabeth,' he said.

I shook my head and he lifted his shoulders and turned away. He said: 'She must be watched. If there is the least indication that she is plotting against you, it must be the Tower for her . . . and most likely her head.'

He came to me a few days later with the news that de Noailles was visiting Elizabeth secretly. It could only be that they were plotting to destroy me.

'Why should de Noailles be working for Elizabeth?'

'He is not,' replied Renard. 'Depend upon it, once he had despatched Your Majesty, Elizabeth would go the same way. She is too naïve . . . too eager for power to see that. His only interest is to put Mary Stuart on the throne.'

'Must there always be these plots against me?'

'Until we are sure that you are safe on the throne, there will be.'

'And when will that be?'

He lifted his shoulders. 'Your Majesty must see that we take every precaution and that while Madam Elizabeth is here, charming the people and being, as she thinks, so clever, we must be watchful. She should be sent to the Tower at once.'

'But nothing has been proved against her.'

'Then we must find out if there is anything to prove.'

I summoned two of my ministers – Arundel and Paget – and told them that the Princess had been behaving in a suspicious manner with the French ambassador.

'Go to her,' I said. 'Discover if there is any truth in these rumours.'

They clearly did not like the task. I noticed that people were becoming more and more careful how they treated Elizabeth. If she could survive, if she did not commit some treasonable act and if nothing could be proved against her, she had a very good chance of coming to the throne. I knew that was what she wanted more than anything. She always implied when I was in her presence that my health was poor and I looked sickly. Though perhaps I imagined that, and it was only myself who compared her healthy looks with my delicate ones. The people had shown that they did not like the succession interfered with. So . . . Paget and Arundel would remember that the young woman they were questioning for treason could be their Queen tomorrow. Naturally they were loth to go to her.

But they did and they came back and reassured me. They had proved without a doubt that de Noailles had made no indiscreet calls on her. She had given ample proof of her loyalty.

I was relieved. It would have worried me considerably to have to send my sister to the Tower.

She asked for an audience again, which I granted, and when she came to me she fell onto her knees.

'Your Majesty, dearest sister,' she said, 'how grateful I am that you have justly given me the opportunity to disprove charges of which I am innocent. I might have been condemned unheard, but Your Majesty is bountiful and loving to your poor subjects, of whom I am the most loyal. I beg of you that you will never give credit to the calumnies that might hereafter be circulated about me, without giving me the chance to defend myself.'

'I will promise you that,' I told her.

'Then I am happy, for I am your loving and devoted servant, and as I would never act against you, nothing can ever be proved against me.'

'You are looking pale,' I said, turning the tables, for it was indeed true. She must have been very worried, and it had had its effect on her.

'I have been grievously ill, Your Majesty. I yearn for the

country air. I wonder if you would grant me permission to retire from Court for a little while.'

I looked at her steadily. Her eyes were downcast; she looked very innocent.

I hesitated. I wondered what Renard would say. As for myself, I should be glad to be rid of her. Her good looks and youth aroused such envy in me, and whenever I saw her, I became more conscious of my own appearance and that my marriage was imminent.

She was so sure of herself, so vain, so confident of her power to charm.

'Where would you go?' I asked.

'I thought to Ashridge, Your Majesty. The air there does me good.'

'Very well. You shall go.'

She fell to her knees once more and kissed my hand.

'Your Majesty is so good to me.'

So good? When I had recently sent Paget and Arundel to test her loyalty? She was appealing in her way, and I was as unsure of her now as I ever was.

I called to one of my women to bring me a box of jewels, and from it I selected a pearl necklace. I put it round my sister's neck.

Her eyes filled with tears, and she went so far as to forget the respect she owed to the Queen and put her arms round me and kissed me. Or did she really forget, and was this another of her gestures?

Then she drew back, as though alarmed by her temerity. 'Forgive me, Your Majesty . . . sister . . .'

My reply was to draw her to me and kiss her cheek.

'You will recover quickly in the healthy atmosphere of Ashridge,' I said; and then I dismissed her.

Renard shook his head over my decision to let her go.

'I would prefer,' he said, 'always to have that young woman where I can see what she is doing.'

* * *

Elizabeth continued to occupy Renard's thoughts. He would not be happy until she was out of the way – either in another country or in her grave. I sometimes wondered whether some charge would be trumped up against her. I must be watchful of that. I did not want to have my own sister's blood on my hands. Marriage was a better idea.

The Emperor evidently thought so too. He suggested that Elizabeth be betrothed to the Prince of Piedmont.

She stubbornly refused to consider this. Of course she did. She wanted the English throne above all things.

Renard was annoyed with her, but I could see that he had a grudging admiration for her, too. I think sometimes he wished *she* were the Queen with whom he had to work. They would have understood each other better than he and I did.

However, there was no way of getting rid of Elizabeth through marriage. She was clearly determined on that.

Christmas had come, and it was in January of the following year, 1554, when Gardiner uncovered the plot.

The news of my proposed marriage to Philip of Spain was leaking out, and the reaction was as I had feared it might be.

The French ambassador called on me. He was clearly deeply disturbed. Did I realize the dangers? he wondered. Philip would dominate me.

I replied haughtily that *I* was the Queen of this realm and intended to remain so.

'Husbands,' replied de Noailles, 'can be persuasive.' He added that his master, King Henri Deux, did not like the match at all.

That was no news to me; I was fully aware that he would dislike it and do all he could to prevent it.

Every day seemed to bring home to me more and more the danger of my position. Though I had been crowned Queen of England, there were others who had envious eyes on that crown. Oddly enough, they were all women. There was Lady Jane Grey in the Tower at the moment, my prisoner; but perhaps she did not want it for herself, it was others who coveted it for her. There was Elizabeth, patiently waiting to step into my shoes; and in France was the young Mary, Queen of Scots, who, by becoming the wife of the Dauphin of France, had made Henri Deux cast speculative eyes in its direction.

This was no news to me. I knew very well that the French would dislike the Spanish match.

My position was as dangerous as it had ever been. There had been no peace for me since that day when my father had decided that he wished to be rid of my mother.

I needed a strong man – someone to care for me, to stand beside me and help fight off my enemies.

Philip of Spain would help me to do that. I should have the might of Spain behind me. It would be a good match.

But the news of my intended marriage was already causing trouble.

I knew that Edward Courtenay was bitterly disappointed. He had pretended to care for me, but I often asked myself if he really did. I had been attracted by him. Who would not have been? He was so good-looking and charming, and his history was so touching. The idea of such a man being prisoner all those years for committing no sin but having royal blood in his veins. It was admirable that, during those years in the Tower, he had educated himself so that he was as polished as any courtier; all he lacked was horsemanship and outdoor skills, for how could he have practised those, confined as he was? Yet I doubted not that in a year or so he would vie with any.

I was fond of Gertrude, his mother, whom I had made a lady of my bedchamber. She was constantly extolling the virtues of her son. So there was another who was disappointed.

I did not realize how deeply this disappointment had gone. I had been hearing rumours about him. He was extravagant; he mingled with a fast set; it was said that this included relationships with loose women. I excused him.

He was a lusty young man and he had been shut away for a long time; in any case I had ceased to regard him as a possible husband. I could see that to marry such a man, just because he was young and handsome, was not the way a queen should act. I had, I confess, been a little over-whelmed by his grace and good manners and his show of affection for me. But I was not so easily deluded. I knew that I was not good-looking, that I showed signs of age, and I should have been a fool if I had not understood that it was my glittering crown which dazzled, not my person.

I was sure I had done the right thing in agreeing to marriage with Philip of Spain. He was not expecting a beauty; what he wanted was a queen, and he would not be disappointed in that respect.

The members of the Council were constantly on the alert, and they knew the Spanish marriage was not going to be popular. Gardiner discovered that a certain Peter Carew of Devon was going through the towns of that county, telling people that they must not allow the marriage to take place. It would be letting the Spaniards into the country. They were a harsh and cruel race, he warned them, and they would be bringing Spanish laws into England. There were sailors in Devon who had come into the clutches of the evil Inquisition and had, by great good luck, escaped. Let the people listen to their stories of hideous torture. The Spaniards would rule England, and the Queen would be merely the wife of a foreign king. There must be no Spanish marriage.

There was only one thing for the Council to do, and they did it. They ordered Peter Carew to come to London for questioning. But Carew realized what was happening and, when he did not come and they sent guards to arrest him, he had already disappeared.

It was disturbing, for there was no doubt that there would soon be revolt in Devon.

Stephen Gardiner came to me and begged an audience. When I received him, I saw at once how grave he was.

'I have news which will shock you,' he said.

'This revolt . . .' I began.

'Carew has escaped, as Your Majesty knows. He is a bold fellow with a colourful past. He has led a life of adventure, and he is the sort men choose for a leader.'

'It is a pity he was not forced to come before the Council. He should have been arrested and brought here.'

Gardiner nodded slowly. Then he said: 'I have discovered what was afoot.'

'Then pray tell me.'

'As the rising was in the Earl of Devonshire's territory, I thought of questioning him.'

'Yes,' I said uneasily.

'He has confessed that he knows of the plot to oppose the Spanish marriage. He says he took no part in it, but when I questioned him he was very ready to tell me about it.'

'He is a weak young man, easily led, and he has become ambitious,' I said.

Gardiner agreed. 'It is good that we have this warning,' he said. 'It enables us to put down the revolt with less trouble than we should have if it were allowed to develop. There are certain people of whom we must be watchful and . . . Courtenay is one.'

I nodded.

'And more dangerous still . . . the Princess Elizabeth.'

'Do you think . . . ?'

'I am of the opinion, Your Majesty, that she is a very dangerous lady.'

It all seemed to come back to Elizabeth.

While I was growing more and more anxious about these rumblings of revolt, the marriage treaty was signed. It had been very carefully drawn up. Our two dominions, England

440

and Spain – which Philip would inherit on the death or abdication of his father – were to be governed separately. Only the English were to hold office in the English Court and government. If I had a child, it was to inherit my dominions with the addition of Holland and Flanders. I was not to be taken out of the country, nor should any children I might have, without my consent and that of the government. England was not to be involved in any wars in which Spain might be engaged, nor was Spain to appropriate English ships, ammunition or the crown jewels; and if I died without children, all connection between England and my husband would cease.

All this seemed fair enough, but there was one final clause, and I think that was what aroused the indignation of the people: Philip was to aid me in governing the country.

It was soon after the contents of the treaty were made public that trouble started in earnest.

The disappearance of Sir Peter Carew had to a certain extent quelled that which was about to take place in Devon. Courtenay had left London. He had not been arrested because he had alerted us to the dangers of the plot; but at the same time he had been guilty of traitorous intent. The plan had been to dethrone me, marry Courtenay to Elizabeth and set her on the throne, at the same time establishing the Protestant religion throughout the land.

There was a rising in the Midlands by the vassals of the Duke of Suffolk. Their aim was to set up Lady Jane Grey and also the Protestant religion.

Courtenay's confession had helped a great deal, and these were suppressed. But there was yet another to contend with, and this proved to be a very serious matter.

It was headed by Sir Thomas Wyatt. He was a headstrong young man from Allington Castle in Kent, and he continued to rouse the men of that county to action.

Wyatt was not unknown to me. He was the son of the

poet who had been a close friend of Anne Boleyn – possibly her lover. I was greatly suspicious of his motives, and I wondered whether his father's love and admiration for the mother had been transferred by him to the daughter.

Every time I heard of these disloyal insurrections, my thoughts went to Elizabeth.

This Wyatt was a man to watch. He was an adventurer such as Peter Carew. They stepped naturally into the role of leader. They were fearless in the first place; they were reckless, too. I supposed it was those qualities which endeared them to others.

As a very young man Wyatt had been in trouble along with Henry Howard, Earl of Surrey, who himself had lost his head just before my father died. They had been wild young men, roaming the streets of London together, taking part in mischievous tricks which had resulted in their being arrested and spending a few weeks in the Tower. As such young men often do, Wyatt had later distinguished himself. This was in military service in Boulogne, and later he had been among those who had helped to defeat the Duke of Northumberland when the latter had tried to set Jane Grey on the throne. It seemed that he had been a loyal subject until the intended Spanish marriage was proposed.

Later I heard more of what had happened. Edward Courtenay was more deeply involved than we had at first realized. He it was who, knowing of Wyatt's dislike of the Spaniards, had invited him to raise men in Kent to join the insurrections. Wyatt was enthusiastic. Long ago, he had travelled to Spain with his father, the poet, who had been arrested and taken before the Inquisition. It was something he had never forgotten, and an intense hatred of Spaniards had been born in him then. He was determined to do everything possible to stop the Spanish marriage, and he, like many others, believed that, with a Spanish consort, Spanish manners and customs would be introduced into the country.

When a number of the conspirators were arrested, Wyatt found himself the head of the revolt. He might have fled the country, which would have been his wisest course of action, but men like Wyatt are never wise. Caution and self-preservation are traits quite unknown to their nature.

Finding himself forced into the position of leader, he rode to Maidstone and there proclaimed his cause. His neighbours and friends from other counties were urged to fight for the liberty of the people which would be suppressed if the Queen married a foreigner.

Renard came to see me in great consternation.

He had his spies placed everywhere, and the most accomplished were in the household of the French ambassador, who, he said, was our most dangerous enemy. The news he had to impart was indeed disquieting.

'King Henri is planning to open a front along the Scottish border,' he told me. 'And he is hinting at giving help to the rebels.'

'He cannot do that!' I cried.

'Why not? The Scots are always ready to come against us. They will welcome him. He has twenty-four warships on the Normandy coast, just waiting until the moment is ripe.'

'Why should he help the rebels?'

'He will help them to defeat your supporters, and then he will step in to perfect his plan.'

'To put Mary of Scotland on the throne. But the rebels want Elizabeth.'

'They are simpletons, he thinks. He will get them to do the worst of the work for him, and that will be the end of them.'

'How dangerous is this? We have suppressed the risings . . all except this one of Wyatt's.'

'It is this one of Wyatt's that we have to watch. The sooner you are married, the better it will be.'

'Wyatt cannot do much against trained men.'

'Wyatt has been a soldier. He is not merely some hothead with a grievance. It is disturbing that the French should be ready to involve themselves in this.'

'I should like to dismiss de Noailles.'

'It would do no good. There would be another, and it is better to have one of whose methods we know something.'

'I shall send Norfolk against them.'

I was confident at this time that the trouble would soon be over.

This was not the case. As Renard had pointed out, Wyatt was a soldier; and, to my horror, it was not Wyatt who was defeated but Norfolk. I was greatly distressed when our soldiers returned to London; they were tired, dirty and hungry; they looked like the defeated army they were. There was great consternation among the citizens. It was clear to them that this was a serious revolt.

Then came the news that Wyatt was preparing to march on London.

It began dawning on me that I was in a desperate situation. I had no army to defend me. I asked myself how far I could trust my Council. I knew them for a group of ambitious men jostling for power. There was a small faction against Gardiner. He – with my support, it is true – was too fervent a Catholic; he was accused of causing trouble by trying to force people to join in religious observances against their will and for which they were not yet ready. Gardiner turned to them and declared that the sole trouble was the Spanish marriage and he had often questioned the wisdom of that.

So there I was, in my capital city, without an army, with a Council who were quarrelling among themselves, and rebels preparing to come against me.

Wyatt's headquarters were at Rochester, where he had gathered men and ammunition and was preparing to march on London. I sent messages throughout the country offering a pardon to all his followers who left him within the next twenty-four hours and returned peacefully to their homes, reminding them that, if they did not, they would be judged traitors.

Then we heard that he was on his way with 4,000 men.

Gardiner came to see me. He was in a state of some agitation. Clearly he felt Wyatt to be a formidable foe. He said he had sent messages to him, asking him to state his demands.

I was astounded. 'This is amounting to a truce,' I said.

'Your Majesty, the situation is dangerous. We have to halt this march on London.'

'I will not parley with him. Let him come. We will face him.'

'Your Majesty does not fully grasp the danger. He is marching on us with his army. The Council has considered the matter. Your Majesty must go to the Tower immediately . . . no, better still, Windsor. You should not be here when Wyatt's men come into the town.'

'They shall not come into the town,' I said firmly, 'and I shall not go to Windsor. I will stay here and face these rebels.'

'It was suggested that you should dress as one of the people . . . and mingle with them so that it would not be known who you are.'

'I shall certainly not do that. I am the Queen, and everyone must know that I am the Queen.'

Renard came to tell me that the Imperial Commissioners were preparing to leave the country. I thought that was wise, as they had been negotiating the marriage contract and the people might turn on them in their fury.

'They wish to come and take their leave.'

'Then bring them,' I said.

When they arrived, I told them to give my best wishes to the Emperor and to tell him that I would write to him and tell him the outcome of this little matter.

They were astounded by my calmness. They believed I

was in acute danger. I might have been, but at that time I was so confident of my destiny that I had no fear.

When they left, I went to the Guildhall. The people, aware of my coming, assembled there.

They cheered me as I approached, and it was heartwarming to hear the cry of 'God save Queen Mary!'

I spoke to them, and I was glad of my deep voice – which some had said was more like a man's than a woman's – as I heard it ringing out with confidence which seemed to inspire them and disperse some of their anxieties.

'My loving subjects,' I cried, 'who I am, you well know. I am your Queen, to whom at my coronation you promised allegiance and obedience. I am the rightful inheritor of this crown. My father's regal state has descended on me. It would seem that some do not like my proposed marriage. My beloved subjects, I do not enter into this out of self-will or lust, but it is my bounden duty to leave you an heir to follow me. It is untrue that harm will come to our country through my marriage. If I thought I should harm that and you, I should remain a virgin all my life. I do not know how a mother loves her child because I have never been a mother, but I assure you that I, being your Queen, see myself as your mother, and as such do I love you. Good subjects, lift up your hearts. Remember that you are true men and brave. Stand fast against these rebels. They are not only my enemies but yours also. Fear them not, for I assure you I fear them not at all.'

As I stopped speaking, the cheers rang out. 'God save Queen Mary!'

'People of London,' I went on, 'will you defend me against these rebels? If you will, I am minded to live and die with you and strain every nerve in your cause, for at this time your fortunes, goods and honour, your personal safety and that of your wives and children are in the balance.'

As I stopped speaking, once more the cheers rang out.

446

It was clear that they were all deeply moved. Gardiner, who had been beside me, looked at me with a dazed expression. Then he said: 'I am happy that we have such a wise Queen.'

The people of London were rallying to my side. The streets were full of men prepared to fight. I was gratified. I knew I had taken the right course. I felt that I had been inspired and that God was showing me the way.

* * *

It was three o'clock in the morning. I was startled out of a dreamless sleep to find Susan at my bedside.

'Your Majesty, the Council are here. They must see you at once.'

I hastily rose. Susan wrapped a robe about me, and I went into the ante-room where the Council were waiting for me.

Gardiner said to me: 'Your Majesty must leave London without delay. Wyatt is at Deptford. He will be at the city gates ere long.'

I replied: 'I have promised the people of London that I will stay with them.'

'It is unsafe for Your Majesty to stay here.'

I was thoughtful for a moment. It was all against my instincts to fly, and yet, on the other hand, if I stayed and was murdered, what good would I be to my faith? It was my duty to restore this country to God's grace, and how could I do that . . . dead?

I was very undecided. My inclination was to stay, because I had given my word to the people of London. But was it foolish?

Only the previous day Renard had congratulated me on my speech to the people at the Guildhall. He said that if I had left London then, Wyatt could have succeeded, and that would have meant putting Elizabeth on the throne and strengthening the Protestant influence in the country. How wise I had been to act as I did, he said. The Emperor would approve.

And now here was my Council suggesting flight.

I said: 'I will decide in the morning.'

Gardiner replied that the time was short. In the morning it might be too late.

'Nevertheless,' I replied, 'I will decide then.'

As soon as they had gone, I sent one of my servants to bring Renard to me. He came with all speed.

'They are suggesting I leave for Windsor,' I told him. 'They say that Wyatt is all but at the gates of the city, and if I stay here and he is victorious, it will be the end of my reign, and me most likely.'

'Your presence here has brought out the loyalty of these citizens,' said Renard. 'If you go, Wyatt will be allowed to walk in. Elizabeth will be proclaimed Queen, and that will be the end of your reign.'

'You are saying that I should stay.'

He nodded slowly. 'I am saying just that.'

So my mind was made up. I should stay.

* * *

London was a city at war. The shops had been boarded up, and all the goods were removed from the stalls. Armed men were everywhere; the drawbridges were cut loose, and the gates of the city were barred and guarded.

We waited in trepidation.

The guns of the Tower were trained on Southwark, but I could not allow them to be fired, even though Wyatt and his men were sheltering there. I had to consider the little houses and the people living in them. How could I fire on my own people? It was no fault of theirs that they were in the line of fire.

Wyatt must have been getting uneasy. One day passed . . . and then another. The bridge was too well guarded for him to cross; if he attempted to storm it, there would be

448

bitter fighting and the village of Southwark would be destroyed. I imagined that at this stage he was wishing he had never been caught up in this rebellion. He had only meant to raise men against the Spanish marriage, and when the others had deserted, he had found himself the leader and it was too late to turn back. He was an honourable man; there was no pillage and looting in his army.

He must have realized that he could not fight his way across the bridge and therefore must leave Southwark. It was with relief that we saw his army on the march, although we knew that would not be the end; he would attempt to cross at another point.

We heard that he was at Kingston. He was in a quandary, for the rain was teeming down, the river was swollen and the bridge had broken down. Nothing daunted, Wyatt set his men to repair the bridge, which, in the heavy rain, took hours; but at length, after much toil and skill, it was sufficiently repaired to allow the men with their ammunition to cross the river.

All these delays and difficulties had had their effect on the men. It is a tribute to Wyatt's leadership that he kept them together. But at least he must congratulate himself. He had arrived with his army – albeit not in the condition it had been in when it left Southwark. But he was now on the Middlesex side of the river; he had successfully crossed, and London lay before him.

I was awakened once more in the night to hear that he had reached Brentford. Several of the guards were in the streets beating drums – the signal for citizens to be out of their beds and to prepare.

Then he reached Knightsbridge.

The Council told me I should go to the Tower, but I refused. I would stay at Whitehall. I knew the people must see me. If I went to the Tower, it would seem as though I were afraid and should have to protect myself. I did not want that. I must show the people that I was prepared to face danger, as they must.

Instinct told me that Wyatt was a desperate man. He must have believed that there were enough Protestants among the population of London to come to his aid, and that someone would open the gates when he had been at Southwark. I believed it was my action in staying with the people of London, and showing them my confidence, which had made them rally to me.

It seemed to me that I had acted on inspiration from Heaven, and I thanked God for those men who were loyal to me on that day. I had come near to a disaster which would have changed the face of history. Wyatt was a strong man with deep convictions; he was a leader, but the odds were against him. Perhaps he had ill luck. Perhaps it was that God intended me to live and fulfil my mission. I believed that, at the time, and I have gone on believing it.

Pembroke was magnificent. He was a skilled general. As Wyatt made his way towards St James's, Pembroke kept his forces in hiding; and when Wyatt's forces had passed along unmolested, Pembroke and his men sprang out and attacked them in the rear. Winchester, another of my good commanders, was waiting ahead for him, so that he was between Wyatt and Ludgate.

The fighting was fierce. I was in the gatehouse, waiting, watching, desperately anxious for news.

A messenger came hurrying in. 'All is lost!' he cried, 'Pembroke has gone over to Wyatt.'

'I don't believe it!' I cried. 'Pembroke is no traitor.'

'Wyatt is close. Your Majesty must take barge at once. You could get to Windsor.'

'I will not go,' I said. 'I shall stay here. Let us pray, and the Lord will save the day for us. I know in my heart that this will be so. I put my trust in God.'

I felt then that He was the only one in whom I could put my trust.

That was my darkest hour.

It was not long before the news reached me. The rumour was false. Pembroke was no traitor, as I had known he could not be. Wyatt's men, dispirited, cold, dirty and hungry after their experiences at Kingston, were no match for my men. They knew it, and when such knowledge comes to a soldier, he is a defeated man.

I wondered what Wyatt's thoughts were as he battled there at Ludgate; he must have realized with every passing second that his cause was a lost one.

Sir Maurice Berkeley called to him to surrender. 'If you do not,' he said, 'all these men whom you have brought with you will doubtless be killed – yourself, too. Give in now. It may be that the Queen will show you mercy.'

Wyatt hesitated, but only for a moment. He knew that he had lost and he gave up gracefully.

Sir Maurice took Wyatt on the back of his horse and rode to the keep where I was watching, so that I might see that the leader of the rebellion was his prisoner.

My first thought was: 'We must give thanks to God.' And, taking my women with me, I went to the chapel, where, on our knees, we gave thanks for this victory.

I was exultant. To me it meant confirmation of my dreams. God's purpose was clear to me. I prayed that I should be worthy to complete my mission.

* * *

Now was the time for retribution.

Wyatt was in the Tower. Although there was no question of his guilt, he was not executed immediately, because it was hoped that he would incriminate others – mainly my sister Elizabeth and Edward Courtenay.

At the Old Bailey, as many as eighty-two persons were judged and condemned in one day. In every street in London hung the bodies of traitors – a grim warning. This continued for ten days, and there were so many executions that men had to be cut down from the gibbets to make way for others. As Wyatt came from Kent, it was thought necessary to let the Kentish people see for themselves what happened to traitors. Men were taken there, and in the towns and villages their bodies were set up on gibbets or in chains.

Renard had told me frequently that the leniency I was inclined to show was dangerous. There would always be such insurrections while Lady Jane lived – and I could see that that was true. I knew I must agree that she be brought to the block.

I was wretched. I should have rejoiced. Our victory over Wyatt was complete, and yet, because it must result in so many deaths, I was unhappy. God had shown me how to act, and I had followed His instructions but I wished there need not be this carnage.

I told myself that these men were traitors, and they all knew the risk they ran when they took up arms against the anointed sovereign. It was the thought of Jane which haunted me, but I knew my advisers were right. While she lived, this sort of thing could happen again. It was better for her to die than that thousands should lose their lives because of her.

So at last they prevailed on me to sign the death warrant.

Guilford Dudley was taken out to the block the day before her. It was unnecessary cruelty to make her watch his execution from a window in the Tower. I did not know of this until after it had happened. There were many of my courtiers who regarded me as a soft and sentimental woman who let her heart rule her head. I should not have forced that cruelty on Jane, for, in my view, it served no purpose. Die she must, but I wanted it to be done with the least possible discomfort to her.

There were many to tell me how she went to her death, how she came out to Tower Green, wondrously calm, her prayer book in her hand, looking very young and beautiful.

And as she was about to mount the scaffold, she asked permission to speak. When this was given, she spoke of the wrong done to the Queen's Majesty and that she was innocent of it.

'This I swear before God and you good people,' she added.

Her women tied a handkerchief about her eyes, and pathetically she stretched out her hands, as she could not see the block.

'Where is it?' she said. 'I cannot see it.'

They said it was the most piteous sight, to observe her thus, a young and beautiful girl, so innocent of blame. I was glad I did not witness it.

They helped her to the block and, before she laid her head on it, she asked the executioner to despatch her quickly, and he promised he would.

Then she said in a firm, clear voice: 'Lord, into Thy hands I commend my spirit.'

I was deeply moved when they told me, and how fervently I wished that it had not had to be.

Others followed her, including her father, the Duke of Suffolk. I did not feel the same pity for him.

On the day Jane died, Courtenay was taken to the Tower. De Noailles was under suspicion. He had certainly played a part in the rebellion, and papers had been found to prove this. But it is not easy to deal with an ambassador. One cannot clap him into prison. We might have insisted on his recall, but Renard was against this.

I do believe that de Noailles was a very uneasy man at that time.

Elizabeth was the one Renard was most interested in. He had always regarded her as the great menace. In a way he respected her. He thought her clever, but that only added to his desire to put her away.

'She must be questioned,' he said to me. 'She has had a

hand in this. She is at the very heart of the plot. She must have known that Wyatt would have set her up as Queen.'

'He insists that it was merely to stop my marriage that he rebelled.'

'He would have stopped that by seeing that you were not here to marry. Depend upon it, his plan was to set Elizabeth on the throne. I tell you this: the Prince of Spain might refuse to come here unless she is put away . . . and Courtenay with her.'

'Courtenay is already in the Tower.'

'And Elizabeth should be there, too. You must send for her to come to London. There will be no peace in this realm while she is free.'

Gardiner added his voice to Renard's. I knew they were right. I did not trust my sister; but I did not believe she would be party to my murder. She knew that I was not strong; I had no heirs; she could come to the throne constitutionally. She was young. Would a woman of her astuteness, her far-seeing nature, not be prepared to wait until she could achieve her desires peacefully and with the people behind her?

However, Gardiner and Renard thought differently. They were sure that Elizabeth would be safe only in the Tower.

I summoned her to Court. The reply was just what I expected. She was too ill to travel. I did not believe this, although she must have suffered great anxiety when she knew that Wyatt had been captured and that he – with Courtenay, who had been paying her some attention – was in the Tower.

I sent two of my doctors to discover whether she was well enough to travel, and they were fully aware that, if they agreed she was too ill, they would be under suspicion.

Elizabeth came to London.

As was expected, she made sure of a dramatic entrance. She was dressed in white and rode in a litter, insisting, truthfully, that she was too ill to come on horseback. She had ordered that her litter should not be covered. Naturally, she wanted the people to see her so that she might win their sympathy.

The people came out to watch her retinue as it passed along the roads. Many were weeping, knowing for what purpose she was going to London, to her death, they thought.

It was only eleven days since the beautiful Jane Grey had walked to the block. Was Elizabeth's fate to be the same? That was what they must have been asking themselves.

Perhaps some recalled her mother, who had lost her head on Tower Green.

I was relieved, though, that they did not shout for her, even though they gave themselves up to tears. The times were too dangerous to show partisanship; there could hardly have been any of them who had not seen the corpses rotting in chains.

They took her to Westminster, whence she sent a plea to me, reminding me of my promise never to condemn her unheard.

I did not answer that plea. I wanted others to question her – not I.

I could not get her out of my thoughts. I reproached myself for refusing to see her. I could not forget that she was my sister.

It was proved that Wyatt had written to her on two occasions: once to advise her to move farther from London and secondly to tell her of his arrival at Southwark; but she was too wise to have replied to either of these communications.

De Noailles had mentioned her in his despatches to France, and these had been intercepted by Renard, so, to a certain extent, she was implicated, if not of her own free will.

Of course, she vowed her innocence. I believed her

because I did not think she would be foolish enough to embroil herself in a revolt which could easily fail, when all she had to do was wait. If I had a healthy child, then she might have reasons, but as it was, I could see none. And Elizabeth was one who would always have her reasons.

I wanted others to decide what was done with her. Renard wanted her out of the way; Gardiner wavered. He was not really in favour of the Spanish marriage, and in this he was alone in the Council. He was of the opinion that, if I married, Philip would dominate affairs. He regarded me with that mild contempt which men often bestow on women. He was loyal but he could not believe that women were capable of government.

He it was who declared that there was no actual proof of Elizabeth's participation in Wyatt's plot. There was no correspondence between them except the letters which Wyatt had written and which had apparently been unanswered. I wondered how big a part his objections to the Spanish match played in his judgements. When the Council decided that the best place for Elizabeth was in the Tower while her case was investigated, Gardiner was inclined to stand out against this; yet when he saw he was outnumbered, he gave way.

Her passage to the Tower was as dramatic as she knew how to make it. Even the elements seemed to work in her favour, for I wished her to be taken by night so that the people might not see her and express their sympathy. I was furious with Sussex, who was to conduct her to the Tower, for allowing her to delay so that she missed the tide and had to go the next morning. It was Palm Sunday, which seemed to make it all the more dramatic. I decided she must go while most people were at church.

Many have since heard of Elizabeth's journey to the Tower, how the stern of the boat struck the side of the bridge and almost overturned, how she was at length taken to the Traitor's Gate to step into the water, her words

456

ringing out to all those about her that they might sympathize with her.

'Here lands as true a subject being prisoner as ever landed at these stairs.'

And the response from the lookers-on: 'May God preserve Your Grace.' Many of them wept, and she turned to them and told them not to weep for her; and there she was, comforting them who should have been comforting her. 'For you know the truth,' she said. 'I am innocent of the charges brought against me, so that none of you have cause to weep for me.'

Then they took her to her prison in the Tower.

But the thought of her haunted me. I believed that, as long as we lived, she would be there to disconcert me.

* * *

So Wyatt, Elizabeth and Courtenay were all in the Tower – Wyatt certain of death, Courtenay and Elizabeth uncertain, but living in fear of it. Life must have been very uncomfortable for de Noailles. He knew that he was watched and suspected. I had no doubt that he would have preferred to be recalled, although that could have offered him little joy, for to be recalled in such circumstances would be an indication of failure.

At about the same time as Elizabeth was being lodged in the Tower, Wyatt was brought to trial, condemned and sentenced to death. Even so, the deed was not to be performed immediately, and the 11th of April was fixed for his execution.

I was told that early that day he asked to be allowed to see Courtenay, who was lodged near him. The request was granted, and at the meeting Wyatt fell to his knees and begged Courtenay to admit that he had been the instigator of the rebellion.

This upset me a great deal, for I remembered how at one time I had thought Courtenay cared for me. How foolish I had been to think a young and handsome man would have tender feelings for an old woman. He certainly had coveted my crown. I felt hurt, but my anger was more for myself for having been so easily deluded than for this vain and arrogant young man. He had touched my feelings rather deeply, for I made excuses for him. He was but a boy, younger than his years, so many of which had been spent in unnatural captivity. It was not surprising that, when he found himself released and saw the possibility of a crown, he became reckless and behaved in such a way as to show a complete lack of judgement.

On the scaffold, when he was face to face with death, Wyatt made a statement in which he took the entire blame for the rebellion and declared that Elizabeth and Courtenay were innocent.

He was a brave man, but brave men are often rash and foolish.

His head was hung high on a gallows near Hyde Park, and his quartered limbs were placed for display about the town.

This was a grim warning to all traitors.

The Spanish Marriage

That was a trying time. My thoughts were of marriage. At last that blissful state, of which I had so often dreamed in the past, was about to come to pass. When I had been a little girl and betrothed to the Emperor Charles, my maids had told me with such conviction that I was in love that I had believed them. Now I told myself that I was in love with Philip, and I was in that state, with the image I made for myself, much as my women had made for me with the Emperor.

I lived in a dream: love, marriage, children. I had wanted them desperately all my life. Now I believed they were within my grasp. I did not remind myself then: I am eleven years older than he is; his father is my cousin. Did that make me his aunt? If there was a shadow in my thoughts, I dismissed it quickly. No, no. Royal brides and grooms were often related to each other.

It was a period of uneasiness. There were murmurs of discontent all over the country. Wyatt's head was stolen, presumably so that it should be snatched from the eyes of the curious and given decent burial. I should have been glad of that – those ghoulish exhibits always nauseated me – but it was a sign of sympathy with the rebels. It meant that Wyatt's followers were still to be reckoned with and were bold enough to commit an act which could result in their deaths.

This was not only a matter of religion. The main grievance was the Spanish marriage – though I supposed one was wrapped up in the other.

A hatred for Spaniards was making itself known throughout the country. Children played games in which Spaniards figured as the villains. No child wanted to be a Spaniard in the games, and it was usually the youngest who were forced to take those parts, knowing that before long they were going to be trounced by the gallant English.

There was the unpleasant affair of Elizabeth Croft. She caused quite a stir until she was caught. She was a servant in the household of some zealous Protestants who lived in Aldersgate Street. From a wall in the house a high-pitched whistle was heard. Crowds collected to hear the whistle in the wall, and then a voice came forth denouncing the Spanish marriage as well as the Roman Catholic religion. This continued for months, and there was a great deal of talk about 'the bird in the wall'.

Susan told me about it. She was frowning. 'People are beginning to say it is a warning.'

'How can there be a bird in the wall?' I demanded. 'And what would a bird know about these matters?'

'People say it is a heavenly spirit speaking through the bird to warn you.'

'Then why shouldn't this spirit speak to *me*?'

'This bird is supposed to be talking to the people, telling them they should never allow the Spanish marriage to take place.'

'That is what Wyatt said, and look what happened to him.'

'I suspect the voice is a human one,' said Susan.

'In whose house is it?'

'Sir Anthony Knyvett's.'

'Has he been questioned?'

'He swears he knows nothing of it.'

'It is silly nonsense.'

'Yes, Your Majesty, but the people gather to listen.'

That voice in the wall continued to be heard for a few more months before the truth was discovered. It was Elizabeth Croft, the servant girl. When she was caught at her tricks, she was sent to prison. Sir Anthony was innocent of any part in it, but the girl did confess that she had been persuaded to do what she did by one of the servants, a man named Drake who was a fierce Protestant and hated the prospect of the Spanish marriage.

Both Renard and Gardiner talked to me about the girl. It was not that she was important in herself but it was dangerous for people to believe, if only temporarily, that a voice from Heaven should denounce my marriage.

What should we do with her? She was a simple girl, I said, no doubt led astray by others – this servant Drake for one. A weaver of Redcross Street was mentioned, and there was a clergyman from St Botolph's Church in Aldersgate also. I could see how the girl had been tempted, and I did not want her to be severely punished. It was enough that the people should know that she was a fraud.

She was taken to Paul's Cross where she made a public confession. This she was more than willing to do, feeling – and rightly so – that she had escaped lightly. After confessing to the trick she had played on the unsuspecting public, she knelt and asked God's forgiveness, and mine, for her wickedness.

She was sent to prison for a while and afterwards released.

But the disquiet continued all through the months that followed. There was even dissension among the Council. Some of them, Gardiner and my good Rochester among them, who wanted a return to the Catholic religion but not to go back to Rome, believed that the interests of the country were best served with the monarch as Head of the Church. Paget, on the other hand, wanted a complete return to religion as it had been before my father had interfered with it. Then there was of course the Protestant element.

In addition to all this was the problem created by my sister. She was still in the Tower, and that worried me. Paget, among others, had often told me that while she lived

461

I was unsafe and that the best gift I could have was her head severed from her shoulders.

Such talk did not please me. I could never forget that she was my sister. I remembered so well the bright little girl with the reddish curls and the shining eyes, so eager to miss nothing. How did she feel . . . a prisoner in the Tower? I doubted she was treated harshly. She would make friends of the gaolers if necessary. She would always make friends of people who could be useful to her, and in view of her closeness to the throne, people would be wary of offending her.

I remembered her protestations of affection when we last met and her plea that I should always listen to her before judging her. I had not done that. I had refused to see her and had been prevailed upon to send her to the Tower.

I discussed her with Susan. I knew that to speak of her to Gardiner or Renard would only arouse their indignation against her, though I could tell them again and again that nothing had actually been proved against her. Wyatt himself had exonerated her, but they would never believe in her innocence.

But *I* believed in it, and as I felt towards her as a sister, I was sure she felt the same towards me.

I said to Susan: 'I cannot be entirely at peace while she is in the Tower. She is a princess, my father's daughter, my own sister. How I wish that we could be friends!'

'Your Majesty should be wary of her,' said Susan.

'I know. I know. But she is my sister. It is for that reason I do not care to think of her as a prisoner in the Tower.'

'Perhaps she will marry.'

'Ah, if only she would marry abroad!'

It was an idea which persisted to haunt my mind.

I discussed it with the Council. Many of them thought she would be safer dead, but marriage did seem a way of disposing of her.

I said: 'I will see my sister. Emmanuel Philibert, Duke

of Savoy and Prince of Piedmont, would be pleased to marry her, I am sure. He would be a good match for her. She would then leave the country; people here would not see her and therefore not consider her as a rallying-point for rebellion.'

The more I thought of the idea, the more plausible it seemed. Emmanuel Philibert was one of those who had been chosen for me long ago, and I had forgotten now the reason why the match was put aside. There had been so many such cases.

So Elizabeth left the Tower and came by barge to Richmond, where the Court was at that time.

I sent for her.

She looked a little pale; her sojourn in the Tower had had its effect on her. It was natural that it should. How could she have known from one day to the next when she might be taken out to share her mother's fate?

She looked at me without reproach, almost tenderly, and I warmed towards her.

I said: 'I greatly regret it was necessary to send you to the Tower.'

'Your Majesty is so just that you cannot endure injustice. I am innocent of all my enemies are contriving to prove against me. Your Majesty will know that my sisterly affection would never allow me to do aught to harm you.'

I nodded and said: 'It is your future of which I am thinking.'

'Your Majesty, I should like to retire to the country. The air of Ashridge has always been beneficial to my health.'

I waved a hand impatiently and said: 'I have a proposition to set before you. You are no longer a child. It is time you married.'

She turned pale and recoiled in some dismay.

'Emmanuel Philibert, Duke of Savoy and Prince of Piedmont, would be a worthy match,' I went on.

463

I saw her lips tighten, and a look of determination came over her face.

'I have no desire to marry, Your Majesty.'

'Nonsense. It is the destiny of every woman.'

'If that is her wish, Your Majesty. For myself . . . I would prefer to remain a virgin.'

'You speak of matters of which you have no knowledge.'

'I have an instinct that the state is not for me. I will not marry.'

She was looking at me steadily, and I could see the defiance in her eyes. Was it because she did not like the idea of Emmanuel Philibert, or was it marriage itself which was so repulsive to her?

I remembered the scandal about her flirtation with Seymour. I had seen her eyes sparkle with pleasure at the admiration of men. Why this sudden, almost prudish attitude? One should not *force* people to marry. My thoughts went to poor Jane Grey who had been starved and beaten and forced to marry Guilford Dudley. But how could I compare Elizabeth with Jane Grey?

If Elizabeth refused to marry, I could not force her. I was disappointed. It was an unsatisfactory meeting, and I dismissed her.

Why would she not marry? Because to marry Emmanuel Philibert she would have to leave the country and she did not want to do that. She wanted to be on the spot for any contingency.

But *I* was going to marry. I was going to enter a state of bliss, and I was sure that anyone who wanted children as much as I did must soon become a mother.

My happiness at the prospect made me lenient. Elizabeth should not be coerced, nor should she be forced; she should not return to the Tower. She was dangerous, of course, and I must take precautions. I knew what I would do. I would send for Sir Henry Bedingfield of Oxborough in Norfolk, who had been a loyal supporter of mine ever since

I had been proclaimed Queen. He had been with my mother at Kimbolton during the last years of her life, and one of the first to rally to my side on the death of my brother. It is such things one remembers. When he came to me, the outcome was by no means certain, and I had been considerably heartened by the sight of him and his 140 armed men. He was severe and serious, but one of those men whom one would trust absolutely and whom a woman in my position wants to have about her. I had made him a Privy Councillor, and I knew I could safely put Elizabeth into his hands.

I explained to him that I wished my sister to be released from the Tower but that a strong guard must be kept on her, and he was the man I was going to trust with the task.

'Sir Henry,' I said, 'I want you to serve not only me but the Princess Elizabeth. I fear there are some who, perhaps in their zealous care for me, might seek to do away with her. I want her to be guarded from such. It would cause me the utmost grief if aught happened to her and, although I were innocent of this, I should feel myself to be guilty.'

'Your Majesty shall have no fear,' he replied. 'I will guard the Princess with my life.'

'Thank you, Sir Henry. I put my trust in you.'

And I did.

Elizabeth complained bitterly, I know, of the stringent measures employed. She did not seem to realize that they were guarding her not only for my safety but for her own.

I was relieved when she had left for Woodstock under the guard of Sir Henry Bedingfield.

* * *

Now that the Wyatt rebellion had been brought to a satisfactory end, Courtenay was removed from the Tower to Fotheringay. I intended that in time he should be released. He was little more than a boy – and a foolish, reckless one. I could not bear to think of that handsome head being severed. Antoine de Noailles had once said he was the most handsome man in England – and he was right. I had seen it in writing when Renard had intercepted some of his letters of Henri Deux. I really wanted to shut him away until he became less significant, and then release him and perhaps send him abroad.

Elizabeth was safe in the care of Bedingfield, and soon Philip would be arriving for our marriage.

But nothing seemed to run smoothly. The dissensions in my Council were growing. Paget and Gardiner were deadly enemies, and Philip appeared to be expressing marked indifference, for he made no move either to write to me or to come to England.

De Noailles . . . that man again . . . had now been forced to accept the almost certainty of our marriage, and it did not please him at all. However, realizing that all his attempts to stop it had failed, he shrugged his shoulders and said Philip and I deserved each other, which was meant, I am sure, to be uncomplimentary.

His brother Gilles, who proved to be a handsome and charming young man, had come to England. I could have wished he was in his brother's place.

He came to see me on a matter quite apart from state affairs. He told me that his brother, Antoine, had a newly born son and he would be so honoured if I would help in the choice of godparents. Antoine would have asked me himself but he was afraid I did not regard him very favourably at the moment.

I was always delighted to be involved with babies and, in spite of the strained relations between the French ambassador and myself, and forgetting his blatant spying during the Wyatt rebellion, I said I should happily have undertaken the part of godparent myself but for the fact that I should shortly be going to Winchester, for what purpose he would know.

Gilles de Noailles bowed politely and smiled, as though

he were delighted to see me so happy. How different from his brother, who had done everything he could to stand in the way of my happiness!

I chose the Countess of Surrey to act as my proxy for the christening, and Gardiner and Arundel were godfathers. My Council was amazed that I could give so much time to this man's affairs when he had proved himself to be no friend to me.

But I was so happy to be involved with a christening, praying all the time that I should soon be more deeply concerned with one nearer to me.

Meanwhile there were more misgivings. I had heard nothing from Philip himself. I had thought that he would write to me, send some token. The uneasy thought came to me that he was having to be persuaded, and I began to fear he might refuse me.

I knew the Emperor wanted the marriage, and that should be good enough. Philip could not disobey him. I did hope that my fears were groundless. I was now deeply in love, although I had never seen Philip. I assured myself that he was all that my romantic heart could desire.

There was whispering among the Council. Where is he? Why does he delay? What does it mean? Is this going to be another of those abortive betrothals? Will the Prince of Spain ever come to England and marry the Queen?

I would not listen to them. There must be some urgent matter which was delaying him. I knew the Emperor was always heavily committed, and naturally he would need the help of his son.

'All will be well,' I said to Susan.

But I could see that she was beginning to look a little worried.

Then, one June day, the Marquis de las Nevas arrived, bringing letters and gifts.

My happiness was complete. He was coming. He would soon be on his way. The weary waiting was over. Soon he would be with me. We should be married, and our happy life together would begin.

There were presents not only for me but for my ladies. There was a necklace of diamonds for me, and with it an enormous diamond with a pearl hanging on a long chain. It was the most exquisite piece of jewellery I had ever seen. I kissed it and told Susan I should love it always because it was a symbol of our love for each other. He also sent me a diamond mounted in gold which had been his mother's, given to her by the Emperor.

'Is it not beautiful?' I cried to Susan. 'And doubly dear to me because it belonged to his mother.'

I had his picture. I thought he was wondrously handsome. They told me he was of short stature. Well, so was I, so we should match well together. I had not wanted a giant such as my father had been. Philip had a broad forehead, yellowish hair and beard, and blue eyes which might have been inherited from his Flemish grandfather; that he had the Hapsburg chin was evident.

How happy I was that night as I lay in my bed and thought of the future! There would be no delay now, and soon I should know that happiness for which I had so long yearned.

News followed. He would soon be on his way. Before he left, he spent a little time in Santiago with his son, Don Carlos. How I should have loved to be with them, to meet the boy. Philip would be a good father, I was sure.

It was touching that he had spent those days with his son, for when he was in England he would be separated from him. Perhaps some arrangement could be made. I could not leave the country. That was one of the penalties of queenship. Don Carlos might visit us. I would be a mother to him.

I could scarcely wait. Soon, I kept telling myself. And this time nothing will go wrong. I shall be a happy wife and mother.

At length Philip left his son and set out for Corunna, from whence he would sail for England.

There was trouble. It seemed there must always be. The English thought the Prince should sail in an English ship. This he refused to do and travelled in his own flagship, the *Espiritu Santo*. It must have looked splendid, upholstered in cloth of gold, displaying his banner. I was apprehensive and prayed that the weather might be calm. My prayers were unanswered, and for a day and night the ship battled against the elements, which must have been a sore trial to Philip, who was wont to be sick at sea. Fortunately in due course the gale abated, and by the time they came into sight of Southampton, the sea was as calm as anyone could wish it to be.

How glad he must have been to be on firm land — and, I hoped, to be brought nearer to me. It was a pity that our Admiral Lord William Howard should have offended him almost immediately. Howard, who prided himself on his bluff frankness, had made some jocular but slighting reference to the Spanish ships. I knew him well. He would have felt impelled to pierce Philip's dignity with what he would call good English humour. Philip would never understand that and would regard Howard's remarks as insulting. Then Sir Anthony Browne presented him with a white horse which I had sent as a gift. It was caparisoned in crimson velvet ornamented with gold. Philip said he would walk, at which Sir Anthony, who was a big man, lifted Philip, who was a small one, onto his horse; and although Sir Anthony kissed the stirrups as a gesture of deference, I cannot think Philip was pleased by the action.

While we were all in a fever of impatience, Philip stayed at Southampton, for the rain fell heavily and incessantly, which made travelling difficult; while there he met members of the Council and the nobility who had been waiting for him.

I feared he was not getting a very good impression of my

country; and people were already beginning to say that the rain was sent by God as an omen.

Philip behaved with wonderful charm and astuteness. He must have been aware of the suspicions which were directed against him. I was delighted to hear that he told the Councillors that he had come to England not to enrich himself but because he had been called by divine goodness to be my husband. He wanted to live with me as a right, good and loving prince. He hoped they would accept this; and they had promised to be faithful and loyal to him.

The more I heard of him, the more I loved him, and I rejoiced because soon we should meet.

What was so delightful was that, after his first encounter with Lord William Howard, he made great efforts to establish a good relationship between them. They chatted together, and Philip did all he could to show an appreciation of Howard's jokes – which was noble of him, because they were not noted for their wit. He ordered that beer should be brought because he said that he wished, while he was in England, to adopt our customs.

This greatly pleased everyone, and I was so happy that my bridegroom was making such efforts to be accepted by my people. I knew how stubborn they could be, but I did believe he was beginning to win them to his side.

We were to meet at Winchester. The weather continued to be appalling. The rain was torrential. When Philip left Southampton, he had to borrow a hat and cloak to cover his magnificent apparel, but even this was not adequate to protect him, and he was obliged to stop on the way to change his garments. What he must have thought of our weather, I could not imagine. I hoped he did not notice the murmuring that it meant God disapproved.

Poor Philip, how uncomfortable he must have felt to arrive in Winchester, his beautiful velvet garments splashed with mud and his bedraggled entourage soaked to the skin.

Fortunately it was dusk when he arrived and, because of

the weather, there were few to see him. He went to the church, and there it was a different story. People had crowded into the building more to get a glimpse of him than to thank God for his safe, if damp, arrival.

After the service of thanksgiving, he went to the Dean's house close to the church. He was to stay there. I was in the Bishop's palace. I was waiting with great impatience. This was to be the most wonderful moment of my life so far. I was wildly excited, and I could not hide my state. Susan was beside me with some of my other favoured ladies. I was aware of their anxious eyes on me.

And then he came . . . escorted by a few of the Spanish nobles who had accompanied him.

My heart leaped with joy at the sight of him. Small he undoubtedly was, and slight, but I had been warned of this, and it mattered not at all. He was wearing a doublet and trunks of spotless white kid. His surcoat was white and silver decorated with gold and silver thread-work. His cap matched it, and in this was a long white feather.

As he came towards me, I was conscious of his handsome looks, his youth, and I was filled with apprehension because I was eleven years older than he and doubtless looked it, particularly after all the trials of the last year. How did I look in my black velvet gown, my petticoat of frosted silver, my headdress of black velvet lined with gold? Was I too sombre? Was he going to be disappointed in me? Never had I prayed so fervently that this might not be so.

Now we stood face to face, smiling at each other. I kissed my own hand and took his. He was determined to follow our customs and kissed me on the mouth. I was so happy. I refused to think of my age and that I was not beautiful. I was the Queen, and this man was to be my husband.

I led him to a canopy of state and sat down with him.

He could not speak English, so I spoke in French, which he understood, and he replied in Spanish, of which I had learned a little from my mother.

I told him how glad I was that he had arrived safely, and he said that he was happy to be here.

I asked him to tell me about the crossing and his journey to Southampton.

It was all trivial conversation for two people who were shortly to embark on what is surely the greatest adventure in life. All the time we talked we were studying each other. I was enchanted. I should have been in a state of ecstasy if I could have stopped myself wondering what effect I was having on him.

He was so dignified. If he were disappointed, he would never betray the fact. He said that he must learn some English, for he felt greatly at a disadvantage.

I understood how he felt, I said, and he would be surprised how quickly he would become familiar with our tongue.

'I hope it will be so,' he said. 'The people will expect that.'

'I will teach you,' I told him.

'Teach me what I shall say to the lords of the Council when I take my leave.'

'That is simple. You could say, "Good night, my lords all."'

It was amusing to hear him struggling with the words. We smiled together, and I was happy.

Then he said he would introduce me to his gentlemen, and I should do the same for him and my ladies.

He called his party to come to us, and they were presented to me. I was immediately struck by Ruy Gomez da Silva, a most distinguished man who, I discovered later, was a very close friend of Philip.

Then we turned to my ladies. Philip kissed them all. I was rather surprised but he said: 'It is an English custom is it not? I am determined to follow the English customs.'

The ladies were flushed and smiling, liking the attention

472

And I smiled with them. I was so happy that everything seemed wonderful.

We parted and I returned to my apartments in the palace. Susan was with me.

'What thought you of him?' I asked.

She hesitated and I looked at her sharply. 'He is handsome – as they said he was,' she replied.

'You sound reluctant to admit it,' I said.

'N . . . no. He is like his portrait.'

'But what, Susan?'

'He is a little solemn.'

'It is a solemn occasion.'

'But perhaps not so when he kissed the ladies.'

I laughed. 'Oh, he is trying to please us all by following what he thinks are our customs.'

'The custom to kiss the ladies . . .'

'He has an idea that we kiss, and he has to do it on every occasion.'

'That is a custom of which you will have to cure him,' she said.

'Susan, you are like the rest. You are critical of all those who are not English.'

'Is that so, Your Majesty? Then if you say so . . .'

I was a little put out because I had the feeling that she did not admire him as I thought she should.

Later that day he called on me. It was dark; the candles has been lighted; he asked to be admitted to my presence, and I was delighted. How romantic, that he should come to me thus, unceremoniously.

'I must speak with you,' he said. 'It is why I have come.'

'I am so happy that you did,' I told him.

'I have just heard from my father. He is giving up the kingship of Naples, and it is to be mine. He does this because he thinks you should marry a king and not a mere prince.'

'How delightful! How wonderful!' I took his hand and kissed it. 'Your Majesty, I am happy for you.'

Philip did not smile easily, I noticed, but he looked gratified.

So I was betrothed not merely to the Prince of Spain but to the King of Naples as well.

By this time a delegation had arrived at the palace; the Council assembled, and with them all the ladies and gentlemen of our households, while a declaration of the Emperor's donation to his son was read out.

The Council was pleased and agreed that it should be proclaimed in the cathedral next day when the marriage took place.

It was a day to which I greatly looked forward but not without a certain trepidation.

The rain had ceased. I looked out of the window. How fresh the earth smelt – how green were the grass and trees. I could catch the sweet scent of flowers below me.

I was in love. Tomorrow would be my wedding day.

I said to myself: This night there is none happier in this land than its Queen.

* * *

It was the feast of St James, which was appropriate, for St James is the patron saint of Philip's country.

The church in which the ceremony was to take place was magnificently decorated with scarlet and cloth of gold.

I was at the church before Philip, having walked from the episcopal palace. I was wearing a gold-coloured robe richly brocaded, trimmed with pearls and diamonds; my coif was decorated with two rows of diamonds; and the kirtle beneath my robe was of white satin with silver tracing. I wore the diamond on the chain which Philip had sent me, and my train was carried by Lady Margaret Douglas.

When Philip arrived, I felt gloriously happy. He looked

magnificent in garments which I myself had presented to him. They were quite magnificent, and I congratulated myself that I had chosen just what suited him; and he had the grace to wear them, which was a compliment to me. But how they became him! The trunk-hose were of white satin worked with silver; he wore a collar of gold, diamond studded, and at his knee was the Garter which had been bestowed on him as soon as he arrived in England.

We took our seats in the two chairs which had been placed at the altar. Gardiner was waiting – with Bonner, the Bishop of London, and the Bishops of Durham, Lincoln, Ely and Chichester.

Before the ceremony began, the Regent of Naples declared to the assembly that his Imperial Master, Charles V, had resigned from his kingdom of Naples that his beloved cousin Queen Mary might marry a king.

Then we were married and when the ceremony was over seated ourselves in the chairs of state while the Mass was celebrated.

* * *

Every detail of that wonderful day stays with me. My memories comfort me when I am most melancholy. I want to keep that day fresh in my mind, for I was never so happy as I was then.

We went back to the Bishop's palace for a banquet. I do not remember what we ate. Philip and I sat side by side. I took covert glances at him, which was foolish of me because I should have known I would be closely watched and everything I did would be reported later. I did wish that my subjects would not be quite so zealous in stressing the point that I was the Queen of this realm and, important as Philip might be in his own country, here he was merely the Queen's consort. Why did they have to make his chair less fine than mine? Why should he be served from silver plate and I from gold? I was fully aware of the cold looks of the Spaniards as they noticed these details.

But I would not let that spoil my pleasure.

When the toasts and expressions of good will towards us were over, Philip and I drank one to the guests; and after that we went to our presence chamber so that the English and Spanish might mingle. Language presented a problem. There was dancing but the Spanish ways were different from ours. I remembered how my father had distinguished himself as the finest of dancers because he could leap higher than anyone else. The Spaniards walked in stately fashion rather than danced, and we English did not call that dancing. I think they were a little taken aback by our cavorting and pirouetting. I had always been fond of dancing and was able somehow to match my steps to Philip's. I have to admit that, stately though he was, he was no great dancer. But I loved him the more for this failing.

The festivities ended earlier than we had expected because of these differences in our speech and customs, and Philip and I were escorted to our separate apartments, where we dined. Afterwards we met at the lodging where we were to spend our wedding night. We were taken there by members of the Council, and when they had conducted us to our bedchamber, they left us.

So we were alone together. I was apprehensive, lest I should not please my husband; if I did not, he did not betray it. Never had I imagined such kindness and courtesy. I was ignorant of the ways of married people and had only shadowy notions of what was expected of me. Philip, I knew, was greatly experienced in these matters. He had been married before, and was already a father. But I was as romantic as a young girl. I had lived with dreams.

I thought a great deal about our first encounter later, when he had gone. I wondered what was in his mind. One would never know with Philip. But I shall always remember his kindness to me, his patience with my ignorance.

And I was able to say to myself on that night: This is love.

Waiting for the Child

When I awoke next morning, it was to find that he was no longer beside me. There was a great commotion outside the door. My women were talking loudly, protesting.

I rose and went out to them.

Several Spanish gentlemen of Philip's entourage were standing there, being held at bay by my valiant ladies. They were trying to explain that it was a breach of etiquette to call on a lady the morning after her wedding.

I said: 'I daresay it is a Spanish custom.' I would ask Philip when I saw him.

I could not imagine where he could be. I wondered if I might ask him what induced him to rise so early. I had hoped to wake and find him beside me. But I did not ask him. One did not ask Philip such things. For all my love for him, I felt there was a barrier between us. But I did discover later that it *was* a Spanish custom for certain gentlemen to come into the bridal chamber after the wedding night in order to congratulate the married pair.

I was learning that the customs of my husband's Court were very different from ours, but at that time I was amused by the differences and told myself how interesting it would be to learn each other's ways.

I was surprised when I did not see Philip all that day. I was told that he was busy attending to despatches he had received from his father.

It was my duty to meet the wives of the gentlemen who had accompanied him, and I began with the Duchess of Alva. She was very elegant and rather alarmed me by her stately demeanour. But I was in love with all things Spanish. It was natural that I should be. I had Spanish blood in my veins. I remembered snatches of conversation I had shared with my mother years ago. She had been brought up in a Court which must have been very like that in which Philip had lived. I thought of how happy she would be if she could see me now.

The Duchess and I got on very well after a while. I suppose she was as nervous of me as I was of her. I had gone to meet her, which surprised her because she had expected to find me seated, and she did not know how to greet me. She sank to her knees and tried to kiss my hand, but I put my arms round her and kissed her cheek.

I meant to be warm and friendly but my manner seemed to disconcert her; however, after a while we were able to speak in a friendly fashion together.

It was very difficult to break through the solemnity of the Spanish, and I could see that this was going to be a problem with Philip. I could never be sure what he was thinking. He behaved with courtesy and gentleness towards me, yet he was never abandoned, never passionate. If I had not deluded myself, I could have feared that our marriage, our love-making, was to him a task, a duty which must be performed.

Later I believed this was so, for when he had gone, people talked more freely of him, and I have to admit that whenever possible I urged them to do so. There came a time when I felt a certain masochistic pleasure in torturing myself, when I wanted to learn the truth about my marriage.

Then I reminded myself that I was old and he was comparatively young . . . that I was to him a kind of maiden aunt.

But for the time being I was blissfully happy.

We left Winchester for London and crossed London Bridge at noon, surrounded by the nobility of Spain and England. We were greeted by the pageantry one grows accustomed to on such occasions; but what pleased the people most, I am sure, were the ninety-seven chests – each over a yard long – which contained the bullion Philip had brought with him.

We came to Whitehall, where celebrations continued. These were, however, cut short by the death of the old Duke of Norfolk. I insisted that the Court go into mourning. Poor Norfolk! The last years of his life had been very melancholy. After narrowly escaping being beheaded by my father, he had been a prisoner all through the last reign; and when I had come to the throne, he had been released but his luck had not changed. He had led an inferior force against Wyatt and had suffered the humiliation of being defeated, which would be heartbreaking for a man of his calibre. So it seemed right to put on mourning for an old friend.

At Windsor the ceremony of the Garter was officially performed, and I was happy to see Philip honoured. I wanted to give him so much, which could seem only very little after all the happiness he had brought me.

Susan used to watch my exuberance with a certain fearfulness. I know I behaved like a young girl in love; but, if I was not a young girl, I was certainly in love, and older people's feelings can be so much stronger than those of the young, particularly when happiness comes to them late in life after much tribulation.

I wanted Philip to have a coronation. So did Renard, who came to see me about the matter and to stress what a good thing it would be.

'He would take so much of the burden from your shoulders. You have too much to contend with. You must see that he is given the status here that he so richly deserves.'

'I would willingly give it,' I said. 'There is nothing I want more. I will speak to the Council.'

I did.

Gardiner said: 'The people would never accept it.'

'I am the Queen,' I reminded him. 'I intend to rule as my father did.'

'It was different in your father's day. It is not long since people flocked to Wyatt's banner. There is your sister . . .'

'I know you want to have her . . . removed . . . but I will not allow that. She is not concerned with this. I am sure the country would welcome a king to help in governing them.'

'The time has not come . . . yet,' insisted Gardiner.

It was a sort of compromise. Not yet, he said. He must mean that we should wait awhile.

I had to admit that he was right, for after that first enthusiasm when we had our ceremonies and pageants, which people always enjoy, they began to display their dislike of foreigners in general and Spaniards in particular. It was said that there were more Spaniards than English in the streets of London. 'England is for the English,' was their cry. 'We want no aliens here.' Those who had come in Philip's train were rich, and that aroused the people's envy. Children called after them in the streets and threw stones at them. Quarrels were picked and there was frequent fighting. The Spaniards began to fear that it was unsafe to go out alone, for they were constantly being robbed.

I was ashamed of my countrymen, but Philip remained calm and as courteous as ever; he would not give up his Spanish household and, as I had provided him with English servants, he kept the two, which must have been a great expense; but as he could not easily dismiss those I had found and would not give up those he had brought, he accepted the cost.

I wished that we could have talked more openly together. I wished I had known what was in his mind. There were constant despatches arriving from the Emperor. Philip would spend most of the day dealing with them. I saw very little of him except in company, and when we were alone in our bedchamber, very few words were spoken.

It was in September when I believed I might be pregnant. I had suffered through my life from internal irregularities, so I could not be sure, but I had a certain exultant feeling within me. I felt blessed, and I said to myself: This is what the Virgin experienced when she was visited by the angel.

This was what I had longed for. A child of my own! Everything I had endured . . . all my troubles . . . they were all worthwhile, if I could hold my own child in my arms.

I was afraid to say anything. I was fearful that it might not be so.

But it must be. Why else should I have this feeling of exultation?

* * *

September passed. Each day I became more sure. I wanted to sing out to the housetops: 'My soul doth magnify the Lord . . . I am to have a child . . . a child of my own. It will be a son. It must be a son.' Oh, what rejoicing there would be! If only the time would pass more quickly. When could I expect the birth? Next May perhaps? The child would be my firstborn. Who knew? There might be others . . .

I could think of nothing but my child.

Susan knew that something had happened. She waited for me to tell her. But I did not just yet, hard as it was to keep a secret. I was afraid that she would remind me of my weakness which had been with me all my life.

'Are you sure?' she would say. 'Can Your Majesty be sure?'

I could not bear that there should be a doubt; and she would doubt, I knew. She would say, like the rest: She is nearly forty years old. She is too old for childbearing. She

481

has her weakness. It is a recurrence of that which we have known before.

No! No! I argued with myself. This is different. I am no longer a virgin. I am a wife . . . a passionately loved wife.

Passionately? Was Philip passionate? How could I know? What experience had I of passion? He seemed eager and loving. He did care for me. He did, I vehemently assured myself.

At last I could not resist telling Philip. We had retired for the night and were alone together.

I said to him: 'Philip, I think it may be so . . . I believe it to be so . . .'

He looked at me eagerly.

'I believe I am with child,' I concluded.

I saw the joy in his face, and my heart swelled with happiness.

'You are sure . . .?'

'Yes, yes . . . I think it may be so.'

'When . . . when?'

'I cannot be quite certain of that. Perhaps next May we may have our child.'

I saw his lips moving, as though in prayer.

* * *

A few weeks passed. I was terrified that I should be proved wrong; but so far I was not.

I had told Susan now. She looked alarmed.

'Why, Susan,' I said, 'you should rejoice.'

She replied, as I knew she would: 'You are sure, Your Majesty?'

'I am absolutely sure.'

'May God guard Your Majesty,' she said fervently.

I knew what she was thinking. I was old . . . too old . . . for childbearing. I was going to prove them wrong. I was not yet forty. Women had children at that age. I was small and slight – not built for the task of bringing children into the world. They would all have to change their minds. I would make them.

I was faintly irritated with Susan. She did not share my pleasure. I would have reprimanded her but I knew it was out of her love for me that she was apprehensive.

Philip said to me: 'The French are plaguing my father. I should be there to help him.'

A cold fear ran through me. 'He will understand that you must be here,' I said.

'Oh yes . . . for a time.'

'It is your home now, Philip.'

He said a little coldly: 'My home is in Spain. One day I shall be the King.'

'That is far ahead, and now that we are married we must be together. The people would never allow me to leave this country.'

He said nothing, but his lips were tight.

I thought: Poor Philip. He is a little homesick. It is natural. Perhaps the Emperor would come and visit us or, mayhap, when the child was born, I could go with him . . . just for a brief visit.

I knew that could never be. But I was in love and about to be a mother, so I allowed myself wild dreams.

* * *

Happy as I was, I thought often of my sister Elizabeth. She was a prisoner at Woodstock under the good, though stern, Sir Henry Bedingfield and I knew how that must have irked her.

From Sir Henry I had learned of a plot to assassinate her. The suspicion came to me that it might have been hatched by Gardiner, who was always an enemy of hers, and I expect he feared what might happen to him if she came to the throne. According to Sir Henry, he had been called away and had left his brother in charge, giving him strict injunctions that Elizabeth must be watched day and night, not only because of what she herself might become involved in but because there might be those who wished to harm her.

A man named Basset, with twenty men, had been found loitering in the gardens, with the obvious intent of doing some harm to my sister. Because of the strict vigilance, the conspiracy had been discovered and the plot failed.

Although she caused me continual anxiety, I should hate any harm to come to her; so she continued to be in my thoughts.

I had never understood her and was always uncertain as to whether or not she would plot against me. Whenever we were together, I felt nothing but affection for her. Perhaps I was guileless, but I believed she cherished sisterly feelings towards me.

And these accusations which were brought against her? Were they true? I wished I knew. I wished I could trust her completely and that she could come to Court so that we might be as sisters should.

I spoke to Philip about her.

I said: 'My sister is much on my mind. It is hurtful that she should be kept under restraint. After all, she is my sister. I want to see her. I want to ask her, face to face, how much truth there is in these rumours that she has supporters who would set her up in my place. If she has hopes . . .' My voice softened and I looked at him appealingly, '. . . they cannot remain . . . now.'

I believe the Spaniards are brought up to hide their emotions. My mother had not been like that. Formal as she could be at times, she had always been warm and loving with me. Perhaps it was not in Philip's nature to show emotion.

He was preoccupied with the subject of Elizabeth. I had noticed that, whenever her name was mentioned, he became alert and gave his full attention to what was being said.

'Bring her to Court,' he now advised.

484

I smiled happily. 'You think that would be a good idea? Gardiner is against it.'

He lowered his eyes. 'Bring her to Court,' he repeated. 'Speak with her alone. Ask her . . . then judge.'

I nodded. 'I should like to see her married.' I smiled at him fondly. 'Everyone should marry. It is the greatest happiness on Earth . . . as I have found.'

A wry smile touched his lips. I told myself it meant that he agreed with me.

I went on: 'Emmanuel Philibert will be here for a few months. He would be a suitable match. It will be better when she is out of the country. While she is here, there will always be people to see her as a rallying-point. There are a great many heretics in the country, Philip, and they look to her.'

'That will be remedied,' he said. 'Send for her. It is the best.'

He asked questions about her, and I told him how, when she had been born, she had been treated with great respect and, when her mother fell out of favour, how her fortunes drastically changed. 'She has lived her life under the shadow of death,' I went on. 'Many times she has come face to face with it.'

I could not help thinking that at one time Philip and his father had been eager to see the end of her. Now he seemed to be more tolerant. I thought: Being in love makes one eager to see the whole world happy . . . even those who may be our enemies.

'It will be different now,' I said, 'because of the child. I believe that, before, she refused marriage because it would have meant her leaving the country.'

'I see her point.'

'But now everything has changed.' I smiled radiantly. I was so happy. Soon my child would be born; and if Elizabeth were married to Emmanuel, I could think of her

485

with pleasure. We could exchange personal, sisterly letters, and everything would be as it should be.

It was wonderful to be in agreement with Philip. How well he understood my feelings!

Sir Henry Bedingfield brought Elizabeth up from Woodstock, and in due course she arrived at Hampton Court.

Before I summoned her, I sent Gardiner to her. I told him that he must ask her to confess her fault and then I would consider her confession and perhaps forgive her.

He came back to me and told me that his interview with the Princess had been unproductive.

He said: 'I told her that she must confess her fault. She replied that, rather than confess to something she had not done, she was prepared to stay in prison for the rest of her life, for she had never committed any fault against Your Majesty in thought, word or deed, and that therefore she could crave no mercy at your hand, but rather desired herself to be judged by law. I told her that you marvelled at her boldness in refusing to confess – for in doing so she implied that Your Majesty had wrongfully imprisoned her.'

'And what did she reply to that?' I asked.

'She said: "She may, if it pleases Her Majesty, punish me as she thinketh good." "Her Majesty says you must tell another tale ere you are set at liberty," I told her, to which she replied she would as lief be in prison as abroad, suspected by the Queen. I said that she implied she had been wrongfully imprisoned, to which she answered that she spoke the truth, would cling to the truth and seek no advantage through lies.'

I listened attentively. Philip wanted to know what had passed between Elizabeth and Gardiner and listened with great interest when I told him.

I learned from one of the women who was in Elizabeth's household and who reported to me that which she thought would interest me that, after the interview with Gardiner, coupled with the fact that I had summoned her to Court,

Elizabeth believed it meant that another charge would be brought against her, and she was sure her enemies were determined to put an end to her. She kissed her ladies fondly, saying it might be that they would never meet her again on Earth.

I was very distressed that she should think this of me when what I wanted was to stop this suspicion between us, and for her to be at Court and that we should be as sisters.

'I must see her,' I said to Philip. 'I should be the one to question her . . . not Gardiner.'

I was delighted that he agreed with me.

'Summon her,' he said, 'and while she is with you I will watch. I will be hidden behind a screen. I would hear what passes between you.'

I thought it was wonderful for Philip to care so much for me and to understand my feelings for my sister far better than others did.

So when Elizabeth was brought to me, Philip hid himself behind a screen placed so that, when Elizabeth stood before me, she would have her back to it. It meant that he could take occasional glimpses at her as well as hear every word that was spoken.

It was ten o'clock at night when she came to me. I could see she was distraught and, having heard of her farewell to her women, I understood that she thought her end was in sight.

I was immediately overcome with pity, remembering the bright child who was the delight and terror of Lady Bryan's life, and I felt a certain nostalgia for earlier days and wished that life could have been different for us all.

She fell to her knees and, before I could speak, began professing her absolute loyalty; she swore by God and the Holy Virgin that she had never been engaged in any plots against me.

I tried to fight the sentiment in myself. She looked very attractive with her red hair falling about her shoulders. I

487

tried to speak sternly. I said: 'So, you will not confess your fault, but stand firmly on your truth. I pray that it may become manifest.'

'If it is not,' she replied proudly, 'I will look for neither favour nor pardon at Your Majesty's hands.'

'You are so firm . . . so fervent in your protestations of innocence that you have been wrongfully accused . . .'

She looked at me with a certain slyness. 'I must not say so to Your Majesty,' she said.

'But you will say so to others seemingly.'

'No, Your Majesty. I have borne and must bear the burden. What I humbly beseech is Your Majesty's good opinion of me, as I am, and ever have been, Your Majesty's true subject.'

'How can I be sure?' I murmured.

Then she seized my hands and burst into a passionate appeal. I must understand, she said, that I was to her firstly a dear sister. She remembered my kindness to her when she was an outcast. That she would never forget. She wanted a chance to prove to me that I had never had a more devoted servant. In the great happiness which had come to me, she thought I and my noble husband would be kind to a poor prisoner who was loyal towards her sovereign and tender towards her sister.

She was eloquent. She was, after all, fighting for her life. She believed at that time that I had brought her up from Woodstock with the purpose of sending her to her death.

I was touched, and hurt that she could think this of me. I told her to rise and I embraced her.

I said to her: 'No more. Whether you are guilty or not, I forgive you.' I took a ring from my finger. It was a beautiful diamond. I had given it to her on my coronation, telling her that, if ever she was in trouble, she was to send it to me and if possible I would help her. It had come back to me at the time she was taken to the Tower, and I had kept it ever since. Now I gave it back to her.

488

There was a radiance about her. She had come to me expecting to be sent to the Tower, and instead she had the pledge of my friendship. Her eyes were filled with tears. I was deeply touched, and suddenly she flung herself into my arms.

'You are once more my sister,' she cried. 'I have your love and I am happy again.'

When she left me, Philip emerged from behind the screen. There was no doubt that he was greatly interested in Elizabeth. His eyes shone and he almost smiled. But it was not easy to know what he really thought of her.

He said: 'You did well. You acted with dignity and tolerance.'

'And what did you think of my sister?'

'I think that much of what I have heard of her is true.'

It seemed an evasive answer, but I was delighted with his approval.

* * *

It was about this time that I noticed one of my ladies behaving in a strange and almost secretive manner. This was Magdalen Dacre. She was outstandingly beautiful – perhaps the most beautiful of all my ladies. She was very tall and made dwarves of some of us, and she would have been remarkable because of her statuesque figure if for nothing else. Magdalen had all the virtues. She was religious and efficient. Perhaps some would say she was a little prim, but I liked her for that. I would not have wished to be surrounded by frivolous women.

I noticed that she was absent on one or two occasions. I asked for her and was told she was resting. She seemed to need a good deal of rest. I wondered if she were unhappy about something.

She was hardly ever present when Philip was there, but I noticed that when he was he treated her with great courtesy. He was courteous to all my ladies, but he did seem especially so towards Magdalen.

I wondered mildly about her, and then I ceased to think of her for something very important was about to happen.

I had not yet achieved my mission, which was to return England to Rome. It was too dangerous to do so at the moment. I did not want to plunge the country into civil war. At the same time I did feel that there should not be too much delay.

The news from the Continent delighted me. Reginald Pole was coming home.

He had been out of favour with the Emperor, for at one time he had made it clear that he opposed my marriage to Philip. I believed that his opposition was due to the fact that he thought I was too old for childbearing and that to attempt it would be dangerous to me. None wanted the return to Rome more than he did, but he believed it could be done without the marriage.

I daresay the Emperor thought that, if he came to England, he would be my chief adviser, which was very likely, and I was not sure that the Emperor wanted that. Reginald would doubtless have returned to England earlier but for these considerations. After all, he was no longer an exile. He had left the country only because he upheld my right to the succession; now I was Queen the way was clear for his return.

And now he was coming.

It was November, and I was now certain of my pregnancy. I was wildly happy, and the thought of seeing Reginald after all these years added to my joy. He was not strong and had had to take the journey by easy stages. There should be a royal yacht at Calais to bring him to Dover.

I was delighted to hear that he had arrived safely in England, and as he made the journey to Gravesend he was in the midst of an impressive cavalcade. At Gravesend the barge I had sent for him was waiting and, with his silver cross fixed on the prow, he sailed to Whitehall.

Gardiner received him at the water's edge, and at the entrance of the palace Philip was waiting for him. I myself stood at the head of the stairs.

With what emotion we embraced! The years seemed to slip away, and I was young again, dreaming of him, telling myself that one day he would be my bridegroom.

That was in the past. How old Reginald looked – yet handsome in an aesthetic way. He was frail, thin and of medium height, but he looked tall beside Philip. His hair and beard, which I remembered as light brown, were now white; but he still had the same gentle expression which I had loved.

'Welcome home,' I said. 'It is wonderful to see you. I know that, now you are come, all will soon be . . . as it should be.'

He congratulated me on my marriage. I raised my eyebrows, reminding him that he had warned me against it.

'I was wrong,' he said charmingly, reading my thoughts. 'It has worked out in the best possible way. I am happy for you.'

He meant it. I wonder if he remembered the plans to get us married, how my mother and his had planned when we were both much younger. But nothing had come of it, and he had gone on his way – indeed he had had no choice, for if he had stayed he would have gone to the block with most of his family. And now I had Philip – whom I would not have exchanged for any man in the world.

It was wonderful to know that he was back, and perhaps even more so to realize what his coming meant, for he had come to help restore the Pope's supremacy in England which, I had convinced myself, was the reason why God had preserved my life and set me on the throne to work His will.

491

Gardiner came up the stairs.

He was to take Reginald to Lambeth Palace.

* * *

My pleasure in seeing Reginald was marred by the change in him. He was still handsome, still noble, but I sensed a deep sadness, and there was in him a bitterness against my father.

We met frequently and there were times when he and I were alone together. Then he talked of his family, all of whom – with the exception of Geoffry, who had tried and failed to take his own life and was now living abroad in exile – had been murdered. What affected him most was the death of his mother, who, he said, had been butchered on the scaffold.

'My mother,' he said, 'was a saint. She was the most pious of women who had never harmed a living soul . . . and to be murdered so.'

I wept with him, remembering so much of my life with her.

'But it is over, Reginald,' I said. 'Life dealt harshly with you and yours, and we do no good by remembering.'

He said: 'I see myself as the son of a martyr, for such was my mother and I shall never forget her.'

'The past is over,' I said. 'Many died and your family among them. We cannot bring them back. We have to think ahead. We have to continue with this great task which God has set us.'

He was certainly zealous in that cause. Three days after his arrival, the two Houses of Parliament were assembled to hear Reginald speak. He told them he had come to restore the lost glory of the kingdom.

A few days later Philip and I were presented with a petition from the two Houses to plead with the Legate to absolve the country from its schism and disobedience.

We were moving towards our goal. High Mass was

celebrated at St Paul's. The Act restoring supremacy to the Pope had not yet been passed but it was on the way.

There was a ceremony at St Paul's at the end of November to celebrate my condition. It was very moving. The Virgin Mary was referred to, and the similarity of our names seemed significant. 'Fear not, Mary,' the angel had said, 'for thou hast found favour with God.'

The fear meant that they were all remembering my age and the dangers of childbirth, even to the young and healthy. They would certainly be remembering the last prince to be born, my brother Edward, whose coming had meant the death of his mother.

I listened to the prayers with emotion.

'Give therefore unto Thy servants, Philip and Mary, a male issue.' I was always a little apprehensive about this manner of giving commands to God. Few would have dared treat me in the same manner! 'Make him comely and in wit notable and excellent.'

All I wanted was a healthy son; and I was the happiest woman in the world at the prospect of having one.

* * *

Christmas had come. I was delighted that my sister would be at Court to celebrate it with me. She did not appear often in public – only when her presence was commanded. Then she was subdued, and there was a secretive air about her. Philip was immensely interested in her. I often noticed his eyes following her.

I told myself: He is a little suspicious of her; he fears she may be plotting against me.

Dear Philip, he was so careful of me, and I was very happy that I had conceived so soon. It was a sign of fertility.

I was feeling quite ill at times but I rejoiced in my suffering. It was all part of pregnancy, which could be very trying to some women. I expected it would be particularly so for me, in view of my previous weakness.

I said to Philip: 'Until this child is born, Elizabeth is the heir presumptive, and I believe she should be treated as such.'

He said he had no objection and was very affable to her, often seating himself beside her and engaging in conversation.

It was a great pleasure to me that they seemed so friendly towards each other but I did feel a little dismayed when Elizabeth was inclined to be coquettish. I thought Philip might have been a little disgusted. He was no Thomas Seymour to smile on or encourage such conduct. But so determined was he to be amiable that he made no objection.

I mentioned to him that he seemed very interested in her, and he replied that she was too near the throne for him to ignore her.

'She seems to be happy about the child,' I said, 'but it has blighted her hopes.'

'She will understand that it is God who decides what is to be.'

'As we all must,' I said.

I put my hand over his, but his lay cold beneath mine. It was his Spanish nature. He did not seem to know how to respond to those little endearments, and therefore pretended he was unaware of them.

I said: 'Philip, you do think it is right to treat my sister as heir presumptive, do you not?'

'We must until the child is born.'

'So thought I. Then she must be seated at my table. And she must receive honours. That is right, Philip?'

'I believe that to be right,' he said.

'I am glad that she will have an opportunity to become acquainted with Emmanuel Philibert.'

Philip nodded gravely.

When it was seen that I was treating Elizabeth with the

respect due to the heir presumptive, there were many to flock around her. Philip's eyes were speculative as he watched her success. If I had not known him well, I should have thought he was interested in her as a woman.

As for Elizabeth, she was in her element. I had never seen anyone recover so quickly, whether it was from sickness or fear of death; as soon as it was over, she seemed able to dismiss it from her mind.

Emmanuel Philibert was paying court to her. She accepted his attentions and then wide-eyed declared that she could never marry. I was irritated with her. She must have known what was expected of her, yet she put on that pretence of innocence which I knew was entirely false.

I sent for her and told her she was foolish. The prince was a good man; she was fortunate that he should agree to marry her.

'My dear sister,' she said, 'I have a repugnance for the state of marriage. I wish to remain a virgin.'

'What! All your life?'

'It would seem so . . . at this time.'

'You are a fool, sister.'

She piously raised her eyes to the ceiling, accepting my judgement. But I could see the stubborn look about her mouth.

Later I consulted Philip.

I was feeling very ill now, and I know I looked wan. Philip was most anxious about me, and I was gratified that he showed such care for me.

He said: 'She should not be forced to marry.'

'It would be difficult to force her.'

He nodded. 'Let her stay. She is watched. No harm can come that way.'

I thought how kind he was, how considerate of others.

I told Elizabeth that the King thought she should make her own decision about marriage.

495

Her eyes lighted with pleasure, and she smiled secretively.

* * *

The Acts setting out the return to Rome were now confirmed, and those nineteen statutes against the See of Rome brought in during my father's reign were repealed.

It was not to be expected that the country would easily change, and there must certainly be dissenters. When Gardiner came to me and told me that the Council were going to enforce the old laws against heresy, I was disturbed.

I questioned this. In my imagination I saw the pale, martyred face of Anne Askew, and I remembered those days when my stepmother Katharine Parr went in fear of her life. Anne Askew and Katharine Parr had been good women, though misguided. I could not bear to think of people being tortured and burned at the stake.

'I think persuasion would be the best way to proceed,' I said.

'Your Majesty, with all respect, when has persuasion ever persuaded? These people are as firm in their beliefs as . . .'

'As you or I?'

'They need guidance.'

'Then let us give them guidance.'

'The Council are of the opinion that the old laws should be enforced. Moreover, it is the Pope's wish.'

'All I wanted was to bring the country back to Rome, for the Mass to be celebrated openly and with due reverence. I must think of this.'

Gardiner looked at me with something like exasperation. Often he had deplored what he thought of as my woman's sentimentality. One did not govern a country on sentiment. If the law of the country was that people should worship in the way it was before my father broke with Rome, then that was how it should be.

I wanted to explain to him that it was different now. Since Martin Luther nailed his ninety-five theses on the church door at Wittenberg, Protestantism had grown apace, and there were many Protestants in England who had flourished under my brother. Would they lightly discard those new beliefs and cheerfully return to the old? They certainly would not, and then . . .

'Let it be gradual,' I said.

'Perhaps you will talk to the King,' replied Gardiner.

He knew that I would. He knew that I sought every opportunity of talking to Philip, and he knew that Philip would doubtless agree with the Council.

I told Philip how gratified I was that we were restoring the true religion. We had come out of the sleep, as someone said, and we were now getting back onto the right course. It was what God had ordained for me, and I was achieving it.

'It is a matter for rejoicing,' said Philip.

'Philip,' I said earnestly. 'I do not wish the law to be harsh.'

He never betrayed his feelings, but I could see his thoughts were much the same as Gardiner's had been and that he believed my misguided sentiments stood in the way of good government.

He said: 'If the people will not come to the truth voluntarily, they must be led to it.'

'How can they be led if they will not listen?'

'When they see what happens to heretics, they will be led.'

'There will always be martyrs.'

'There will always be heretics and they must be removed.'

'I remember Anne Askew. She was a good woman, but

497

misguided in her views. They racked her. They burned her at the stake.'

'You must understand. A heretic denies God's truth. What is there for him . . . or her . . . when they are brought before their Maker? It will be hell fire for them . . . eternal fire. That which is felt at the stake will be nothing compared with what is to come.'

I covered my face with my hands. 'I wish it need not be,' I said.

'There must be examples.'

'Each person must be given a chance to recant.'

Philip nodded. 'That should be. And for the death of one, think of the thousands who will be saved by his example. It is easy to talk of martyrdom, but when the flames are actually seen to consume the bodies of those who sin against God, men and women will question their beliefs. It is the way to turn people to the truth.'

He persuaded me, and in January, when Parliament was dissolved, the way ahead was clear.

I wanted every person to have a chance to save him- or herself. All they had to do was turn from the new learning to the old, true religion. I wanted all to know that I would be a loving monarch if my people would obey the laws of the land. I wanted no trouble. I wanted them to regard me as their mother. I wanted them to know I loved them and that, if I agreed to punishment – and this applied particularly to heretics – it was for their own good.

I said that all those who had been imprisoned at the time of the Wyatt rebellion should be released. I thought often of Edward Courtenay, with whom I had at one time considered a marriage. How fortunate I had been to escape that! In spite of his Plantagenet blood, he would have been a most unsuitable husband. How different Philip was!

I said he should be released from Fotheringay, where he had lived virtually as a prisoner since his release from the Tower. But he must not stay in England, of course. That could be unsafe. He and Elizabeth might plot together. She had sworn she was loyal to me, and I tried to believe her, but I would never really know Elizabeth. She was shrewd. The perils through which she had passed would have made her so. I must remember her dangerous flirtation with Seymour, which might have had dire results.

So Courtenay could go free only if he left the country. He went, with the injunction that he must not return to England without permission.

It was in February of that second year of my reign that the first heretic was burned at the stake for his religious opinions. His name was Rogers, and people gathered at Smithfield to watch him burn. In Coventry the rector of All Hallows Church was burned and at Hadleigh Rowland Taylor, a well-known adherent to the Protestant cause, met the same fate. He was the parish priest and much loved, a man of great virtue, apart from his stubbornness in religious matters. He had protested violently when a priest had been sent to perform Mass in his church. His arrest and sentence to the stake had followed. But the most prominent victim was John Hooper, the Bishop of Gloucester and Worcester.

I was very distressed. Why could they not accept the truth? All were given the chance to. All they had to do was deny their faith and accept the true one, and they would be saved.

I did remember how I had clung to my faith and how I had put myself in danger by my firm adherence to it. But that was the true faith. I laughed at myself. These poor people deluded themselves that theirs was the true one.

Because Hooper was so well known, there was more talk about him than the others. He had been such a good man, people were saying: he had a wife who had borne nine children. I knew this. But he had been remonstrated with and given every chance. He had been arrested some time before on some petty charge, because Gardiner had intimated to me that he was a dangerous man. He believed so fervently in his style of religion, and people were moved by his eloquence and inclined to follow him.

Hooper had been in the Fleet Prison for some time, and he had made it known that there he had been treated worse than if he had been a slave.

Gardiner saw how distressed I was that this man had suffered death by burning, and he insisted that he had done much harm with his preaching and writing, and would have done more if he had been allowed to live. He had been offered every chance.

The day before his death, Sir Anthony Kingston had gone to him and begged him to recant, for to do so would save his life. But he would not. He said he would rather face the flames.

'He was a foolish man,' said Gardiner.

'Aye,' I replied, 'but a brave one.'

I was deeply disturbed that there should be this religious persecution in my reign. I had wanted to be good to all my people. I almost wished that I was back in the past, when I was without responsibilities, even wondering who was seeking to destroy me.

Now the power was mine to destroy others, I could not rest. My nights were haunted by memories of my step-mother Katharine Parr. She came to me in dreams, side by side with Anne Askew.

'All these heretics have to do is recant,' I continually reminded myself. If they did, they would be received with joy. Is there not greater joy in the sinner who repents? They should have instruction. They should have time to learn. I would insist on that.

I was pleased when one of the Franciscans preached at Court, pointing out that burning at the stake was not the way.

I said to Philip: 'He is right.'

500

But Philip did not think so. In his native country the Inquisition flourished. It had a beneficial effect, he insisted. People lived in fear of it. Only the reckless and foolhardy wanted to pit themselves against it.

After that sermon, there was a lull for a while, and then the arrests began again and the burning continued.

What was happening threw a cloud over my happiness.

It was April, and I believed that the birth of my child was imminent. I was to go to Hampton Court, where arrangements were being made for my confinement. Soon, I told myself, I should forget my troubles. In a few weeks from now I should have my child.

I then embarked on the most extraordinary and heart-breaking time of my whole life.

The first weeks at Hampton were peaceful. I was glad of the custom which decreed that a queen should retire and live quietly with her women, awaiting the great event.

Here Jane Seymour had come before me. She had given birth to a boy, and that had killed her – yet she had been young and healthy and ripe for childbearing, it had seemed.

Susan said I must not think of Jane. She had not been taken care of after the birth. *She* would see that I had every care.

And so we waited. I had the cradle placed in my room so that I could see it all the time. It was very elaborate and splendidly decorated – worthy of the child born to be King.

My dearest hope was about to be realized, and it seemed as though the days would never pass. I said to Susan that time seemed to have slowed down.

'It is ever so, when one is waiting,' she replied. 'Very soon your time will come.'

I talked all the time of the child. 'He will be a boy, I know it . . . a perfect boy. I can see him, Susan. He will be like Philip. That is how I would have him. But perhaps he will be tall . . . as my father was . . . although I am small and so is Philip . . . but sometimes children take after

501

their grandparents. The child's grandfather was a big, fine man. I should like my son to be like him . . . as he was in his youth before . . . before . . . And my father's grandfather, Edward IV, was a big and handsome man.'

'Be the child large or small, you will love it just the same,' said Susan wisely.

'How dare you call my child "it", Susan?'

'We do not know that it will be a boy. It is wise at such a time to see what God will send.'

'I should love a girl, of course. But it is a boy that everyone wants. A King . . . not a Queen . . . but if the child is a girl, we might get boys after.'

Susan raised her eyes to the ceiling. She did not approve of my having a child at all. She thought I was too old and not strong enough. I could have been angry with her, but I knew all she thought and all she did was out of love for me.

The waiting went on. The weeks were passing. What was wrong? Sometimes I would look out of my windows and see people gathered some little way from the palace. They were waiting for the announcement.

'Let it be soon, O Lord,' I prayed. 'And give me a son. That is all I need for my happiness. Is it asking too much? The lowest serving woman can have sons . . . many of them. Please God, give me a son.'

But the time was passing, and my prayers were unanswered.

At the end of the month a rumour circulated that I had given birth to a beautiful baby boy. Bells were rung, and the people were already celebrating in the streets. All through the morning the rejoicing went on, but by afternoon the truth began to be known.

There was no child. I was still waiting.

May had come, and there was still not a sign. To my secret alarm, the swelling in my body, which I had convinced myself was my child, began to subside.

Susan had noticed. She did not mention it but I knew

she was thinking that I had had such disorders before. The swellings had not been so great and they had subsided more quickly. A terrible fear began to dawn on me that what I had experienced was not pregnancy but a return of my old complaint.

At last Susan spoke of it. 'It is as it was before,' she said. 'I have never been so swollen before.'

She agreed and tried to comfort me. 'Perhaps the child will come at the end of May.'

I clutched at the hope. But I was growing melancholy. I did not see Philip. I told myself that it was a Spanish custom not to see a wife who was about to give birth until after the child appeared.

I felt certain pains such as I had suffered before, but I knew they were not concerned with childbirth.

The people were growing restive.

Where is the child? they were asking. Could there have been a miscalculation so great as to be two months late? Rumours began to circulate. Was the Queen dead? Where was the child? Had the Queen given birth to a monster?

And I stayed in my apartments, seeing none but my own women, and I felt as though my heart would break. I was too old, too small . . . something was very wrong.

One of my household sent a woman to me. She was of very low stature and not very young; she had just given birth to three babies and had regained her strength in a week. The babies were brought to show me. They were all strong and healthy.

It was a comfort to see her, but in my heart I began to accept the truth. There was no child. I had suffered from the symptoms which had been with me for a greater part of my life; but perhaps because of my great need, my great desire to bear a child, I had forced my body to show the outward signs of pregnancy.

But I would not give up.

The midwife said: 'We have miscalculated the time. It will be August or September.'

I wept bitterly. I clung to Susan. I said to her: 'They say this to soothe me. In their hearts they know there will never be a child. Susan, don't lie to me. It is true, is it not?'

She looked at me sadly, and we both began to weep.

The Queen is Dead: Long Live the Queen

If Philip was disappointed – which I am sure he must have been – he did not show it.

I felt not only desolate but intensely humiliated. I had believed myself to be with child, and there was no child. I could imagine the manner in which I was being discussed in the streets of the cities and villages, and even in the tiny hamlets; all over the country they would be talking of the child which had never existed.

Philip was always mentioning his father, who needed him badly.

'He has missed you from the day you left,' I said. 'I understand that.'

'He has many commitments. I should be with him.'

He was looking at me with the faintest dislike in his eyes. Oh no, I told myself, not dislike. It was only that terrible disappointment. He had so much hoped that we should have our child by now. Was he thinking that I was incapable of bearing children? I knew I was small; I was not attractive; I had been old when I married him. How did I please him as a lover? I did not know. Such matters were not discussed between us; they just happened. Was that how lovers behaved? I wondered. Did I disappoint him? He had already had a wife; he never spoke of her. I heard rumours that sometimes he went out at night with some of his gentlemen, that they put on masks and went about the town, adventuring. There were bound to be rumours.

If only I had a son! I often thought of my mother. How often had she prayed, as I was praying now, for that longed-for son who would have made all the difference to her life? My father would never have been able to treat the mother of a male heir to the throne as he had treated her . . . not even for Anne Boleyn.

How strange that my story should be in some measure like hers!

'I must return,' said Philip. 'I have sworn to my father that I should do so . . . when the child was born.'

Any mention of the child unnerved me.

'But,' I stammered, 'there may still be a child.'

'You have been under great strain. You need a rest. You could not attempt such an ordeal . . . just yet . . . even if . . .'

I knew what he meant: Even if you can bear a child. He did not believe that I could.

And I was beginning to wonder, too.

I felt humiliated and defeated.

'I would come back . . . as soon as I could,' he said tentatively.

'Philip!' I cried, suddenly wanting to know the truth which I had tried not to see for so long. 'Do you truly love me?'

He looked startled. 'But you are my wife,' he said, 'so of course I love you.'

I felt comforted, forcing myself to be. He must go if he wished. I knew. I could not detain him, and even if I succeeded in doing so, it would be against his will.

He was nostalgic for Spain, as I should be for England if ever I left it.

It was natural that he should want to go.

'I shall return,' he said.

'I pray God that you will ere long,' I answered.

* * *

So he was going. He had said his absence would be brief, but I wondered. What reasons would there be for keeping him away? I was filled with foreboding. The terrible drama

506

of the last months had left its mark on me. I felt I would never believe in true happiness again.

We were at Oatlands — we had had to leave Hampton Court for the sweetening — and I had come there from London. I should accompany Philip to Greenwich, for I wanted to be with him as long as possible.

It was the 26th day of August. The streets were crowded. I was not sure whether it was to see me or because it was the day of St Bartholomew's Fair. I was not strong enough to ride and was carried in a litter.

I noticed the people's looks, though they cheered me loyally enough. No doubt they were wondering about me and the baby which had never existed. I knew there must have been fantastic rumours. There was one I heard about a certain woman — and even mentioning her name. It was Isabel Malt, who lived in Horn Alley in Aldersgate. She had given birth to a beautiful healthy boy at that time when I was waiting for mine. It was said that a great lord had offered Isabel a large sum of money for her baby if she would part with him and tell everyone that the child had died. The baby was to have been smuggled into Hampton Court and passed off as mine.

These wild rumours might have been amusing if they were not so tragic; and unfortunately there will always be those to believe them.

If I had had a child, I wondered, what rumours would have been created about him?

I had never been so unhappy as I was at that time. As I rode through those crowded streets and met the curious gaze of my people and heard their half-hearted, if loyal, shouts, I thought I would willingly have given my crown for the happiness of a loved wife and mother.

It had been arranged that Elizabeth, who was to be a member of the party come to bid Philip farewell, should travel by barge. I did not want to have to compete with her for the cheers of the people. I felt that she, with her young

507

looks and easy manners, would have commanded the greater share of the acclaim – and, worse still, it would have been noticed.

I took barge with Philip at the Tower Wharf and was beside him as we sailed down to Greenwich.

The members of the Council accompanied us, and I noticed how ill Gardiner was looking in the torchlight, for it was dusk. I was glad of the gloom. I did not want the bright sunlight to accentuate the ravages in my face which the last weeks had put there.

There came the moment when we must say goodbye.

Philip kissed all my ladies, as he had when he arrived, and I was reminded of that day and yearned to be back in that happy time.

At last he took his leave of me. He kissed me with great tenderness, and I tried to tell myself that he was as grieved at our parting as I was; but I knew in my heart that he was not. I was aware that, if he had greatly desired to stay, he would have found excuses for doing so. He gave no sign of his pleasure in leaving, and his features were set in a mould of sad resignation.

I felt the tears in my eyes and tried to suppress them. But I could not do so. Philip would hate tears.

I clung to him. He responded stiffly and then, murmuring, 'I shall be back ere long,' he left me.

I stood lonely and bereft, watching him depart. I would not move. He stood on the deck, his cap in hand, watching me as I watched him.

And there I stayed until I could see him no more.

I had lost my child, and now my husband was taking with him all hopes of happiness.

* * *

I think I must have been the most unhappy woman in the world.

Sullen looks came my way as I rode out; a pall of smoke

hung over Smithfield, where men were chained to stakes and died because they would not accept the true faith. I had not wanted that. 'Persuasion,' I had said. Was this persuasion?

Gardiner had died. He had left me to reap the harvest and had not stayed long enough to see what effect it would have.

I was lonely and helpless. This was my mission. I had completed it. I had brought the Church back to Rome but there was little joy for me.

I was ill most of the time. My headaches persisted. My dreams were haunted by the screams of people chained to the stakes in that Smithfield which had become a Hell on Earth.

It had to be, I assured myself. The Council said so. Every man had a chance to recant and save his life. They were all offered mercy. Most of them preferred martyrdom, and the fires continued. It had become a common sight to see men and women led out to be chained to the stakes, and the faggots lighted at their feet.

It was a black day when Nicholas Ridley, Bishop of London, and Hugh Latimer, Bishop of Worcester, went to their deaths. They had been tried and sentenced in Oxford, and the stakes were set up in the ditch near Balliol College.

It must have been a pitiable sight to see such men led to their deaths. They came out to die together.

The scene was later described to me. I did not want to hear of it but I had to know. Two such men . . . noble, good men in their ways, though misguided, to die so!

Latimer presented an impressive sight to the watching crowds, in his shabby frieze gown tied at the waist with a penny leather girdle, a string about his neck on which hung his spectacles and his Testament. I could not bear to think of this infirm old man shuffling to his death. But they said he had such nobility of countenance that the crowds watched in silent awe.

Nicholas Ridley, who came with him, presented a contrast.

He was about fifteen years younger and an extremely handsome man. Why . . . oh why? If only they would renounce their faith! But why should I expect them to do that? I would not have renounced mine.

I could not bear to think of those two men.

Neither of them showed fear. It was as though they were certain that that night they would be beyond all pain, in Heaven.

And as the faggots were lighted at Ridley's feet, Latimer turned his head towards him and said: 'Be of good cheer, Master Ridley. We shall this day light such a candle, by God's Grace, in England, as I trust will never be put out.'

The power of words is formidable. There would be people who would never forget those. They would inspire. There would be more martyrs in England because Ridley and Latimer had died so bravely.

Latimer, being old and feeble, died almost immediately; Ridley lingered and suffered greatly.

There were two more to haunt my dreams.

* * *

My great consolation at that time was Reginald. I spent hours with him. He had done so much in aiding the return to Rome. I was hoping that in time he would come to be Archbishop of Canterbury now that Cranmer was in prison.

It seemed to me that that was a post which would suit him. He had more understanding of Church affairs than those of government.

While we talked, I often found myself slipping into a daydream, wondering how different my life might have been if I had married him as my mother and his had wished.

In spite of his saintliness, there was a strong streak of bitterness in his nature. It was understandable. His happy family life had been completely changed because my father had desired Anne Boleyn and had thrust aside with ruthless ferocity all those who had stood in his way. And so many had.

It was that which had changed the course of our lives, and Reginald could not forget it.

I was right. The martyrdom of Ridley and Latimer had had its effect. No one could have witnessed such a spectacle without being deeply affected by it. There was murmuring all over the country.

I was so unhappy that I fell into fits of melancholy. I was tired and spiritless. I longed for Philip. His absence was to have been brief, he had said, but in my heart I knew that, once he had gone, he would not hurry to return.

Here I was, barren and lonely, having to face the fact that the child I had so desperately wanted was nothing but a myth.

Why had God deserted me? I asked myself. When had He ever given me aught to be thankful for? Why should I be so ill-used? Those were dangerous thoughts. I must subdue them. I must, as my mother would have said, accept my lot and keep my steps steadily upon the path of righteousness.

It was inevitable that there should be plots; and there was one which could have been very dangerous.

Every few weeks someone was accusing someone. It was often proved that a person had a grudge against another or someone had made a certain remark which could have been construed as treason; but when a conspiracy was discovered which involved the King of France, that was a serious matter.

It was by great good fortune that this came to light before it had gone too far, because one of the plotters lost his confidence in the success of the rebellion and went along to Reginald to confess what he knew.

His name was Thomas White, and his part in the scheme was to rob the Exchequer of £50,000.

Reginald had been sceptical at first, but when White explained that he was friendly with the wife of one of the tellers in the Exchequer who had promised to get impressions made of her husband's keys, he took it seriously.

Robbery was one crime, treason was another; but it emerged that robbery was a preliminary to the greater plan. The money was needed by Sir Henry Dudley to get together an army of mercenaries who would be banded together in France and who would cross the Channel to attack the south coast.

This Sir Henry Dudley was the distant cousin of the Duke of Northumberland who had set Jane Grey on the throne. The Dudleys were a formidable family, and the fact that he belonged to it made him a figure of importance not only in my eyes but in those of many others.

If only Philip were here! I needed a strong man beside me, for it had become clear that the plot was far-reaching. I wondered whom I could trust among those around me. I could rely, as I knew from the past, on my dear friends Rochester and Jerningham, and I asked them to choose men whom they could trust to investigate what was going on.

It was revealed that the French ambassador, de Noailles, who had always caused much anxiety, was fully aware of what was happening and was reporting it to his master, on whom they were relying for help. John Throckmorton, a relative of Nicholas who had sent the goldsmith to warn me of my brother Edward's death, was one of the leaders of the plot and that threw suspicion on Nicholas.

The magnitude of the scheme was alarming, involving the French as it did. Plans for landing and taking the Tower of London were revealed, and they had all been drawn up very carefully.

I was very tired and sick. I almost longed for death.

Meanwhile the conspirators were brought to justice. The object of the plot had been to despatch me as I had despatched Jane Grey, and to set up Elizabeth, who would marry Courtenay.

I did not believe for one moment that Elizabeth was aware of this. She would not be so foolish. She knew the state of my health and that it would be wiser to wait. Surely I could not have long to live? I did not wish to. If Philip would return to me and I could have a child, then only would life be worth living. But deep within me I feared that would never be. I was too old. I had this illness in my inner organs. It was what had plagued me all my life. I tried to fight against the conviction that it had made me barren; and I fought hard to reject the idea because I could not bear to accept it.

It was said that Sir Anthony Kingston was involved in the conspiracy. He was in Devonshire and immediately commanded to come to London to stand trial with the others.

I was to learn that he died on the journey to London. It was rumoured that he had killed himself rather than face trial.

The prisoners were tried and questioned. Only John Throckmorton proved himself to be a brave man and, even when racked most ferociously, he refused to betray any of his fellow conspirators and declared he would die rather than reveal anything. The others were less brave and implicated others, some of them men in high positions.

Executions followed and there were further arrests.

The Council urged that Elizabeth be brought for questioning, but I would not have that. I believed she was loyal to me, and I did not want them to trump up a charge against her. Apart from my sisterly feelings towards her, I feared that, if she were harmed in any way, the people would rise in strength against me. She had won their hearts. I had always known that her popularity far exceeded my own.

I wanted nothing now so much as to be left alone with my grief and melancholy.

* * *

The burning of Protestants continued. It was only when some notable person was led to the stake that it was an event.

So it was with Cranmer.

As Archbishop of Canterbury, Cranmer had played a big part in my father's affairs and had been one of the prime movers in the break with the Church of Rome; and it was thought that it would be safe and wise to be rid of him.

He was a man of great intellectuality but such men are often less brave than others. Cranmer was not a brave man . . . not until the very end. The return of papal authority must have filled him with terror, for he would know that one who had been at the very heart of the break would find himself in a difficult position.

I was pleased when he signed a declaration agreeing that, as Philip and I had admitted the Pope's authority in England, he would submit to our views. That should have been enough; and doubtless it would have been but for his position in the country and the effect he would have on so many people.

I had said that those who admitted their heresy and turned to the true faith would be free. But there were politics to be considered as well as religion and, much as I deplored this, I was overruled.

If only Philip had been here, I said, over and over again; but I knew that if Philip were here he would be on the side of the Council. Yet I deluded myself into thinking that he would have stood by me. I *had* to delude myself. It was the only way to bring a glimmer of hope into my life.

Cranmer signed two documents. In one he agreed that

514

he would put the Pope before the King and Queen; and in the other he promised complete obedience to the King and Queen as to the Pope's supremacy.

This should have saved him, but his enemies were determined he should die. He was too important to be allowed to live; and he was condemned and taken out to the stake.

Face to face with death, martyrdom descended upon him. He addressed the people, telling them that in his fear of death he had signed his name to certain documents. He had degraded himself by doing so, and before he died he wished to proclaim his faith in the new religion.

The faggots were lighted and, as the flames crept up his body, he held out his right hand and said in resonant tones: 'For as much as my right hand offended, writing contrary to my heart, it shall be punished therefor and burned first.'

He stood there, his hand outstretched while the flames licked his flesh.

All over the country they were talking of Cranmer.

'Where will it end?' they were asking. 'What next? Will they bring the Inquisition to England?'

Sullen anger was spreading.

I had done what God had intended I should, but it had brought me into ill repute.

There was no comfort anywhere. Reginald was ill and growing very feeble; I could not believe he would live long. And still Philip did not return.

* * *

Why did he not come? I wrote to him: 'I am surrounded by enemies. My crown is in danger. I need you.'

But there was always some excuse.

His father had now abdicated in his favour, and he was King of Spain in his own right. This seemed a good reason to keep him away. I made excuses for him to others, but in my own chamber I said to myself: He does not want to come. I am his wife. Why does he not want to be with me as I do him?

He had never loved me. Once more I had deluded myself. He had gone through the motions of being a husband; and I, feeling so deeply myself, had been aware of the lack of response in him. But I would not admit it. I had tried to believe because I so desperately wanted to.

I was deeply upset by the burnings. I did not know what I should do. It was God's will, I told myself continually. This was what He had preserved me to do. Those who died, I assured myself, were doomed to hell fire in any case. They were heretics, and heretics are the enemies of God. They must be eliminated before they spread their evil doctrines.

I concerned myself with the poor. I would go to visit them in their houses, talk of their problems with them, take them food and give them money if they needed it.

It comforted me to some extent. It helped to shut out the ghostly cries that echoed in my ears, the smell of burning flesh which seemed constantly in my nostrils.

Cranmer, Ridley, Hooper, Latimer . . . I could not forget them. They were men I had known, spoken with. I had liked some of them . . . and I had condemned them to the fire. No, not I. It was their judges. I would have pardoned them. But the ultimate blame would be laid on my shoulders.

Apart from Reginald, my greatest comfort was in my women. There was Susan, of course, and Jane Dormer was another whom I particularly liked. Jane was betrothed to the Count of Feria, a gentleman of Philip's suite, and one of his greatest friends. When Philip returned to England with his entourage, Jane was to be married, so she and I had a great deal in common at that time, both awaiting the return of a loved one.

My fortieth birthday had come and passed. How the

516

years pressed on me! If Philip did not return soon, I should be too old for childbearing.

I still cherished the hope.

Why did he not come? I asked myself again and again. Always it was the same answer when I wrote to him pleadingly: 'I will come soon . . . as yet there are duties which keep me here.'

He wrote that he must go to Flanders to celebrate his coming to power there, as well as in Spain.

There were malicious people to bring me news of those celebrations. Philip was playing a big part in them. He was giving himself up to pleasure. It was difficult to imagine Philip's doing that. He had always been so serious when he was with me.

'Why does he not come?' I kept demanding of Susan and Jane. 'What can be keeping him all this time?'

If they were silent, I would make excuses for him. His father had renounced the realm in Philip's favour, I reminded them. He was no longer merely the Prince of Spain but the King. He had his obligations.

But I was worried. Reginald could not help me. He was very ill, and I was discovering that he was not a practical man. He was clever and learned, but I needed advice.

I was desperately worried about the burnings, in spite of the fact that I told myself it was God's will. I heard terrible stories of wood which would not ignite properly, of people who were scorched for hours before they finally passed away. Some of the screams were terrible. Men talked of Cranmer, Ridley, Hooper and Latimer, but there were humble folk, too . . . the unlearned who had been led astray. Having been on my errands of mercy, disguised as a noble lady with no hint that I was the Queen, I had learned something of the lives of these people. I felt it was wrong to send them to a fiery death simply because they were ignorant and saw themselves as martyrs.

If only Philip were here! But he upheld the Inquisition

in his land. He would bring it to England, and persecution would be intensified then.

To whom could I turn?

I decided to send to Flanders to find out the real cause for Philip's continued absence. Were those stories of his adventurings true? I could not believe them. But then, just as I had never understood my sister Elizabeth, I did not understand Philip either. I was too downright, I supposed. I was at a loss with those people who showed a certain front to the world when they were secretly something else.

At the same time I sent a messenger to the Emperor. I had the utmost respect for his judgement. I had always regarded him as one of the most shrewd leaders in Europe, possessed of great wisdom.

I wanted him to be told of the heretics who made martyrs of themselves and the effect it was having on the people. I had always wanted to persuade . . . to coerce perhaps . . . and only rarely impose the final penalty. The Emperor might give me his views. There was another point. People varied. What the Spaniards accepted, the English might not. I wanted him to know that there was discontent throughout the kingdom and that even the most faithful to the old religion felt a repugnance towards the fiery death – particularly for men who had led good lives – men such as Hugh Latimer, for instance.

Why did I expect Charles to understand? On his orders, 30,000 heretics in Flanders had been either beheaded or buried alive. And Philip? What did he care for those people? The numbers who had died in England since the rules were introduced were infinitesimal compared with those who had suffered at the hands of the Inquisition.

No, the Emperor would think, with Philip and some members of my Council, that I was a foolish woman, and that a woman needed a man beside her if she was to rule with a firm hand.

I was ready to agree. If only he would come!

He had so many commitments now, he wrote. As soon as it was possible, he would be with me. It was only duty which kept him from me. Duty! Paying homage to beautiful women in Brussels! Was that duty?

I was told that Ruy Gomez da Silva had told our ambassador that Philip could not come because his astrologer had prophesied that, if he returned to England, he would be assassinated. Therefore he felt it wiser to stay away. After all, the Spaniards had been treated rather badly when they were in England. They had been shunned almost everywhere; they had been robbed and often attacked. It was small wonder that the King was inclined to listen to his astrologer.

I was ill . . . sick with disappointment. My women were anxious about me. They thought of everything they could do to amuse me for a while, but I was not amused. Even Jane the Fool could not bring the slightest smile to my lips.

I was with Susan and Jane Dormer one day when they began to chide me for my listless attitude. I was not eating enough; I was staying in my apartments, brooding.

'It will be different when the King returns,' I said.

'Your Majesty should try to enjoy what is here for your pleasure.'

'My heart is with my husband,' I replied. 'You must know that.'

'But he does not come, Madam,' said Jane Dormer sadly.

'He has too much with which to occupy himself.'

I caught a glance which passed between them. Susan's lips were a little pursed. Jane lifted her shoulders slightly. It was as though Jane were asking a question. I distinctly caught the faint shake of Susan's head.

'What have you heard?' I demanded.

Jane flushed scarlet. Susan was more self-contained.

She said: 'I doubt little that Your Majesty does not already know.'

'Then why is it that you have decided not to tell me?'

They opened their eyes wide and looked at me, assuming innocence. But I knew them well, and I guessed there was something they were keeping from me.

'Susan . . . Jane . . .' I said. 'Have you joined the ranks of my enemies?'

'Your Majesty!'

'You are hiding something from me.'

'But Your Majesty . . .'

'Susan, what are you afraid to tell me?'

'Oh . . . it was nothing. Just idle gossip.'

'Concerning me.'

They were silent.

'And the King . . . was he concerned?' I persisted.

Susan bit her lip. 'It is all nonsense. There will always be rumours.'

'And these rumours?'

Susan looked at Jane and Jane at Susan. It was Susan who spoke. 'They are saying that the King will never come back.'

'Why should he not?'

'They are saying, Your Majesty, that he prefers to be somewhere else.'

There was silence. Jane fell to her knees and, taking my hand, kissed it.

'Oh, Your Majesty,' she said earnestly, 'I wish all could be well with you. I pray he will come soon and show how he loves you . . . and that there will be a child.'

'I pray for it, Jane.'

'I, too, Your Majesty,' added Susan.

I looked at her. There was an expression of infinite sadness on her face. I had known Susan for many years. She was one of those most dear to me. I trusted her. I knew of her love and devotion.

'You do not believe that he will come, Susan,' I said. 'And you know something which you are afraid to tell me.'

She could not dissimulate. She was my honest, open Susan.

She drew a deep breath and said: 'There are rumours. But there are always rumours.'

'And these rumours? Come. Since they are only rumours, we need not believe them if we do not wish to.'

'That is so, Your Majesty.'

'Then tell me what you have heard. It is not good that I should be kept in the dark.'

'Your Majesty has suffered. Only those of us who have been near you know how much. I cannot bear to see Your Majesty suffer . . . and to remain deluded.'

'Deluded? What of these rumours? They concern the King. You must tell me.'

Still she was silent.

'Susan,' I commanded. 'Tell me.'

'There are women, Your Majesty. The Duchess of Lorraine is his mistress.'

I tried to smile. I heard myself saying: 'The King is a man, Susan. It is the way of men. I am not there. He wants me, of course. I am his wife. But we are separated. We should not take these women any more seriously than he does.'

I was amazed at myself, surprised that I could speak calmly when I was seething with jealousy within. It was hard to pretend. He should be faithful. We were married. We had taken our sacred vows. But I knew this rumour was true. A mistress! How was he with her? Not as he had been with me . . . courteous . . . like a stranger. We must try to get a child. Just that. No real love, no passion. Was that how he was with her? But he would not be with her because of the urgent need to get a child. He would be with her because that was where he wanted to be.

And this was why he did not come to England.

I knew that was not all. Half of me said, Do not pursue

521

this. It is only going to make you more unhappy. But if there was more to know, I must know it.

'What else, Susan?' I asked.

'There is nothing else.'

'Usually you are truthful, Susan. It is one of the qualities which have endeared you to me. Come, do not disappoint me. What else have you heard?'

'One cannot trust the French,' she said.

'No. But sometimes they make some pertinent comments. What is their verdict on my marriage?'

She was silent and looked as though she were on the point of bursting into tears.

'I insist on knowing, Susan.'

'The French ambassador told the Venetian ambassador that Philip has said that England is nothing but a costly nuisance. He does not like the people and he does not want to return to it.'

'That cannot be true.'

'Your Majesty asked . . .'

'Yes, I asked because I like to know what tales are being circulated. What else, Susan? You are still holding something back.'

She paused; she held up her head and a certain defiance came into her eyes. I knew she did not like Philip because she blamed him for my unhappiness.

She said: 'It is that King Philip is hoping to have his marriage annulled.'

It was out, and now it was difficult for me to hide my dismay. They knew me too well, both of them. They had seen my exultation. I had talked to them of the perfections of my husband, of my perfect marriage, of my hopes. I could not disguise my misery from these two who knew me so well.

I sat very still and covered my face with my hands. There was a deep silence in the room. Then I felt them at my feet. I opened my eyes and saw them both kneeling there. There were tears on Jane's cheeks, and Susan looked stricken.

'It is only gossip, Your Majesty,' said Susan.

'Only gossip,' I repeated. 'Yet it has a ring of truth . . .'

They saw now that there was to be no more pretence. It was no use. They knew of my love, of my hopes. They had been with me during those terrible weeks when I was awaiting the birth of a non-existent child. They had been through it all. They had suffered with me.

I could no longer hide my true feelings from them. They were my very dear and trusted friends.

Susan spoke first. 'Your Majesty must not grieve. It is better to look at the truth.'

'Better to say I deluded myself,' I murmured, 'that he did not care for me, that he never did.'

'It is often so in royal marriages, Your Majesty . . . and in the marriages of those who are high born.'

'But sometimes love comes,' I said.

They were silent.

'He is a great man,' I said.

'Your Majesty is a great Queen,' added Susan.

I put out my hands and touched their heads gently.

'You should not grieve, Your Majesty, for one who would betray you,' said Susan.

I did not answer. Did she know that she was uttering treason against the King? But she was safeguarding the Queen.

'He was not what Your Majesty believed him to be,' she went on.

'He was all that I believed him to be.'

She was silent for a moment, then she burst out: 'You thought he was so solemn . . . so pure . . . so chaste. It was never so. Why, he tried to seduce Magdalen Dacre.'

'Magdalen Dacre!'

'Yes. She told us. She was horribly shocked.'

I remembered how I had noticed the girl because she

was so tall. They would look incongruous together, I thought inconsequentially. Ludicrous. Perhaps that was what appealed to him about her. But she was exceptionally beautiful. I remembered there had been a time when she had been subdued and always seemed to absent herself when Philip was there.

'It was at Hampton Court,' said Susan, who, having begun, seemed to find it difficult to stop. 'She was at her toilette. There was a small window. He must have seen her as he passed. He tried to open the window and put his arm into the room. Magdalen rapped him sharply and told him to be off.'

'She did not tell me.'

'She would not have grieved you.'

'Perhaps it would have been better if I had known.'

There was no pretence now. I could not hide my misery from them, and they would not have believed me, however good a job I made of it.

'He gave me no sign . . .' I said.

'He was particularly courteous to her afterwards.'

'He bore no grudge,' said Jane, as though calling my attention to something in his favour.

'Oh, Your Majesty,' said Susan, 'you must not be unhappy. There are such men. They know not the meaning of fidelity. It is better not to care too much. We heard how he used to go off with a group of friends. They were of a kind.'

'I had heard rumours and not believed them.'

'They used to sing that song about the baker's daughter,' said Jane.

I closed my eyes. So they knew! All my people knew, and I was the only one who believed he loved me!

'What song?' I asked.

Susan said quickly: 'It was a silly little rhyme . . . nothing . . . nothing . . . I have forgotten it.'

I caught Jane's wrist. 'Tell me the rhyme,' I commanded.

'Your Majesty, I . . . I can't remember.'

'Tell me,' I said coldly.

So she told me.

The baker's daughter in her russet gown
Better than Queen Mary – without her crown.

The humiliation! The pain of rejection! My happiness had been nothing but an illusion. It was a phantom creature of my imagination to mock me now. It was created out of nothing . . . like the child of whom I had dreamed, for whom I had planned . . . a will o' the wisp . . . to taunt me and to leave me desolate.

I wanted to be alone with my sorrow. It overwhelmed me. I could share it with no one.

'Leave me,' I said.

'Your Majesty . . .' began Susan, but I only looked at her coldly and repeated: 'Leave me.'

So I was alone . . . alone with my wretchedness, staring the truth in the face as I should have done many weary months before. I had conceived a dream, a flimsy figment of my own imagination. It had nothing to do with reality. I had duped myself; and I had been seen to be duped by those around me. There would be some who laughed at my gullibility and others who kept silent and protected me from the knowledge because they loved me.

At length I rose. I went to that chamber where his picture hung.

How I had loved it! He stood erect, as he always did to disguise his low stature. His face was handsome with his fair hair and beard and his firm Hapsburg chin. I had stood many times before this picture, glowing with pride and pleasure, while he had been romping with some low woman of the town. The baker's daughter who was better than Mary . . . without her crown, of course.

I found a knife and I slashed at the picture. I felt better

than I had for some time. The knife pierced the canvas, and still I went on cutting.

Susan came in.

She must have heard me come here. She was terribly anxious and feared what effect the revelations had had on me.

She saw at once what I had done.

'Have it taken away,' I said.

'Yes, Your Majesty.'

Gently she took the knife from me and hid it in the pocket of her skirt.

The next day the picture was gone, but my unhappiness remained.

* * *

I was ill after that. No one was surprised. My periodic illnesses had become commonplace . . . too frequent for anyone to notice.

I spent long hours alone. I brooded on the past. I recalled incidents, our being together, our love-making, which had been conducted in a manner to resemble a stately pavane. There had been no joy in it, no laughter, no fun. It was a ritual which had to be borne – on his side – for the sake of an heir.

As for myself, I had not known it could be any other way. How could I, ignorant as I was of such matters? Now I wondered how it had been with the Duchess of Lorraine, the baker's daughter and all the others.

I stormed . . . to myself, of course. I wept. I talked to him as though he were there beside me. I told him what he had done to me. He had humiliated me, used me, slighted me, and never had he loved me.

I remembered how he had been with Elizabeth. He had said she should not be forced to marry. Did *he* plan to marry her when I was dead? He surely could not be thinking of annulling our marriage so that he could marry my sister? Dispensation could, of course, always be obtained for the powerful.

How empty my life was! For the happiness I craved I would have exchanged twenty crowns.

But one cannot mourn for ever. I must meet my Council. The country was unstable. The burnings were deplored in several quarters. I was blamed for them. Families all over the country were cursing my name.

I wanted to talk to someone. I wanted to explain how distressed I was. My task had been to bring England back to Rome, and that I had done, but there were sullen looks everywhere. There were murmurings against me.

Only those close to me, the people who really knew me, gave me their love – and mingled with it, I think, their pity.

I told myself that I hated Philip.

* * *

News came from Italy. Edward Courtenay had died.

I was deeply moved. He was so young. So handsome he had been. I could have been in love with him. Then Philip had come, a King, a ruler, a strong man. Poor Courtenay! What chance had he had then? I thought of all those years when the Tower had been his home; it was commendable that he had educated himself, but there was more needed than education. To have married him would have been an even greater disaster than my marriage with Philip.

Would he have loved me any more? Not he. I was too old. Love had passed me by until I was too old to understand and enjoy it. I had nothing to offer but a crown. A low-class baker's daughter was more attractive than I . . . if my crown were taken away.

But with it, of course, I had been a glittering prize.

I knew poor Courtenay had found it hard to live in exile. Right up to the time of his death he was pleading to return. I would have granted his request but the Council was

527

horrified at the prospect. Often they had pointed out how dangerous such people could be. With Courtenay, his good looks made up for his lack of sense, and he was a member of that dynasty which, now it was no longer the ruling family, had been ennobled with the sanctity of that which was and now is no more. Oh yes, the Plantagenets had become holy now their age was past. Had people loved them so devotedly while they lived? Would the Tudors be as revered when they had passed away?

So Courtenay had wandered about Europe, dreaming of home and perhaps a crown. It was tragic to be born within reach of it – even when the chances of attaining it are remote – and to spend one's life in endless striving for the unattainable.

Yes, the Council had been right. It would have been folly to have allowed him to return.

So the golden boy had died in Padua. He was buried there, and all his dreams of glory with him.

* * *

Philip was writing to me. Such tender letters they were. He desired to return but events delayed him. However, he was coming. There was so much he wished to discuss with me. Our enforced separation had gone on too long.

How could I help it if my melancholy lifted, if I began to dream again?

The rumours had been false, I told myself. He loved me. He implied it in his letters. There had certainly been weighty matters to occupy him. Now he wanted to talk with me that we might act together, which, as husband and wife, was natural for us.

Perhaps I was not so guileless as I had been, for while a part of me wanted desperately to believe, there was another part which knew why he was so eager to express his affection.

He needed help.

Well, should not a wife help her husband? It should be her joy and privilege to do so.

The fact was that he was coming home. I should see him again. I studied myself in my mirror. There were dark circles under my eyes, and wrinkles round them. I was an old woman. But the news had brought a certain radiance to my face, and I assured myself I looked younger.

Susan said I did. She was anxious, though. She believed that Philip would hurt me again as he had before.

I knew why he was coming. He wanted help against the French.

There were times when I did not care that he came for this reason. It was only important that he was coming. We should be together again . . . lovers, and perhaps this time there would be a real child. A child would make up for everything.

I was arguing with myself again. Some women of my age had children. Why should not I? I prayed fervently. I wanted the whole country to pray with me. But I did not ask them to. I could not have borne the humiliation. They would have tittered when and where they dared. They would have sung 'The Baker's Daughter'.

But I was a desperate woman, longing for the love I never had.

I went to see Reginald. He was very ill, but there were days when he was lucid and it seemed that all his old power returned to him. He could not walk now, but he still studied. That was his pleasure in life – as, I imagined, it always had been.

He kept abreast of what was happening in Europe and, because of the years he had spent there, was in close contact with Rome and those who, like himself, held the office of Cardinal.

I said to him: 'Philip writes of coming home.'

'To England?'

I nodded.

'Ah, yes,' went on Reginald. 'It is the war. I deplore it. The Emperor and the King of France fought for years – each wanting to rule the Continent. They will never achieve this . . . either of them. Perhaps one succeeds for a few years . . . and then the other. It will go one way and then swing back. It always has. I cannot see why they do not understand it always will.'

'It has kept us apart. Philip has his duties and now that he is the King . . .' I shook my head sadly.

'I was against the marriage,' he said. 'You remember, I warned you. You should not have married. You could have reigned alone. The people never wanted Philip. They will never accept him with a good grace. They hate foreigners.'

'People seem to hate those who are not of the same nationality as themselves – and sometimes they hate people who are. There is too much hate in the world.'

Reginald was silent for a few moments; then he said: 'And now there is a new force in Europe . . . this new Pope.'

'He is an old man. I heard that he was eighty. Surely that cannot be? How could they elect a man of that age?'

'He is no ordinary man. And he has had eighty years of experience which few men have, and he uses what he has gleaned through the years to his advantage.'

'They should have elected you, Reginald. You should have been Pope.'

'My dear Mary, I am a sick man.'

'So they chose this old man!'

'You have not seen him. He has the energy of youth and the experience of old age. A man who can combine the two is a rarity, but such is Cardinal Caraffa who is now Paul IV. It is unfortunate that he has a grudge against Philip.'

'How could Philip have aroused his animosity? It was not very wise of him, was it?'

'It would have been if the Cardinal had failed to be

elected. Philip tried to prevent that and so, I fear, has earned the Pope's enduring enmity.'

'A man of God will forgive,' I said.

Reginald smiled wryly. 'The Pope will try to drive Philip out of Europe and to achieve this is ready to make an alliance with the French.'

'All my life I remember it. There was an alliance between my father and the King of France . . . and then they were enemies and there was an alliance with the Emperor. Then he quarrelled with the Emperor and was the friend of France. How much are these alliances worth, Reginald?'

'A great deal while they last. Philip is disturbed.'

'That is why he is coming home. He will talk to me. It is what he wants.'

'I will tell you what he wants. He will want England to stand with him. He will want you to declare war on France.'

'War! I hate war! There are enough troubles here already. The drought has not helped. The people fear famine, and when that threatens they turn against those who in their eyes are wealthy and well fed. There has been trouble since we turned to Rome. Oh, Reginald, there are times when I am so unhappy. The people no longer love me. I think they are waiting for my death . . . hoping for it . . . that they may turn to Elizabeth.'

'She would take the country away from Rome.'

'She would do what the people wanted her to.'

'She has heard the Mass.'

'Yes . . . but showing her reluctance. She sways with the wind. Which way do you want me to go? What is the best for me? she asks herself. And that is the way she will go.'

'There are some who think she should be questioned.'

'I cannot believe she would ever harm me.'

'You are too trusting.'

'Yes,' I agreed, thinking of Philip. 'It may be that I do not employ subterfuge as some people do.'

He put his hand over mine. 'You have done well,' he

said. 'Remember you used to say you had a mission? God had chosen you to bring England back to His true Church? You must rejoice, for you have done that. Always it will be remembered that it was in your reign that England returned to the Church of Rome.'

It was pleasant to be with him. I wanted to talk of the old days when I was a child and I had first known him. He had seemed so noble then. I liked to think of our mothers talking confidentially over their needlework, match-making for us.

If I had married Reginald when I was young and had wanted to, how different my life would have been. It would surely have been a very suitable and happy marriage.

But it did not come to pass; and now Philip was coming home because he wanted my country to join his in the war against the French.

* * *

We were disturbed by the menace of another rebellion. This time it was Thomas Stafford. It was very disconcerting to me because the young man was Reginald's nephew.

Reginald was very upset about it. He talked to me about Thomas, who had renounced the Catholic faith. When he was on the Continent, Reginald had made great efforts to bring him back to it – but in vain.

Thomas's mother, Ursula, was the daughter of my dear Countess of Salisbury; thus she was Reginald's sister. So the young man had royal blood on that side of the family; but his father was the third Duke of Buckingham who was descended from Thomas Woodstock, third son of Edward III. So . . . Thomas had royal blood on both sides, and he had the temerity to consider that his claim to the throne was greater than mine, for he declared that, by marrying a Spaniard, I had forfeited my right to it.

It seemed so recklessly stupid that one felt one should ignore it, and, as Thomas Stafford was abroad, we did for some time. It had seemed just one of the minor irritations I was doomed to suffer.

Gradually we began to see that it was not so trivial. This was when the English ambassador to France sent despatches home which indicated that Thomas Stafford was being received with respect by Henri Deux, who was giving him encouragement, and had even promised him two ships to help him.

Ruy Gomez da Silva arrived in England. It was February and bitterly cold.

I was delighted to see him, because I knew that his coming meant that Philip would soon follow.

Ruy Gomez was a typical Spanish nobleman. He was a master of courtesy, as Philip was; but Ruy Gomez had an ease of manner, a way of flattering with his eyes and paying unspoken compliments which made one feel attractive even though one knew to the contrary. He was a very gracious, charming gentleman.

He asked for an audience immediately on his arrival and, of course, I granted it with alacrity.

Susan warned me that, underneath all the charm, here was an astute diplomat who should be carefully watched.

He talked pleasantly and easily of the journey, the crossing and the health of Philip, which was good.

'His Majesty has been completely immersed in his duties, which were onerous, and now that the Emperor has passed his dominions to his beloved son, those duties are increasing.'

'We shall have much to discuss,' I said.

'The French are causing a great deal of trouble,' Gomez told me.

'There are always some to cause trouble, and often it is the French.'

'The King needs all the assistance he can get.'

He did not actually say that Philip was coming to ask me

533

to give assistance, but he implied it. Though, of course, I knew that already.

'The Council and the country would not be in favour of our being involved in war at this time,' I told him.

He gave me the most flattering of smiles. 'You are the Queen,' he said.

'It would be necessary for the Council to agree.'

'The French are no friends of England.'

'It seems to me that no country is a friend of another.'

He looked at me reproachfully. 'But our countries, Your Majesty, are united by the marriage of yourself and the King.'

'That is so,' I agreed.

'And it is because the King relies on your love and loyalty that he will tear himself away from his duties to come to you.'

'It is long since I have seen him.'

'His duties have kept him, most reluctantly, from your side.'

I thought: Fêting the beautiful women of Brussels? Enjoying a liaison with the Duchess of Lorraine?

'And now he will come,' I said, 'because he needs help.'

'He has yearned to be with Your Majesty. As I stress, it is only duty which has kept him away from you.'

'And now duty bids him come to me.'

'It is his love for Your Majesty which will bring him.'

His eyes were shrewd. I knew what he was telling me in his subtle way. He was sounding me. Would I and my Council be prepared to declare war on France? If so, Philip would come to England and we would work together on that project. If not, he would be wasting his time in coming.

I tried to stifle the wretchedness I was feeling. It was better to be ignorant when knowledge brought so much pain.

He was watching me closely. He would have to report to

Philip. Was it worth his while to come? If there was no hope, he would find some excuse to stay away. If there was hope, he would come and persuade me.

That was not true, I admonished myself. He was my husband. He wanted to be with me. Of course, his duties were extensive; he had a kingdom to govern. I had allowed people to poison my mind against him. When he came, he would assure me that he loved me and that it was only his overwhelming duties which kept us apart.

For a moment I looked steadily at Ruy Gomez da Silva. I could not face the truth. I had to see Philip.

I said: 'The French are as great a menace under Henri as they were under François.'

He nodded. That was good enough. Philip would come.

* * *

I was at Greenwich. The news had come that evening. Philip had landed at Dover.

It was wonderful to see him again. I embraced him warmly, and he smiled at me affectionately. I was a little concerned, because he had aged considerably. Yet in a way that made me feel better, for I knew that my looks had not improved since his departure. There had been too many sleepless nights, too much bitterness.

As soon as I saw him, my heart softened towards him. I told myself romantically, foolishly, We shall start again.

I ordered that the bells of London should ring out and the Tower guns fire their salutes. And we rode together into the capital. There was a noticeable lack of rejoicing in the streets. I fancied I could smell the smoke from the Smithfield fires. There were a few faint cheers and a great deal of silence.

The citizens no longer loved me, and they distrusted my husband. Reginald would say he had been right. There should never have been a Spanish marriage.

I had prepared banquets and masques to welcome Philip

but he displayed little interest in them. He had never had any great enjoyment in that kind of activity.

When we were alone together, he was subdued. He told me he had been concerned in affairs of the Continent, and the election of Paul IV had been a shock to him.

I said that a man such as he was, a firm upholder of the true faith, should be beloved by the Pope.

'This Pope is an ambitious man,' he said. 'He should never have been elected.'

'I wish that Reginald had become the Holy Father,' I said.

He did not answer.

And so we retired. It was not quite as it had been before. I felt I was outside the scene, looking on at myself and my husband. There was no spontaneous love. Did I imagine it or was he as one performing an onerous duty? In the past it had been necessary in the hope of getting an heir. That reason was there no longer. He regarded it as an impossibility, though hope lingered with me. But now he must perform his duty for the sake of getting England to declare war on France.

It was not for such purposes that love was meant.

I half deluded myself. I suppose, when one has been so deprived of love as I have, one snatches at even a pretence of it.

The next day, when I was introduced to the ladies and gentlemen of his entourage, I received a shock.

A tall and beautiful woman was presented to me, and I was immediately struck by her radiant good looks.

'The Duchess of Lorraine . . .'

I felt sick. He had brought her with him! Oh, how dared he! How could he be so blatant?

She was kissing my hand, lifting her dark-fringed eyes to my face, studying me, no doubt seeing me as the plain, unwanted wife. I looked at her coldly, nodded and passed on to the next who was being presented to me.

I was wondering what he had said of me. People talked indiscreetly during intimate moments. I was angry, but most of all very sad.

* * *

Susan and Jane Dormer understood. They were indignant.

'It is nothing,' I said to them. 'Kings have mistresses. They are not serious entanglements.'

'Do they bring them in their trains?' demanded Susan.

'Often, I suppose. It just happens that we have heard her name mentioned. He does not know that.'

I turned over in my mind what I should do. Should I confront him with the fact that I knew who she was? Should I demand how he dared bring his mistress to my Court? Or should I feign ignorance?

But how should I receive the woman? I could not endure it. I would have her sent back. On the other hand, if I did, there would be more whispering, more titters. Pretend I did not know? I had been living a life of pretence for so long, shutting my eyes to the truth.

I could not bring myself to be civil to the woman. Yet I did not see how I could order her to go.

Sometimes I was on the verge of telling Philip I would not have his mistress here, but I did not.

When we were together, when he showed affection for me, I was still able to deceive myself. It was because I so earnestly wanted there to be love between us.

He talked a good deal about the iniquity of the French. They must be defeated. They were the enemies of England as well as of Spain. I must see that the sooner England declared war on them the better.

This was why he had come. Not to be with me. I knew it and still I wavered. There were moments when I completely deluded myself. I wanted him with me. I wanted to please him.

He was getting exasperated because I was shelving the

537

question. It was urgent, he said. The French were laughing at us. They were working against us as they always had.

I said I would speak to the Council.

The verdict was non-committal. We were not in a position to go to war. The Exchequer was alarmingly low. The people were not in a mood to suffer taxation.

It seemed as though Philip had come in vain.

My attitude towards the Duchess of Lorraine was becoming very strained. I wondered whether people noticed. No one mentioned it to me. But at several banquets I cut her when she approached me, and I always insisted that she be seated as far from Philip as possible.

Susan came to me in distress one day. She had friends who were always ready to pass on news, and she thought it her duty to garner it and sometimes tell me.

She explained that she had heard that, at the French Court, they were laughing about the *ménage à trois*, and there was speculation as to how the Queen would deal with her beautiful rival.

'It is an impossible situation,' I said. 'I do not know what to do.'

Susan was forthright. She had already expressed her disapproval of Philip's behaviour with Magdalen Dacre, so she did not hesitate to do so now.

She said: 'Your Majesty should send her away.'

I frowned. I said: 'But she is in Philip's entourage. It would not be good manners for me to interfere with his private circle.'

'In the circumstances,' she said, 'Your Majesty should remember that you are the Queen. He had no right to bring her here but you have every right to dismiss her.'

'How could I?'

'Simply by telling her that her presence is no longer required at your Court.'

'Philip would be angry.'

'Your Majesty is angry.'

I said: 'I think you may be right.'

I pondered on it for a few days. I almost spoke to Philip, and then found I had not the courage to do so. I was afraid he would leave me. He was already becoming impatient about the delay in agreeing to make war on France.

Eventually I did it. I sent a message to ask her to leave, as her presence was no longer required at my Court.

She was a discreet lady. A few days after receiving the order, she left.

* * *

I was not sure what would happen. There was a feeling in the Council against war. As for myself, I wavered. There were times when I wanted to please Philip beyond everything; there were others when I reminded myself that he had not come to see me but to persuade England to declare war on France.

He made no comment on the departure of the Duchess of Lorraine. I was glad of this, although I should like to have known what his true feelings were. I had come to the conclusion that I would never know much about this strange, cold man I had married.

He seemed to be obsessed by the need to bring us into the war with France.

I am not sure what would have happened but for the Stafford affair.

Reports of the latter's activities were coming in from our people in France, and it was clear that what had seemed just another little plot was really dangerous, due to the increasing involvement of the King of France.

Stafford was becoming more vociferous. It was clear that the influence of the French King was making him very confident. It seemed as though Henri might be using Stafford as he had attempted to use others before; this put a new aspect on the matter.

Stafford was declaring that the Spanish marriage was a

539

disaster and that the Spaniards were preparing to land in England, bring in the Inquisition and make England a vassal of Spain.

I knew how inflammatory such talk could be. He called himself 'the Protector', and he had supporters in England who were already urging people to rise and fight the Spaniards who were dragging the country into war.

He landed in Yorkshire and took possession of Scarborough Castle. It was a foolhardy thing to do. His forces were pitiably small and lacked the means to fight against us. It was hardly a battle.

He was soon captured and brought to London, where he was tried and hanged and quartered at Tyburn.

That was the end of the Stafford rebellion, but it changed the minds of those waverers on the Council.

The French part in the affair was apparent, and we had to make it clear to them that we would not have them meddling in our affairs.

So Philip achieved his object through Stafford rather than through me.

England was at war with France.

* * *

Those were happy days. Philip was in high spirits. Well, perhaps that is an exaggeration. Philip could never be in high spirits; but let me say he was pleased. He looked better, and he had the air of a man whose mission is accomplished.

I was expecting him to declare his intention to depart, and when he did not and seemed to be happy to be with me, my joy was boundless. I had come from the depth of despair to the heights of happiness.

He discussed military preparations with me; and the only time he left me was when campaign strategy had to be worked out with the generals, in which he said I should not be interested.

Ruy Gomez da Silva had left soon after Philip arrived. He had returned to Spain to raise the necessary army and funds for the proposed war.

I was as happy as I had been in the first days of my marriage. I was believing once more in the love of Philip. He wanted to be with me, I told myself. He was finding it difficult to tear himself away. When he had conquered the French, he would return to me, and we should live happily together.

As for the Duchess of Lorraine, she was just a memory to me – and, I hoped, to Philip. There was no question of philandering now. There would have been no time for him to indulge in such things. When he was not with his generals, he was with me.

I threw myself into the task of raising money to support the army.

It was wonderful to share a project. We talked of it incessantly. There was even time for a little hunting, and with Philip beside me that was a great joy. I found such pleasure in being in church with him. A fervent devotion to religion was something we shared. He was as eager to attend the service as I was, and to worship together brought us even closer, I was sure.

I knew that every day he asked if there was any message from Ruy Gomez. I tried not to think of it. He did not mention it, but I knew he was eagerly awaiting the return of his friend.

And then at last the news came. Ruy Gomez da Silva was in the Channel, and with him was the Spanish Fleet. They were ready to go into battle.

From the day Ruy Gomez was sighted, Philip was all eagerness to be gone; and only ten days later, he was ready to leave.

He was to join the Spanish Fleet at Dover. I was wretchedly unhappy and wanted to be with him as long as possible so, sick as I felt, I insisted on making the journey with him from London to Dover.

I cherished every moment of those four days we spent on the road. We halted three times and that last night at Canterbury was a bittersweet one for me.

I could scarcely bear to look at the ship which was going to take him away from me, but he could not hide his eagerness to be gone. It was his duty, I told myself. He had to defend his country. It was not that he wished to leave *me*.

He bade me a tender farewell, but even then I could not help being aware of his impatience to be gone.

Sadly I stood on the shore, watching until I could see the ship no longer.

I had a terrible presentiment that I should never see him again.

* * *

Before Philip left, he asked Reginald to look after me.

'I know your regard for each other,' he said. 'It is rooted in the Queen's youth. You alone, Cardinal, can comfort her.'

The trouble had begun just before Philip left. The Pope, who had made himself Philip's enemy, declared he was deeply dissatisfied by the manner in which the return to Rome had been conducted in England. I had to admit he had some cause for complaint. I had thought it would be a simple matter and that, once the law was changed and the Pope acknowledged as Head of the Church, everything would be as it had been before the break.

There were certain facts which had escaped my attention. With the break and the introduction of Protestantism, many of the churches had been destroyed; the monasteries had been dissolved, and their lands sold or given away. The Exchequer was very low, and the war with France was depleting it further. It seemed to the energetic Pope that we were not really trying; and for this he blamed Reginald.

It was unfair. Reginald had never forgotten his duty to Rome. He had been placed in a very difficult position when the Pope and Philip had become enemies, for as a cardinal he owed his allegiance to Rome. We had brought England back to Rome, and now the Pope regarded us as his enemies, for friends of Philip were enemies of his. Moreover, Paul had allied himself with France – so we were at war with him.

Paul blamed Reginald, who was supposed to be my guide and counsellor, and he had allowed me to be persuaded to join the alliance with Spain against him.

The Pope was withdrawing all his legates from Philip's dominions, and that meant that Reginald himself was recalled. He was to be replaced by Cardinal William Peto.

To add to his tribulations, Reginald was accused of heresy. This was absurd but typical of the fiery Pope. He was good to his friends but could not hate his enemies enough, it seemed; and, having decided that Reginald was serving Philip and myself, he was determined to destroy him.

His next move was to command Reginald to appear before the Inquisition. True, he had been appointed Archbishop of Canterbury, but in the Pope's eyes he was guilty of heresy because he had not succeeded in bringing England back to Rome as he should.

I am sure Reginald was not afraid of facing the Inquisition; he would never fear bodily torment or even death; but he was bitterly wounded by the Pope's treatment of him, for he had always been a loyal son of the Church. It was the break with Rome which had made him an exile; his entire life had been changed because he had been faithful to his beliefs. My father had loved Reginald dearly before the disagreement between them; it would have been easy for Reginald to have denied Rome and kept my father's favour. What a different life he might have had if he had done so! But he had been true to his faith . . . and now, to be accused of heresy . . . it was more than he could bear.

He was seized with tertian fever and became very ill indeed. He had been ill for a long time but now he seemed to have lost something of himself. He became vague and suddenly, in the midst of a discussion, he would seem to lose his way and wonder what we were talking about. He would wander through the Court, unsure of where he was going. It was very sad to see him.

I felt I was losing one of my dearest friends – for already he seemed more dead than alive.

Life was so unhappy. I had to create dreams. And as we passed into the autumn I began to believe that I was pregnant.

I did not tell anyone at first. I could not forget the humiliating experience when everyone had been awaiting the birth of the child which had never been conceived.

I clung to the thought. I knew it. All the symptoms were present. I must be so this time. God would not desert me again.

When I told Susan, I saw the look of horror dawn on her face before she set her features into joyous lines.

'Your Majesty, can it really be so?'

'It is, Susan, I know it. Everything points to it.'

'Then . . . it is wonderful news. It will give Your Majesty new life.'

'What I have always wanted, more than anything, Susan, is my own child.'

'Yes, Your Majesty, I know.'

'As yet I shall tell no one.'

She could not hide her relief.

'No,' I said. 'Not even Philip. I will wait awhile.'

'It is best,' said Susan.

'But I am sure,' I said firmly.

I had to be sure. It was the only thing which could draw

544

me out of the morass of misery into which life had plunged me.

* * *

I had thought I had touched the very depth of misery, but there was more to come.

We were at war. The people said we were fighting Spain's war. We had not the means to finance a war. The Council had been against it. It was only when the Stafford affair had exposed the perfidy of the French that they had reluctantly agreed to declare war on them.

Now we were reaping the harvest.

One of the greatest blows I had been called upon to suffer had come upon me. The French had taken Calais. It was the final humiliation. That this should have happened in my reign! I was more deeply wounded than I could express. Calais had always meant something to the English. It was the gateway to France, and we had always seen the need to keep it well protected. It had been in our possession since it was taken by Edward III in 1347, and he had won it after a twelve-month siege. Always its importance had been recognized.

And now it was in the hands of the French; and all because we had become involved in a war which we did not want, which would bring us little good, and into which we had gone largely because I wished to please Philip.

It was no use telling me that our garrison had behaved with the utmost bravery – at the end only 800 of them holding out for a week against 3,000 troops of the Duke of Guise.

We had lost Calais, and in my heart I blamed myself.

Not even the thought of my pregnancy could lift my spirits.

* * *

There was silence in the streets. They were burning people at Smithfield and all over the country. They are heretics, I said. It is God's will. He has set me on the throne for this purpose, and I am carrying out that purpose to the best of my ability.

But I was failing. The Pope said so. Pamphlets were being issued illegally. They condemned me. They called me a Jezebel. They said I had brought misery to my country. No man was safe from the accusations of heresy and the fire.

One of my greatest enemies was John Knox. This fanatical misogynist poured forth his hatred for my sex, and what infuriated him so much was to see a woman in control. Having hated Mary of Guise in Scotland and Cathcrine de' Medici in France, simply because they were women of power, he turned his attention to me. He regarded himself as the great reformer, the guardian of the people's conscience. In his opinion only papists were more to be despised than women.

He thundered forth in his pulpit, and he had only recently brought forth his *First Blast of the Trumpet against the Monstrous Regiment of Women*. It was banned in England but this did not prevent reckless people bringing it into the country.

I was indeed the Jezebel. According to my father, I had been a bastard. I had no right to the throne. God must be punishing England for her sin in allowing a woman to reign over her. He referred to my 'Bloody Tyranny'.

It was then that people began to call me 'Bloody Mary'.

I was deeply unhappy. People were dying for their faith, it was true. But how many more had suffered, and as cruelly, in my father's reign? Yet no one had hurled abuse at him. He had sent them to their deaths because they disagreed with him; I had done so because these victims had disagreed with God's Holy Writ. Why should I be so stigmatized when none had questioned him?

There was disaster everywhere. Calais lost, and my people and my husband deserting me. My friends were dying round me. What had I to live for? Only the child which I deceived myself into thinking I carried in my womb. I had to. It was my only reason for living.

I was ill. There was no disguising the fact. I suffered from the same fever which had attacked Reginald. He was dying. Every time a messenger came from him, I feared it was to announce his death.

News came that the Emperor Charles had died. I felt deeply depressed. I had not seen him since my childhood, but I had always felt that he was there to help me in my need. He had not always done so, I know, but it had been comforting to know that he was there . . . a friend.

Everything around me was changing. I wrote to Philip begging him to come to me. I knew now that the swelling in my body was due to dropsy.

Yet another disappointment, but those around me had never believed it was anything else.

I left Hampton Court for St James's. Something told me I had not long to live.

Philip would not come to me. He was too deeply involved elsewhere. He deplored the loss of Calais. 'But we shall recover it,' he wrote. He had made me name Elizabeth as my heir, for, as he pointed out, if I did so, that would avoid the possibility of civil war.

He did not say he was expecting my death, but I guessed that he was. He would have been told of my increasing infirmity . . . of my poor dropsical body which had succeeded twice in deluding me into thinking I was about to become a mother. He told me Reginald Pole would comfort me. Did he not know that Reginald, wandering in a shadowy world of his own, was past giving comfort to anybody?

Susan and Jane Dormer were with me. Jane was very beautiful, young and in love with the Count of Feria, who

547

was soon to be her husband. I rejoiced with her and hoped she would know all the happiness which had been denied to me.

I had asked her not to marry until Philip came back.

Now I thought, when will that be? Dear Jane must not wait so long. I told her so. 'You are fortunate,' I added. 'The Count is one of the most charming men I ever met and, Jane . . . he loves you. That is wonderful.'

Jane turned away to hide her emotion. In the depth of her own happiness, she would understand how I had suffered from my loveless marriage.

When one knows that death is close, one looks back over one's life and sees events with a special clarity.

I have made so many mistakes. Yet I cannot see where I could have acted differently, except perhaps in my emotions, my tendency – in love only – to look upon what should have been clear to me and distort it to fit my own needs and desires. Why could I not have accepted our marriage as one of state? So many women of my kind had to do the same. I had been too old for marriage. Why did I not see that? If I had not married, everything might have been different. I would have ruled single-mindedly. I would not have been seeking to please him and so led my country into war. I should have acted on my own judgement.

Had I succeeded in the mission God had set me? I was not sure. We had returned to Rome but not very securely. I could not see into the future. I wondered what my successor would encounter. She would be ready though. Her hands were already stretching out for the crown.

Elizabeth's accession now seemed to be a certainty, and people were ready for that. They were waiting for me to die, for they believed England would be a happier place under her. It had certainly not been happy under me.

The weeks were passing. I was becoming more and more

feeble. I did not see Reginald. He was too ill to come to me and I to go to him.

I heard that people were calling at Hatfield. I knew that Philip had sent orders to the Spaniards in the country to pay respectful court to Elizabeth.

So he was expecting my death . . . and he did not come.

It had occurred to me often that he was interested in Elizabeth. I remembered the occasion when he had hidden behind a screen that he might study her. I remembered the look in his eyes . . . speculative . . . a little lustful? I had not recognized it then, but now I knew what it meant. When I was dead . . . he saw himself a suitor for Elizabeth's hand.

I did not want to live. I was aware of that so strongly at that time. She had always been my rival, this vitally attractive, unpredictable sister, so much cleverer than I, always alert for her advantage. And she would succeed me. There was no question of that now.

There would be no burnings at the stake which had made me so unpopular. Even the staunchest papists did not like them. England was determined that the Inquisition should never be allowed on its soil.

'Bloody Mary' they called me. I could hear the screams of the people as the flames licked their limbs. I could smell the pungent odour of burning human flesh. I called on God to forgive me. I had thought it was His will – and my people hated me for it. Bloody Mary! That awful epithet rang in my ears.

They blamed me, they reviled me . . . only Mary . . . Bloody Mary. Yet others had committed greater crimes. Some 300 people had been burned at the stake in my reign. Nobody blamed those who had murdered thousands in the name of the Holy Office of the Inquisition! Isabella, Ferdinand, Charles, who had buried people alive in Flanders – 30,000 of them. Yet I, who was held responsible for sending 300 to the stake, was Bloody Mary.

It was small wonder that I welcomed the prospect of death. What was there for me here?

The Court was growing more and more deserted. Why stay with a woman who was almost dead?

What should I be remembered for . . . the cries of martyrs, smoke rising from the fires which had been lighted at their feet because they denied the faith which I had imposed on them?

I was tired of life and my people were tired of me. It was time I went.

Susan was with me, so was Jane. They would not leave me. There were other faithful women, too.

Susan tried to cheer me. But nothing would cheer me.

They brought me materials so that I could write, for thinking of the past could draw my mind from the present. Susan was not sure that that was right for me.

'Sometimes it makes you so sad,' she said.

'There are many wounds that trouble my oppressed mind,' I told her. 'And there is one which is greater than any.'

Susan said: 'If the King knew you were so ill, I am sure he would come.'

'Do not let us deceive ourselves, Susan, my dear friend. If he knew how ill I was, he would do just what he is doing now, only perhaps he would renew his attention to Elizabeth. But I was not thinking of Philip then. I was thinking of Calais. When I die, they will find Calais lying upon my heart. I lost it, Susan. I lost it because I wanted Philip. I wanted to please him . . . to keep him with me. Always I have suffered through my affections.'

'Not always, dear lady. You have not suffered through us who have always loved you and will do so until you die.'

I turned to Susan and embraced her. Then I took Jane into my arms and wished her all the happiness I had missed.

'And that,' I added, 'is a great deal.'

They left me, and I took up my pen and wrote.

They are all going to leave the Court. To them the Queen is dead. So I shall write no more, for soon they will be at Hatfield crying: 'Long live the Queen!'

Bibliography

Aubrey, William Hickman Smith, *The National and Domestic History of England*

Bagley, J. H., *Henry VIII*

Bigland, Eileen (Edited by), *Henry VIII*

Bowle, John, *Henry VIII*

Chamberlin, Frederick, *The Private Character of Henry VIII*

Erickson, Carolly, *Bloody Mary*

Fisher, H. A. L., *Political History of England*

Froude, James Anthony, *The Divorce of Catherine of Aragon*

Froude, James Anthony, *History of England*

Guizot, M. (Translated by Robert Black), *History of France*

Hackett, Francis, *Henry VIII*

Hackett, Francis, *Francis the First*

Hume, David, *The History of England*

Hume, Martin, *The Wives of Henry VIII*

Hume, Martin, *Two England Queens and Philip*

Lewis, Hilda, *I am Mary Tudor*

Lingard, John, *History of England*

Luke, Mary, *Catherine of Aragon*

Mattingly, Garrett, *Catherine of Aragon*

Pollard, A. F., *Henry VIII*

Pollard, A. F., *Thomas Cranmer and the English Reformation under Edward VI*

Prescott, H. F. M., *Spanish Tudor. The Life of Bloody Mary*

Prescott, William H., *History of the Reign of Philip the Second*

Ridley, Jasper, *The Life and Times of Mary Tudor*
Salzman, L. F., *England in Tudor Times*
Scarisbrick, J. J., *Henry VIII*
Smith, Lacy Baldwin, *Henry VIII*
Stephens, Sir Leslie, and Lee, Sir Sidney, *The Dictionary of National Biography*
Stone, J. M., *The History of Mary I Queen of England*
Strickland, Agnes, *Lives of the Queens of England*
Trevelyan, G. M., *History of England*
Wade, John, *British History*
Waldman, Milton, *The Lady Mary*
White, Beatrice, *Mary Tudor*

The Courts of Love
Jean Plaidy

Born into the Courts of Love, she sought to create her own.

Eleanor of Aquitaine was dazzling, sensual and beautiful and when she met Henry Plantagenet he bore no resemblance to the noble knights of her girlhood. Careless of dress, dogmatic and arrogant, Henry captivated the passionate Eleanor.

But when Henry strove to subdue his bride, the inevitable strife began . . .

'Jean Plaidy is one of the country's most widely read novelists.' *Sunday Times*

FONTANA PAPERBACKS

Victoria Holt

The supreme writer of the 'gothic' romance, a compulsive storyteller whose gripping novels of the darker face of love have thrilled millions all over the world.

and others

FONTANA PAPERBACKS

The Lady in the Tower
Jean Plaidy

Obsessive love turns into murderous hate.

Anne Boleyn was destined for distinction. The possessor of a quality more exciting than beauty, she was soon noticed and desired even by the King himself.

But Henry VIII was sometimes sentimental and always ruthless, a man with absolute power over those around him – including Anne, impetuous, reckless, heading for danger and realizing it only when it was too late . . .

FONTANA PAPERBACKS

Fontana Paperbacks: Fiction

Fontana is a leading paperback publisher of fiction.
Below are some recent titles.

- ☐ SHINING THROUGH Susan Isaacs £3.99
- ☐ KINDRED PASSIONS Rosamund Smith £2.99
- ☐ BETWEEN FRIENDS Audrey Howard £3.99
- ☐ THE CHARMED CIRCLE Catherine Gaskin £4.50
- ☐ THE INDIA FAN Victoria Holt £3.99
- ☐ THE LAWLESS John Jakes £2.99
- ☐ THE AMERICANS John Jakes £2.99
- ☐ A KIND OF WAR Pamela Haines £3.50
- ☐ THE HERON'S CATCH Susan Curran £4.50

You can buy Fontana paperbacks at your local bookshop or
newsagent. Or you can order them from Fontana Paperbacks,
Cash Sales Department, Box 29, Douglas, Isle of Man. Please
send a cheque, postal or money order (not currency) worth the
purchase price plus 22p per book for postage (maximum postage
required is £3.00 for orders within the UK).

NAME (Block letters)_____

ADDRESS_____

_____